Also by Danielle Steel

* Published outside the UK under the title PASSION'S PROMISE

For more information on Danielle Steel and her books, see her website at
www.daniellesteel.com

Danielle Steel

Winners

CORGI BOOKS

TRANSWORLD PUBLISHERS
61–63 Uxbridge Road, London W5 5SA
A Random House Group Company
www.transworldbooks.co.uk

WINNERS
A CORGI BOOK: 9780552159128 (B format)
9780552159135 (A format)

First published in the United States
in 2013 by Delacorte Press
an imprint of The Random House Publishing Group

First published in Great Britain
in 2013 by Bantam Press
an imprint of Transworld Publishers
Corgi edition published 2014

Addresses for Random House Group Ltd companies outside the UK
can be found at: www.randomhouse.co.uk
The Random House Group Ltd Reg. No. 954009

Penguin Random House is committed to a sustainable future for
our business, our readers and our planet. This book is made from
Forest Stewardship Council® certified paper.

MIX
Paper from
responsible sources
FSC® C018179

Printed and bound in Great Britain by Clays Ltd, St Ives plc
Typeset in 12/15.5pt Adobe Garamond by Falcon Oast Graphic Art Ltd.

6 8 10 9 7 5

To my beloved children,
Beatrix, Trevor, Todd, Nick,
Samantha, Victoria, Vanessa,
Maxx, and Zara,
May you be forever blessed,
lucky, and happy,
And may you have the strength,
courage, and perseverance
to be winners!

I love you so much,
Mommy/DS

'What blesses one
blesses all.'

–MARY BAKER EDDY

WINNERS

Chapter 1

Lily Thomas lay in bed when the alarm went off on a snowy January morning in Squaw Valley. She opened her eyes for just an instant and saw the thick snow swirling beyond the windows of the house her father had rented, and for a fraction of an instant, she wanted to roll over and go back to sleep. She could hear the dynamite blasts in the distance to prevent avalanches, and just from a glance, she knew what kind of day it was. You could hardly see past the windows in the heavy blizzard, and she knew that if the mountain was open, it wouldn't be for long. But she loved the challenge of skiing in heavy snow. It would be a good workout, and she didn't want to miss a single day with one of her favorite instructors, Jason Yee.

She and her father came here every year during Christmas break. They celebrated Christmas at home in Denver, flew to San Francisco where her father visited friends and did some business, mostly with venture capital firms in Silicon Valley, and then they drove to Squaw. It was a tradition Lily loved, and good skiing. They'd been coming here since she'd started downhill racing when she was a little kid. She had won bronze in the Junior Olympics three years before, at fourteen. And she was training for the next Winter Olympics, in a year. This time she was hoping to win the gold.

Lily gave a last stretch in her warm, comfortable bed and got up to take a shower. She glanced out the window and saw how heavy the snowfall was. There were two more feet of fresh snow on the ground than there had been the night before. She grinned, thinking of the morning that lay ahead. The heavy snow might slow them down a little, but Jason always pushed her hard, which was what she liked about him. She loved skiing with him, and he was more fun than her regular Denver coach, who'd been training her for the Olympics since she was twelve.

It had been her father's idea for her to start skiing, and then racing, when he saw what a natural she was. He had loved to ski at her age. He had been mostly self-taught, and had a passion for it, and had skied on whatever skis he could afford. After his simple beginnings in a mining town in Pennsylvania, he had made his fortune in his early twenties, speculating on the commodities market and later investing in high-risk deals that brought enormous returns. Since then he had been investing more conservatively, and his fortune was secure and would go to Lily one day. She never thought about it, although she knew how fortunate she was. Her father always preached discipline and hard work, and Lily was a lot like him. She was an outstanding student and a talented athlete. She was a junior in high school and hoped to go to an Ivy League college. And in the meantime she trained for the Olympics every day, at a grueling pace. She had been the joy and main focus of her father's life since her mother died when she was three. Bill Thomas lived for her, and Lily adored him.

Bill Thomas had gone to a state college in Pennsylvania. His father had been a coal miner and died when Bill was in his teens. He knew what poverty looked like at its most extreme, and all he had wanted as a young man was to provide a better life for the family he hoped to have one day. A scholarship to Harvard Business School had changed his life. He had used the MBA he earned there, and his own entrepreneurial sense, to achieve everything he had set his sights on as a boy. His mother never lived to see him graduate, and his brother had died in a mine accident at nineteen. Only Bill had escaped into a better world, and he never forgot where he came from, and what he had achieved. He was brilliant in business, and at fifty-two, he had fulfilled his dreams, and worked at home now, managing his investments, and spending as much time with Lily as he could. He had been both father and mother to her for fourteen years, and was infinitely proud of her.

Lily showered and dressed, and appeared at the breakfast table a few minutes later, in her ski pants, thermals, and bare feet. Her long dark hair was still wet from the shower, and her father was sipping a cup of coffee, as he looked up at her with a smile.

'I was wondering if you were going to sleep in. It looks nasty outside.' As he said it, they both heard the dynamite go off again. The chairlifts weren't moving yet, but Lily was sure they would soon, at least for a while.

'I don't want to miss the day,' she said, putting brown sugar on the oatmeal he had ordered for her, from room service at a nearby hotel that provided food and maid service to the house they rented every year. 'I love skiing with Jason, Daddy,' she said, as he uncovered the rest of what he'd ordered for her, scrambled eggs, bacon, and whole wheat toast. 'I can't eat all that,' she said, making a face.

Lily was lean and athletic and in fantastic shape, and she was as beautiful as her mother had been, with the same lavender-blue eyes, dark hair, and creamy skin, and a wide smile that mirrored his own. Bill was as fair as she was dark and looked younger than his years. He had never remarried and had no desire to, as long as Lily was at home. He had dated the same woman for the past two years. Penny was devoted to her career, had never married, and had no children, and she traveled so much for her PR business that it never bothered her that the most important woman in Bill's life was Lily, and most of the time he was busy with his daughter and had little interest in anyone else. He and Penny had an unspoken arrangement that worked for both of them. When they had time and were in the same city, they spent an evening together, and other than that, they had their own lives. Neither of them wanted more with each other than they had. And they had fun whenever they got together.

Penny was a good-looking redhead, and she worked hard at maintaining a spectacular body that she had 'enhanced' here and there. Bill always enjoyed having her on his arm when they went out. She was younger than he was, but not so much that he felt foolish when they were seen together.

They had even managed a couple of trips, usually to resorts she represented so she could kill two birds with one stone. He had never suggested a future to her, nor did he plan to, and she was an independent woman who didn't seem to want one with him, or anyone else. She was forty-two years old, and Lily liked her, and knew that Penny was no threat to her. Her father rarely involved his daughter in his dating life – they spent their family time alone, as on this vacation. And during their time in

Squaw, Penny was at the opening of a new resort in St. Bart's, and Bill had never invited her to Squaw Valley with them on their annual trip. He liked spending the time with Lily – she was so busy with school and friends, sports, and after-school activities when they were at home. He dreaded when she'd leave for college and was trying to talk her into going to school in or near Denver, although Lily had her heart set on the Ivy League in the East, and had the grades to get in.

'Are you sure you want to go out today?' he asked, as she took a bite of the eggs and then nibbled a strip of bacon.

'They'll probably close the mountain early. I want to get in as many runs as I can before they do,' she said, then stood up to go finish dressing.

'If it gets too bad, I want you to come in,' he reminded her. He admired her skill, and her discipline, but he didn't want her taking crazy chances in ugly weather. But she was a sensible girl too.

'I know, Daddy,' she said with a dazzling smile as she looked over her shoulder. 'Don't worry, we'll be fine. Jason knows the mountain better than anyone here.' It was one of the reasons why Bill had hired him years before. He wanted Lily to have fun, but he wanted her safe above all. He had lost her mother and didn't want to lose her as well. Lily's mother had been driving too fast the night she hit a patch of ice in Denver and died at twenty-five, leaving Bill widowed, with a three-year-old child. He protected Lily as if she were made of glass.

She was back ten minutes later, with her sweater on over her thermals, ski pants, hiking boots, and her Olympic team parka and helmet over her arm. She left her skis, boots, and poles in a locker at the base of the mountain every night, and she had to take a shuttle bus to meet Jason there now. She put her parka on and zipped it up. Bill was sitting at his computer checking the commodities market, and then looked up at her with a grin.

'You look mighty cute,' he said, smiling broadly. The Olympic team parka and helmet said she was a hotshot, and they were a status symbol on any slope. Just looking at her, he was proud of her all over again. 'And come in if the weather gets any worse,' he reminded her, and she bent to kiss him on the top of his head on her way out.

'We will,' she said happily, and waved her gloves at him from the doorway, and then she was off to get in as much skiing as she could before the mountain closed. He was sure it would by midday, and so was she.

He stood up and watched her from the window, and saw her get on the shuttle bus to the base. She didn't see him, and he felt his heart tug as he gazed at her. She was so beautiful and so young, and she looked so much like her late mother they could have been sisters. It still tore his heart out sometimes. She would have been thirty-nine years old if she were still alive, which was hard to imagine.

In his mind, she would be young forever, hardly older than Lily was now at seventeen. He went back to his computer then, and hoped that Lily would come in early. The snow seemed to be getting worse, and he knew there would be a veil of fog at the top of the mountain. Only the worst diehards would venture out today, like Lily. She had her mother's looks but her father's grit, stubbornness, and determination. Because of it, Bill was sure that her skill and relentless training would win her the gold in the next Olympics.

While riding the shuttle to the base, she had time to text her boyfriend Jeremy and best friend Veronica. Both were on the ski team with her, and were practicing in Denver that day. She had no time to make friends with anyone who wasn't on the Olympic team, and she and Veronica had known each other since nursery school. Jeremy answered her with a quick 'I love you.' Veronica didn't answer, and Lily guessed she was still asleep.

Lily met Jason, as promised, at the lockers. He was wearing his ski school jacket, and next to her Olympic team gear, they looked very official, as they put their skis and boots on, left their shoes in a locker, grabbed their poles, and headed toward the lift. They were both wearing goggles in the heavy snow. Jason glanced at her with a grin, as they showed their passes to the chairlift operator and he nodded. There were three other people waiting for the lift ahead of them, and it had just started operating only minutes before. Two others were already high in the air on the chairs as Lily glanced at them. It was exhilarating to be out on a day like this, and she loved the challenge of skiing through the heavy snow. Jason admired that about her – nothing ever stopped her.

'You either have to be crazy to go out on a day like this,' Jason said, laughing, 'or very young, or both. I don't think the mountain will be open long.' But they both knew it was safe, if the chairlift was operating, otherwise they'd have closed it down. And only the most skilled would brave the mountain today, and she and Jason both qualified for that. He was an astounding skier, and so was she. He had won national championships at her age, and he was an excellent teacher too. She always learned something new from him, which added to what she learned from her Denver coach, who was a taskmaster.

'I guess that means I'm crazy,' Lily said happily. 'My dad thinks we're nuts too.' They could hear the dynamite blasting again, as Lily got on the first available chairlift, and Jason waited for the next one, right behind her. Lily felt the same thrill she always did, as the chairlift went high in the air, and she looked down at the trees and virgin snow. There was not a single skier yet on the slopes, and she could tell that part of the mountain was closed as they headed toward the top. The wind was whipping her face, and she enjoyed the peaceful silence as the chairlift hummed along, and then she heard another crack of dynamite, unusually close by. It sounded like they were right next to it, which surprised her, and at exactly the same moment, as they approached a ravine, from a great height, she saw a long snake whip through the air, like a giant rope above their heads. She looked up at it and felt herself falling fast at the same time. She didn't even have time to understand that the cable that held the chairlift had just broken, as she plummeted down, into a deep hole in the snow. When she landed, all she saw was white, and her eyes closed as she fell into a deep sleep. She never had time to turn and look at Jason, while they free-fell past the trees, and he landed in the ravine. Jason was dead the minute he hit the snow.

Chapter 2

Bill watched the prices on the Dow Jones all morning, and then read *The New York Times* and the *Wall Street Journal,* which he had delivered to him by the hotel that serviced the house. He glanced out the window now and then and saw that the snow had gotten denser, and he could no longer see the mountain through the fog. He couldn't even tell if the chairlift was operating, or if they had closed the mountain. But he was sure that if they hadn't yet, they would soon. Bill was sure that she was safe with Jason, who knew the mountain like his own pocket, but Bill hoped she would come in soon. The weather was just too bad.

He often met her at the base at lunchtime, and decided to meet her there now. He was sure she'd be exhausted after several runs in the thick snow. Even at her age, it was heavy going, and required strength and concentration. He was hoping to talk her into a nice lunch, and maybe a swim in the hotel pool that afternoon, or a massage, which sounded good to him too. He got out his jacket and put on a cap and boots, as he heard sirens in the distance. He looked at his watch to see if it was noon, but it was only eleven-thirty, and then he saw a helicopter speed past their windows, followed by a second one, and he wondered if someone had gotten lost in the fog at the top of the mountain, or injured. It was an unpleasant feeling, thinking that someone might be hurt, but he was reassured it wasn't Lily, since she was with Jason.

He drove his rental car out of the parking lot a few minutes later, an Escalade that had been perfect for the drive from San Francisco, and headed toward the base of the mountain, and when he got there, he saw several ambulances, police cars, and two fire trucks parked helter-skelter, and the ski patrol heading out on snowmobiles and pulling sleds. Bill was instantly concerned as he parked and got out of his car, and hurried over to ask a police officer what had happened. He could see then that the chairlift wasn't operating, so they had obviously closed the mountain. And one of the helicopters whirled past them as he noticed how many rescue vehicles there were. Far too many for one injured person.

'Accident at the top?' Bill asked the officer, as he noticed people standing around with worried expressions.

The officer pointed to the chairlift, and as he did, Bill could see that the line was slack, and at first didn't understand why. The operator was standing talking to some of the paramedics, and there was a cluster of people from the ski patrol conferring with them in somber conversation.

'The cable broke. We don't know what happened yet. The ski patrol is up there. They're bringing the first people down now.' Bill felt his blood run cold as he said it. All he could do was pray that Lily had gotten to the top before it broke. 'The weather isn't helping. We've got a lot of fog up at the top.' The choppers had disappeared into it, and were no longer visible from the base. The officer then asked Bill to step aside. There was an area they had designated for people to wait, behind a line of yellow tape, and he pointed Bill toward it.

'My daughter's up there,' Bill said in a strained voice, as the icy snow and wind whipped his face. He could only imagine how bad the weather was at the top of the mountain, and seeing the injured people on the ground made it worse.

'Is she alone?' The officer sounded concerned, as more fire trucks with paramedics arrived on the scene.

'She's with an instructor from the ski school. Jason Yee.' The officer had already seen Jason's name on a list of casualties but said nothing to Bill. 'Her name is Lily Thomas. She's wearing an Olympic ski team parka and helmet,' Bill said, choking back tears of terror.

'I'll radio the patrol and the choppers,' he said quickly.

'We're having a tough time with the fog and the trees. The visibility is right down to the ground. We've only gotten two people down so far. If you wait over there, sir' – he pointed to the designated area again – 'I'll let you know as soon as we get word.'

Bill nodded and went to stand with a cluster of anxious people who had arrived while Bill was talking. Two of them were parents of ski instructors who were on the mountain, and there were a handful of others who looked panicked. Most of the people on the scene were rescue workers, and a fleet of snowmobiles had raced past them only moments before. All available instructors had been mobilized to join the ski patrol in the search for injured people. The operator wasn't sure how many had gone up in all since most of them had day passes. All he knew was that the chairlift had jammed for an instant, and the next thing he was aware of was that the cable had gone slack, and the chairs had gone down one by one. Someone in the group said it had sounded like a crack of thunder, louder than the dynamite they'd been detonating, which had stopped now. All Bill could hear around him were the rescue vehicles arriving and men shouting.

It was another hour before a sled sped down the mountain with men from the ski patrol all around it. Bill couldn't stop himself and raced forward, but he could see instantly that it was a young boy, who looked dazed as they lifted him into an ambulance on a backboard, and he heard someone say that both his legs were broken, but he was alive. His older brother was brought down on a sled, with a tarp covering him. He was dead. They had pulled him out of the ravine on ropes. The younger brother had fallen into a snowbank right before it. It was rapidly turning into a grim scene as Bill watched, overwhelmed by panic. There was no news of either Jason or Lily. He was unaware of the tears rolling down his cheeks as he waited, and more than once he couldn't stop himself and went to remind the police and firemen of where he was standing and that Lily was wearing the jacket and helmet of the Olympic team, so they could identify her quickly when they found her.

The ski patrol at the top were in constant radio communication with the men at the base, and warned them when people were coming down and what condition they were in. Only three survivors had come down so far, all suffering from hypothermia, and two people had been killed. But so far Lily was among neither the injured nor the dead. Only one man had escaped without injury. He was suffering from exposure and frostbite, but from what they could tell, he had no broken bones, and had fallen into a snowbank from the low part of the chairlift. All Bill could hope now was that Lily would be one of the lucky ones. Bill kept thinking of the night her mother had been killed, when the police showed up at his front door. She had gone to meet a friend for dinner, and died instantly when her car hit the ice and she ran into a tree.

And then as another sled appeared, with ski patrol flying alongside it, he saw the familiar jacket and helmet. He raced toward it, as the men pulling the sled shouted at him to get out of the way. He stepped aside just in time and saw her face, deathly pale, with her eyes closed. She was covered with tarps and thermal blankets, the sleeve of her jacket had been cut off, and they had run an IV into her arm. Bill was next to the sled instantly, as the paramedics called out to one another and slid her into the ambulance. She was unconscious. Bill jumped into the ambulance with her. He told them rapidly that he was her father, and no one objected. The doors slammed as soon as he said it, and they drove away at full speed, as two of the paramedics took her vitals.

Her temperature was icy, which one of the paramedics explained to him might have kept her alive, in spite of her injuries. They didn't know what condition she was in yet, but were assuming she had back and neck injuries from the position they'd found her in, sprawled like a rag doll in the snow. The atmosphere in the ambulance was tense as they put more thermal blankets on her and heating pads to try and warm her up. Fortunately, she had been in the snow for only a few hours, longer might have been disastrous, but she wasn't out of danger yet by any means. Her blood pressure was alarmingly low as her father watched her with a look of devastation and gently touched her hand. She never stirred as they continued to monitor her, and the ambulance flew toward the hospital at full speed, with its siren on. They were there in minutes, and a team was waiting in the parking lot for her. She was the fourth victim of the chairlift accident to come in.

Lily was rushed straight into the trauma unit, with Bill running behind them. A nurse stopped him at the door.

'You'll have to stay in the waiting room, sir,' she said firmly, as his eyes blazed fire at her. No one was going to keep him from his daughter in the condition she was in. She looked more dead than alive. And as the nurse stopped him, they were already cutting Lily's clothes off, while a team of doctors and nurses worked on her.

'That's my daughter in there,' Bill said with a grim look, trying to force his way past the nurse. 'You'll have to carry me out,' he said bluntly.

'That can be arranged,' the nurse said with a look of equal determination. 'You can't go in.'

'Watch me,' he said, and shoved past her through the trauma unit doors. He found Lily in the first treatment room, already naked, with monitors attached to every part of her, and electrically heated blankets being used to warm her up. 'How is she?' he said in a hoarse voice to the doctor closest to him, who was too busy to answer, and shot a meaningful look at a resident to get Bill out before he got in their way. They were trying to save her life. She was young and strong, and they hoped they had a decent chance, but nothing was sure, and they hadn't evaluated her injuries yet. They were dealing with the hypothermia, and her blood pressure. She was hardly breathing, and they were going to intubate her. And they wanted Bill out of the room for that.

'You can't stay in here,' one of the doctors said tersely, as the resident took Bill's arm and led him out of the room with a strong hand. This time Bill didn't fight him, he was overwhelmed by what he'd seen. Lily didn't even know he was there – she was still deeply unconscious, and had been since they rescued her from the snow.

The resident led him into the nearby waiting room, and Bill sat down, deathly pale himself. 'Are you all right?' the resident asked calmly, and Bill nodded, but he wasn't. He was terrified Lily was going to die, just like her mother. She had looked like she was barely clinging to life in the treatment room. 'We're going to do everything we can for her,' he reassured him, and Bill stared at him with panic in his eyes.

'What happened? What's broken?' he asked in a trembling voice.

'We don't know yet. We're trying to assess that now.'

'Her head?' Bill asked in a choked whisper.

'The ski patrol reported that she had her helmet on when they found her. We're more concerned about her neck and spine.' Bill nodded silently, and dropped his head into his hands, as the resident sat down in a chair across from him. 'We need a history on her. How old is she?'

'She just turned seventeen.'

'Allergies?'

'None.'

'Medical problems? Heart? Lungs? Surgeries?'

'Nothing. She's fine . . . or she was . . . ,' he said, as tears filled his eyes.

'Any history of drugs – anything we should know?' Bill shook his head miserably.

'How soon will you know what her injuries are? How far did she fall?'

'From the high point of the chairlift. She just missed the ravine. Her instructor wasn't as lucky,' the young doctor said grimly.

'Jason?' Bill was shocked – he hadn't heard that yet.

'They found him before they found your daughter. She was deep in the snow. The only good thing about that is that maintaining her body at such a low temperature kept the swelling down on her injuries. That could be helpful. I need to get back in now,' the resident said quietly. 'We have an orthopedic surgeon coming in to evaluate her. And we have a neurosurgeon on call, if we need one.'

'Who are they?' Bill panicked again. 'I'm not going to

let just anyone operate on her,' Bill said, suddenly fierce – he was a lion ready to defend his cub. 'I want to know who they are. Can we fly someone in?'

'That won't be necessary. We have an excellent team here, the best there is.' He looked insulted, and Bill didn't care. He wanted the finest doctors he could get for Lily. If she needed surgery, he didn't want some local quack bungling it. They were at the most state-of-the-art hospital in Tahoe for trauma and orthopedic injuries, but he wasn't ready to trust anyone with his child.

'We may not have time to bring someone else in. We need to stabilize her, and do X-rays and exams, and scans. They're doing that now. As soon as we know something, the head of the trauma unit will come out and talk to you.' He stood up then, trying not to appear nervous. Bill seemed as though he was going to throttle him if he didn't come up with the right answers, or if they couldn't save the girl. The resident had no idea if they would be able to save her, but it wasn't looking good when she came in. The ski patrol and paramedics who had found her had thought she was dead at first and were stunned when they found a pulse.

He left the room then, and Bill sat going crazy for two hours. He thought of calling Penny, but didn't really want to talk to her. They had a good time together, but even after two years they weren't that close. He had no idea who to call, and had never felt so alone in his life, not since a night fourteen years before, when Lily's mother died. But he wasn't going to let that happen to Lily.

He was ready to try to force his way back into the treatment room when the chief trauma doctor came out. He looked like a college kid to Bill, and there was a tall, dark-haired man with him. He was wearing a lab coat, with his name embroidered on the pocket, it said 'Ben Steinberg, M.D.,' and he appeared to be a little older than his colleague, in his late thirties or early forties. He introduced himself to Bill immediately, and said he was an orthopedic surgeon.

'How's my daughter?' Bill asked in a voice raw with worry and grief.

'We're trying to stabilize her. We need to get her body temperature up, before we can do any kind of intervention on her. We're assessing her injuries. She's still unconscious, which is partially due to the hypothermia. She was in the snow for several hours,' he explained. 'We don't know the extent of any internal injuries yet. She has a broken arm, and a spinal cord injury, but we don't know the implications of that yet either. We've done preliminary X-rays, and a body scan, but they're not conclusive. My partner is a neurosurgeon, and I'd like her to come in to evaluate your daughter for us.'

'What does that mean? And what kind of spinal injury? Is she paralyzed?' Bill looked like a cornered bull as he said the words, and Ben Steinberg realized he needed to handle him with kid gloves. The resident had warned him of that, but he could see now the level of Bill's anxiety for his daughter. He seemed like he was going to lose control any minute. He couldn't bear what was happening to her.

'We don't know any of that yet, which is why I'd like a neurosurgeon to evaluate her. My partner is one of the best there is. I called her a few minutes ago, and she's coming in. We need a little more time to stabilize Lily anyway. We need to get her warmer and her blood pressure up before she could tolerate surgery.'

'I haven't agreed to surgery,' Bill reminded him. 'And I asked you if she's paralyzed.' His eyes blazed into Ben's.

'It's hard to assess with her unconscious, but there appears to be limited function of her legs. We need to determine the degree of the injury before we can give you a reliable answer. We just don't know the full extent of her injuries yet.'

'When is the neurosurgeon coming in, and why the hell isn't she here yet?' He was impatient for everything – for answers, but mostly for help for Lily.

'She should be here in fifteen or twenty minutes. I just called her,' Dr. Steinberg said calmly. He sympathized with Bill's concern about his daughter, and he had a soothing manner, but nothing was going to satisfy Bill now except the news that Lily was out of danger, and no one could tell him that, not even a neurosurgeon. She had had a very serious accident, and there was no way of telling yet if she would survive it.

'May I see my daughter?' Bill asked, with agony in his eyes, and the orthopedic surgeon nodded. He hated to have her father see her in the condition she was in, but he didn't have the heart to deny him. And maybe it would help him understand her fragile state. She was hanging on to life by a thin thread.

Bill followed them wordlessly into the trauma unit. Lily had been moved into the trauma ICU, and there were two nurses and a doctor with her, checking her vital signs, and doing a neurological assessment before the surgeon arrived and would need the information. Lily was still covered by several electric warming blankets, her long dark hair was in a surgical cap, and her face looked ghostly. She had a breathing tube taped in her mouth, and a machine was helping her breathe. She had IVs in both arms, and monitors attached to her limbs gave them the information they needed, and would sound an alarm if her heart stopped or she stopped breathing.

Bill was even more shaken the moment he saw her. There wasn't an inch of her that he could hold or kiss, all he could do was watch her, and gently touch her good arm with his finger. The other arm was in a cast, and a nasty bruise had begun to show on one side of her face, where she had fallen. Bill just stood there crying quietly, and a few minutes later a nurse led him from the room.

There was nowhere for him to stand without getting in their way, and as much as he wanted to be with her, he didn't want to interfere with what they were doing. He had no illusions about how dire her situation was. He sat down in the waiting room again, and the nurse offered to get him a cup of coffee or something to eat. He just shook his head and laid it back against the couch and closed his eyes. After seeing her, it was almost impossible to believe she would live. And for the first time in fourteen years, he prayed.

Chapter 3

Jessie Matthews had been running all afternoon. Her days off were always like that, but it was inevitable with four young kids, and she loved it. Her oldest son, Chris, was eighteen now and allegedly more independent. He had a driver's license and a car, but he still needed help with everything. He still consulted his parents on minor and major decisions, needed help with term papers and school projects, emptied the fridge, and forgot to do dishes. Jessie did his laundry, and he asked her for romantic advice. And he loved playing basketball with his dad when he had time. Both his parents were busy. His mother was a neurosurgeon, and his father, Tim, was an anesthesiologist. They usually took turns with their schedules, except for emergencies, which happened often, and then they were both out at the same time. Chris stayed with his younger siblings and drove them around whenever he had to. He was going to college in the fall and hoping to get into either UC Boulder or the University of Denver, for the skiing. He could hardly wait to go. And Adam, his eleven-year-old brother, said he couldn't wait for him to leave too. It seemed sometimes like they had been arguing with each other since the day Adam was born, or very shortly thereafter, although they were seven years apart.

Heather was fifteen, and a sophomore at the same school Chris attended. She and Chris got along fairly decently, except when she said he was acting like a jerk or a pig or refused to drive her somewhere because he wanted to see his girlfriend. But they'd been doing better since she'd been in high school, which was a relief to their parents.

And Jimmy was everyone's joy, at six. He had been a 'slip' on Jessie's part, five years after Adam, but she and Tim were infinitely grateful for it now. He was the most affectionate child she'd ever seen, and he made everybody laugh. He loved his entire family. He was the sweetness and comic relief in the group. Tim had forgiven Jessie instantly for adding a fourth unexpected child to their already-strained finances, the moment he saw him. Jimmy was impossible to resist, and everyone who knew him loved him. His whole perspective on life was colored by the fact that he had never met anyone who didn't like him. Strangers in line at the supermarket fell in love with him, and he made friends wherever he went. Even homeless guys on the street smiled at him, when Jimmy stopped to say hello and ask them how they were.

Tim was just waking up when Jessie came in with the groceries. She had used her day off to do a million errands, dropped Heather off to do some shopping she wanted to do, and took Adam for a haircut he didn't want and was furious about. Now she still had two loads of laundry to do, and she had promised to cook dinner. She and Jimmy were unpacking the groceries, when Tim walked into the kitchen in his pajamas, with a yawn. He had been up all night with four surgeries back to back, and didn't get home till ten A.M. He put on a pot of coffee, and helped her put the groceries in the fridge.

'Looks like you had a busy day.' He smiled at her over Jimmy's head. It was the same smile that had made her heart race for all these years. They had married in medical school at twenty-four. And nineteen years and four kids later, they were still very much in love, and it showed. Adam rolled his eyes and looked disgusted whenever they kissed, and Chris and Heather looked embarrassed. Jimmy thought it was funny and had shown a picture of his parents kissing, at show and tell, that Jessie didn't know he had taken. There was nothing improper about the picture, and his class thought it was funny. Tim and Jessie both knew it was rare for people to still be that in love with each other after nearly twenty years, but their kids thought it was normal.

'Sorry I didn't give you a hand today,' Tim apologized as Jessie put away the empty bags, and Jimmy went upstairs. 'I was dead to the world.'

'It's fine, you had a rough night last night.' She could see that he was exhausted.

'It was a little dicey,' he admitted, as he poured himself a cup of coffee and sat down at the kitchen table. 'I had a nasty compound fracture, an eighty-seven-year-old woman with a broken hip, a perforated appendix, and a woman who delivered twins at thirty-two weeks. We almost lost one of them, but the neonatal guys worked a miracle and saved him, and then the mom hemorrhaged and almost bled out, and they saved her too. And there were only two anesthesiologists on last night – two of the others were on vacation, and three were sick, so we couldn't call anyone in. Crazy night.' It often was for him, but she knew he loved what he did.

'My phone must be out of order. I managed to get through a whole day without being called in for an emergency today. It was nice.' She smiled at him, and bent to kiss him where he sat as he put an arm around her waist. She still had the same slim figure she'd had when she met him, even after four kids. She had long blond hair she wore in a braid most of the time, big blue eyes, and a dusting of freckles, which made her look like a kid.

'What's on the agenda for tonight? Any chance we can drop the troops off at their friends' and steal a night of romance without Chris and Adam threatening to kill each other, or Heather needing a ride?' he asked hopefully, and she laughed.

'Not a chance. Heather's going to the movies with friends, and I said I'd drop her off. I think Chris has a date. Adam is spending the night at Parker's house, and we have to get him there. And I promised to take Jimmy bowling. You can come with us if you want. I've been promising him all week, and I didn't have the heart to postpone it again.'

'Terrific,' he said with a rueful smile. 'I was hoping you'd suggest we go bowling.' He pulled her onto his lap for a kiss just as her cell phone rang.

'Dr. Matthews,' she said, as she pulled her mouth away from Tim's. It was her official voice, but she was smiling at him, and she could see on her BlackBerry that it was Ben. They had shared an office for the past ten years, since Tim had convinced her to move to Tahoe after Adam was born. They had lived in Palo Alto before that, and she had just joined a group at Stanford Hospital, and leaving it had been a sacrifice for her. But she did it for Tim and her kids, even knowing that she wouldn't have the same professional opportunities at Squaw Valley that she did at a teaching hospital like Stanford, but she liked their life here now. Tim was happy, and it was great for the kids. And her work was interesting even here. Her specialty was spinal cord injuries, and she had several challenging cases every year. She and Tim had both gone to medical school at Harvard and done their residencies at Stanford. And they both loved the healthy country life at Lake Tahoe. Tim was always happiest outdoors, more so than Jessie, who missed the city a little. But they went to San Francisco occasionally for a weekend.

Tim saw her frowning as she listened to Ben, and she glanced over at Tim with a look of surprise. 'I heard the sirens, but I figured it was a car accident in the bad weather. I've been so busy, I haven't turned the radio on all day.' And then she listened to him again, and asked a number of questions. Tim could tell it was a spinal cord case, and he could see an evening of bowling alone with his youngest son in his immediate future. She looked serious when she ended the call, after promising she'd get there as soon as she could. She stood up and looked at Tim then, with a shocked expression.

'A chairlift cable broke today. I don't know how I missed hearing about that. Several deaths, a number of injuries. Ben has a seventeen-year-old girl with hypothermia and an SCI. He needs me to come in,' she said apologetically.

'I got that,' he said, as he stood up and kissed her.

'Will you take Jimmy bowling? I promised. I told them I'd make tacos tonight too. I bought a bunch of frozen pizzas if you don't feel like cooking. I'm really sorry. I thought maybe I'd get away with a night off too.'

'I'll manage. You think you'll be operating tonight?'

'Sounds like it. Ben says they're stabilizing her now, and still assessing her. If she's stable, we'll go in. If not, we may have to wait till tomorrow. It doesn't sound too good. She fell off the chairlift at the high point. The instructor she was with was killed.'

'I wonder if they'll call me in too,' Tim said, glancing at his own phone, but there were no messages, and he assumed some of the other anesthesiologists had come back on duty.

'I hope not. If they call you, Chris will have to drive Heather and Adam and babysit for Jimmy, which will screw up his date and he'll be pissed.'

'I'll do my best not to spoil his evening,' Tim said, as Jessie went upstairs to change. She was wearing torn jeans and an old sweater, and Ben had sounded anxious for her to come in as soon as she could to help with the evaluation. She was back downstairs five minutes later, with her hair brushed and in the braid, wearing a turtleneck sweater, black jeans, and boots, and she grabbed her heavy parka off the hook in the front hall. She looked a little more serious than she did in an old sweater and torn jeans, but she still looked very young for forty-three.

'I'll call you as soon as I know what I'm doing, and if I'll be there all night.' She kissed him on her way out, and a few minutes later she was in Tim's Jeep, heading to the hospital. She left her van for him, since he'd need it to drive the kids. She noticed that the roads were icy, and she drove carefully on the way to the hospital. She was already thinking about the patient Ben had described to her, and the people who had been hurt in the chairlift accident. It was one of those things that could happen in a ski resort, although you prayed it never would. Just thinking of it made her shudder, and worry about her kids. All of them were avid skiers, especially Chris and Adam. What if it had been one of them on the chairlift today? She pushed the thought from her mind as the car started to skid and she got it back in control. She was used to driving on snow and ice, and she pulled into the hospital parking lot a few minutes later, parked Tim's Jeep, and walked into the hospital. She went to her locker to change into her white coat with her name on the pocket, and she slipped it on over her sweater and jeans. She was in the trauma unit five minutes later, examining Lily and listening to Ben as she did. Lily was stable but still unconscious, and she agreed with his diagnosis of the case. He suspected a T10 spinal cord injury. If he was right, Lily would never walk again. Jessie wanted to operate on her that night to do all they could.

Ben went to the waiting room with her so they could explain it to Bill. He was sitting on the couch, with his head leaned back against the cushions and his legs stretched out. He looked as beaten as he felt. He opened his eyes as soon as they walked in, and Jessie met his eyes with a serious expression and introduced herself. Ben told him that she was the neurosurgeon they'd been waiting for. Bill did not look pleased when he saw how young she was.

'Is there a more senior member of your group?' he asked bluntly, and Jessie looked momentarily stunned. No one had ever asked her that before. But she could see how distraught he was over his daughter, and she understood. She spoke to him in a gentle voice.

'We are the senior members of the team,' she said, indicating Ben. 'We've been in practice here for ten years.'

'What did you do before that?' he questioned, with eyes that probed hers.

'I was in a practice at Stanford Hospital, where I did my residency.' Ben appeared offended, but Jessie didn't. She had kids the same age as Lily – Ben was a bachelor with no family.

'Where did you go to medical school?' Bill asked her with an intense, aggressive glare, and Jessie could see Ben bristle at the question.

'I went to Harvard,' she said quietly, as Ben objected.

'This is ridiculous. Dr. Matthews is one of the most respected neurosurgeons in the state. People send their spinal cord injury cases here to consult with her. I went to UCLA, if you want to know that too. And I did my residency at UCSF in San Francisco.' He was furious at

43

Bill questioning their credentials, but Jessie didn't blame him. She would have wanted to know the same things if someone was going to operate on one of her kids.

'I have a son almost the same age as Lily. I understand how you feel,' she said compassionately, but Bill wasn't reassured. He was too frightened to be gentle or even civil with either of them.

'How do I know you know what you're doing?' he asked her, and Jessie didn't flinch.

'You don't. You have to trust us. We don't have a lot of choices here. I'd like to operate on Lily tonight, Mr. Thomas. If you'd rather wait until tomorrow to check out our credentials, I understand, but I think it will benefit Lily if we operate sooner. The swelling could get worse, which is liable to do further damage to her future motor function.'

'What does that mean?' He narrowed his eyes at her, and he did not look pleasant.

'We don't know how extensive the damage is. She has a spinal cord injury, but the scans and X-rays don't tell us everything we need to know, about nerve damage, for instance. If her injury is "complete," she won't walk again.' She knew she had to be honest with him. He looked as though he might faint. 'If it's incomplete, we have a chance. I'm hoping it's incomplete, but I won't know until we get in and take a look. But we can wait until tomorrow morning if you prefer. I'd rather not, but

I defer to your wishes.' She was putting the full burden of responsibility on him.

'And if you don't know what you're doing, you cripple her for life, and she's paralyzed. Is that it?' he said angrily. But he was angry at the fates that had allowed this to happen, the same fates that had betrayed him before, and now it was Lily. There were tears bulging in his eyes, so Jessie forgave him his harsh words. Ben didn't and had a strong urge to grab him and shake him, which he resisted.

'Let's assume I know what I'm doing,' she said in a calm voice.

'Is her life at risk in the surgery?'

'We don't have a choice here,' she explained simply. 'The only variable is when. And that's up to you, Mr. Thomas.' He nodded and ran a hand through his hair with a look of anguish.

'I swear, if you kill her, I'll kill you,' he said and seemed as though he meant it. Ben was about to intervene, but Jessie stopped her partner with a quelling glance. She was not afraid of Bill Thomas and could handle him herself.

'I understand that's how you feel,' she said firmly. She had a soothing voice, but Bill was beyond that now. He was crazed with fear for his little girl. 'Why don't you think about it for a while? I'll be here. I'm not going anywhere.' She and Ben left the waiting room and went back to check on Lily, who was remaining stable in poor condition, and then they went to the cafeteria for coffee.

Jessie had a feeling it was going to be a very long night. She wanted to call Tim and see how he was doing, but she also wanted to know her plans before she did.

'How can you let that asshole talk to you like that?' Ben said in a fury, handing her a cup of coffee. He was incensed.

'He's a father, Ben. She's his only kid, according to the chart. He lost his wife. He's terrified he's going to lose his kid, or that she'll be paralyzed. Maybe you have to be a parent to understand.' She took a sip of the steaming coffee, and they agreed that the hospital made the worst coffee on the planet, but they drank it anyway – they always did.

'He threatened to kill you!' Ben said, with all his feathers ruffled. 'He acts like we just got out of med school.' And then he laughed. 'I think you impressed the hell out of him when you said you went to Harvard. What did he expect? You got your degree on the Internet?'

'He's desperate,' she said, as they finished their coffee and went back upstairs. Bill was waiting for them outside Lily's cubicle in the ICU. There was no change, and Jessie didn't expect there to be until after surgery. It was Lily's only hope.

'All right, you can do it,' Bill growled at her. 'You can operate on my daughter, but I swear, if . . .' He didn't finish the sentence this time, and Jessie nodded.

'I'll get the paperwork drawn up.'

'When are you going to do the surgery?' he asked nervously. He would gladly have given his life for Lily's at that moment, or any other.

Jessie had already checked and knew there was an operating room available. She glanced at her watch. 'We need time to prep her. I'd say in about two hours. I want to review the scans and X-rays and tests again with Dr. Steinberg,' she said, looking at Ben, and he nodded.

'How long will it take?'

'It's hard to say. About eight hours, maybe longer. It could be as long as twelve. It depends on what we find once we go in. It's a delicate procedure.' He hated the choice he had made to use an unknown doctor, with no time to check her out. But Ben was right – Harvard and Stanford had impressed him. He just hoped he had made the right decision. He didn't want to take the risk of waiting longer, particularly if waiting could cause more damage. He was putting Lily's life in this woman's hands. 'We'll do everything we can,' she reassured him again.

'Thank you' was all he said in a trembling voice, and went back to the waiting room, as Jessie went to look at the X-rays with Ben, and a nurse drew up the papers. She took them to Bill on a clipboard a few minutes later, and he signed them with tears rolling down his cheeks. The nurse took the clipboard from him, without a word.

Jessie sent Tim a text message while she consulted with

Ben. 'Patient in extremis. Crazed father. Surgery in an hour. See you tomorrow. Love, J.' His answer came back a minute later.

'Good luck. I love you, T.' She smiled and slipped her phone back into her pocket, and hoped that Tim had taken Jimmy bowling, but she didn't want to write back and ask. She and Ben had a lot to discuss before the surgery. He would be assisting, and they formulated a surgical plan as the trauma ICU team prepared Lily for surgery.

Bill sat in the waiting room, feeling like he was living a nightmare. He went to see Lily just before they rolled her away to the operating room. He bent and kissed her forehead as his tears fell on her face. Jessie was already upstairs waiting for her. Bill went outside to get some air for a few minutes after they took Lily to the OR. He stood in the parking lot, crying in the night. It was freezing cold, his tears stung his eyes and cheeks. Minutes later he nearly slipped on a patch of ice as he walked back into the hospital. It was the worst night of his life. He lay down on the couch in the waiting room and closed his eyes. He was wide awake and all he could think of was Lily. He hoped the neurosurgeon knew what she was doing and could repair Lily's injuries. He lay there all night willing her to live and walk again.

Chapter 4

Adam, Heather, and Jimmy were all home for dinner when Chris left for his date. He stopped to say goodbye to his father in the kitchen, as he was taking two frozen pizzas out of the oven. One of them was slightly burned. And they all complained about the burned pizza, and went back upstairs until the rest of dinner was ready, while Tim put the pizzas back in the oven and lowered the heat, to keep them warm.

'Have fun, Dad,' Chris teased him, and Tim glanced at him with a pained grin.

'That's not funny,' Tim said ruefully. 'I guess I should have ordered pizzas.' And then he looked seriously at his son. 'Drive carefully, it's cold as hell out there tonight. The roads are going to be icy.' They all had snow tires on their cars, but he never liked Chris out driving in bad conditions, and the temperature had dropped dramatically that night. The day's snowfall had turned to ice, but Chris was unconcerned.

'Becky's mom is cooking dinner, and we're going to stay at her place and watch a movie.' Tim knew she lived a few miles away, and was somewhat relieved, although Chris still had to get from their house to hers.

'Just be careful,' Tim warned Chris, and checked the pasta he was making, as Chris left. He heard the front door close and then started to put dinner on the table. He had made a salad to go with it, and the three younger children thundered down the stairs five minutes later when he called them, and took their usual seats at the kitchen table. Jimmy looked disappointed when he saw the pizzas and the pasta.

'Mom said she was going to make tacos,' he said, helping himself to a slice of pizza, as Adam took half a pizza for himself, and put a mound of pasta on his plate.

'She had to go to work,' Tim explained, passing the food around. They ate everything, and he said he'd drop Heather and Adam off as soon as they cleaned up the kitchen. 'And we are going bowling,' he said to Jimmy, who grinned happily at his father. He looked pleased as he left the table, and they all went upstairs to get ready to leave. Tim got Jessie's text then, and responded. He knew it was going to be a long night for her, and hoped she wasn't too tired. She hadn't even gotten dinner before she left, but that's what their lives were like. One of them was always rushing off to work, to respond to an emergency. They were used to it, and so were the kids. It was relay-race parenting at its best.

Twenty minutes later Tim dropped Adam off at his friend's house. He'd been invited to spend the night, so Tim didn't need to pick him up, and Heather asked if she could stay at her friend's too, so he and Jimmy were on their own for the night. They were at the bowling alley half an hour after they left home, and as soon as they got there and rented shoes, Jimmy asked for a Coke. Tim got one for himself too, and popcorn for both of them, and they started bowling, and Tim showed his son some of the fine points of the game. They had a good time and left the bowling alley at ten, which was a big treat for Jimmy to be out so late. And he loved being with his dad.

'I want to be a doctor like you one day, Dad,' Jimmy announced out of the blue as they walked back to the car, and Tim smiled at him.

'That's a big decision,' he said, as he unlocked the car, and settled Jimmy on the backseat and put on his seat belt. It had gotten even colder while they were at the bowling alley, and the ground was slippery under his feet as he walked around to the driver's seat. He was worrying about Chris again, and hoped he got home all right. He hated the fact that he was driving, and worried about him at night, and he knew Jessie did too. He smiled at Jimmy in the rearview mirror, started the car, and drove slowly out of the parking lot. He drove home cautiously, as he and Jimmy chatted. Jimmy was asking his father questions about medical school, while Tim kept his eyes on the road.

'Let's make root beer floats when we go home,' Jimmy suggested, and Tim smiled at him again in the rearview mirror just as they pulled up to an intersection. The light was green, and Tim pulled ahead – as he felt the car start to skid on a patch of ice. He was concentrating on what he was doing and never saw the car barreling toward him at high speed. The teenage driver started to skid at the same time and hit the brakes, which made the skid worse. He lost control and hit Tim's car at high speed as Jimmy watched in horror from the backseat. There was the fearsome sound of crashing metal as their car spun like a top and hit the stoplight, while the other car hit a tree. It was over in minutes, and the night was silent around them. There was no sound as Tim sat slumped forward, and Jimmy didn't say a word. The air bag had opened, and Tim was burrowed into it, and all Jimmy could see was a trickle of blood running from his father's ear.

Jimmy sat there unable to move or speak, and then he heard sirens, and policemen opened the car door and pulled him out. They sat him in the police car because it was so cold outside, and one of them asked him if he was okay, while the other officer checked their car and then the car that had hit the tree.

'I think my dad is hurt,' Jimmy said in a small,

terrified voice as the officer knelt on the ground and talked to him.

An ambulance came a few minutes later, and the paramedics took him to the hospital to have him checked. 'That's the hospital where my mom and dad work,' he explained. He had already told them his name and address. 'Can I wait for my dad to come with me? He's hurt,' he said to one of the paramedics as tears slid down his cheeks.

'We're going to bring him in a little while,' the paramedic explained. 'We want to talk to him first about what happened,' he said, and Jimmy nodded. His head hurt, he had bumped it sideways on the car door when the other car hit them. Another ambulance screamed past them as they drove away. Both cars had been totaled, and the driver and the passenger in the front seat of the other car had been killed. So had Tim Matthews. But all Jimmy knew as they took him to the hospital was that his daddy would come later and his mom was already at the hospital, at work. He knew they'd pick him up there. He was scared and shaken up but sure his dad would come soon, and his mom would find them.

The paramedics from the ambulance took him into the emergency room on a stretcher, and the pediatrician on duty examined him, as the paramedics explained to the chief resident what had happened. He looked shocked when the ambulance driver told him Tim Matthews had been killed. He knew Tim and Jessie. He said nothing about it to Jimmy when he came to talk to him. He said they were going to call his mom to come and pick him up. He had a slight concussion, but no other damage. Jimmy had been lucky that night, a lot more so than his father. The resident went to get Jessie's number from their roster then and called her cell, but all he got was voicemail. He didn't want to say too much in a message, just left his name and cell phone number, and to please call him immediately. But she hadn't returned his call by midnight, and they decided to admit Jimmy to pediatrics, for lack of a better solution.

'My dad will be here soon,' Jimmy assured him, and the resident said he was sure he would be, and they would wake him when his mother or father came to pick him up. A nurse took Jimmy up to pediatrics then, and they helped him change into pajamas with dinosaurs on them and put him to bed. He was still waiting for his dad to pick him up when he fell asleep.

Chapter 5

The surgery took longer than Jessie had hoped. It had gone as well as could be expected, but she didn't have good news. The spinal cord injury was a T10, and was 'complete,' which meant that the spinal cord had been severed irreparably. Had it been 'incomplete,' there would have been hope that Lily could regain feeling and function in her legs. But the fall had been too severe. Jessie repaired all that she could, but there was no way Lily would regain use of her legs with a 'complete.'

Ben closed for Jessie, and they walked out of the operating room at seven A.M., eleven hours after they started. It had been a very long night, but at least Lily's chances of survival were good, barring postoperative complications. She was taken to the recovery room, where she would spend the rest of the day, and from there she would go to the ICU until her general condition improved. The only good news they had to report to her father was that the injury was not farther up her spinal cord. She had lost the use of her legs, but her other functions would be normal. Her diaphragm and breathing were not compromised, which would have been far more complicated and dangerous for her. She would have full use of her arms and could eventually lead a normal life, even if from a wheelchair. Considering the severity of the fall, it could have been much worse, or she could have not survived it at all. Jessie was hoping she'd make a good recovery after several months in rehab. But it was too soon to explain all that to Lily's father. For now, what he needed to know was that his daughter had survived the surgery, her chances of recovery were excellent due to her age and good physical condition, her heart had held up well in the surgery, and she had a long life to look forward to. The bad news was that the severing of her spinal cord was complete. And Jessie already knew how hard her father would take it. She probably would have in his shoes too. And now she had to face him and tell him.

He was dozing when she and Ben walked into the waiting room. The lights were off, and he was the only one in there. One of the nurses had given him a blanket and a pillow, and he stirred instantly when Jessie touched his shoulder, and looked sympathetically at him. She was exhausted.

'Mr. Thomas . . .' She roused him gently and he sat up immediately with a terrified expression.

'How is she?' He was panicked, and couldn't read Jessie's expression.

'She did very well in the surgery. She's in the recovery room. We're going to keep her there today, to see how she does. If she comes out of the anesthetic well, we're going to take the breathing tube out today and let her breathe on her own. Her lungs weren't compromised. The injury was farther down her spine.'

'How are her legs?' He got right to the point, and Jessie knew she had to tell him.

'She's not going to regain full function,' she said quietly.

'What does that mean?' He was too tired to be angry now, only scared. 'Will she walk again?' It was all he wanted to know. He couldn't imagine Lily living life in a wheelchair, not his beautiful Lily, who was going to win the gold.

'I don't think so, not with a T10 injury. She'll have full use of her arms and other functions, but the severing of her spinal cord was complete, and there is too much nerve damage in the area to regain full function.'

'Are you telling me that she'll never walk again? That she'll be paralyzed forever?'

'There is constant ongoing research in spinal cord injuries. We can't repair completes now, but that doesn't mean we won't be able to one day. She's very young and could benefit from that research.' It was an oblique way

Danielle Steel

of telling him that medical science currently had no way of repairing the injury Lily had sustained. Jessie had done all she could. Conceivably she could have babies one day, she could lead a full life, and she could have a profession, and a family, but she would do it from a wheelchair. Jessie was confirming his worst fears.

'Never mind the research,' Bill said, standing to face her. 'Can you do anything to make her walk after this? Further surgeries? Bone grafts? Something? Anything?' Jessie shook her head, and he let out an animal sound that was almost a howl of grief. But at least his child was alive. She hadn't died in the accident or the surgery, and she easily could have. He turned to face Jessie then with an angry expression. 'I don't believe you. You just don't know what you're doing. I'll take her anywhere I have to, New York, Boston, Europe. There has to be someone who can repair the damage to her spine.'

'I don't think so, Mr. Thomas. I don't want to hold out false hopes. But she can lead a very good life just as she is. She'll need rehabilitation, but one of the best rehab hospitals in the country is right in your city. Lily will be able to make an amazing adjustment and adapt to her new life. And we can't lose sight of the fact that it's a miracle that she's alive, given the injury she sustained.'

He sat down on the couch again with his head in his hands. The room was reeling. He couldn't even imagine Lily's future. It was a cruel turn of fate for her to wind up in a wheelchair for the rest of her life. He wasn't going to accept it. He would take her all over the world if he had to. Whatever it took, he was going to find someone to fix her. He looked up at Jessie then with anguished eyes.

'I'm not going to let this happen to her.' Jessie knew better than anyone that he had no choice in the matter, any more than he had control over the cable on the chair-lift breaking. It had happened, whether he wanted to face it or not. And for now he was in denial about the consequences of the accident for Lily. Jessie stayed and talked to him for a few more minutes and told him that he could see Lily in a few hours, when she was awake. She suggested that he go home and get some sleep for a while – they would call him if anything happened. But he was determined to stay. He didn't want to leave until he saw Lily. And then Jessie and Ben left. Her conversation with him had not gone well, but it was what she had expected. She suspected that it would be a long time before he was able to face the truth.

Jessie turned her cell phone back on as they came out of the elevator and were walking into the lobby. It had been a long, hard night of intense concentration and back-breaking work, and all she wanted to do now was go home, take a shower, and go to bed. She listened to her messages on the way to her car, and was surprised to hear that she had three from a resident in the ER and two from the police. Her heart nearly stopped as she suddenly

59

thought of Chris. Had something happened to him on the road the night before? But she had no messages from him or Tim, so it couldn't have been about him. She was puzzled as she called the resident in the ER, and as soon as he answered, he asked her where she was.

'In the parking lot. Why? I just walked out of an eleven-hour surgery on an SCI. I warn you, I'm not in great shape, if you want me to look at a patient. Is it someone from the chairlift accident yesterday?' She was willing to examine a patient, but there was no way she could perform surgery again right now. She was exhausted.

He hesitated before he answered. 'Your son was in a car accident last night, Dr. Thomas,' he said, sounding awkward. It was exactly what she'd been afraid of, and all she wanted to know was how bad it was.

'Chris?' she asked, panicked. He could hear the terror in her voice.

'No, Jimmy.'

'How is that possible? He was with his father. No one called me.' Except the police. And suddenly she added confusion to panic. 'Where is he? Did you admit him?'

'He's upstairs in pediatrics. He's fine. He has a mild concussion.'

'Then why did you admit him? Where's his father?'

'I . . . why don't you come in?' She started back toward the hospital at a dead run, as she hung up and called Tim.

It went straight to voicemail, and then she called the number on the message from the police. A sergeant answered, and she told him who she was and why she was calling.

'I think something happened to my husband and son last night. I got a message from the police. I just picked up the message. Is there someone who can tell me what happened?'

The sergeant hesitated, not wanting to tell her over the phone, but he had no choice.

'There was an accident last night. They were hit by a car and skidded on the ice. Your husband's car hit the stoplight. Your son is fine.' He steeled himself for his next words and hated having to say them to her. 'I'm sorry, Mrs. Thomas. Your husband was killed on impact. We went out to the house, but there was no one home.'

'I was working,' she said in a small voice. 'Oh my God . . .' And where was Chris? Why hadn't he called? 'Where is he? . . . my husband . . . where . . .' She felt completely disoriented as she walked into the ER.

'He's at the morgue,' the sergeant answered. Without thinking, she closed her phone. She couldn't bear what he had just said. It couldn't be true. Tim was home with the kids. He had to be. What would he be doing at the morgue? And then the resident spotted her and walked toward her. He recognized her immediately, even though she didn't know him. She was the star neurosurgeon in Squaw. He came to tell her how sorry he was, and she nodded blindly and let him take her upstairs to pediatrics, where Jimmy was dressed and wearing the clothes he'd been wearing the night before, and she could see that he had a bruise along the side of his face where it had hit the car door. She folded him into her arms and held him, grateful that he wasn't dead or seriously injured, and then she looked at him with devastated eyes.

'Daddy forgot to come and get me,' he said quietly. 'We got hit by a car, and he hurt his ear. It was bleeding, and they took me away in an ambulance.' He tried to tell her everything at once. 'The air bag opened, just like you said why you don't let me sit in the front seat.' She listened and had no idea what to tell him, or that his daddy hadn't hurt just his ear, and hadn't forgotten to pick him up. He was at the morgue. The sergeant's words were still ringing in her ears. 'Can we go home now?' She nodded, unable to speak. She helped him put on his coat, and the resident from the ER walked them to her car.

'Can you drive?' he asked her with a look of concern, and she said yes in a small voice. She could drive. She just couldn't think. She didn't understand what had happened, and she knew it couldn't be true. Tim would be at home, making breakfast for the others. She put Jimmy in the backseat of the car, and tried to pretend everything was normal on the drive home, although she was shaking violently. And as soon as they walked into the house, Chris ran down the stairs with a look of panic.

'Dad and Jimmy didn't come home last night,' he said, before he saw Jimmy. 'I knew you were operating so I couldn't call you, and Dad didn't answer his cell.' And then he saw Jimmy standing behind their mother, with the bruise on his face. 'Where's Dad?' Chris asked both of them, as confused as she was. She didn't answer, and both boys were staring at her with a look of terror in their eyes.

'He's not here,' she said, vaguely. 'He's out. I'll make breakfast,' she said, with no idea how to do it. And then she asked Chris to pick up Heather and Adam and bring them home.

'Did something happen to Dad?' he asked her, and Jimmy answered.

'We got in an accident. A car hit us. Dad hurt his ear, it was bleeding, and I bumped my head.' He showed him the bruise, and Chris didn't question him further, or his mother. He left the house without a word, and twenty minutes later all four of the children were in the kitchen, looking expectantly at her. Chris had told them what he knew on the way home, which wasn't much.

'Is Dad okay?' Heather had asked him with concern, and Adam was annoyed that he had had to leave his friend's house just as they were about to eat breakfast, but

Chris said they had to go home right away, and for once Adam didn't argue. He could sense that something was wrong, and his older brother looked scared.

Jessie sat down at the kitchen table with them. She had wanted to tell them all together, but now she didn't know what to say. It was too much for her. None of it made sense. How could he die from being hit by a car? Jimmy had survived it. Why hadn't he? She knew none of the details, but they didn't matter. All that mattered was that Tim was dead. It was unthinkable as she looked into her children's eyes and started to cry.

'Something terrible happened last night. I don't know how it happened.' She looked at Jimmy as she said it, and pulled him onto her lap. He sat there and clung to her. 'Daddy was killed.' She sobbed the words, and all three of the other children put their arms around her and hugged each other and began to cry. It made no sense. It couldn't be true, but it was. She always worried about Chris driving at night, but not Tim. She had assumed he would be there forever. She had never thought something would happen to him. They sat in the kitchen, crying and holding each other for a long time.

And then she called Ben and told him and asked him to come to the morgue with her. The police said she had to identify him, but Ben did it for her – she didn't want to see him like that. She wanted to see him and touch him and hold him, but she didn't want to remember him dead. She couldn't bear it. She couldn't believe he would never come home again.

They went to the funeral parlor and made the arrangements, and then Ben took her home. He told her not to worry about Lily Thomas, that he would go back to the hospital and check on her and cover for Jessie – she should stay home with her kids. But Jessie was too responsible to let him do that, and said she would go to the hospital with him. She owed it to her patient and her father. Ben said he'd pick her up, and at five o'clock she left the children and told them she'd be back soon. Chris's girlfriend had come over, and two of Heather's friends. Adam was playing a video game, unwilling to believe what had happened, and Jimmy was asleep in his parents' bed. Jessie had been lying next to him before she left the house again with Ben.

When they got to the hospital, Lily had been moved from the recovery room to the ICU. The breathing tube was out, and she was sedated, but she was awake. And medically she was doing well. Her father had been in to see her, and the nurse with Lily said he had gone to the cafeteria to get something to eat. Jessie checked Lily's chart and prescribed several medications. She was satisfied with her progress, and Ben promised to check on her again that night.

They were just leaving, when Lily's father stepped out of the elevator and looked at them both with a distraught expression, but he spoke to Jessie, not Ben.

'I don't believe what you told me this morning,' he told her firmly. 'You may have gone as far as your capabilities, but that doesn't mean that someone else, with greater skill, can't repair the damage that was done.' For a moment Jessie didn't answer, and then she nodded. She was willing to let it go at that. She knew full well that no doctor was going to be able to restore full function to Lily, but Bill Thomas wasn't ready to accept that yet. In time he would – he would have no other choice. 'I'm lining up consultations with other doctors in London and New York. I heard about a neurosurgeon in Zurich who specializes in spinal cord injuries. And I want to take her to Harvard.'

'I understand,' Jessie said with a nod. 'I probably would too. Dr. Steinberg will come back to see her later.' He saw that Jessie looked vague and distracted, and he interpreted it as fear of the other consultations and what they would say.

'And what about you? You're not coming back tonight?' He looked outraged, and Jessie was apologetic.

'I'm sorry, I can't. I'll come back tomorrow.'

'Don't you think that as her neurosurgeon, you should see her tonight too?' He was instantly hostile and aggressive.

'If she has a problem, I will,' Jessie assured him. 'I'll call in and speak to the resident, and Dr. Steinberg will come in immediately if anything comes up. I think she'll be fine. I'm sorry, I have to be with my children. I'll be back tomorrow, as soon as I can.' Bill was furious as he pushed past her, and without a word, she got into the elevator with Ben, and looked like she was going to collapse. Jessie knew it had been a mistake to come in. Although she had wanted to see Lily, Jessie wasn't up to it, or to dealing with Lily's father's implications that she hadn't done a good job and didn't know what she was doing.

'You should have told him,' Ben said through clenched teeth. It had taken all his restraint not to grab the guy and tell him what he thought of him. He acted like he could control the world, and he couldn't. He had been incredibly rude and hard on Jessie, but all she wanted to do now was go home to her kids and comfort them. She wanted to lie on her bed and cry for the husband she loved so much and would never see again. Ben drove her home, and she thanked him when she got out of the car. He watched her walk into the house, and cried all the way home himself. He couldn't believe Tim was gone, and he couldn't even imagine how hard Jessie's life was going to be now without him, and how empty. All she ever did was work and spend time with her husband and kids. They hadn't had time for a social life in years, and rarely saw friends, just each other. Tim had been her best friend. Ben's heart ached for her and her kids. It was a terrible time for all of them.

Bill Thomas was still steaming when he walked back

into the ICU. He had convinced himself that Jessie was incompetent, and now she was being negligent too, not planning to visit Lily again that night. It was the least she could have done, as far as he was concerned. He noticed the nurses talking in hushed whispers with a serious expression as he passed the desk.

'Is Lily okay?' He was worried that something had happened and they were talking about her.

'She's fine,' one of the nurses reassured him, and she could see how angry he was. He had already told them that he would see to it that his daughter would walk again. 'We were just talking about Dr. Matthews,' one of the nurses explained, and seemed upset.

'What about her?' he said unhappily. 'She's not even coming back to see Lily tonight. She says she has to be with her children,' he said with contempt. 'Maybe she should decide if she's a mother or a doctor. Being a neurosurgeon isn't a part-time job.'

The nurse was shocked by what he said, and it was obvious he didn't know what had happened, and she thought he should. 'Dr. Matthews's husband was killed in an accident last night. A car accident. He was an anesthesiologist here, and a very dear man. It happened when she was operating on Lily. She only found out this morning when she left. Her youngest son was injured too.' Bill looked startled by what she said, and then embarrassed. He had no idea how to respond.

'I'm sorry . . . I didn't know . . .' He remembered what he had said to her. He believed it, but he recognized that his timing had been awful. 'I'm very sorry,' he said again, and went back to see his daughter. He was haunted by what the nurse had said and remembered how he had felt the night Lily's mother died. And competent or not, which remained to be seen, his heart went out to Jessie. And as he looked down at Lily, sleeping peacefully in her hospital bed, for the first time he forgot about whether or not she would walk again and was just grateful she was alive.

Chapter 6

As promised, Jessie came back to check on Lily in the morning, after having breakfast with her kids. She couldn't eat, but they picked at the cereal she put on the table. She hadn't slept all night, and she looked it, when she arrived in Lily's room in her white coat, looking pale with dark circles under her eyes. She smiled as soon as she saw Lily, who was mildly sedated for pain, but awake. She was responding well to the medications.

'How are you feeling, Lily?' Jessie asked her gently as she stood next to her. She had read all the entries in her chart carefully at the nurses' desk before she came in. Lily had had a few minor problems, and some discomfort, but she was doing remarkably well. She was young and strong. And it was much too soon to tell her the implications of her injuries, so she didn't know yet, and Bill hadn't said anything to her either. She needed time to recover from the surgery. She didn't know either that she would have to go to rehab when she was released from the hospital, to learn a whole new way of life, and adjust to her injury. Jessie was not planning to broach the subject with her for some time, although she had been candid with Lily's father. What Lily needed now was time and healing. Jessie used all her energy and discipline to focus on her patient.

'I'm okay,' Lily said quietly. She was alert enough to know that she had sustained a very serious injury – she just didn't know the realities of her future. 'Thank you for everything you're doing for me,' she said, and Jessie was touched.

'That's what I do.' She asked about some pain the chart said Lily had had the night before, but it was normal for her to have considerable discomfort, despite the paralysis in her lower trunk and limbs.

'How soon can I go home?' Lily wanted to know, which Jessie thought was a good sign.

'Not for a while. Let's get you feeling better first,' she said noncommittally. But she also knew that it was typical of patients with any illness or injury to feel that if they could just get out of the hospital, they could leave the problem there. Lily was going to be taking this problem with her, for the rest of her life. But what Jessie planned to tell her, when she was ready to hear it, was that in spite of her complete spinal cord injury, she could still lead a full life in almost every possible way, and others had done it before her. She needed to be shown what she could do, not just what she obviously couldn't, and she would learn all that in rehab. Jessie was going to recommend that she stay at Craig Hospital in Denver for three or four months. She knew it would come as a blow to Lily and a shock to her father, but Jessie wanted her to make the best possible adjustment. She hoped to have her there within a month, if all went well.

Jessie spent nearly an hour with Lily, just talking and observing her for small medical details while seeming to just be casually chatting, and then she left and Lily dozed off. Jessie ran into her father at the elevator as she was leaving, and Bill was getting off, on the floor of the ICU. He seemed surprised to see Jessie, and mumbled awkwardly for a moment, which was unlike him, as he looked into her eyes, which were two deep pools of pain. She was far less cheerful now that she was not at her patient's bedside, and he could see how distraught she was. Jessie was deathly pale.

'I . . . the nurses told me about your husband yesterday . . . I'm really sorry . . . and about the things I said . . . I was just upset about Lily. I still am, and I want to get all the consultations I can for her when we leave here. Someone, somewhere must have some new space-age, state-of-the-art procedure that will help her walk again. We can't just give up and let her sit in a wheelchair for the rest of her life. That would be a tragedy for her,' he said grimly, but his tone with Jessie was considerably gentler than it had been the day before.

'It's only a tragedy if we treat it that way,' Jessie said firmly. She was stronger than she looked, even in her own dire situation. She was still a supremely competent medical practitioner, and her patient's needs and best interests were at the forefront of her mind at that moment. 'Her life doesn't have to be a tragedy, Mr. Thomas.' She wanted him to see that too, not just Lily, because he would inevitably influence how Lily felt about herself. If she lived in an atmosphere of despair, it would affect her deeply, and Jessie didn't want that for her, or for any of her patients, no matter how catastrophic their accidents had been, or their injuries as a result. And an upbeat attitude about what lay ahead was essential to her recovery now. It was part of why she wanted Lily to go to Craig Hospital, to get her life going again, in the best possible way. 'She can still lead an amazing life, and we want her to, Mr. Thomas. There is a huge range of things she will be able to do – drive a car, go to college, learn a profession, go into politics, marry, and have babies. The only thing she can't do is use her legs. The rest of her is still intact. We just need to refocus her goals.' There was more to it than that, but Jessie wanted to stress a glass-half-full theory, or even entirely full or close to it, rather than a glass-half-empty mood of catastrophe, which Lily would pick up on rapidly and respond to, either way.

Bill's face looked tense and angry again when he answered, 'She's not going to be skiing again, or going to the Olympics. She will never win a gold medal now, and she's been training for that for five years. She'll never dance or walk again, she won't walk down the aisle at her wedding, and how many guys do you think are going to marry a girl in a wheelchair, no matter how beautiful she is?' There were tears in his eyes. It had been all he could think of since Lily had been in the accident, and even more so after Jessie's prognosis after the surgery that she would never walk again.

'The right one will marry her. I did my residency at Stanford with a man who had a spinal cord injury similar to Lily's. He was in a wheelchair, and he wanted to do neurosurgery because of what had happened to him. He got married around the same time I did, and last I heard he had six kids. He married a wonderful woman, also a physician, who is crazy about him. She's at the forefront of SCI research, probably because of him. Great lives can still happen after an accident like this.

'I'm not telling you it's easy, and I won't lie to Lily either, but I have seen personally what people can achieve. With the right attitude and training, Lily will be able to do great things. And it could have been even worse. She's paraplegic, not quadriplegic, she has full use of her upper body and upper limbs. She won't have to run a wheelchair by using a breathing tube, although some of the people who have to do that are remarkable too. And more important, she's alive.' A number of people on the chairlift hadn't been as lucky, and there would be several funerals in town in the coming days. Others had been killed who had come to Tahoe just to have some fun and ski, as Lily had.

'I'm not going to just let it end there,' Bill said with determination. 'I'm starting to contact the experts in spinal cord injury around the world.' The implication was still there that Jessie was a small-town doctor, and others were more capable than she. But Lily's injury was what it was, and no one would be able to change that or reverse it, until research came up with new solutions, hopefully in Lily's lifetime since she was so young, but not yet. Jessie had already done, and was doing, all that anyone could, whether Bill recognized that or not. He still was in denial, and wasn't ready to give up. Jessie knew that ultimately it would be hard on Lily if he was not able to accept the realities of his daughter's life. But she also knew that it was early days yet, and sooner or later he'd have to face the truth.

Bill Thomas was a fighter and used to getting what he wanted. He had achieved remarkable things and was not ready to give up on this. And he would have done anything in the world for Lily. Jessie admired that in him, no matter how rude and disagreeable he was to her. Unlike Ben, she understood his motivations and his feelings and sympathized with him. He was fighting for Lily, not for himself, and he thought he was doing the right thing, even if it meant riding roughshod over Jessie. She was the bearer of bad tidings, and he didn't want to hear bad news. No one did, and some people accepted it better than others. Bill didn't. He wanted the very best recovery he could get for Lily. He wasn't malevolent, he was just rough around the edges when things didn't go his way.

'I'm sorry about your husband,' he said again, and Jessie nodded, trying not to cry at what he said. It was easier to talk about Lily than herself. And she was exhausted after two nights without sleep, which made everything even worse. 'I lost my wife in a car accident when Lily was three. It's a terrible thing,' he said gently. 'I know how you feel.' Her emotions overwhelmed her then, and in spite of her best efforts, tears spilled from her eyes and ran down her cheeks. She wiped them away with one hand, as he looked at her sympathetically. 'I hear you have four kids. I'm sorry for all of you. At least you have them. All I have is Lily. She's my whole world.' His eyes were damp as he said it, and they stood looking at each other for a long beat, momentarily partners in loss and grief. It was a singular kind of pain, and Jessie had never hurt so much in her entire life. Her whole being had been intertwined with Tim. They had spent every waking hour together when they weren't working, and had been perfect partners in raising their kids. She couldn't even imagine a life without him. And every time she thought about it, she wanted to scream in terror. How was she going to live without Tim?

She left Bill and the hospital a few minutes later. She had assured Bill that Ben Steinberg would be monitoring Lily closely and let her know if he needed her to come in. Tim's funeral was the next day, and for now she needed to be with her kids. This time Bill didn't complain.

She was home a few minutes later, and all four of her children had stayed home from school, and her neighbor Sally McFee had come by and brought them food. Everyone wanted to help. Chris and Heather were sprawled in the living room, watching daytime TV, Adam was in his room, lying on his bed and staring at the ceiling with a blank expression, and Jimmy was sitting next to Heather, sucking his thumb, which he hadn't done since he was three. They were a forlorn group, and Jessie looked no better as she walked in. Sally showed her what she'd put in the fridge for them. It was a mountain of food that none of them wanted to eat, but Jessie appreciated the thought. Everyone in the neighborhood felt terrible for them. Tim had always been the nicest guy they knew, and had even been helpful with their kids, not just his own. He was always willing to drive carpool, have their kids spend the night, or help a friend. Jessie looked at Sally with devastated eyes, and then Sally hugged her and they both cried. Jessie knew without saying it that her life would never be the same again.

They talked about the accident at the chairlift then, just to change the subject, and Jessie mentioned that she had a patient who had been one of the people who had fallen off. Sally and her husband knew two of the ski instructors who had been killed. They compared it to a similar accident that had happened more than thirty years before. The chairlift had been well maintained, but it was just one of those fluke accidents that happen, and sweep lives away, and alter other lives irreversibly, like Lily's. It was fate, like Tim's death two nights ago. And now Jessie had the rest of her life to face without Tim. After Sally left, Jessie went upstairs to pull out clothes for the kids to wear to their father's funeral, and something for herself. She looked into Tim's closet then, to find something decent to put him in, even though the casket would be closed. She had promised the funeral parlor she would drop off a suit for him to wear, and as soon as she opened the closet door and looked at the clothes he would never wear again, she just stood there for a minute, sank to her knees, and sobbed.

While Lily slept that morning, which she still did most of the time, Bill went back to the house to take care of some things. He called Angie, his assistant in Denver, and gave her a list of calls to make for him. He had told her about the accident by e-mail, and she was horrified by the news, and anxious to do whatever she could. She adored Lily and was dedicated to Bill. He gave her the names of neurosurgeons all over the world that he wanted to check out, and he said he had no idea when they'd be coming home. It was too soon to tell.

And after Bill spoke to her, he called Penny in St. Bart's. The accident had happened two days before, but he hadn't had the time or the heart to call her. She wasn't part of his family life, and although she had known Lily for two years, they weren't close.

He was planning to leave Penny a voicemail, and thought it unlikely she would answer, and was surprised when she picked up. He hadn't wanted to give her news like this in a text, and for a moment he wanted to hear her voice. He had called no one until then, except his assistant a few minutes before.

The moment she heard his voice, Penny could sense that something was wrong. She felt guilty for not having called him from St. Bart's, but she had been intensely busy for the past week. For her, work always came first – it was a choice she had made with her life twenty years before. At forty-two, she had never married or had children and had no regrets. Her clients were her kids. Her business meant everything to her, and that suited Bill, who wasn't prepared to give more than he had. Lily owned his heart. And there had never been serious room for anyone else in it, since his wife died.

'Something wrong?' She could hear instantly the somber tone of his voice when he said her name.

'Yeah, very much so,' he said, as tears filled his eyes and he cleared his throat. He didn't want to get emotional with her, he just wanted to let her know, but it was comforting to hear her on the phone. They knew each other well after all. 'Lily had an accident in Squaw.' He told her what had happened then, and Penny was horrified. He didn't tell her the doctor had said she would never walk again – the rest was bad enough, and he didn't believe it yet.

'Oh my God, I'm so sorry. Do you want me to fly out? I was leaving tomorrow anyway. The opening went really well,' although it seemed irrelevant to both of them now, in the face of what he had said. She had been planning to stop in New York to see a client there on the way back, and another in Chicago, but said she was more than willing to come to California and drive to Lake Tahoe to be with him instead. He was touched by the offer, but it didn't feel right to him. He wanted to focus on Lily and no one else. 'Will she walk again?' Penny went right to the obvious question, and Bill sounded hard when he answered.

'Of course she will.' He had no intention of sharing Jessie's prognosis with her. He thought it was wrong anyway. And he didn't want Penny thinking of Lily that way – it would make it all too real. 'I've got Angie looking up a list of neurosurgeons to consult. We want the best care we can get. This is a backwater town, although the surgeon is supposedly pretty good, she's Harvard trained, but not as sophisticated as doctors in big cities. I want to take Lily for some other consultations when we leave here.' Penny could sense that there was something he wasn't telling her. Bill had put on his toughest voice, and she wondered if they had given him bad news. If it was about Lily, he wouldn't take it easily.

'That makes a lot of sense,' Penny said quietly, and didn't press him further about it. 'She's lucky to be alive. Is there anything I can do?' she asked, sounding wistful for a minute. She would have liked to be there for him in a crisis like this. She liked Lily, and Bill, but she was also aware that he never let her into the inner sanctum of his life, and he was even less likely to now when Lily needed him so much. There hadn't been much room for her before, and there would be even less now. It was just the way he was. Lily was the center of his universe, and Penny was just a place he visited from time to time.

Marriage or even living with a man had never been her goal. And too much time with anyone, or intimacy, made her uncomfortable as well. Her career was easier to manage than a man who might take over her life and try to control her. Like Bill, she had fought hard to improve her life and establish her business. Her own security and independence were more important to her than close personal bonds. But when she heard the sadness in his voice, she was sorry he wouldn't let her be there for him. Still, she wasn't surprised. That wasn't the kind of relationship they'd shared, which was strictly meant for good times, and nothing else.

'I'll let you know if there's anything,' he said kindly. 'For now, she just has to get strong and heal. She came through the surgery very well, but it was only yesterday. I'll call you when I can,' he promised, but she doubted that he would. She could hear it in his voice. She was on the outside now, and always had been, except for the occasional nights they spent together when Lily was out, or on trips. Bill Thomas had very successfully compartmentalized his life and guarded his heart from anyone but his daughter.

'I'll talk to you soon. Give Lily my love,' she said as they hung up. She sent her love to Lily, but had never offered it to him, nor did he want it for himself. They had no commitment to each other, and had preferred it that way. And for an odd moment after they ended the call, Penny had the feeling that he had just said goodbye to her and their relationship. She wasn't sure, but she could sense that he wanted no distractions now from his helping Lily to recover. And Bill had the same feeling as he sat looking out the window in Squaw Valley, at the chairlift that had broken two days before and changed their lives. The entire area had been cordoned off, and a large part of the mountain was closed and would stay that way for some time until they solved the mystery of what had happened and why.

Lily developed a fever that night, which wasn't unusual after surgery, and Ben called Jessie to report it to her. They had just come back from the funeral parlor, where the entire medical community of Squaw Valley, and several others, had come to pay their respects to Tim. Parents of their children's friends were there, men who had played tennis and softball with Tim when he had time. There were people Jessie didn't even know he knew, and others who only knew her. She was shocked by how many showed up, and she felt drained when she got home and Ben called. And her children looked miserable too. The casket with their father in it had been there, but at Jessie's request, it was closed. It would have been too much to see Tim lying there. She was sure that she would have lost control and become hysterical if it were open, and she didn't want her children having the memory of him that way. What Jimmy had seen that night after the collision was bad enough, and he was still talking about the blood coming from his father's ear, which Jessie knew was from the head injury that he had sustained and that had killed him.

'I'll come in,' Jessie said with a sigh when Ben called her about Lily's fever. It was fairly high, and something to watch, but not unusual in the circumstances, but Jessie wanted to see her anyway to be sure. She was responsible and diligent even now, no matter how hard for her.

'You don't have to,' Ben reassured her. 'I'll stick around for a while.' His girlfriend Kazuko had come to the funeral parlor, and Ben was going to be one of the pall-bearers the next day. Kazuko was a nurse he had met at UCSF, and they had lived together for years. She had come to Squaw Valley from San Francisco with him, and the living arrangement they had seemed to work. He was two years younger than Jessie, and at forty-one, he still didn't feel ready to get married. Jessie and Kazuko had talked about it several times, and Kazuko had given up hope that he ever would. She was forty-six years old, totally devoted to him and didn't seem to care if they got married now. She said she felt too old to have kids, and had given up the opportunity, to be with him. She worked at the hospital in radiology, had dozens of hob-bies, and spoke fluent Japanese, although she'd been born in the States. She and Ben had gone to Japan several times, and he had learned Japanese too. They were avid skiers, which was what had brought them there in the first place, and Ben loved their life in Squaw Valley. Ben had grown up in L.A. and said he never missed it. Mountain life suited him far more than it did Jessie, who still missed city life occasionally, and the cultural life it offered, after her years in Boston and Palo Alto, near San

Francisco, and growing up in New York before that, but she had come to Lake Tahoe for Tim and never looked back.

When Jessie got to the hospital to check on Lily, she was sleeping, and Bill was roaming the halls, worried. Jessie examined her and was satisfied that it was a minor but ordinary complication of the surgery, and she and Ben agreed, but she felt better for having seen her.

'How are your kids doing?' Bill asked her before she left. He had been surprised that she'd come in, but Lily was a major case, and although she trusted Ben implicitly, she wouldn't have been comfortable if she hadn't seen her herself. She didn't say it to Bill, but he understood and was impressed. If the news she had given him weren't so bad, he might have liked her better than he did. As it was, he resented what she'd said about Lily never walking again.

'My kids are okay, I guess,' Jessie answered his question. 'As okay as they can be right now. It doesn't seem real to any of us yet,' and as she said it, she realized that that was how he felt about Lily's accident. It took time to absorb the reality of change into one's life, especially changes as major as the ones that had just happened to all of them.

'Thank you for coming in.' He knew the funeral was the next day, and her showing up at the hospital to check Lily's fever was a sign of her meticulous diligence.

She reassured him again about Lily, and then left, and went home. The children were painfully quiet, and the house was eerily silent since the accident. It was hard to imagine laughter there again. The older children were distraught. Jimmy was already sound asleep in his mother's bed, and Adam was playing video games on the TV, with a glazed look. They all felt as though they were underwater, moving in slow motion.

Tim's mother was alive in Chicago, but had dementia, and wouldn't understand what was going on, so she didn't come. Jessie had lost her parents years before, fairly young, so the children had no grandparents to share their grief with them. All they had now was their mother.

The funeral the next day was even worse. It had a horrifying unreality to it, as the priest talked about Tim and the choir sang 'Ave Maria,' while Jessie and her children cried. Almost every medical practitioner, nurse, and technician in Squaw was there. Jessie recognized hundreds of faces but wouldn't remember any of them later. The pallbearers were all fellow anesthesiologists he worked with, and Ben, and Chris had asked to be one of them too. It nearly ripped out Jessie's heart as she watched him and realized for the first time, as her son helped carry his father's casket, that he was now a man. He had just turned eighteen. And this was the most awful rite of passage of all.

They went to the cemetery afterward and buried Tim in the frozen ground. Someone had told her that the two teenagers who had died in the accident, in the other car, were buried the same day, and those who had died in the chairlift accident would be buried in the coming days. And as everyone went back to Jessie's house afterward, it began to snow again, big fat flakes of snow that looked like something in a snow globe or on a Christmas card. She stood outside their back door for a minute, to get some air, and to escape all the people who had come to pay their respects, and she looked up at the sky and thought about Tim. It was impossible to believe she would never see him again. She couldn't imagine a world without him in it, and tears rolled slowly down her cheeks, as they had for days. She shivered in the cold and went back inside, knowing, as she had since it happened, that her life would never be the same.

Chapter 7

It was February, and Lily had been at the hospital for over a month, before Jessie felt ready to release her. She had made a good recovery, and responded to the medications and treatments well. They were mostly for bladder and bowel control, and would be important for her in her life as a paraplegic, which was a concept her father still hadn't accepted. He had been in consultation with neurosurgeons around the world, and had identified four he was planning to take her to, in Zurich, London, New York, and Boston. Jessie was familiar with their names and reputations, and the research they had done or been attached to. The only one of the group she knew personally was the doctor Bill had contacted at Harvard, who was the head of neurosurgery at Massachusetts General Hospital. Jessie had studied under him in medical school, and had remained in touch with him. She had never consulted with him about a patient until now. All of her cases so far were clear-cut, and although many of her patients came from other places and had been injured while skiing in Squaw Valley, most of them had only wanted referrals to physicians in their hometowns when they went back. None had ever embarked on a pilgrimage like the one Bill was planning, and Jessie had some concerns about Lily traveling so extensively as soon as she was released. But Bill was mindful of that as well. He had chartered a private plane for the journey, and booked suites in the best hotels. He had asked Jessie if she thought a doctor should travel with them, and implied heavily that she should do it, but that would have been impossible for her. She couldn't leave her children so soon after their father's death, nor her other patients in Squaw Valley, who needed her as well. Instead, Jessie suggested he take a nurse from the neurosurgery ICU, and she selected one carefully and discussed it with her.

Jennifer Williams was thrilled to make the trip, and Lily liked her. Jessie assured Bill that she trusted Jennifer implicitly, and he made his plans to leave Squaw on Valentine's Day. Their departure just happened to fall on that day, due to the schedules of the neurosurgeons they would be seeing, and the availability of the plane. They were planning to fly out of Reno, and would be getting there from Squaw Valley by limousine. Bill's assistant in Denver had carefully made all the plans and handled all the details. Jessie still felt that the journey would be futile, but she didn't try to discourage him, and she assured him that she would be available by phone for consultation with any of the doctors. And they had already received from Jessie all of Lily's records and test results electronically. Given what they showed, Jessie was surprised that they were willing to meet with him, but Bill Thomas was an important man, and he had pulled all the necessary strings to get in to see them. Jessie knew by then just how stubborn he was. They had had several showdowns in the past six weeks, when he continued to assure Lily in no uncertain terms that she would walk again. Jessie felt it was irresponsible of him to do so. Two days before they left, Lily brought it up with her.

'This is it, isn't it, Dr. Matthews?' Lily had asked her quietly, while sitting in a wheelchair in her room. She had already begun therapy at Squaw, and Jessie had agreed on a treatment plan with the therapists at Craig Hospital when she got back to Denver. That was crucial for her now, to help her adapt to her new life. Her old life was gone forever, despite what her father said.

Lily had begun calling and texting her friends at home once she felt better. She had called Jeremy and Veronica, both of whom were horrified by what had happened to her, and she had called some other friends. But suddenly there was a vast chasm between them and Lily, and everything they talked about was something she would no longer be able to engage in, like their Olympic training on the ski team, and all of her friends were on the team. And just as it had been for her, it was their whole life. With her accident, she had become an outsider instantly. Even their recreational pastimes would be difficult or impossible for Lily now, dancing, skating, skiing, sports. And for three or four months after they got home, Lily would be in rehab, and they would have to visit her there. They promised Lily they would, but she already felt left out of their activities when they called her, and without training for the Olympics, there would be a huge hole in her life. Her coach had called to encourage her, after talking to her father, and assured her that she would not be too old to win the gold in five years, if she missed the Olympics the next year. Her father had assured her coach that she would make a full recovery. Bill had told no one that her spinal cord injury was complete or that she was paralyzed from the waist down and would stay that way. Given what her father said, her coach was sure that she would recover, and Lily hadn't told her friends the full extent of her injuries either. Her father had told her not to. Her eyes looked sad as she put the question to Jessie, who didn't understand immediately what she meant when she asked her if 'this was it.'

'Here in Squaw? Yes, it is.' Jessie smiled at her after her morning visit. She had grown attached to her, more than she usually did with her patients. Lily was a lovely girl, and the blow of what she was facing would weigh heavily on her for a while, Jessie knew, particularly with her father's attitude. He still had reality to face and hadn't yet. Jessie hoped that for Lily's sake he would soon. It would make it easier for Lily once he did, and they could move forward into the business of leading life in the best possible ways. For now, he was still clinging to the past, and urging Lily to do the same, which wasn't good for her.

'You'll be busy once you get home,' Jessie said to her. 'At Craig, with school, with your friends. You've got college ahead of you too.' She was trying to get Lily to look forward instead of back.

'I didn't mean that,' Lily said sadly, with a look of resignation. 'I meant, this is it,' she said again as she pointed to her legs, strapped into the wheelchair so they wouldn't slip off when the chair moved. She had no control of them whatsoever, as though they belonged to someone else, and she felt nothing below her waist. Jessie paused for a long moment after she asked her the question. Bill had given her strict instructions not to tell Lily she would never walk again, but Jessie was a responsible physician, and she knew what the other doctors were going to tell them, particularly the one in Boston, whom Jessie knew and had called herself. He agreed with her prognosis to the letter and had sensed Bill's refusal to accept it. Jessie had confirmed that to him. 'I'm never going to get out of this chair again, am I?' Lily asked her bluntly. She had suspected it from everything that had been said, but her father kept telling her otherwise, with incredible determination, and he had never lied to her before. It was confusing her now, and Jessie could see it. Lily was more ready to face the truth than her father was.

'There's a lot of research in this area,' Jessie said. 'Spinal cord injuries are of interest to a lot of people. And stem cell research has given everyone a lot of hope.' Lily's eyes were boring into hers. She didn't want to hear about the research, Jessie knew – she wanted to hear the truth from her. Jessie's voice was serious when she spoke. 'For now, yes, this is it. They're going to teach you a lot of ways to deal with it and improve your skills at Craig.'

Lily had a powerful lower body from skiing. Now they were going to strengthen her upper body, so she could use her arms in new ways, to guide her wheelchair, or help herself. Her father had ordered her a state-of-the-art feather-light wheelchair for their trip. It was one of the best ones made. And Jennifer would be there to help her.

'Lily, there's no reason why you can't lead an amazing life from now on. Not just a good life, an amazing one. I really mean that, and I believe you will. I'm not telling you it will be easy at first, and it's a big adjustment, but you can do this. New doors are going to open up to you, which you don't expect now. You may not be able to win the gold at the Olympics, and in fact you can't, but you can win the gold in your life, which matters more. You're a winner, Lily, I know you are. You just have to hang on for the ride now, and see where this takes you.' Lily nodded, with tears in her eyes.

'My father keeps saying I'm going to walk again, and I know I won't. He doesn't want to believe that,' she said, as the tears spilled onto her cheeks. She had a lot to face now, and all of it from a wheelchair, forever. It was overwhelming for a seventeen-year-old, or anyone, and Jessie respected her enormously for trying, and in some ways being more mature than her father.

'He loves you very much,' Jessie said quietly, trying to explain the agonies of parenthood to her in a few words, but Lily understood that herself.

'I know. You don't think I'll walk again, do you?' she asked Jessie, who couldn't lie to her. She hadn't yet, but she had avoided the obvious as much as possible, at the request of Lily's father.

'No, I don't. Unless the research they're doing now changes something,' she said again. It was the best she could offer, and had been from the beginning, given the location and extent of Lily's injury.

'Then why is my dad taking me to all those doctors all over the world?' She wasn't looking forward to being poked and prodded by four more doctors. She trusted Jessie, even if her father didn't, and she knew she was right. She had sensed it all along. Her legs were too dead to ever come alive again, no matter what her father said.

'Because he's hoping that I'm wrong. I'm not sure I

blame him. I'd probably do the same if it were one of my kids. It's always good to get other opinions and learn something more.' She tried to be respectful of what Bill was doing, at least to his daughter, although as Lily's physician and surgeon she would have preferred to see her go straight to Craig and start rehab, and not wear herself out traveling. But they were doing it in optimal conditions, so she had no serious medical objections, just philosophical ones. And she would have hated to see Lily cling to a hope that wasn't real. But Jessie could tell now that she wasn't, only Bill was, and he wasn't Jessie's patient. His refusal to face the truth was something he would have to deal with himself. Jessie knew that the doctors and physical therapists at Craig would do all they could for Lily. And sooner or later Bill Thomas would have to face the facts.

'I'm going to miss you,' Lily said in a small voice and wheeled her chair over to where Jessie was standing, to hug her. And then she choked on the next words: 'Thank you for saving my life.' It was something Bill hadn't been able to say to her. Jessie's eyes filled with tears as she hugged her. So much had happened since she and Lily had met. It had been a life-altering time for her as well, with her husband's death. They had both lost a lot in the last six weeks, and the benefits, if there were to be any, and the blessings weren't obvious yet.

'Will you stay in touch?' Jessie asked her gently. She

normally didn't ask that, except medically, but Lily had come to mean a lot to her. She was a very special girl, Bill was right about that.

'I promise.'

Jessie was glad they had had the opportunity to talk without her father around, which was rare. He seldom left Lily alone in the hospital, and he intended to do the same once they got home. Jessie realized that ultimately his deep concern might become oppressive for Lily, but he was still getting over the shock of what had happened, and it would probably take him a long time, just as it would for her to get over losing Tim. Now, every time Chris drove somewhere, or every time her cell phone rang, she had her heart in her mouth. She knew it would be years before she trusted life again. The worst had happened, and now she was terrified for her kids. Just as Bill was about Lily. It was their burden to bear, and Jessie knew it wasn't easy for their kids.

Lily's departure from the hospital, six weeks after the accident, was emotional for everyone who had cared for her. Nurses came to say goodbye and give her little gifts. The resident kissed her goodbye, Ben wished her good luck when he joined Jessie to see her off. Lily hugged Jessie hard and thanked her again, and there were tears in many eyes, as Lily waved from the window as the limousine drove away to take them to Reno. They were flying to

London for their first consultation on the list of four. Bill had wanted to schedule one in Germany as well, but after reviewing her records, the doctor had refused and said he would be wasting their time.

Lily's wheelchair was in the trunk of the car, and Jennifer, the nurse Bill had hired, was with them, excited about the trip. She was twenty-seven years old and had never been to Europe or the East before. She had gone to nursing school at USF, and then returned to Lake Tahoe, where she had grown up. This was a big adventure for her, and she and Lily chatted while Bill talked on his BlackBerry. He had let his business slide in the last month and a half and was paying closer attention to it again.

Jennifer gasped when she saw the plane that was waiting for them in Reno. It was a Boeing Business Jet, and incredibly luxurious once they stepped inside. Bill carried Lily easily onto the plane and set her down in one of the large, comfortable seats. There was a living room, a dining area, and two bedrooms, which Bill had wanted so they could rest. They were expected to be in London in ten hours, which was seven A.M. local time. Their consultation with the chief neurosurgeon at King's College Hospital was set for the following morning. And he had booked two suites for them at Claridge's. He had high hopes for the meeting, and was even willing to stay in London, if the doctor suggested treatment there for her.

Lily watched two movies, and then Jennifer helped her settle into one of the bedrooms. The bathroom was difficult for her to negotiate with the wheelchair, and Bill had to carry her in and out and lay her gently down on the bed afterward. Lily slept for the rest of the trip, she still tired easily, and Jennifer took her vital signs, but she was fine, and did well on the flight.

They were whisked through customs and immigration at Heathrow, and Jennifer pushed Lily's chair. A Bentley was waiting to take them to Claridge's, and their accommodations were comfortable and elegant. Lily was dying to get out, but her father wanted her to rest. She called Veronica, but she was out training on the slopes, and her phone was on voicemail, so Lily sent her a text and said she couldn't wait to see her. They were due back in Denver in ten days, depending on how things went on their medical tour.

They spent the day in the suite, resting and watching movies on TV. And the next morning, after breakfast in Lily's suite, they went to King's College Hospital, to meet with the first doctor her father had lined up. He looked old and serious as he examined Lily. He had already studied all of her records, and could have given them the prognosis without seeing her, but Bill had insisted on a consultation in person, and to have Lily seen by the experts. After the examination, Lily went to the waiting room to sit with Jennifer, while her father conferred with the doctor. Lily wanted to stay in the room, but her father preferred to talk to him alone. The doctor was somber and to the point.

'I'm very sorry, Mr. Thomas, but I concur entirely with the neurosurgeon who operated on your daughter. With a T10 complete spinal injury, she will not regain use of her legs. It's medically impossible. I don't want to hold out false hopes to you or Lily. She needs to focus on rehabilitation now and getting on with her life. Many great people have conducted productive lives as paraplegics and from wheelchairs. Your president Franklin Roosevelt was one of them. I think that's important to stress to Lily now, rather than fostering false hopes that can only disappoint her.'

Bill was crushed and angry again at what he said. He thought he was old-fashioned and a defeatist, and Jessie had obviously influenced him with whatever she put in her report. He looked annoyed when he came out of the doctor's office, and Lily said nothing. She had understood the doctor's opinion of the situation from the questions he asked her, which were the same as Jessie's in the past six weeks. Lily had no illusions now after talking to her. Only her father did. She asked if they could go to Harrods to do some shopping, since they had time before they left for Switzerland the next day. And she had been to Harrods before, and liked shopping there.

Her father dropped her off with Jennifer and said

he'd wait in the car. He had some calls to make to New York. But Lily wasn't prepared for how difficult it would be to shop from the chair. She was jostled by the crowds, and had people's elbows and purses in her face. Salespeople spoke to Jennifer and not to her, and ignored her even when she asked them direct questions. She couldn't try anything on – it would have been too complicated. It was frightening and upsetting and a taste of what life would be like now. It was the first time she had gone out in the world in her wheelchair, and Jennifer could see how upset she was when they went back to the limousine. Lily was near tears, and her father looked surprised at how rapidly they emerged. Lily had felt claustrophobic in the crowds and returned to the car empty-handed.

'Well, that's a first,' her father said, smiling at her. 'You didn't buy anything?' She usually liked to shop, like other girls her age, and she and Veronica often went shopping when they had a day off from the team.

'I didn't see anything I liked,' Lily said quietly, and asked to go back to the hotel, and Bill seemed surprised.

'Do you want to go out to lunch?' She shook her head.

All she wanted to do was disappear. Her first venture into the world at Harrods had been a disaster, and had brought the realities of her future home to her with the force of a wrecking ball.

They went back to Claridge's and ordered room

service, and Bill could see how unhappy she was, although he didn't fully understand why. He hadn't seen how difficult it had been for her at Harrods, and Jennifer was intimidated by him, so she didn't say anything. She left Lily alone with her father and had lunch in her room. She didn't want to intrude on them. Jessie had made an excellent choice in picking Jennifer for the trip. She was a good nurse, and very discreet. And Lily liked her.

'Baby, it's going to be all right,' her father said sooth-ingly as they waited for lunch in her suite. He had sensed that her attempt at shopping had not gone well. 'You're not going to be in that chair forever, and you can go shopping all you want when you get back on your feet.' He meant well, but what he said made it even harder for her. She felt like Alice in Wonderland in the dream, or Dorothy in *The Wizard of Oz.*

'Stop it!' she shouted at him, which stunned him. 'Stop acting like I'm going to walk again! I know I won't. You're the only one who thinks I will,' she said and broke into a sob, crying inconsolably, as he tried to comfort her, to no avail.

'Sometimes it only takes one relentless person who believes,' he said to her. 'I'll never give up, Lily. I'll do whatever I have to, to get you walking again.' He believed it, but Lily no longer did.

'You can't,' she said, still crying. 'My spinal cord is severed, Daddy. My legs will never walk again. I'm going to be in this stupid chair forever. Why can't you understand it and accept it? I don't want to go to all these doctors. They're all going to say the same thing.'

'Until we find one who doesn't,' he said quietly. 'That's the one we're looking for.' He was looking for the holy grail. It sounded crazy and unreasonable to her.

'I want to go home,' she said miserably.

'We will. Just give me another week, and then we'll go back to Denver.' But once they did, she would be in rehab for several months, and he hated that idea. But Jessie had insisted on it, and he'd agreed. All the arrangements had been made. They were waiting for her at the rehab hospital, where she was being admitted the morning after they got home. Lily was dreading it too. It sounded like prison to her, with everyone in wheelchairs, and probably no one her age. She missed her friends. Six weeks in the hospital in Squaw Valley had been enough, too much in fact. She just wanted to go home.

When their lunch arrived, Lily only picked at it, and afterward Jennifer distracted her by playing cards with her for several hours, and then they watched a movie on the TV in the suite. It was a long, boring day, and Lily was sad when she went to bed that night. Bill had gone to bed early too. He didn't want to tell her, but he was depressed by what the British doctor had said. It was just more of the same and not worth the trip. He was determined to hear better news at their next stops.

The neurosurgeon in Switzerland said exactly the same thing. His examination was cursory, and his opinion had been formed before they got there, based on all Jessie's reports and tests. Like the doctor in London, he couldn't understand why they'd come. They were out of his office in less than an hour, and although they had two of the best suites reserved at the beautiful Hotel Baur au Lac, Bill decided to leave for New York that night, and had Angie move up their appointment in New York. She made it for the following afternoon. Bill was beginning to think they would do better with doctors in the States. They were too traditional and old-fashioned in Europe, and had nothing innovative to offer. He had high hopes for their meeting in New York, and the one in Boston. They had come up with nothing encouraging here.

He told Jennifer and Lily they were leaving that night, and after an early dinner in the suite, they left for the airport, and took off for New York, and landed at midnight local time in New York. The time difference was in their favor, so they gained six hours and were at the Carlyle in half an hour. Lily had slept for most of the flight, and she and Jennifer ordered dinner from room service and played cards when they arrived. Lily and the young nurse got along very well. Jennifer made everything easier for Lily and was good at distracting her with cards, games, fashion, or gossip magazines. She had made the trip much happier for her, and provided female companionship as they flew from city to city.

Later, Lily texted Veronica in Denver, to tell her they were in New York. Veronica texted her back right away. She was at a party with lots of cute boys, and she couldn't wait for Lily to come home. Lily couldn't wait either. It had been the longest, hardest two months of her life. And she missed her home, her old life, and all her friends, and told Jennifer how happy she'd be to see them again.

Chapter 8

The apartment was dark, as Joe Henry sat at his handsome English partner's desk in the library of his home. He had lived in the same apartment in New York with his wife Karen for the past fifteen years, ever since their sons grew up and they had sold their townhouse on East 81st Street. And for the past six months, Joe had been alone. Life never turned out the way one had expected. The years of empty nest had taken a toll on Karen and their marriage. She had been lost without their boys, both of whom were now in their thirties. One lived in Atlanta, the other in Cleveland, and both worked for large corporations, were married, and had children of their own.

Karen had gotten into Eastern religions in order to fill the void in her life, while Joe continued to work on Wall Street and spend too little time at home. And once the boys left for college, he had spent even less time with her. He understood that now, but hadn't before. He had used their children being gone as an opportunity to work harder and expand his business. He had taken on a partner, with disastrous results, while Karen began taking trips to India and spent first weeks and then months at an ashram. She had found a guru whom she followed devotedly, and had less and less and less in common with Joe. Then she had taken a film class at NYU, and had begun making documentaries to help expand the work and exposure of her guru, and by then she was traveling to Tibet and Nepal, and for the last ten years she had rarely been at home.

His business, a hedge fund, had expanded exponentially with his new partner. New clients had been added, they were handling larger investments than Joe ever had before, and then the roof fell in. His partner had invested badly, in ways that Joe knew nothing about, and concealed it from him. For months Joe had worried about being prosecuted, and narrowly escaped federal charges. His partner hadn't been as lucky, and had been convicted of embezzlement and wire fraud. They had lost a fortune for their clients, but the FBI had realized that Joe was innocent. He had been gullible and naïve and trusted a man who was a brilliant sociopathic con.

They had settled countless civil lawsuits before his partner went to prison, and now whatever savings Joe had had were wiped out, his reputation shot forever, his career ended in disgrace. Karen had decided it was the opportune moment to move to Nepal. She had left six months before, after filing for divorce. All Joe had left was a small nest egg he was just barely able to live on, and he was planning to sell the apartment. He had virtually nothing to leave to his sons, and Karen had wanted nothing from him when she left, not even the photographs that were evidence of their history and long marriage. According to Karen, she had been resurrected and reborn into a new life and wanted nothing from her past. She didn't even maintain contact with their sons. Joe thought she had gone a little crazy, but unlike him, she was happy, so who was he to say she was wrong? He hardly recognized her when he saw her before she left. She had a long mane of snowy white hair, which had been prematurely white since her twenties, and she'd been wearing a simple orange robe, like a Buddhist nun. She looked incredibly peaceful, and she had told him she was planning to make more documentary films about her guru. She had become a person he couldn't relate to and no longer knew.

Since the previous August, Joe had been alone in the apartment. His business was closed, his debts had been settled, his partner was in prison, his wife was gone. And at fifty-eight, he knew there was no way he could rebuild any of it. His long-respected career in finance had ended in shambles, and he hadn't had the courage to face or even contact his friends in nearly two years, since his partner's crimes had been exposed, and his own gullibility and foolishness. He was just grateful he hadn't wound up in prison with him. And it was inconceivable to him to find another woman, or even want to, or explain why his wife had preferred to become a Buddhist nun rather than stay with him. His partner had been dishonest, and his wife crazy with some sort of midlife crisis, after years of lack of attention from him, but whatever the reasons or the excuses, life as he had known it was over, and there was nothing left for him to look forward to. He would be remembered as a fool if not a crook, like his partner.

He saw his sons from time to time, but they rarely came to New York. They were married to nice women, had happy, stable marriages and children, and liked the cities where they lived and worked and the worlds they had there. Joe felt completely superfluous to them, and of no use or interest. They didn't need him. He had visited both of them during the holidays, one at Christmas and the other one at Thanksgiving, and in both cases felt he had become an object of pity and not respect.

He hadn't bothered to turn the lights on in the apartment on a dark night in February. He was sitting at his desk with nothing to do there, as he did so often now, out of habit. He had nothing to occupy his time anywhere, and no one to talk to now that Karen was gone. He had lost contact with everyone, even his closest friends. He didn't return their calls, and eventually they stopped calling, which was a relief. He was too ashamed. He had just put the apartment on the market, he needed the money to live on, and he had no idea what to do, or where to go after that.

As he thought about it all, which he did every night now, and had for many months, he unlocked a drawer in his desk, and quietly slipped the gun he kept there out of its case and held the weapon in his hand. It was loaded, and he sat holding it for a long time. This wasn't the first time he had done that, but he hoped tonight would be the last. He had had enough. Through force of circumstances, bad luck, and his own mistakes, he had become entirely redundant. He served no useful purpose, to his children, his clients, his ex-wife, or himself. His life was completely useless, and exiting now would be a mercy for him, and probably not even surprising to his children. They seldom called him, and he couldn't blame them. When they did, he had nothing to say. He had no relationship with his grandchildren, whom he saw too seldom, and lived too far away for him to be engaged in their lives in a meaningful way. Nothing in his life mattered to him now. He was ready. He cocked the trigger, and slowly raised the gun to his head. And then, as in a very bad movie, the phone rang. It was after midnight, and the number that came up on his phone was unfamiliar to him. Probably a wrong number. No one ever called him at that hour. In fact, no one called him at all.

The phone continued ringing, and then, both annoyed

and curious, he set the gun down. He was in no hurry, but he didn't want to lose his nerve again, as he had several times before. He couldn't go on any longer. He wanted out. It was time. But just this one last time, he answered the phone.

'Hello?' His voice sounded ghostly, he hadn't spoken to anyone in several days. He hadn't even left the apartment, and he had had two stiff scotches that night to steel his nerve.

'Joe? It's Bill. I'm sorry to call so late. I just flew into town from Europe. You haven't called me in ages, but I wanted to let you know I'm here.' It took Joe a minute to find his voice. Bill had been one of his closest friends. He was six years younger than Joe, but they had gone to business school together, and Bill had given him good advice at the beginning of the mess with his partner, and then, too embarrassed to call him again, Joe had faded away, as he had done with everyone else. It was hard to lose the respect of his colleagues and friends, and he knew he had, although Bill had always been a good friend, and hadn't been judgmental when he gave him advice. And some of what Bill had suggested had helped Joe extricate himself with less damage than there might have been otherwise. Bill knew the late hours Joe had always kept, so he had dared to call him at that hour, which he wouldn't have done with someone else. 'How are Karen and the boys?' Bill added, and Joe let out a long slow sigh, as he realized they hadn't spoken in a year. He sat staring at the gun on the desk, in the light of the streetlamps outside.

There was so much to tell him to bring him up to speed that Joe didn't know where to start. He had let Bill know when his ex-partner went to prison, but Joe hadn't contacted Bill again after that. 'What are you doing in town?' was all Joe could think of to say at first, by rote, responding with a question instead of answering Bill's inquiry about his wife and sons.

'I'm here with Lily. It's a long story,' Bill said, sounding tired. 'I was wondering if you want to have dinner with us tomorrow night. Karen too, of course, if she's in town.' Bill thought she was more than a little wacky now, but after all, she was Joe's wife, and he had liked her in the past, before she found her guru, traveled to India, and became somewhat nuts. He had great respect for Eastern religions, but Karen had seemed 'off' to him for years.

'She's not here,' Joe said quietly. 'We're divorced. I just got the final papers last week. She's living in Nepal.'

'Oh dear.' Bill wasn't entirely surprised. 'I'm sorry to hear it. But she's been on that path for a long time,' he said practically, and thought Joe was better off, although he wasn't sure how Joe felt about it.

'Yes, she has. And the boys are fine. Still in Cleveland and Atlanta. We finally settled all the lawsuits, I'm sorry I didn't keep you abreast of that. It was a royal mess, and it closed down the business, but at least it's over. And

Roger is in prison, where he belongs. Actually, it's been kind of a clean sweep. No wife, no business, no career.' He wanted to add 'no future' and 'kids who don't need me,' but out of pride if nothing else, he didn't want his old friend to know how depressed he was. The gun lay gleaming in the light from outside, and Joe ran a finger gently along the barrel, planning to pick it up again and use it at the end of the call.

'I'm sorry you had such a tough time,' Bill said sincerely. 'I should have called, but somehow time slips by for all of us, I guess.' It was a poor excuse, but they both knew it was true.

'What about you? How is beautiful Lily?' Joe asked, as he thought of her. She had always been a golden child. She was years younger than his children, who were in their thirties, but he could still remember how thrilled Bill had been when she was born, and ever since, justifiably so. He had never met as enchanting a child and, later, young woman.

'I'm actually here for her,' Bill said in a somber voice. It was late for him, after the trip from Europe, and he knew he didn't have to put a good face on it for Joe. They had always been honest with each other. Or at least that was what Bill thought. Joe had been his closest friend at Harvard, and for many years thereafter, and he had deep affection for him. 'She had an accident in Squaw Valley six weeks ago. We've been there ever since.'

Joe was worried the moment Bill said it. 'Is she all right? Was she still training for the Olympics?' He had gone to the junior games with Bill three years before, when she won the bronze medal in downhill racing, and Joe had had a great time there with Bill.

'She'll be all right, but she's not training for the Olympics right now,' Bill said, sounding tense. 'The chairlift broke at Squaw, the cable snapped, she had a hell of a fall. She has a spinal injury, Joe,' Bill said in a choked voice, fighting back tears again, which happened to him too often now. 'A bad one.'

'Oh my God,' Joe said, unconsciously pushing the gun away from him. 'How bad?'

Bill started to say she would be fine, as he had for the last six weeks to everyone who asked him, but this time he was honest with his old friend, and himself. 'I don't know. That's why we're here. She was operated on by a woman in Squaw Valley. I don't know if she's any good. They say she is, but she's a small-time local doctor, and who knows? I just took Lily to London and Zurich, and it wasn't good. We're seeing someone here tomorrow, and I'm taking her to Boston after that. Her spinal cord is severed, and she's in a wheelchair for now. It's been a hell of a shock. She's dealing with it better than I am, but it's hard on her too. She's been through a lot.' Joe could hear the tears in Bill's voice, and his heart ached for both of them. Compared to his problems of a life gone awry, a failed marriage and business, this was infinitely worse. It was a young girl's life.

'You've been through a lot too,' Joe said in a voice full of emotion and compassion. 'What can I do for you?' Bill had always been there for him, now Joe wanted to do the same for him, even if all he could do was lend moral support.

'Nothing. We'll see what the doctors have to say. I'd love to see you tomorrow, though, if you'd like to join us at the hotel for dinner. Lily hasn't been out yet. She just got out of the hospital a few days ago. And I think it would be embarrassing for her to go to a restaurant in the chair.' He had never asked her about it, but it was how he felt.

'Of course. I'd love to see you. I'll be there. What time?'

'Why don't you come at six o'clock so we can talk? I want to catch up on all your news too, and how everything shook out in the end.' It seemed ridiculous now that he hadn't spoken to him in a year. They had been such good friends and still were. It was odd the way life sped past you sometimes and you lost touch. Bill felt as close as ever to him now as they talked.

'I'll be there,' Joe assured him. 'And Bill,' he hesitated for a long minute, 'thanks for calling. You'll never know how much it meant.'

'I feel the same way. I really needed to talk to someone

tonight. I'm glad you were up. Thanks, Joe. I look forward to seeing you tomorrow,' he said in a voice full of emotion.

'So do I,' Joe assured him, and they hung up. Joe looked at the gun on his desk and felt as though he had just woken up from a nightmare. What Bill and his daughter were going through was so much worse. Joe felt guilty and self-indulgent as he picked the gun up, removed the bullets, and put it back in his desk. He locked the drawer with a shudder, thinking about what he had almost done, and what it would have been like for his children, and the person who found him. He felt now as though someone had thrown cold water in his face. Maybe Karen wasn't the one who was crazy – maybe he was. One thing was for sure, he knew, as he stood up and walked away from his desk – whatever happened, he was not going to do that again. All he could think about now was Bill and Lily, and hoped he could do something to help them. He owed him an even bigger debt than he had before, when Bill had advised him about his business. This time, without even knowing it, with his well-timed phone call, Bill had saved his life.

Chapter 9

The doctor Bill took Lily to in New York at the Hospital for Special Surgery was even more discouraging than the two in London and Zurich. He took the time to explain to Bill at length and in detail why Lily would never walk again. He made diagrams and showed him models, he pointed out where the damage was on the X-rays and scans, and he described the effect an injury at that location would have on her legs. The only good news, as they had told him before, was that it was low enough that her lungs and diaphragm were not involved. He spent over an hour with Bill in his office, and when they left, Bill had no illusions that their meeting with the neurosurgeon in Boston would be any different. He had hoped that one of these surgeons would either tell him that she would recover, or offer to operate on her again and give her back her legs. He knew now that that wasn't going to happen, and why. Barring a miracle in stem cell research,

Lily was going to be in a wheelchair for the rest of her life. Bill had to fight back tears when they left his office, and Lily was strangely calm. With each doctor they saw, even though they didn't discuss it in front of her, she could see from her father's expression that Jessie had been right. Lily had believed her and understood it earlier in Squaw Valley. Her father hadn't. He had had to drag her halfway around the world to three other doctors in order to begin to understand.

'I think my dad is finally getting the message,' Lily said to Jennifer when they got back to the hotel. He had looked deeply depressed after the meeting with the surgeon.

'How are you doing?' Jennifer asked her. 'Holding up, with all these doctor's visits?'

'I'm okay,' Lily said quietly. 'I just want to go home now. Although I'll miss you when I do.' She smiled at the young nurse. Jennifer was leaving to go back to Squaw Valley as soon as they took Lily to Craig Hospital in Denver, the day after they got home.

'I'm going to miss you too,' Jennifer said honestly. It had been an incredible trip for her, to London, Zurich, New York, and Boston tomorrow, staying in fancy hotels in fabulous suites, ordering room service, and flying around on a private jet, even if they didn't see much of the cities they were in. She knew she'd never do anything like it again in her life, and it was an experience she'd always remember, and maybe tell her children about one day. She was sorry there hadn't been better news for Lily about her prognosis, but neither she, Jessie, nor Lily had expected there to be, only Bill.

'Do you want to go out for a while?' she suggested that afternoon. It was a sunny day, although it was cold in New York, but not as cold as it had been in Europe or Squaw Valley when they left. It was nearly March and almost felt like spring, although people had said the weather would get colder again. But for now she thought it would do Lily good to get out and get some air, instead of going to doctors, watching TV, and playing cards all day.

'Yeah, okay,' Lily said, and Jennifer helped her put her coat on. Bill had bought her a parka in Squaw Valley when her Olympic team jacket had been destroyed. And he had bought her some clothes for their trip to Europe and New York since all she had had with her were ski clothes. She was wearing jeans and a sweater, the new red parka, and running shoes she'd brought to Tahoe in case she worked out in the gym. He hadn't found much for her in Tahoe, and Lily didn't really care. She had plenty of clothes at home.

Jennifer wheeled her into the hotel elevator, after letting Lily's father know they were going out, and he thought it was a good idea too for her to get some air. He suggested they do some shopping on Madison Avenue, or go to Barneys, and handed Jennifer his credit card. He still hadn't understood how impossible it had been for her at Harrods, and trying anything on would have been a major ordeal. It took her a long time to get dressed, although she had already learned how to help Jennifer do it, and she was good at maneuvering into her chair now. Her arms were getting stronger, but shopping was no longer going to be the fun it had been before her accident.

The two young women set out on Madison Avenue, and looked into the shops, but they didn't go into any of them. They went almost as far as Barneys, and then turned around and came home. It had been invigorating, but it upset Lily to realize that she was now below people's line of vision, and they looked right over her. If they spoke to anyone, they spoke to Jennifer, who was at eye level with them, while Lily was completely ignored.

'It's like I don't exist. They don't even see me,' she complained to Jennifer on their way back to the hotel. 'No one talks to me. They talk to you.' Jennifer knew that what she was saying was true, and had noticed it herself.

'I think people get embarrassed when they see someone in a wheelchair,' Jennifer said thoughtfully. 'They don't know how to react.' At the hospital, they always spoke to people in wheelchairs, but out in the world she had seen that no one did.

'It feels weird, like I became invisible all of a sudden.'

And she was just as uncomfortable when they got in the elevator at the Carlyle again, and she was at waist level to everyone in it. They looked right over her head and never looked down. And when Jennifer maneuvered the chair out of the elevator, they looked away. She could see that Lily was upset when they got back to the suite. It was a whole new world she had to adjust to, and the way people reacted to her in it.

And when Joe saw her at six o'clock when he came to visit them, he almost burst into tears. Lily was so young and so beautiful, and she was sitting in the wheelchair in the living room of the suite. In spite of what Bill had told him, seeing her that way was a huge shock. He tried not to let it show, but he was very distressed, particularly knowing how vital and active she had been before. After all, he had seen her win a bronze medal in the Junior Olympics, and now she was in a wheelchair, and would be forever. It was easy to understand why her father was so upset. The two men left to chat in Bill's suite, while Jennifer flipped through a magazine and Lily texted her friends.

'How did it go at the doctor today?' Joe asked him when they left Lily's suite.

'Not well,' Bill said with a deep sigh. 'I started this trip thinking I could find someone to save her legs and her ability to walk, but it's been bad news at every stop. I don't think it will be much better in Boston tomorrow.

We're going back to Denver tomorrow night, and I have to put her in a rehab hospital there the next day. She's going to be in rehab for three or four months.' Bill was looking seriously depressed, but happy to see his old friend, although he thought he looked considerably older than he had a year ago. Joe had been through enormous challenges, and it had been even harder than Bill realized. If he had known that his friend had been on the verge of suicide, he would have been shocked.

'Why don't I come out and see you, while Lily is at rehab? I don't have anything to do here. Maybe I can give you a hand with something out there, or just keep you company for a few days.' Bill looked relieved as soon as he said it, and loved the idea. He dreaded Lily being at the rehab hospital and not at home, and he knew he was going to be lonely without her, although he planned to visit her every day.

'I haven't thought about it yet, and didn't want to. But I may have to build some ramps and things to make life easier for Lily when she gets home. Our house really isn't accessible for a wheelchair. I may have to put in an elevator too. I was hoping I wouldn't have to, but it sounds like I will.' It was the least of their problems, but something he knew now that he'd have to do. It was the beginning of acceptance for him. 'Maybe you can give me some ideas.' He was going to hire an architect if he had to, but he liked the idea of Joe visiting him while Lily was away, maybe even for a few weeks, since she would be at Craig for three or four months, which seemed interminable to him. He had never even let her go to sleepaway camp as a child.

'Just tell me when you want me to come out, and I'll be on the next plane.' Bill looked pleased when Joe said it, and then they talked about Joe's failed business and the embezzlement until dinnertime. They talked about Karen too, but there was less to say. She had told him she wanted a divorce, filed the papers, and left, with very little conversation about it. She said the marriage was over for her, and that was that. But he seemed to be dealing with it, and had made his peace with what she'd decided, although it was painful for him. Joe mentioned in passing while they talked that he had no desire to get involved with anyone else now. He felt too old, he said, to start again, or even have a relationship. He hadn't dated in more than thirty years, and his marriage to Karen had ended in too much disappointment for him to want to try again. Bill said he understood. He wasn't feeling particularly romantic these days either. All his thoughts were focused on Lily, and nothing else. And Joe knew he hadn't had a serious woman in his life since Lily's mother.

The three of them had dinner together in Bill's suite. And when Lily went back to her own suite, she maneuvered the wheelchair deftly, and the two men watched her with a sorrowful expression. After she was gone, Joe gently patted his friend's shoulder as Bill fought back tears.

When Joe left Bill that night, he promised to come to Denver in the next few weeks, as soon as Bill called him, and Bill assured him that he would. He was relieved to have seen his old friend. He had known him for twenty-six years, since business school, and Bill had known Karen for just as long, since Joe had already been married when Bill met him. It was strange to think how life turned out sometimes. Now he was widowed, Karen was living in Nepal and India with her guru, Joe's business was in the tank, and he'd been the smartest guy Bill had known at Harvard, and Lily was paraplegic. Who could have imagined any of that? Nothing had happened as Bill had hoped, and he was exhausted when he went to bed that night, after the discouraging meeting with the neurosurgeon that morning. And they had one more the next day. They were getting up early to fly to Boston, and then home that night. All Bill could hope was that the doctor at Mass General would have something hopeful to say. If he didn't, as far as Bill was concerned, Lily's life had been destroyed when the chairlift fell in Squaw. He couldn't see it any other way.

Chapter 10

A pretty woman with shoulder-length dark hair was the center of a celebration at the breast cancer clinic at Mass General that morning. The doctors and nurses who had taken care of her for the past year were there, and her peer counselor who had guided her through the hardest year of her life. The woman being celebrated was Carole Anders. She had completed her treatment, and had been declared cancer free after a year of chemotherapy and radiation, a double mastectomy, and a hysterectomy. She hadn't had breast reconstruction yet, and didn't want to. She felt that for now she'd been through enough surgery, and she'd heard from others that there was a risk of infection or complications with implants, and she just didn't want to take the chance. She wore prosthetics in her bra, and no one saw her undressed now anyway. Her husband had walked out on her six weeks after she'd been diagnosed with cancer, which she'd been told was not unusual, but it had been a hell of a blow. He just couldn't deal with what she was going through, and had started an affair with a woman in his office. It had been Carole who ultimately filed for divorce. Carole had gotten through it with the support of the medical staff at the breast clinic, her counselor, and her friends. Her husband had been a no-show for the entire event. He hadn't even called her when she had the hysterectomy and the mastectomy. He just couldn't deal with it. But Carole had, and she had come through the whole experience with flying colors, emotionally and medically, and now she had a clean bill of health.

Carole's mother and older sister had both died of breast cancer, so she had been at high risk. But she intended to survive what she'd been through. Her sister had refused to have a mastectomy, which Carole thought made a difference, and her mother had been diagnosed too late. Thanks to annual mammograms since she was thirty, because of her history, they had detected hers early, at thirty-seven. She had just turned thirty-eight, and the good-looking cut of her dark brown hair, in a shoulder-length pageboy, was a very expensive wig she had bought at a theatrical hairdresser in New York. It had been worth every penny she spent. Her own hair had only just begun growing again, and was peach fuzz all over her head under the wig. Her peer counselor had told her about the theatrical wig store in New York, and had been invaluable to her in countless ways, particularly during the breakup of her marriage, and then the divorce. Her peer counselor's husband had left her after she was diagnosed too. As Carole said, it had reduced her to nothing more than a statistic, and made her husband of five years seem pathetic. And her treatment had been an issue for him too, because he wanted to have children, and Carole no longer could. The whole experience with him had left her so disillusioned that she had no desire to even date, let alone get involved in a relationship. She never wanted to go through anything like it again. Surviving cancer was enough.

Despite grueling treatments and two major surgeries, Carole had managed to miss almost no work. Her boss in neurosurgery, and another in orthopedics, had been incredibly supportive and had adjusted her schedule to fit her medical needs. She was a psychologist specializing in young people recovering from trauma involving spinal cord injuries. She had a Ph.D. from Stanford and had done her internship there, and then came to work at Mass General, and she loved what she did. The kids and young adults she worked with were terrific, and continuing to stay active and engaged had gotten her through her own illness, and now it was behind her. But she had never really stopped living in the last year. She had gone to cultural events, museums, and movies, continued her work, and seen friends whenever she could. Everyone who knew her was impressed at how well she had come through it, in spite of the additional challenge of the divorce. Carole was a strong, cheerful person, with a positive attitude about life. And it was contagious in her work. She was able to infuse her patients with excitement about their lives, and a will to live, in spite of what they'd been through. She was a woman who practiced what she preached. And everyone at the breast clinic was happy to be celebrating her.

She was in great spirits when she arrived at her office two hours later than usual. She had warned her secretary she'd be late, to allow for time for the celebration they had planned for her. And best of all, she was cancer free. Her last tests had been immaculate.

'How was the party?' Janys, her secretary, asked her. She knew where Carole had been and was thrilled for her. Everyone had been rooting for her all year. Everybody loved Carole, and it was easy to see why.

'It was great,' Carole said happily, and glanced at the copy of her schedule on Janys's desk. Carole was extremely organized and liked to make full use of her time. 'What have I got this morning?'

'You have a meeting with Dr. Hammerfeld, about three new patients he has coming. But he's running late. He's with some people now.'

'One of my new patients?' she asked with interest, but Janys shook her head.

'This is just a consultation. A family from Denver. They're on their way back there and admitting her to Craig,' Janys explained.

'It doesn't get better than that,' Carole said with an approving look. 'Why are they here?'

'Looking for a miracle, I think. It's a T10 injury.'

'Complete or incomplete?' Carole asked.

'Complete,' Janys said with a serious look. She had seen Lily go into the doctor's office, with Jennifer and her father. And Janys and Carole both knew that with a complete spinal cord injury, there would be no miracle. Dr. Hammerfeld was delivering the news at that moment, and Carole went to her office to return some calls. Dr. Hammerfeld hadn't asked her to join them, as he wouldn't be following the case. It was just a one-time meeting. And while Lily dressed in the examining room, he dealt the final blow to her father in his office.

'There's nothing we can do,' he said solemnly, and Bill nodded, with a look of despair. He was used to hearing it by now. 'What made you come here?' The tests were so conclusive that Bill's visit didn't make a lot of sense.

'To be honest, I really wasn't sure about the neurosurgeon who did the surgery, and her diagnosis. I thought it was possible that she was wrong and made a mistake.' With that, the doctor looked at Lily's chart again to see the surgeon's name, frowned, and then looked back at Bill.

'You had one of the best neurosurgeons I know. In fact' – he said, with a small wintry smile – 'she trained with me, although she didn't do her residency here. She's a very fine surgeon, and I've referred cases to her over the years.' Bill nodded – everyone had had high praise for Jessie. But the bottom line was that Lily was paraplegic and would never walk again. He would have gone to the devil himself if that could have helped. And the doctor could see how desperate Bill was, but reiterated that there was nothing they could do to help, and their focus had to be on rehabilitation now. Bill tried not to look as heartbroken as he was, when he left the doctor's office. Hammerfeld had been his last hope, for now anyway. Now they had to go home, and start the long road to rehabilitation. Bill pretended to be cheerful, and got Lily into the car.

They went back to the hotel to check out, picked up their luggage, and he called Joe because he had promised he would, and told him what the doctor had said. Joe felt badly for him and he could hear how emotionally wrung-out Bill was. The surgeons they had consulted had destroyed his hope of Lily walking again. Joe gently reminded him how lucky they were that Lily was alive.

And two hours later they left for the airport, and took off for the four-hour flight to Denver. It was the end of a long, discouraging trip. It hadn't gone the way he hoped, and Lily was tired of being examined and poked and prodded. All she wanted now was to go home, even though it was only for one night. And then she had to face a whole new environment again, and a hospital of a different kind. She was so tired after the day in Boston, and all the traveling they'd done before, that she fell asleep as soon as they took off, and Jennifer woke her as they were about to land. Lily opened her eyes with a start, smiled at her, and as soon as they were in the car, she texted Veronica. She had promised to come by that night. She texted Jeremy too, but he hadn't answered her in several days. It was only eight o'clock in Denver when they landed, and Lily couldn't wait to see Veronica, after two horrible months away.

They were almost at the house when Veronica answered Lily's text and said she was having dinner with her parents, studying for midterms, and they wouldn't let her go out, since her grades sucked, as usual. All she cared about was training for the Olympics, and she had never done well in school, unlike Lily, who had successfully managed both. Lily was disappointed when she got the message – she hadn't seen Veronica for so long. She promised to come by the next day, but Lily answered that she would be at Craig the next day, which was why she had hoped she would come by that night, like old times. She had no idea what it would be like to have visitors at Craig, if she would have a roommate or not, and what the rules about visitors were. Veronica texted back that she'd come to see her at Craig soon, she just couldn't get out tonight.

She still hadn't heard from Jeremy – his texts had become more and more infrequent in recent weeks, and he had cooled off noticeably since the accident. And Veronica had hinted a couple of times that he was interested in someone else. She didn't want Lily to be shocked when she got home. It hadn't been a serious romance with Lily, but they'd had fun for the last six months, before the accident in Squaw. And Lily didn't have many illusions that he'd be faithful to her while she was in rehab for four months, but he hadn't broken up with her, so as far as she knew they were still dating, whatever that meant now. He was one of the best-looking and most popular boys on the Olympic downhill team, so she realized there was a possibility he might not stick around, but she hoped he would. She texted him again from the car but got no response.

The limousine that had picked them up at Denver International Airport drove them to the Cherry Hills Village section of South Denver, where they lived. Lily looked excited as she saw the familiar streets. She turned to glance at her father, and he was looking out the window of the car with a sad expression. He had never expected to bring Lily home from their annual trip to Squaw Valley in a wheelchair, and she was just glad to be home.

The driver pulled up in the circular driveway in front of the house, and Angie was waiting for them. She had stayed to see if there was anything she could do to help. The driver got the wheelchair out of the trunk, and Jennifer and Bill helped Lily into it, and she turned to smile at Angie, who tried not to show the emotion she felt as she watched her. Seeing Lily in the wheelchair nearly broke her heart. The housekeeper who came in the daytime had left food for them in the fridge, which Angie mentioned cheerfully as she followed them into the house.

'Hi, Angie,' Lily said with a slow smile. She was tired after the trip.

'Hi, Lily,' she said, trying not to look as sad as she felt, watching Lily roll herself into the house, and Bill squeezed Angie's shoulder as he walked past her. It had been a long, hard two months.

And once in the house, Bill had to help maneuver the wheelchair up three steps into the front hall. It was a large, handsome house, filled with beautiful antiques and expensive art. Jennifer tried not to look as impressed as she was, but after the hotels and the plane, she wasn't surprised. They lived an amazing life, although she realized that even they weren't exempt from unexpected hardships, like the death of Lily's mother and Lily's accident in Squaw.

Lily stopped at the entrance to the living room, and

would have had to go down two steps to go into it, so she turned and went to the kitchen instead. There was a swinging door that she couldn't manage, and Bill held it open for her. Angie was taking out the food the house-keeper had left for them for dinner, and Lily rapidly found that she was bumping into everything. The table, chairs, and island in the center were an obstacle course for her. She had to lean into the fridge to get something to drink, and the counters were the wrong height. She had suddenly become a misfit in her own world, and she couldn't reach the faucets at the sink to wash her hands. She looked upset and rolled up to the table, and helped herself to some cheese and fruit, and told her father she wanted to go upstairs. There was a long elegant flight of stairs that she couldn't negotiate, and he had to carry her, while Jennifer carried the chair. It confirmed to Bill that the house was going to be impossible for Lily to live in unless he made a number of changes. Otherwise she would be a prisoner in their home, unable to move from one place to another without help.

While Bill carried Lily upstairs, Angie left discreetly and Lily settled into her room like a warm embrace. Everything was pink silk and satin, there were flowered curtains, and the thick wool carpeting that had always seemed so cozy was hard to negotiate with the chair. She pulled herself onto her bed and called her friends, while Jennifer unpacked for her. Bill had showed Jennifer a guest room nearby, where she was to spend the night before she went back to Squaw Valley the next day.

Lily was disappointed that Veronica couldn't come over, and she tried calling her just to talk, but couldn't get her. And Jeremy still hadn't answered her text. He called her two hours later, after Jennifer had helped her take a bath and get into bed between fresh, clean sheets. It felt wonderful to be in her own bed.

'When did you get home?' Jeremy asked casually, as though he hadn't gotten her latest texts, and she'd been on an ordinary trip, instead of a journey to hell and back with a month and a half in a hospital for a spinal cord injury, major surgery, and a weeklong jaunt around Europe and the East to see doctors for examinations and consultations.

'About two hours ago. Do you want to come by?' She was dying to see familiar faces, and she realized now how much she had missed everyone on the ski team and at school, and she couldn't go back to school until the end of May. She would be dependent on them to visit her while she was at Craig. There was a long pause after her question, and she had a sudden feeling that their conversation wasn't going to go well.

'I'm kind of busy,' he said, in response to her invitation, 'and Lily, I guess we need to talk.' She could sense what was coming and closed her eyes, waiting to hear what he would say. But more than anything, she knew why. The word was out among her friends. She was in a wheelchair, and although she hadn't said it, they had guessed that she was liable to stay that way. 'I've . . . I've kind of been seeing someone else . . . you've been gone a long time.'

'And now that I'm back?' She wanted to force his hand and see what he said. At least she'd know where she stood. She was trying to face the realities of her life, and didn't want to delude herself about him either. She needed to know what and who was real and who she could count on. More than ever, it was important to her now.

'You're not really back, though, are you? Aren't you going to rehab tomorrow?' He made it sound like she was going to jail, and she felt that way. 'I kind of think we need to let things go with us, don't you? I've been meaning to tell you for a while.' He sounded embarrassed but not really apologetic. Clearly, a girlfriend in a wheelchair was more than he could handle, and she was sure he wouldn't be the only one. She suddenly felt like a pariah.

'Yeah, I guess you're right,' she said, trying to sound cavalier about it and not as hurt as she was. 'Well, take care. Thanks for calling me.' She hung up before she started to cry, which would have been mortifying. She sat staring into space, still holding her cell phone in her hand for a long time. She wondered if anyone would ever want her now.

And downstairs Bill had just called Penny. He felt an

obligation to call her now that he was home. He had hardly spoken to her in the last two months. She sounded surprised to hear from him and asked him where he was.

'We just arrived from Boston two hours ago.' He had told her about the round of consultations he was planning, but he hadn't spoken to her since, and that had been three weeks ago. He just never had time to call her, and he didn't really want to. The only thing on his mind was Lily, and the miracle cure he had hoped to find.

'How did it go?' Penny sounded sympathetic and concerned.

'Not very well,' he said honestly, and she could hear the discouragement in his voice.

'I'm sorry, Bill,' she said sincerely. 'What are you going to do now?'

'They're admitting her to Craig tomorrow. She'll be there for three or four months while they teach her what she needs to know.' He sounded near tears as he said it, and Penny's heart went out to him. 'Maybe we could have dinner sometime next week.' She wanted to ask him why, but she didn't. There was clearly no room for her in his life. There hadn't been much before, but there was even less now. After not hearing from him for three weeks, she knew she was the last thing on his mind, and she hadn't been a high priority before.

'I'm actually leaving for Kenya tomorrow, for three weeks. I've been asked to do the PR for a new chain of hotels there, for an organization that plans safaris. It's an exciting project. I'll call you when I get back.' By that time she wouldn't have seen him for three months. With Lily's accident, their pretense at a relationship had become absurd, and he was aware of it as well.

'I'm not sure what kind of energy I have for us right now,' he said honestly. 'This thing with Lily has been rough, and it's not going to get better for a while.' She could sense that there was more to what he was saying to her, and she wasn't surprised.

'What are you saying?'

'I like spending time with you, Penny, but you have a busy life, and I have a kid who has to adjust to the idea that she may be in a wheelchair for the rest of her life. I need to be here for her.'

'You always have been,' Penny said simply. 'But I understand. It sounds like there's no room for us.'

'I think that's right,' he said quietly. He had never been in love with her, and having to think about her now felt like too much. She had figured that out when he called to tell her about the accident, from Squaw. She knew how devoted he was to Lily, and what a dedicated father he was. Not having children of her own, it had always been hard for her to understand the major role Lily played in his life. 'I'm sorry,' he said, sounding exhausted. He had never in his life felt as emotionally drained as he had since the accident.

'I expected it would work out like this,' she said, sounding adult about it. She didn't seem very upset. 'I always did, and particularly now.'

'I think it's going to be rough for a while.'

'I'm sorry this happened, to both of you. Try not to take it too hard. There's only so much you can do.'

'That's not so simple to do. I just want to make it easier for her.'

'You will. You're a terrific father,' she said, and he laughed.

'And a lousy boyfriend. Is that what you mean?' He sounded good humored when he said it, and she laughed too.

'Something like that. Take care, Bill.'

'Thanks, you too. Have a good trip.'

'I will. Give my love to Lily,' she said, and a minute later they hung up. It was over, and they both knew it, and had been for two months, or maybe even before that. Their arrangement had been convenient, and fun sometimes, but they had never been in love with each other. And as he thought about it, he wondered why 'take care' always sounded like 'goodbye.'

He turned off the lights in the kitchen, went upstairs, and found Lily sitting on her bed, looking dazed, with her cell phone in her hand.

'I just got dumped by Jeremy,' she said with a serious expression as her father walked into the room.

'So did I, by Penny,' he said with a rueful smile, 'or maybe I dumped her. I'm not sure which. Anyway, it's over. She said to send you her love.'

'Are you sad about it?'

'A little,' he said honestly. 'But it wasn't a big deal.' But two years was a long time, and he liked her. She was a familiar figure in his life, and he would miss her a little, though probably not too much. 'What about you? Are you upset about Jeremy?'

'Kind of,' she admitted, 'but I'm not really surprised. Did Penny dump you because of me, because I got hurt?' She waved vaguely at her wheelchair, and he understood.

'Not really. It was never really right. She travels all the time, and she works hard. And it's not easy being with someone who doesn't have kids. They never understand.'

She nodded. She knew that about Penny too. She was a lot different from her dad. 'I think Jeremy dumped me because I got hurt.' It was easier to say than 'because I can't walk.'

'In that case, he's a jerk, and you're better off without him. Some really great guy is going to love you one day, and it won't matter to him at all.' He hoped that would be true.

'I'm not so sure,' she said with a wistful expression. She couldn't imagine a guy who wouldn't care that she was in a wheelchair, despite everything Jessie had said. It sounded good, but she didn't know if that was true. And it mattered to Jeremy. She could hear it in his voice.

'Where's Veronica?' Bill was surprised not to see her. The two girls were inseparable most of the time.

'Studying for midterms. Her parents wouldn't let her go out. She said she'd come see me at Craig.' Bill hoped she would and was disappointed she hadn't come that night, after everything Lily had been through. He was worried that Lily's friends were going to let her down. And he knew it was going to be hard for her if they did. He hated all that she was experiencing, the disappointments and the heartbreak along with everything else. It was a lot for her to face, but he also knew that kids that age weren't sure to come through.

'Well, we both got dumped, but we have each other. It's a start,' he said, smiling at her, and then kissed her and left the room as Jennifer walked in, suggesting they have a last game of cards. She had been a good friend to Lily and a wonderful traveling companion for the past week.

'I'm going to miss you,' Lily said sadly when Jennifer settled her for the night and turned off the lights.

'So will I,' Jennifer said with a smile. 'You and your father have spoiled me forever. My miserable apartment in Truckee with three roommates is going to be hell after this. I'm going to feel like Cinderella after the ball.' She smiled as she said it, and Lily looked up at her with big eyes.

'I'm nervous about going to Craig,' she admitted.

'Don't be. You'll have everyone wrapped around your finger in no time, and you might meet kids your age. Maybe even cute boys.' Lily nodded, trying not to think about it, but it was like going back to the hospital again, and all she wanted to do now was stay home, in their comfortable house, and see her friends.

She lay in bed, thinking about it for a long time, and finally she was so exhausted, she fell asleep.

Chapter 11

Jennifer helped Lily get ready the next morning, which was a major feat in a bathroom that wasn't built for a wheelchair. There was no special seat for her in the shower. Angie had forgotten to order one, so Jennifer held her up, and they both got soaking wet. The bathroom was a mess by the time they were through. But Lily was a good sport about it.

Her father carried her down to breakfast, and Jennifer and Lily had repacked the night before, with the kinds of things she'd want to wear at Craig. Jennifer quietly put away Lily's ski clothes. There was a whole closet of them, with her jackets and uniforms for the Olympic ski team. She knew it would upset Lily to see those. Instead, she gave her jeans and sweaters, some warm jackets, and three pairs of Nikes. She had tried to choose things that would be easy for her to put on.

Lily ate a light breakfast, and then the cab came for

Jennifer for her flight to San Francisco. She was changing planes there and taking another flight to Reno, and one of her friends was picking her up and driving her back to Squaw Valley. She had given Lily a warm hug before she left and thanked Bill for everything. And after she was gone, he looked at Lily. He had a knot in his stomach, and Lily didn't say anything, but she had one too. She was dreading going to rehab, but she knew it was what she had to do.

Her father carried her out to the car, and put her wheelchair in the trunk with her suitcase. She had a tote bag with her iPod, some DVDs and CDs, her laptop, magazines, and books. And her father had assured her that she would have a private room. They had told him that families were expected to be involved, and there were even accommodations if he wanted to stay there, but since they lived so close by, he and Lily agreed that it didn't make sense for him to stay at the hospital, which seemed more reasonable for people who had come from far away. And in spite of everything she'd read about Craig on the Internet and from all the literature they'd sent them, Lily didn't know what to expect, and she was scared.

She knew that most people went to Craig anywhere from one to four months after their injuries, so she was right in the normal range, almost two months after her accident had happened. The material they had sent said that the average age of their patients was thirty-eight, more than twice her age, 75 percent of them were male, and their most common age range was eighteen to twenty-five. Half of their patients' injuries were motor-vehicle related, only 10 percent were sports injuries, and they admitted no patients under the age of sixteen. So she was going to be at the lower age range of their patients. And a tutor had been arranged for her, so she could keep up with school. As a junior, this was an important year for her, and she had already missed almost two months. She was hoping to finish at Craig by the end of May, so she could attend the last few weeks of junior year at school. It would depend on how well she did in rehab.

She was going to have extensive physical therapy, and there was a long list of classes to help her function efficiently in the real world. But she had also read that more than half their patients had incomplete spinal injuries, which meant that they were less impaired than she was, since her SCI was complete. There were also patients at Craig with brain injuries, but Lily would be participating in groups and classes with other spinal cord injury patients. And the literature showed that she was expected to work very hard in order to achieve independence and be able to lead a productive life in spite of her injury. The medical referral had been made by Jessie, and all of Lily's medical records had preceded her there.

Although they had created a friendly rehab setting, it was a hospital above all.

Most of what she would be doing was physical therapy to get the functional parts of her body strong and healthy. They were going to teach her how to travel on an airplane alone, how to manage when she got back to school, and if she wanted it, she could have driver's training in a special vehicle. They had swimming pool therapy and an amazing assortment of recreational activities, some of which appealed to Lily, even a special course in scuba diving. The one that had inevitably caught her attention on the list was skiing. She had no idea how they were going to pull that off, but it was obviously of interest to her. They also had field trips and outings and attended cultural events, but some of them sounded too adult to her. She was more interested in seeing her friends, hanging out, going out with them, or listening to music, like any other kid her age. She just hoped her friends actually did come to visit her, as often as they could and were willing.

Lily was silent on the ride there. Craig Hospital was in Englewood, five miles from downtown Denver, and very close to Cherry Hills Village, where they lived. And as far as she was concerned, they arrived there much too quickly. Her father got her chair out of the trunk and helped her into it, and a minute later he wheeled her into the lobby, carrying her suitcase. There was a sign, which directed them to admissions. Her father gave them his insurance card and his credit card and signed her in. And they gave her her room assignment, and told them where it was. She had the private room her father had promised her, and they handed her a key. The woman at the admissions desk had been very friendly, and told Lily where to go for her schedule once she had settled in. And as Lily looked up at him, she saw that her father looked as nervous as she felt. He hated leaving her there. He couldn't bring himself to part with her even for a few weeks, and now it had come to this. At least she would be nearby, so he could visit her anytime, although it sounded like they were going to keep her busy. The whole point of her being there was that she had much to learn. And Bill realized that he had a lot to do in the house, to make it livable for her when she returned. He had seen, even in a few hours the night before, that the steps in the entrance hall, the layout of the kitchen, her bathroom, and even her bedroom were going to be too difficult for her.

Lily's room assignment was on the second floor in the west building, which had several cafeterias, including a large one in the basement. There were plenty of places and opportunities to eat, which was the least of Lily's concerns. Mainly she was nervous about meeting the other patients and the therapists who would be working with her, and learning what would be expected of her. This suddenly seemed a lot harder than qualifying for or training for the Olympics.

Her father lingered for a few minutes and helped her unpack her suitcase, and he noticed that everything was built at heights that worked for her from a wheelchair. The closet was easily accessible, the bathroom had everything she needed. It reminded him that he'd even have to redo her closets, since she could no longer reach anything that was hanging, and the shelves were too high for her as well.

After they'd unpacked, Lily went to the office she'd been instructed to go to, to get her schedule, and she saw that she had physical therapy that afternoon, swimming after that with an evaluation of her pool skills, driver's ed if she wanted to take it, or alternately a massage, and she was scheduled to meet with her tutor at six o'clock. She had a full afternoon. They were allowing her the morning to look around and get situated, and they gave her a list of all the locations where she could eat, with a caveat that patients were discouraged from eating in their rooms. Socialization was highly encouraged. And there were crafts courses, movies, chess, and an assortment of activities offered at night. Bill was impressed when she showed it to him, and then reluctantly he decided to leave. She kissed him goodbye outside her room, and he promised to call her later and drop by that night. He knew that the house was going to be empty without her, and there were tears in his eyes as he drove away. He felt like he was abandoning her, but he knew that in the long run this was going to be good for her. He just wished that the accident had never happened. It was no one's fault, which had already been determined, it was just a fluke, but a cruel turn of fate.

Lily decided to go back to her room, after her father left, and listen to her iPod. She was feeling anxious, and she knew it would relax her to listen to some music. She wanted to call Veronica, but she realized she was in school. Lily had her cell phone with her, so she could call and text her father and her friends and they could reach her.

She had her eyes closed and was listening to the music, with the door ajar, and was startled, when she opened her eyes, to find herself looking at a boy in a wheelchair in the doorway. He was watching her and was about her age. He had long, straight blond hair, and he seemed curious about her, as she took the earpiece out of her ear.

'Hi,' she said, looking at him shyly. 'I'm Lily.' She noticed that he had long legs, and was wearing what looked like golf gloves with little sticks on them, and he was using a battery-operated wheelchair rather than the manually operated one she used that she had to roll herself. His was operated by a joystick, and he moved it deftly to enter the room. He smiled at her as he did. He was a good-looking boy.

'I'm Teddy. I wondered who was getting the private room. I have one too. But that's only because I've been here longer than anyone else.'

'How long have you been here?' They were curious about each other, and he looked at ease as he moved around the room.

'Since I was two,' he said nonchalantly, and she looked startled. 'I'm just kidding. I've been here for a little more than two years. I have a C5 and 6 injury, complete. I was in a riding accident. They let me come here at fifteen, with special permission. And I've only been here for two years because my parents are afraid to take me home. My diaphragm is compromised,' he said blithely, 'so sometimes I can't breathe. Like when I get a cold. So that's everything about me. Oh, and I'm seventeen. So what brings you here?' She knew from what he'd said to her that he had a cervical injury that was farther up the spine than hers, which was why his diaphragm and lungs were involved. She wondered if that was why he had the sticks on his gloves, and it made her suspect that his arms might be involved too, but she didn't want to ask.

'I had a freak skiing accident,' Lily said carefully as she saw him glance at the CDs on her desk and nod approval. He seemed very much at home, but it wasn't surprising after two years. It sounded sad to her that his parents were afraid to take him home. She couldn't imagine her father leaving her there a minute more than he had to. 'Where are you from originally?' She was intrigued by him, and happy that they were the same age. He had a handsome open face and gentle eyes.

'Philadelphia. They don't come to visit me either. My mother is always running around to horse shows, and my father runs a bank. They are *very important people*!' he said with a Philadelphia Main Line drawl, and she laughed. 'Where are you from?'

'Here,' she said simply. 'Denver.' He nodded.

'I like your music. So what kind of freak accident did you have?'

'I fell off a chairlift, when the cable broke.' He made a face and looked sympathetic.

'Ooh, that sounds nasty. And scary. I flew over a jump, without the horse. I usually rode better than that. So where's your SCI?'

'T10,' she told him, which was considerably lower than his, which was why she didn't have the respiratory complications he did and had full use of her arms. 'Complete,' she added, in the vocabulary she had learned in the last two months.

'So here we are, at Camp Craig. You can go kayaking, canoeing, fishing, scuba diving, swimming, sail a Hobie Cat, play Foosball, billiards, and table tennis, take acting classes, learn to use blow darts, use a sip-and-puff pole or a sip-and-puff rifle, take singing lessons, go hiking, or hot air ballooning. We go to amusement parks in the summer, and learn to plant a garden. I take art classes, and unfortunately, in addition to all that, at our age, they make you go to school. I'm a junior, what are you?'

'Me too,' she said, smiling at him. 'I saw skiing on the list too.'

'You must be incurable, if you want to go skiing again.'

'I was training for the Olympics,' she said softly, and he looked sympathetic again.

'Yeah, there's skiing, but I haven't tried it. I don't qualify. They have horseback riding too, but I figured I'd quit while I was ahead.' There was certainly enough to do, and she couldn't imagine how they fit it all in. 'And they have massage therapy and acupuncture, which I kind of like,' he admitted. 'And they have a dentist, a dermatologist, and an eye doctor. Full service rehab, the best one in the country,' he said proudly, 'otherwise I wouldn't be here. My parents always sent me to the best camps too. Anything to keep me busy and get me out of their hair.' He said it matter-of-factly, and it sounded sad to her. 'Do you have brothers and sisters?' he asked with interest, and she shook her head. 'Me neither. Maybe we were twins who were separated at birth,' he suggested, and she laughed. He glanced at the clock on her wall then and saw that it was noon. 'We should probably go to the cafeteria before everybody else gets there. The food is pretty good.'

She noticed that he was trim and in good shape, which wasn't always the case with spinal injury patients, she had discovered. Some had a tendency to put on weight from being sedentary, but he looked young and fit, and had powerful shoulders and upper arms. She had noticed that her own arms were getting stronger from rolling her chair herself when no one pushed her. 'I'll show you where the cafeteria is,' he offered, and she followed him out of the room. He was faster because his chair was motorized, and he had to slow down for her. He looked happy to be talking to her as they rolled along side by side.

'Are there a lot of kids our age here?' she asked him. It was nice having a guide and made being there seem less scary.

'Some. The population changes all the time. Sometimes it's younger people, sometimes older. We're still among the youngest ones here, since the lower age limit is sixteen, but almost no one stays longer than four months. Their goal is to get you home. They must have forgotten to tell my parents that when they checked me in.' They had been to visit him once in two years, but he didn't say that to Lily. He had become kind of a permanent fixture at Craig, since he had nowhere else to go. The holidays had been tough the first year, but he was used to it now. He had just spent his third Christmas at Craig.

The cafeteria was a large, friendly room, with tables set up for four and six people, and some for two. They were encouraged to eat in groups and meet new people.

'There are usually about fifty SCI inpatients living here at any given time, so we all know each other pretty well,'

Teddy told her, as they went to order their lunch, which would be brought to them on trays. Teddy and she were both on the full meal plan, and he ordered a healthy lunch, and she did the same, before they went to a table. There were already a number of other people at tables around the room, including technicians and therapists and medical personnel who were eating there too. 'Did I tell you we play volleyball and basketball?' he added, and she smiled. He was a one-man welcoming committee and made it sound like a luxury cruise, although it was still one she would rather have not been on. But it was certainly better than she'd feared, and she was happy to have met someone her age so soon. And Teddy seemed hungry for the companionship of his peers.

'I'll introduce you to my friends when they come to visit. The kids from my ski team said they would come by too,' she volunteered, and Teddy looked skeptical.

'Don't count on it, Lily,' he said gently. 'People mean it when they say it, but they're busy in the real world. They stop coming after a while. It's like we're shut away, and they forget. Whenever people leave here, they say they'll come back and visit, and they never do. And I think it makes people who don't have injuries uncomfortable to come here. It freaks them out to see us and realize it could happen to them. Don't expect your friends to come here too often. They just don't. I've seen it a lot in two years.' He sounded philosophical about it, and he didn't want her to be disappointed and was sure she would be.

'Maybe you could come to visit at my house sometime, after I go home.'

'My wheelchair is pretty heavy,' he said practically, 'and you have to have a special van.'

'Maybe we could borrow one from here.' She felt sorry for him if his parents never came to visit him, and had left him there for two years. It didn't sound like he was going home anytime soon. 'My dad can figure it out. He's good about stuff like that.'

'He must be a nice man,' Teddy said quietly. 'Mine sure isn't. When they explained what kind of care I needed once I got home, they decided to leave me here. They say it's safer for me.'

'Is that true?' she asked, as she finished her sandwich and took a bite of an apple. She was careful about what she ate now. She didn't want to gain weight from lack of exercise.

'Maybe,' Teddy admitted, 'if I get sick, or catch a bad cold. I can't clear my lungs, so someone has to do it for me. I can't cough and clear my chest on my own because of the C5 and 6. But how big a deal is that?' Apparently it was to them, or they'd have taken him home. She knew her father would never do that to her, but not everyone was like her father. 'Where's your mom, by the way?'

'She died when I was three. In a car accident. I live alone with my dad.'

He asked to see her schedule then, and she showed it to him. He gave her the lowdown on the different therapists, and warned her that the physical therapist they'd assigned her to was a tyrant.

'Oh great,' she said, looking discouraged, 'just what I need.'

'He used to be in the Marines, and he runs his sessions like boot camp. But he's terrific actually. He got me using my arms. They said I'd never be able to use my shoulders again, and thanks to him, I can.' She had noticed that he used the sticks attached to his gloves to do everything she could do with her hands. He was incredibly able with them and could feed himself with ease. He surprised her even further when he told her he liked to draw. 'I've been painting for two years. You might like the art classes here too. But you must be kind of a jock if you were on the skiing team. If you are, there's plenty for you to do. But believe me, Phil will get you going. He makes everyone do upper body work to strengthen their arms. I hated him for the first six months, but now he's my best friend. He just looks tougher than he is.'

'You're scaring me,' she told Teddy, and he smiled. 'I've never wanted to be a Marine.'

'You don't have to be,' he explained to her. 'All you have to do is work hard. If you slack off, he pushes you, but if you do your best in your sessions with him, that's all he wants. He hates slackers and quitters. You don't look like either one to me.' And he could see she was in great shape, with a totally athletic body that hadn't melted yet. It had only been two months since her accident, and she hadn't lost her muscle tone, although they both knew she would eventually in her lower limbs, which was why Phillip Lewis would want her to develop everything above her waist, which was the level of her injury. 'I'll go with you if you want,' Teddy volunteered, and she liked that idea. She didn't want to go to boot camp alone. She felt like the new kid in school.

He took her to the therapy rooms after lunch, and went to look for Phil. Teddy found him a few minutes later, and brought him over to meet Lily, who looked at the physical therapy instructor with trepidation, while he and Teddy chatted. Just as Teddy had said, they were obviously friends. And Lily could see why Teddy had said he looked like a Marine drill sergeant. He wore his hair in a buzz cut, he was powerfully built, and he stood erect with precision and discipline. And as soon as Teddy left them, promising to catch up with her later, Phil took a careful look at her upper body. He had read her records before she got there and knew she'd been in training for the Olympics on the ski team. She had the body of a downhill racer, long and lean, with good muscles in her legs and thighs, but now she was going to need her arms.

'You want to be able to go wherever you want, for as long as you want. And you won't be able to do that with weak arms,' he explained. He had her do some exercises that were more tiring than she'd expected, and then he had her lift weights until her shoulders and arms were screaming. And after that he laid her on a mat and worked her legs for her. By the time he got her back into the wheelchair, she felt as if she could hardly move, but she noticed that she moved with greater ease.

She only had a fifteen-minute break, and then she had to report to the pool, and she was happy to see Teddy there. They had him in a harness, and lowered him gently into the pool, and he looked like he was having fun. They were working with several other people, and then they helped Lily into the pool, and after the workout she'd had with Phil, it felt great. She spent an hour in the pool, while they watched her swim, and then she was scheduled for a massage. She fell asleep on the table, and by the time she got to her room after that, all she wanted to do was go to bed. She groaned when Teddy appeared in the open doorway. He was in great spirits, and delighted with his new friend.

'Ready to rock and roll?' he said cheerfully. He had become her official tour guide and new best friend.

'Are you kidding? I'm ready to sleep for the next twelve hours. You're not kidding that this is boot camp.' But she was beginning to enjoy the challenge of how far she could push herself. It was going to be an interesting few months, if she survived.

'They push the younger ones harder. They figure we can take it,' Teddy said with a wry grin. 'We have tutoring at six o'clock.'

'Can we skip it?' she asked hopefully. She was genuinely exhausted.

'Not if you plan to graduate and go to college,' Teddy said, and she groaned again. 'I was supposed to go to Princeton like my father and grandfather, but I'd rather go to art school, if I ever get out of here. I'm still relatively on track, although I suck at math.'

'So do I,' she said as she followed him out of the room again, and went to meet their tutor, who was a pleasant, friendly woman from one of the local public schools. She had already gotten all of Lily's assignments from her school, and they agreed on a study plan for her, with meetings with the tutor every day. She had work to catch up on from the last two months, and several papers due.

They didn't get to dinner till seven-thirty, and when they did, Lily checked her BlackBerry for the first time all day. She'd been too busy to even think about it till then. She saw that she had a text from Veronica, who said only 'Too much homework. See you tomorrow. Love, V,' another one from a friend from school who said she'd come on Saturday, and one from her father that said 'See you at 8. Love, Dad.' She had half an hour to eat before he came. She ordered chicken, a baked potato, and steamed vegetables, and followed Teddy to a table where two boys were sitting who were in their mid-twenties. Teddy knew them both and introduced her. Their names were Bud and Frank, they were both good-looking and seemed athletic. Bud said he had had a diving accident the summer before. Frank had been in a car crash in L.A. on New Year's Eve. They both had injuries similar to hers and were fun to talk to. Teddy was the only one she'd met so far who didn't have full use of his hands, but he managed extremely well.

They were having a lively conversation at dinner, when she saw her father walk into the cafeteria, looking for her, and she waved at him. She introduced him to her new friends, and they sat and chatted for a while, and she told him about her day. He was happy to hear she'd met with the tutor, and impressed by all the rest. It was obvious that they were pushing her hard, but she looked livelier than he'd seen her in two months. He wondered if Jessie was right, and it was good for her to be with young people who were struggling with the same things. He asked her if any of her friends had made any plans to visit her, and he was disappointed to hear they hadn't, particularly Veronica. Teddy didn't comment, but Lily could see he wasn't surprised. He had predicted it at lunch.

And then she and her father went to sit in the living room. Family visits were encouraged, so everyone was welcoming to him, and there were several other family members there who were staying at the family facilities at Craig. She told him that Teddy's parents had been to visit him only once in two years, and Bill was horrified at how people could be so negligent of their own child.

'He seems like a nice kid,' Bill said easily. He was glad she had found a friend, someone her own age whom she could relate to, whose struggles were even greater than her own.

'Could we have him to the house sometime, Dad?'

'Of course.' He didn't hesitate.

'We'd have to borrow a van. We can't fit his chair in our car.' He had seen the heavy motorized chair that Teddy used, and he agreed.

'I talked to Joe today, by the way. He'll be here this weekend.'

'That'll be nice for you, Daddy,' she said, smiling at him. It was hard for either of them to believe this was only her first day. They both felt as though she'd been there for a month. And he didn't say anything to her, but he was meeting an architect in the morning about the changes he needed to make in the house for her. Among other things, he wanted to put an elevator in. Otherwise, she'd be trapped on every floor until someone could carry her up or down, and it was likely to be him. With an elevator, Lily would have autonomy in the house. Joe said he'd help him get the construction project organized. Joe had always loved renovating and building houses, and he had built a spectacular weekend house in the Hamptons, which they later sold. Helping with the construction was something he could do for Bill, and for Lily too. He wanted to do anything he could to help them both, and lighten the load on Bill.

'How long will he stay?' Lily asked him.

'Maybe a couple of weeks. He doesn't have much to do in New York. And with his apartment on the market, he doesn't want to be there while they show it. So he's happy to come out here,' Bill said about his old friend. Lily knew he'd had some kind of business problem, but she didn't know the details, and her father didn't volunteer them, out of respect for Joe. 'We'll come to visit you after we play golf on Sunday.' He would have liked to take her out, but her counselor had encouraged him to leave her there so she could enjoy some of the weekend activities with the other patients, which was better for her. He felt guilty not rescuing her, though.

Bill left at nine o'clock, and she went back to her room alone. A nursing aide came to help her shower and get ready for bed, and by ten o'clock she was lying in her bed exhausted. It had been a busy first day, but she was more comfortable than she'd expected. She closed her eyes, thinking of everything she'd done that day and all that Teddy had told her, and soon she was asleep. She didn't even remember to set her alarm. But Teddy had told her that an aide would wake her if she overslept, and there was a call button next to her bed if she needed anything during the night. There were always nurses on duty. It was a hospital after all, even if it felt like boot camp to her.

Chapter 12

Lily's second day at Craig was even busier than the first one. She had physical therapy again, a class that showed her how to get around a kitchen, which was something she hadn't been too efficient at before the accident either, and had never had to be. She went swimming again, went to driver's ed, and met with her tutor, but she hadn't had time to do her assignments. The tutor told her to be sure and do them over the weekend, and she and Teddy made a date to study together. And Veronica finally showed up. Lily met her in the living room, and Lily noticed how ill at ease she seemed. It was the first time she had seen Veronica in more than two months, and Veronica looked shocked when she saw Lily in the wheelchair. The accident was finally real to her.

All Veronica talked about was training with the team. She described everything their coach was doing and how hard they were pushing. And by the time she left, Lily wanted to cry, and realized how much she missed skiing and always would. She felt totally left out of the life they had once shared, and she wouldn't have admitted it to anyone, but she was almost sorry Veronica had come. She had told her father not to come so she and Veronica would have more time to visit, and now she realized that that had been a mistake. At the end of the visit Veronica walked out of the hospital, free as a bird, and Lily felt like she was in prison, and she was more acutely aware of her injury than ever. Seeing and listening to Veronica made her feel like her life was over. She had been told by her counselor how normal it was to be angry and feel the loss of her life as she had known it. And all she felt was devastation after Veronica's visit to the hospital. She was crying when she rolled back to her room, and she ran into Teddy on his way to his. He stopped with a look of concern when he saw her.

'Are you okay?' he asked, and she was embarrassed that he'd seen her crying.

'No,' she said honestly.

'What happened?'

'One of my friends came to visit, my best friend.' She started crying again after she said it. She didn't want to explain it to him. 'All she talked about was the ski team, and training, and what everyone is doing.' She sobbed and wished he could put his arms around her, but the look in his eyes was as warm as an embrace.

'I'm sorry, Lily. Some people just don't get it. I feel like that sometimes when people talk about their families and what a good time they have together.' He rolled slowly back to her room with her. 'Do you want to watch a movie?' he suggested. 'I could watch with you.'

'No, I'm okay.' She smiled through her tears and helped herself to a tissue and blew her nose. 'She's always been my best friend. And she looked so nervous, visiting. I don't think she'll come back.'

'She may not,' he said, honest with her too. And maybe it would be better if she didn't, but he didn't say that to her. He could see how hard the visit had been for his new friend. They talked for a while after that, and then he went back to his own room, and Lily called her father, and he could hear that she was upset.

'Did something happen?' She told him about Veronica's visit then, and he felt bad for her. There was so little he could do to make things easier for her. Nothing, in fact. They talked for a while, and she felt better, and then she called for the nursing aide to help her get ready for bed. It had been a long day.

Bill called Jessie Matthews in Squaw Valley the next day. He told her that Lily was at Craig now, and she asked about his visits to the neurosurgeons they had seen. Jennifer had visited her when she got back and had thanked her for the opportunity, but they didn't discuss how the consults had gone.

'They all agreed with your prognosis,' Bill said sadly. 'And Dr. Hammerfeld at Mass General sang your praises. But they all said the same thing about Lily's injury being complete and what that means.'

'I thought they would. How is Lily doing at Craig?'

'She sounds very busy, and she's trying to catch up on her schoolwork now. They have an amazing program, and she met a very nice boy her age. They seem to have made friends with each other. Her boyfriend dumped her when we got back, and her old friends aren't making much of an effort to visit. She misses the ski team. It's all a big adjustment for her.'

'And for you too,' Jessie said sympathetically.

'I'm going to make some changes to the house before she comes home. It won't work for her the way it is. And how are you?' he asked her, knowing that her life had been radically altered too.

'We're okay. We're managing. It's hard for the kids.'

'It can't be easy for you either,' he said kindly.

She sighed when he said it. It hadn't been. It was hard to believe Tim had been gone for two months. 'All you can do is the best you can. Let me know how Lily's doing. I think she'll learn a lot of good things at Craig. It's a very impressive place.'

'I can see that it is. I just hope she comes home soon.' He was lonely without her, but Jessie hoped he let her stay long enough to really benefit from what they offered.

That day Lily got an example of some of the more unusual but very useful things they taught. One of the instructors shepherded four of the younger women into a specially fitted van, and they were each secured while they were inside. All of them were in wheelchairs like Lily's and had full use of their arms. They were all several years older than Lily, but it was a good chance for her to meet them in a small group. They headed downtown to a shopping mall, with many stores.

'What are we going to do there?' one of the women inquired, but it was nice to get out of the hospital for an outing.

'We're going shopping,' the instructor informed them. When they arrived, the driver carefully lowered each wheelchair from the van.

The outing was to teach them to negotiate shopping in small stores, and it had been prearranged. It was to give them confidence, show them how to maneuver their wheelchairs, how to get the attention of salespeople, and even how to try on clothes, and not allow themselves to be ignored. It was a little chaotic in the first store, especially with four of them in chairs, but by the second and third ones, they were getting better at it, each of them bought something, and all of them were having a good time. They chatted animatedly with each other as they went from store to store. It reminded Lily of her disastrous outing at Harrods with Jennifer and how insignificant she had felt while salespeople ignored her and she got jostled by everyone. The instructor said they were going to a department store next week. It was the most fun Lily had had since the accident, and she felt successful when they went back to the hospital after lunch. And Phil Lewis had a surprise for her at the physical therapy session too.

'What's on our agenda for today?' she asked, with a feeling of dread. She'd had so much fun shopping with the other women that she wasn't in the mood to play boot camp with him again, but he had other plans.

He had turned on a flat-screen TV and slipped a DVD into a machine. 'We're going to watch movies today,' he said simply, and Lily watched as the film came on. It explained about the Paralympics, which was a form of Olympics, held right after the normal Olympic Games, winter and summer and in the same location, only this was for physically impaired people with injuries such as hers. She watched coverage on several events, and was suddenly mesmerized when she saw people downhill racing on skis, fitted with a seat and device like a chair. It was called Alpine skiing, and looked fast and dangerous and exciting. The ski was a monoski in some instances, or a pair of skis, and the poles had little skis on the tips for balance. And the skier sitting on the chair came down the run at full speed. It was an exciting event and didn't look easy to do. There was Nordic cross-country skiing too.

Lily watched several events and sat riveted until the end of the DVD.

Phil turned to her after he took the DVD out of the machine. 'I thought that might be of interest to you.' He had read her file carefully and knew she'd been training for the Olympics.

'When do they do it?'

'Every four years, just like the regular Olympics. The next one is next year, in March. They have winter and summer games. There are five categories in the Winter Paralympics. I thought the chair racing could be something for you. You'd have to do a lot of work to train, but you're capable of it, if you were on the Olympic downhill team.' Lily was silent for a long moment as she stared at him.

'I want to do it,' she said with a determined look.

'You'll have to work on your balance, and you need to work on your upper body anyway. It's something for you to think about.' He had shown it to her to inspire her, and interest her in new goals that she could achieve. She had never imagined after her injury that she could ski again.

'I want to do it!' she said again, and Phil nodded. He had hoped she would.

'Then we'll work on it.' It was the carrot he was going to use to push her hard. And she did everything he asked of her that afternoon. She was still excited about it when she met Teddy at the pool. She told him all about the race she'd seen on the film. It looked every bit as fast and exciting as downhill.

'I've heard about it. Are you really going to do it?' He looked happy for her. She'd had a great day.

'I'm going to try. Why don't you enter an event?' she said, trying to include him.

'I'm not really good at any sport. I was into horses, but not much else.'

'Why don't you ask Phil if there's an event he thinks would work for you?' She had seen a sledding event that she thought Teddy could do, although he was vulnerable to the cold, so he'd have to be careful.

She was still talking about it at dinner after they met with their tutor, it was all she could think about, but she didn't say anything to her father when he came to visit her that night. She was afraid that he would object. He didn't want her to get hurt again. But she could hardly sleep that night, thinking about the Paralympics, and she talked to Phil about it again the following afternoon. She didn't realize it, but her upper body was already getting stronger after a few days, and he was pleased. She had a lot of spirit, and she worked hard at everything she did. When they reviewed her case at the end of the week, all her instructors agreed that she was doing well, and they were sure she was going to succeed.

And that weekend she caught up on her schoolwork with Teddy. Veronica had said she would come by on

Saturday afternoon, and Lily was relieved when she didn't. She didn't want to hear her talk about the Olympic team again. It was just too hard, but still, Lily missed her old friends.

A group of ten of the patients at Craig went to the movies on Saturday night, and sat in a row of wheel-chairs, eating popcorn and laughing at the movie. At first it felt weird, but after a while she enjoyed it, and Teddy had gone with them. And on Sunday her father and Joe came to visit after they played golf, as he had promised. They stayed for dinner, and Bill was in better spirits when they left.

'She's a brave girl,' Joe said to him.

'Yes, she is,' Bill said proudly, 'and it's a remarkable place. They teach people to lead full lives, in spite of their injuries. It looks like they do a very good job.' He could see that Lily had already learned a lot in less than a week, and she looked healthy and well, better than she had since the accident, and she already seemed more confi-dent as a result of what she was learning. Everyone he'd seen had a positive attitude, and they appeared to have a good time at what they were doing.

'I know this sounds odd,' Joe said, 'but I kept thinking while we were visiting, why don't you build a place like that, on a smaller scale?'

'Why would I do that?' Bill asked, with a startled look. 'They're the best there is.'

'I can see that. But a lot of the patients are older than Lily, and they have an entire medical facility that you wouldn't have to provide, and they work with brain-injured people too. And they have a research component you also wouldn't need to do. If you watch them, the younger ones all gravitate toward each other, and their needs are different from the adults'. The older patients are trying to get back to careers they had before, and jobs, or functioning as heads of families. What if you built a rehab facility geared only to young people, even younger than Lily? Someone said that Craig only takes them from sixteen upward. There must be kids with spinal cord injuries too. I know there's a rehab hospital for children, but you could do something really special. You could take kids from ten to twenty, or ten to twenty-two, or even younger, with just enough medical care to meet their actual needs, and only take them when they are ready for rehab and not before.

'The whole program could be geared to young people, all their activities, art, music, everything they do at Craig, but without the broader age span and maybe with a particular emphasis on sports. You could do it in a very high-end way, but on a smaller scale, and set up scholarships in Lily's name. You could even work in tandem with Craig in some way, and offer things that they need for their younger patients, and pass your patients on to Craig when they were too old for your facility. It might be a terrific complement to what they offer. And you could keep it smaller and make it a very special place. It might be a wonderful thing to do in Lily's honor.

'You could have a sports program that would excite all of them and have instructors there to train for competitive sports.' Lily had mentioned the Paralympics in passing, and Joe thought it was a fantastic idea. 'You could hire some of the best people in the country. You have the money and the access. It's something to think about. Not to compete with Craig or the children's hospital, but as a different, additional facility where appropriate. They might even like the idea. I'm sure they get kids under sixteen that they can't accept into their program, but you could take into yours.' Lily had told Joe at dinner that there was a rehab hospital for children in Denver, but he had something far more sophisticated in mind.

Bill looked at him as they stopped in front of his house. 'I may be crazy, and it would be an enormous undertaking, but I like the idea. Now what do I do?'

'Start thinking about it, and talk to some of the people you've met who've been helpful to you. You've learned an awful lot about spinal cord injuries since Lily's accident. Put it to good use, not just for Lily, but for others like her. Focus on kids her age and both younger and a little older. I think this is something you could really do.' Joe looked excited about it, and inspired, and suddenly so did Bill.

Bill was thinking about it as they walked into the house. They had a glass of wine and talked about it some more, and the idea was gnawing at Bill as he went up to bed. He still wondered if it was a crazy idea, but he felt as though something were pushing him to do it. He tossed and turned all night, and when he woke up at six in the morning, he knew he had to do it. The blessing in Lily's accident had just come clear. He was going to call it The Lily Pad, and he was going to build it in Lily's honor. It was going to be a whole rehab center, just for kids.

Chapter 13

Bill was still excited about Joe's idea when he came down to breakfast in the morning, and found Joe at the kitchen table, reading the paper with a cup of coffee. Joe glanced up and saw that Bill looked like he'd already had ten cups of coffee. He paced around the kitchen with fire in his eyes.

'The market must be either severely up or down for you to look like that,' Joe teased him. He hadn't seen his friend that excited in years, or maybe ever, and surely not recently since Lily had gotten hurt. Bill was totally alive.

'I'm going to do it,' he said, helping himself to a mug of coffee, and taking a sip of the steaming brew with narrowed eyes. His mind was racing at full speed.

'Do what?' Joe stretched out his long legs. He was enjoying staying at Bill's and being in Denver. It was the perfect antidote to his lonely life in New York, with nothing to do and no one to talk to.

'What we talked about last night. The center for kids with spinal cord injuries. Like Craig, only entirely geared to young people. It could feed right into what they're doing at Craig for a slightly older age group. I'm going to call it The Lily Pad. I don't know why, but I just feel I have to do this. It's the right thing to do. I don't know a thing about building a rehab center, but if we find the right people to run and staff it, we could create a fantastic place.' Bill loved the idea, and Joe could see how excited he was. He was a man with a vision. And when Bill got started on something, he didn't stop. It was how he had made his fortune, built on genius, guts, and sheer grit. And he had what it took to pull it off, unlimited money, and the courage to do something new. And knowing him, Joe was certain he wouldn't stop until he had built the best center for kids in the world.

'It could be amazing,' Joe said, looking excited about it too. Bill was brilliant at solving difficult problems and achieving the impossible, excellent at execution, attention to detail, and follow-through. 'I'd love to help, if you need someone to do research on the project or make contacts. I've got the time,' Joe reminded him. And Bill knew he had the skill in spite of the recent fiasco in his career. 'I don't know anything about hospitals, but I can learn, and business is business, whatever you're selling. You'd need a great medical chief of staff, but there's got to be a lot of administrative work with something like that.' Bill nodded, his mind going in a thousand directions, and the doorbell rang while they were talking. He had completely forgotten the meeting with the architect, to make the accommodations he needed for the house for when Lily came home.

Steve Jansen was young and had done projects like this before. He had been recommended by two other architects. He walked through the house, pointing out changes that needed to be made that Bill hadn't even thought of. And they picked a spot for the new elevator. It meant losing a walk-in closet on each floor, one of which was full of files and luggage, which he could put elsewhere, and the other with Lily's ski equipment which she no longer needed. It gripped Bill's heart when he opened the door and saw her ski gear, and he closed it again quickly with tears in his eyes. He didn't want Lily to see any of that either, so he was glad the closet would disappear. Steve assured him that he could get everything done within two months, and have it ready before Lily came home.

He suggested installing a discreet ramp in the foyer, with a handsome brass railing to match the decor, and a similar one in the living room, lowering the island in the kitchen and moving the sink, making easier access to the fridge, and completely remodeling her bathroom with a special shower and tub and a lowered sink. Bill wanted everything in the house convenient, comfortable, and accessible to her without making it look like a hospital ward, and Steve completely understood. Joe was fascinated as he watched the meeting proceed. They walked each floor of the house. By the time Steve was finished with the remodel, there wouldn't be a single unmanageable feature for her. He even suggested lowering the stove and kitchen cabinets and counters. It wasn't going to be inexpensive, but it was worth every penny to Bill. He had seen on the single night she was home how difficult the house was for her now. At first he hadn't wanted to change anything in their home, because it meant accepting that Lily would be in a wheelchair forever, but he realized now that she would be, until something changed in the research everyone talked about. Making their home fully livable for her was his gift to Lily, and Steve was impressed, as was Joe. Bill had made an enormous shift in a matter of days, after seeing her blossom at Craig.

Bill poured them each a cup of coffee at the end of the meeting, and they stood in the kitchen, while Steve explained that everything was going to be high tech, state of the art, with black granite in the kitchen and pink marble in her bathroom. It was going to be beautiful when it was finished, not just functional, in keeping with the standards of the home they lived in, which was magnificently done. It was a high standard for Steve to meet, but he assured Bill he was equal to the job, which was what Bill had been told.

And then Bill had an idea. 'What would you think of a live-in center for spinal cord injury kids, on a high-end scale? Does that sound insane to you?' Bill asked him out of the blue, and Steve looked intrigued.

'You mean like Craig?'

'Yes, and no. Same patient base, but younger and not as broad. Only spinal cord injuries, not brain injuries, and not all the hospital-based medical features they offer, and for younger kids, the ones who don't qualify for Craig now. We wouldn't hospitalize them during their recovery, but *only* for rehab. I mean a real inpatient learning center for young kids and adolescents, and maybe kids in their early twenties, entirely geared to them, a major sports program, arts, music, as well as rehab, and everything they need to know about how to reintegrate back into school or college, and find internships in the mainline workforce, everything for kids, only they'd have spinal cord injuries. I want it to have everything a noninjured kid would want, only designed just for them. Craig is geared for slightly older kids and adults, although they do a fantastic job, and I like the fact that they add so much fun to it. They have an incredible recreational program. But I would want ours to be *only* the activities that appeal to kids.'

'You mean sex and drugs?' Steve quipped, and they both laughed.

'No, I mean good clean fun. But their kind of fun.

Craig has to offer a much broader range to appeal to everyone. I know there are activities there that Lily won't be interested in, although they offer a lot that she'll like too. I just want to narrow the focus here and lower the age. They have an incredible family facility too, and that takes a lot of space and real estate, and I don't want to go there yet. Maybe with the young kids, we can have double rooms where their moms could stay with them, but it would take too much space to set up a family facility like Craig's. They've been at this for forty or fifty years. I don't want to compete with them, I couldn't, and I wouldn't want to. That would be pointless. I want to add some of what they can't or don't do, or do less of. And for the right patients, we could just refer them to Craig. And maybe they would want to send really young kids to us, other than for what's offered at Children's Hospital here in Denver. We could try to offer something different and more than either facility provides. I don't know. Joe suggested it, and I thought about it. I got inspired last night. I just wondered what you think of the idea, and what kind of facility it would take.' Bill had no idea, but that wasn't stopping him now.

Steve looked intrigued as he mused about it for a minute. It was an extraordinary idea, and he could sense that Bill was the kind of man who could deliver on it and who followed his dreams. The house he lived in, and the career he had had, and his enormous success, were proof of that, more than Steve even knew. Joe knew Bill more intimately and had no doubt that he would follow through if he fell in love with the project. To Bill, the dream was already real.

In Bill's mind, it was not unlike a school, where you had younger children, older ones, middle range, high school, and a few college age, and maybe kids like Lily and others mentoring them, to show what you could achieve. They could have a program set up with Craig, where their patients could volunteer with the younger ones to give them hope.

'You can build anything you need, of course, from scratch,' Steve said thoughtfully. 'We can design whatever you want and conceive of. You could get operative a lot faster, though, if we could use an existing structure and adapt it to your needs, rather than building it from the ground up.' And then he thought of something. 'Have you ever been out to the La Vie resort?' Bill shook his head. He'd never heard of it, and had no idea what it was. 'It was kind of a cool idea. It's called La Vie, but their motto was "La vie est belle." Life is beautiful. It was built by a Frenchman. I met him a couple of times. He had a vision of a spa in the States, kind of like something in the Alps. I think he originally thought about building it in Wyoming or Montana but decided on Denver because it was easier to get to.

'It's a rambling place, on thirty acres, and he spent a fortune on the structures. There are some gorgeous houses on it, big ones. He was intending for people to just come there and rest for an extended period of time. There was a fabulous spa, an enormous gym, some smaller houses, a good-size office complex that doesn't look like one. I think he built it to house fifty or sixty guests at a time, and he wanted the spa and sports facilities to be a membership-only setup, like a health club for locals. It was a great idea, kind of nirvana in the mountains. He sank a bundle into it.

'And then the economy fell apart, here and in France. They closed a few months after they opened. It was really a shame, I loved the idea, and the structures are beautiful. It looks like a private estate. And it was standing empty the last time I heard. I'm not sure, but I think the bank was going to foreclose on it. I don't know if it has by now. Last I heard he had hung on to it. I don't know if it changed hands in the meantime or not. I always thought it would make a beautiful home for someone with a lot of adult kids, kind of like a family complex, or one of those art or writing colonies, something like that. Anyway, it's an amazing place. If it's right for you, it would be a great start and save you a lot of time. I don't know who owns it now, but I could find out.' Bill looked mesmerized by what he said.

'I'd like that very much,' Bill said quietly, and Joe

smiled. He could see the wheels of Bill's mind turning a thousand miles an hour. 'Where is it?'

'About ten miles out of town. I don't think anyone ever realized it was there. It was a gorgeous piece of land, and it opened and closed so fast, no one ever knew about it. Kind of like Brigadoon. I'll check it out. If nothing else, it's a valuable piece of property, with some beautiful houses on it, and at the right price it would be a great investment. It may have been overpriced if he tried to sell it, which may be why it hasn't sold. I think the French guy got the land fairly cheap at the time, but he spent a fortune on it, with beautifully built structures. It was his dream apparently. It's a shame it didn't work out. Bad timing more than anything, I think, although he sank so much into it, I don't know how he would ever have amortized the investment. People do that sometimes, and get carried away, and then the bottom falls out.'

Steve had seen that with houses he had designed for people, where they just spent too much on it, and never got their money out when they sold. He tried to keep his clients from doing that, but some people had big dreams, and didn't have the money to back them up. He knew that wasn't the case with Bill. 'If I remember correctly, the guy who built La Vie had a spa in France, and a hotel in St. Bart's, so he should have known what he was doing. Maybe it's different in the States, where a lot of people lost money on investments when the market plunged. I'll let you know what I hear. And I'll send the plans over for your remodel in a couple of days. It's going to be great,' he said with a warm smile. He was sorry to hear about his daughter's accident, but Bill was doing wonderful things for her, while respecting the look, feel, and quality of the house. There was going to be nothing institutional-looking about it. It wasn't going to be depressing, just practical for her, and beautiful to look at. Steve was excited about the job, and so was Bill. But Bill was already thinking about what Steve had said about the defunct spa called La Vie. He couldn't stop himself. As soon as Steve left, Bill called Hank Peterson, a commercial real estate broker he knew, and asked him to check it out.

He was working at his desk, when the broker called him back two hours later. 'Interesting place you found,' he said to Bill. 'I don't know why I never heard of it. It could have a thousand uses. And it's on a fair amount of land.'

'Who owns it?'

'I'm not sure. Apparently the bank was going to fore-close on it a year ago for unpaid mortgage, and the owner came up with the money at the last minute. I don't know where it stands now. I think the original owner still owns it, although no one's been there in three years. They closed almost as fast as they opened. I haven't seen it, but someone in my office has and says it's quite a place. It's a little off the beaten track, but not that far. Do you want me to check out the status of the ownership?'

'Yes, I would,' Bill said coolly, not wanting to show too much interest, but his heart was pounding as he listened. He knew this was the right place, for a project he hadn't even known he wanted to undertake a day before.

'Do you want to take a ride out to look at it?' Hank suggested.

'Sure,' Bill said, feigning a calm he didn't feel. He felt like Kevin Costner in *Field of Dreams* when he hears the voice that says 'If you build it, they will come.' He was usually more practical than that, but he felt as though it was destiny that Steve Jansen had told him about La Vie, at this particular moment in time.

'When do you want to see it?' the broker said casually.

'I'm free now. If you have some time.'

'I can meet you there in an hour.' He gave Bill the directions, and Bill went downstairs to find Joe, who was on his computer, writing to his sons, to let them know he was in Denver with Bill. He said he hoped they were well, and he was having a good time. He told them both about Lily's accident, to explain why he'd come out. One of his sons had written back immediately to say how sorry he was about Lily.

'Want to go for a ride?' Bill asked him offhandedly. Joe smiled at him – he knew him better than that. Bill had something up his sleeve. He had a look on his face like a cat that was about to pounce.

'What are you up to?'

'I want to take a look at that spa Steve talked about this morning. The French guy still owns it. Or the broker thinks he does, he's not sure. It must be costing him a fortune to service the mortgage. The bank almost foreclosed on it last year. Let's take a look, before I get too wound up about it.' But they both knew he already was. And there was another call he wanted to make before he went out there.

'I'll come with you,' Joe confirmed, as Bill went back to his office.

He sat down at his desk and called Jessie. He figured she was probably busy with a patient or in surgery, and he was surprised when she came on the line very quickly.

'Is Lily okay?' She sounded worried.

'She's fine, or at least she was when I saw her last night. Thank you for taking my call so quickly.'

'I thought something might have happened.' Jessie always assumed the worst now, ever since Tim, especially about her kids.

'A friend of mine suggested something to me last night, and I wanted to talk to you about it.' He went right to the point. He knew that she was busy. 'It sounds crazy to talk about, but I can't get it out of my head. What would you think about a residential rehab center for SCI kids, really young ones, and adolescents, younger than the ones they take at Craig, and with their low age range as our higher age, with very specific focus and everything geared just for them? Not a major medical facility combined with it, like Craig, but just rehab, with everything a kid, teenager, or college age kid could want. Not with all the bells and whistles Craig can offer, that's a real medical facility, but straight rehab with whatever medical care is needed, but no ICU facilities, for instance. If we needed acute medical care, we could transfer them to Craig or another hospital. This would be pure rehab for kids and young people, state of the art, high tech, with everything we could offer. What do you think? Other than that I'm crazy, I think that's a given.' He laughed at himself, and she joined him. She was bowled over by everything he had just said.

'It's an incredible idea.' And he was right, it didn't duplicate what Craig was doing or even the local rehab hospital for children. It was just different enough to be interesting, particularly for younger kids, who were much harder to place in rehab. Most rehabs needed to focus on older patients, but there were plenty of younger SCI patients, and even at Lily's age, some of the programs were too serious for them, in order to have wide appeal to all ages.

'I'd also like to offer free scholarships to those who need them, can't afford to pay, or aren't covered by insurance.' She liked that idea too. There were plenty of people who could not afford extended stays in rehab, or to go at all, if they couldn't pay or make up the difference, or justify it to their insurance. And facilities like that were expensive. 'So what do you think?'

'I think it would be a remarkable gift to the SCI community if something like that existed. Craig is the best one of its kind we use, and some patients don't fit their profile, although they're very reasonable about who they take. I had a nine-year-old patient last year who didn't work out at the children's rehab where we sent her, whom we had a terrible time placing. We just couldn't get the right fit, and something as individualized as you're describing would be a tremendous asset in treatment planning. Some parents even try to do the rehab themselves. I think what you're talking about would be a terrific solution. Beyond amazing. Are you really thinking of doing something like that?' She could tell he was, or he wouldn't have called her.

'I wanted to know what you think.' He had come to respect her more and more, particularly after his tour of other neurosurgeons with Lily.

'I think it's a very ambitious project, because I can't imagine how you would do it, and it would cost a fortune. But I love the idea.' She sounded excited as she said it.

'I have friends here whose daughter had juvenile diabetes,' he said. 'They built a hospital for her, which is now one of the best diabetes facilities in the country. Sometimes a project like this is what you have to do, or all you can do, if you can't change what happened.' His voice was filled with emotion, and she understood. But there were very few people who could afford to make such a grand gesture, to include others in the same situation. She suspected that Bill could afford to, and might even have the drive to do it and see it through. He seemed like an incredibly creative and determined person, and she had come to respect him a great deal. He had made a heroic shift in his thinking, once he accepted Lily's situation.

'I think what you want to do is admirable,' she said, sounding moved, and somewhat dazzled. It was hard to imagine achieving what he hoped to do, or having the money to do it. But that was the easy part for him.

'The problem is that I have no idea what I'm doing. All I have is heart and money. We would need expertise in order for this to work. I would want to hire the best doctors and therapists in the country.' And then he asked her a question she didn't expect. He was full of surprises. 'If I do this, would you run it and be the medical director?' She was stunned when he asked the question.

'I'm a surgeon, not an administrator,' she said honestly. 'You could get someone a lot more competent than I am for what you want to do.'

'You could practice in Denver, and still do surgery in a hospital here. But this would need someone absolutely tops to run it, who really knows what's needed.' She had to admit she loved the idea, and his excitement about the project, but it was impossible for her.

'I couldn't do it to my kids. They've already been through so much, losing their father. I couldn't move them away from here. Besides, they'd kill me. This is their home, they love it here, they grew up in Tahoe. And it's a good place for them to be and for me to practice.'

'I had to ask,' Bill said apologetically. 'I would have been a fool not to.' And he was no fool. He was one of the smartest men she had ever met. And she loved what he was trying to do. 'Will you help me find the right people to run it, if I actually pull this off? Which remains to be seen. Right now it's just a crazy pipe dream.' But she thought it was a good one.

'I'll do my best. I'll think about it.' She was going to mention it to Ben, her partner. His situation was less complicated than hers, he had no ties except to Kazuko, and no children. And Kazuko might even like to work there. Bill didn't need a neurosurgeon to run it, although it might have been better. A good orthopedist could work too. But there were other neurosurgeons she could suggest. The problem would be finding someone who would be willing to relocate to Denver. She wasn't, and couldn't. She was too tied in to Squaw Valley. And even if Tim had been alive, she couldn't have done it. He loved Lake Tahoe as much as their kids did. He would never have been willing to move, nor would her children, she knew.

They all thought Lake Tahoe was the best place on earth.

'I'll let you know how I'm doing,' Bill said. 'I'm going to see a property this afternoon. This may all come to nothing, but it's worth a look.' And she knew that building a rehab center for kids was part of his process of acceptance of what had happened to his daughter, just on a much bigger scale than most people could consider or even conceive of. But it was a healthy sign that he was thinking in this direction, even if his project never happened. It was a noble thought.

'Keep me posted,' she said, and they hung up. She didn't expect to hear from him again anytime soon, or maybe ever on that project. But she was intrigued by it, and mentioned it to Ben late that afternoon, after she saw her last patient of the day. She told him what Bill had in mind and that he had asked her if she would ever move to Denver and run it, and she had said she couldn't.

'That's some wild idea he has there,' Ben said, looking at her. She seemed so worn out these days, she was burning the candle at both ends, working too hard, and no longer had Tim to share the load with the kids. She looked sad all the time now, and he hated to see it. 'He must have more money than anyone on the planet if he's considering something like that,' Ben said, visibly impressed.

'I think he can afford it. What about you?' she asked her partner. 'It might be fun to help start something like that.' He was quick to shake his head.

'I'm happy here. I don't have big ambitions to reinvent the wheel. I put people back together when they get hurt. I'm not star material like you are, Jessie. I never wanted to be. I'm a good doctor and a good surgeon, and I like my small-town life. That would be a big job, if he pulls off an SCI center for young kids. And a lot of headaches.' She thought it sounded extraordinary. 'You should think about it,' he told her with a serious look.

'I can't, Ben. I couldn't do that to my kids. I can't move them to Denver after what happened to Tim. That's traumatic enough without a new city, new schools, leaving their friends and the house they grew up in. Besides, they wouldn't let me.'

'He'd probably pay you a fortune to do it,' Ben said practically.

'That wouldn't make a difference to the kids.'

'No, but it would to you.' They both knew that she had lost half their income when Tim died and he had left no insurance. He had meant to, but just hadn't gotten around to it. They were both so busy, and young enough not to worry about dying yet. So now all she had to support them was her work, with four kids to feed and educate. But she shook her head with determination. 'I've been thinking,' Ben said quietly. 'At some point, you should go back to Stanford.' She looked startled when he said it, and a little hurt.

'Are you trying to get rid of me?'

'No. I meant what I said. You're a star, Jess. You don't belong here. You never did. I know you moved here for Tim, and you get some good cases occasionally, like the Thomas kid, but you should be in a big teaching hospital, where you can shine and get the challenges you deserve. I love working with you, but sometimes I don't think it's fair to you. I always thought that, when Tim was alive, and you wanted to be here to make him happy. Now you have to think of yourself. And your kids will be gone in a few years, sooner than you know. You deserve a bigger life than this, and a bigger forum to work from medically. You ought to think about going back to Stanford.'

She smiled at her partner. 'Jimmy won't be going to college for another twelve years. I've got a lot of years left here, and then I'll be too old to make a move. I'll be fifty-five years old, and they don't want old docs at Stanford – they want bright, fresh new ones, with innovative ideas. I'm afraid you're stuck with me, Dr. Steinberg,' she announced, and he looked at her regretfully.

'I'm not stuck, Jessie, you are. You should think about this guy's offer, if you won't go back to Stanford.'

'Who knows if he'll ever do it?' she said sensibly. 'He's on some kind of euphoric high after his kid's accident. It's all part of the grief process for him, probably more fantasy than reality. I can't get caught up in other people's dreams, Ben. I've got my own reality. And mine is four kids to support, who want to live here, where they grew up.'

'Don't let them run your life, Jess. You have to think of yourself too.'

She laughed at what he said. 'Spoken like a man with no children. Believe me, I wouldn't want to be the one to tell Heather Matthews she's moving to Denver. She'd put a contract out on me. She nearly did yesterday because I ironed her blouse wrong and shrank her jeans. Tim always did the laundry better than I do. God save me from fifteen-year-old girls. I'd rather face a firing squad than tell her she's moving to Denver.' She laughed again, thinking about it, just as her BlackBerry rang. It was the hospital telling her that her post-op patient from the day before had spiked a fever. She said she'd be there in five minutes. 'Anyway, I think it would be fun for you.' But it was more work and commitment than Ben wanted. He liked to work hard and play hard, and he had never been as driven about his career as Jessie, but she couldn't do it either, for four very good reasons, her children. All she could do to help Bill was suggest other neurosurgeons to him, who might be interested in the job. *If* he ever did it. She hurried out of the office then, with a wave at Ben.

And after that she had to get home to her kids, help with homework, do laundry, pay bills, and cook dinner. And maybe come back to the hospital again, since she was on call. The days were long for her now, and the nights were longer, with no help from anyone except Chris, her oldest son. And when he left for college in the fall, it would be a nightmare. All she could see ahead of her now was a long, long road, of hard work, and sadness without Tim. And all of it showed in her eyes and her worn expression of grief.

Bill and Joe met Hank Peterson at the property that they had discussed, ten miles out of town. It was exactly thirty-four acres, and the structures on it were as beautiful as Steve had said. There was a very large main building that was impeccably finished and looked like a large French country manor. All the details were exquisite. It had lovely French windows and a mansard roof, and a wide porch around it. There were orchards that had gone unattended and were rotting, and what had been extensive gardens were overgrown. The house was only a few years old and in perfect condition inside. The roof was sound, with no sign of leaks.

Bill counted twenty bedrooms in the main house, all of them lovely, with their own bathrooms. The owner had spared no expense on the construction. There were a few pieces of furniture here and there, but essentially it was unfurnished. The broker said the contents had been sold off in an auction in order to raise money for the mortgage. There were large common rooms, four of them, and a state-of-the-art kitchen and, on a lower level, a maze of offices.

There was a second building with twelve bedrooms, and a similar setup. And a third one that looked as though it might have been the spa, with rooms for massages, steam rooms, a sauna, a hot tub, and a small lap pool. And three more buildings farther out that could have been dormitories for the staff, or offices. There was a large gym, in a building of its own, an enormous garage, and several smaller outbuildings that looked like they were for equipment. And at the back of the property was a greenhouse that was very pretty and was a jungle of overgrown plants. There was an outdoor cooking area, a little stream that ran through the property, and a small stable with a corral. It had everything Bill could have wanted, and it was easy to see the love and care and money that had been poured into it. He could sense easily how disappointed, and even heartbroken, the owner must have been when it failed. Bill made no comment as he walked through it. He didn't want the broker to see how excited he was.

'Do you know yet who owns it? The bank or the original owner?'

'Apparently the owner. I checked. The bank is close to foreclosing on it, and they figure they'll have to any day. But he's still making payments, barely. He doesn't want to sell it. Yet. But the bank says he'll have to sooner or later.' Like vultures, they were waiting to grab it. And it made Bill sad for the owner when he saw how beautiful the place was and all that had gone into it for naught. And it was wasted now, standing empty and unused.

'Do you know how much he's got in it?' Bill asked with the appearance of casual disinterest.

'He paid five million for the land, and whatever it cost him to build it. I don't know how much, but it looks like he spent a bundle. Good way to lose your shirt. I think you'd probably get it if you make an offer. Officially it's not on the market, but the bank thinks he'd take a decent offer.' Bill was quietly trying to calculate how much the owner must have spent on the two main houses, the four smaller buildings, and all the sheds and outbuildings, the gym, and the garage. It had been a very expensive project, and bad luck for him that the economy had folded almost at the same time. He figured that in another city he could easily have spent ten or even twenty million dollars on the structures, in California or New York. In Denver maybe five to seven, along with the cost of the land.

Bill walked the entire property with Joe, and made very little comment. This was one of those things that was happening by instinct for him, straight from the gut. He still wasn't certain he could put a rehab center together, but once he had the place, that much would be sure, and he could always sell it later. And all the structures were in excellent shape because they were new. They had thirty-two bedrooms for patients, he had counted, twice that if they put patients two to a room, and the bedrooms were a good size. Each had its own bathroom that would have to be refitted for handicap needs. And there were buildings for staff dormitories, and for offices, a garage, a gym, and a spa. They had everything they needed to get started, in fact more than enough. And it was a beautiful place. The owner had had the ground leveled before he built, and there were smooth broad paths that would work for wheelchairs. Bill knew, as he glanced around, it was the place. He hadn't even looked for it. It had found him.

He walked back to the car without saying anything to the broker, and then turned with a cool expression.

'I'll make an offer,' he said simply, as though he didn't really care one way or the other. The broker nodded.

'How much do you have in mind, since it's not on the market?' He expected Bill to make a lowball offer that wouldn't impress the owner enough to sell it, that was just rolling the dice to see what would happen. People did that sometimes, trying to buy on spec and then make a profit on a fast sale. The property had potential for that, particularly with a foreign owner in distress.

'Eight million,' Bill said in a noncommittal voice as the broker stared at him. Bill knew it would be a great deal if he could buy it for that, and that the owner would counter. He was willing to pay ten. And the existing structures would save him a lot of time instead of looking for property where he'd have to build from the ground up.

'I'll write it up,' Hank said, suddenly anxious. 'Where will you be later today?'

'At home,' Bill said calmly.

'I'll drop it by so you can sign it, and I'll present the offer tomorrow.' It was one of those fluke deals that had fallen out of the sky and was what every realtor dreamed of. A solid buyer who had the money, a good offer, and a seller who needed the sale. Except neither of them was sure if the seller really wanted to get rid of the property, and looking at it, Bill realized there was a good chance he didn't, which was why he was offering a very decent price. That kind of money would have to be tempting, even if the owner loved the place, and it was a business that had failed in a bad economy, and he lived five thousand miles away. Bill hoped reason would prevail, not sentiment. And so did Hank.

Bill and Joe drove back to Bill's house, and Bill turned to his friend with a long, slow grin. 'So what do you think?'

'That you're the most amazing man I've ever met. I thought you were a little crazy when I met you at Harvard. Now I know you are. Crazy as a fox. I hope you get it. It's perfect for what you want to do.'

'We'll see what happens.' He was playing his cards close to his chest. He was desperate to buy it, but didn't want to admit it, even to himself.

Hank came by at four o'clock with an offer for Bill to sign, for eight million dollars for the La Vie property. He saw the owner's name and didn't recognize it. Hank said they were faxing the offer to France. And they had given him three business days to respond. It was an all-cash offer, as is, with inspections of course, to make sure there were no hidden problems. But Bill couldn't foresee any. Hank had requested a bank reference on Bill, to include in the offer, and Bill's banker had faxed it to him, in vague terms, that assured the seller that the prospective buyer was real, solvent, and not playing games.

Bill said nothing to anyone about the property for the next three days. And he and Joe barely spoke of it. They were the only ones who knew. And on Thursday morning, he got a call from Hank. He spoke in a conspiratorial tone.

'The seller countered at twelve.' Bill didn't hesitate for a heartbeat. He had expected it, and he was pleased with the counter. His greatest fear had been that the owner of the property would say it wasn't for sale. It had a price, and they were getting there.

'Counter at ten,' Bill said in a businesslike voice. 'Fifteen-day closing, after inspections. And it's my final offer. It's an all-cash offer, after the inspections clear and the title search.' It was a nice clean deal for the seller. He'd have to pay off the mortgage, and the rest was all his. In fifteen days he could have the money, and Bill would own thirty-four acres of what had once been La Vie, and would become The Lily Pad. But he didn't have the property yet, and knew the deal could still fall through.

Hank was at the door twenty minutes later with Bill's counter-offer to sign. He looked more excited about it than Bill did, and Joe burst out laughing when Hank left the house and Bill closed the door behind him.

'You're going to give the guy a heart attack.' Joe couldn't stop laughing. 'He's never dealt with anyone like you before. You can practically see him drooling over the commission he's going to get out of this, if the seller takes your deal. For everyone's sake, I hope he does.'

'So do I.' Bill grinned at him. He was just as aware as Joe of how anxious the broker was. And Bill wanted the property.

This time the response came back in twenty-four hours, and Hank sounded like he was going to faint when he called.

'He accepted your offer.'

'He'd have been a fool not to,' Bill said coolly. 'Let's get the inspections lined up right away.' He had his bank wire the money into an escrow account. And five days later, they had all the inspections completed. The structures were sound, the title was clear. The deal went through without a hitch, and fifteen days after his offer had been accepted, thirty-four acres north of Denver, on a beautiful little property, were his. The Lily Pad had been conceived.

He went out to see it again with Joe, once the deal was closed. They walked around the property as Bill silently imagined what it would become. He didn't know how long it would take, and he had a lot to learn in the coming months, but he knew that one day it would be The Lily Pad and his dream would come true. Joe was still astounded, and Bill was too. It had happened so quickly and easily. It wasn't just about the money, it had been the right time for everyone involved – that was key.

With Bill's exciting new acquisition, Joe was sorry he was going back to New York in a few days. It had been a very interesting visit and a healing one for him. He felt better, and he hated the thought of going back to his lonely life in New York. He wished he could stay longer and watch Bill develop his project, but he didn't want to overstay and impose on his friend.

'I still have to find a doctor to run the place,' Bill said as they walked through the main building, examining it again. 'I need a medical director and an administrator.' Then he stopped walking and looked at Joe. 'Do you have any interest in running the business end of a rehab center for kids?' he asked. He had faith in Joe's business sense, his ability as an administrator, and his loyalty.

Joe was beaming as he asked him. 'I thought you'd never ask. I'd love it, Bill. I know even less than you do about rehab, but recent catastrophe notwithstanding, I think I can run the business end for you. And if I can't, I'll let you know.' Bill had every confidence he could, and doing so would give Joe back his confidence in himself.

'You'll have to move out here,' Bill warned him.

'My apartment in New York is on the market anyway. I'm done in New York. It's too depressing for me there now. I'm ready to move out. I'll go back and wrap up. Or actually, I'll look for an apartment here before I leave, and then I'll know what to ship out. I can be back in a couple of weeks. And the kids can visit me here. They don't have to come to New York, and I usually visit them anyway. It's too complicated for them to travel with their kids.'

As Bill and Joe drove back to the house, The Lily Pad had a home, and an administrator. Now all it needed was a medical director, a staff, a mission statement, a program, and patients. Bill and Joe had their work cut out for them. They were going to be busy with The Lily Pad for a long time. Joe was thrilled. Bill had just given him a new lease on life. It was hard to believe that only weeks before he had been desperate, and now he had a new city, and a job. Bill's call that night had been providential and had saved his life.

Steve Jansen, the architect, called Bill that night. He had been meaning to call for several days, but was busy with plans for Bill's remodel, and several other projects, and hadn't had the chance.

'I'm sorry I didn't get back to you about that property I mentioned to you. I've been jammed. I've got bad news, though.' Bill couldn't imagine what it was. 'I checked on it a few days ago through a friend of mine who's a realtor.

The property is in escrow. Apparently someone made an offer on it. I don't know if it will go through, but it looks like we missed it,' Steve said apologetically, and Bill laughed.

'No, we didn't. I bought it, thanks to you. It's perfect for what I want to do, just as you thought it would be. So hurry up on the remodel, we have work to do!' There was a long silence on the other end.

'Are you serious?' Steve was stunned.

'I am. It officially became mine yesterday. The Lily Pad is going to happen,' he reassured him. 'I want to go out and look at it with you next week, to get an idea of what we need to do.'

'I'd be happy to do that,' Steve said in an awed voice. 'You don't kid around, do you?'

'No,' Bill said, 'I don't.' And now all he had to do was tell Lily what he was going to do, and find a medical director to run the place. And work on it like a madman after that.

Chapter 14

Lily stared at her father in disbelief when he visited her at Craig after the sale went through and told her what he'd done.

'You did *what*?' For a minute, she didn't understand what he was saying. It was so far out.

'I bought a thirty-four-acre piece of property ten miles out of town, with a bunch of beautiful houses on it, to build a rehab center for SCI kids from age ten or twelve to whatever age we decide. Like Craig, only even more focused on young people, and especially for younger kids. And I'm calling it The Lily Pad.' He was smiling from ear to ear. Lily still looked like she didn't believe what he had said.

'Are you nuts, Daddy? You don't know anything about running a rehab.'

'No, I don't, but other people do. We're going to hire them to help kids and young people who need rehab after injuries like yours. And we're going to make it the most exciting, inspiring place they've ever been, while teaching them how to live with their injuries and lead good lives, just like here, and what you're doing now.'

'Why?' She stared at him, looking confused.

'Because I love you, and I want to honor you, and other kids who are as brave as you are, like your friend Teddy, and little kids, anyone who needs what we're going to offer them. And for those who can't pay, we'll make it free.' Tears filled her eyes as she listened to him, and then she threw her arms around his neck, and held him tight.

'Daddy, I'm so proud of you,' she said in a choked voice. 'It's a beautiful thing to do. Who's going to run it?'

'I don't know yet. I asked Jessie to help us find the right people. I offered her the job, but she said she can't leave Squaw Valley because of her kids.' Lily nodded. That made sense to her, but she was disappointed Jessie couldn't do it.

'Can I help you?' Even more than he had hoped, Lily was excited by the idea. She was thrilled and in awe of her father.

'I'd love you to. We're going to need lots of advice from you and other young people, about the kinds of things you would want to see there. I want lots of feedback from you. Lily, I'm doing this for you, because of you.' It was his way of facing what had happened to her proactively, and Lily understood that.

After her father left, she and Teddy sat in her room and listened to music that night. They weren't supposed to isolate, and were encouraged to spend their free time with the others, but sometimes she and Teddy liked to just hang out together and talk, with no one else around. He had been right about her friends – they never came to visit her. They always had an excuse not to, and instead of calling her, they texted her, 'Sorry, I can't come by today . . . see you tomorrow,' and tomorrow never came. 'Oops. running late. catch you next time.' 'My mom won't let me go out . . . my car broke down . . . I have exams . . . I have practice . . . My dad won't let me drive the car.' They had a thousand excuses not to visit her in rehab. Maybe it was just too hard for them, but it was a lot harder for her. It was what Teddy had predicted at the beginning. He had seen it happen to others in the past two years. He had seen very few friends come through and stick around. And Veronica, her best friend, was the worst offender. Lily got the feeling that she was trying to be Lily now, on the ski team, and with their friends. And she had seemed so fake the one time she did come to visit. She didn't even feel like a friend now, just someone Lily used to know. Now Teddy was becoming her best friend. He knew what she was going through, and they had that in common. They spent hours talking to each other, like sister and brother, about their dreams, their fears, and their goals.

Her father had asked her not to say anything about what they were doing yet, until they got further along with the project, and then he wanted to come and talk to the administrator at Craig and explain it to him too. Right now it was in its earliest form. But she shared all her secrets with Teddy, she trusted him and knew he wouldn't spill the beans.

'You're not going to believe this,' Lily said to Teddy in a whisper, in her room. It was the most exciting secret she'd ever had, and her eyes were bright as she looked at him.

'What??' He thought she was going to tell him that her dad had a new girlfriend, or that Veronica was pregnant and had to drop off the ski team, or something juicy like that. They lived on shreds of news here from the outside world, about people who were leading full lives. Lily felt like she was in a cocoon sometimes, although she was learning important things. She missed being at school and out in the world, with all its daily mundane events and high school dramas. But at least she knew that her time here was finite. With Teddy's parents refusing to take him home, he was stuck here indefinitely, in rehab, shut away from the outside world.

'My dad is starting a rehab center for SCI kids,' she said to Teddy with wide-open eyes. He stared at her in astonishment, and for a moment he looked confused.

'He is? Why?'

'To help people. He already bought the place. It's going

to be for little kids, and kids our age and maybe a little older. He has to find someone to run it, but he says it's beautiful. He's calling it The Lily Pad.' She was very proud of her father, and Teddy could see it. Sometimes he envied her the relationship they shared. He had never had one like that with his parents, who had been cool and distant even before the accident. Now they called him once a week, told him what they were doing, and promised to visit him sometime in the future, and never did. Something always came up. It was as though they were afraid even to see him, let alone bring him home. He wondered if they felt guilty about it, or just didn't care. And here was Lily's father, not just there for her, but wanting to help other kids. It was hard for Teddy to imagine. 'He says I can help decide what kinds of activities they offer there. And he wants to talk to you too.' Teddy looked excited to hear it.

'We need more art,' he said. 'Art that kids can do, and sophisticated stuff too. I want to work in oils. They want me to use acrylics because the fumes from oil paints bother people, but I get better textures with oils.' He had been working the acrylics to look like oils, and Lily had seen what he could do with the little sticks attached to his gloves. It was incredible. He had real talent that transcended his disability, and in spite of his limitations, he used his arms surprisingly well. 'We should have a band too. A *real* band. The kind of music we listen to.'

'I told Dad we need a great sports program. He said the property he bought has a fantastic gym. I told him about the Paralympics, but that only happens every four years like the Olympics. We could have some kind of games that happen *every* year, with medals and awards.' They talked about it for a long time.

'I'd love to teach little kids to draw,' Teddy said wistfully. 'I want to be an art teacher when I finish school, for kids with special needs.' He wanted to go to college, and major in fine arts, but so far his parents refused to discuss it with him, and because of his cervical injury and breathing issues, they didn't like him going on field trips either. And they thought being tutored at Craig was enough. Teddy didn't agree, and he was planning to apply to college in the fall, whether they agreed or not.

It was past their normal bedtime when Teddy left her room that night. Lily called her father and told him how excited she was, without mentioning Teddy, and he was thrilled. She shared a bunch of new ideas with him about sports, music, and art.

'We'll talk about it more tomorrow,' he promised. 'And I can't wait to show you the property. Sleep tight, baby. I'll see you tomorrow.' He couldn't wait for her to come home, and for Steve to finish the remodel of the house so she'd be happy there. And now there was so much he had to do.

*

Bill called Jessie the next day to tell her the sale had gone through and the property was his. She was incredibly impressed at the speed with which he'd moved, and his seriousness about the project.

'Now I need a medical director so I know what I'm doing. If you won't do it, I still need you to help me find the right people. At all levels. I'd be happy to pay you a consulting fee. I'm flying blind in this.'

'I would be too,' she assured him. 'I've never run a rehab center.' She smiled at the thought. 'And you don't have to pay me. I'll try to think of some people who would be right for you. I talked to my partner about it, but he doesn't want to leave the Tahoe area either. I do know a woman who'd be terrific as your resident psychologist. You'll need one of those to deal with the emotional issues. I worked at Stanford with her. She's at Mass General now, affiliated with Harvard Medical School, and brilliant at what she does. She deals with SCI kids to help them with the adjustment. Her name is Carole Anders. Did you and Lily meet her when you were there?'

'No. We only met with Hammerfeld for the assessment.'

'That makes sense. Carole was sick for a long time last year. She had some serious medical issues, but I hear she's okay now. I haven't talked to her for a while. You should call her. It's hard to drag people away from there because of the prestige, but what you're doing is right up her alley, so you never know. And she might be willing to consult. She's a terrific woman, you'd like her.' She gave Bill her number. 'I'll see who else I can come up with. She's not a potential medical director, but she would be an important member of the team, if she'll do it.'

'Would you consult for me?' Bill asked humbly. 'Maybe come out and look at what we're doing when we get farther along, if you have time?' Her advice would be invaluable.

'Of course. I'd love to do it. And I'd like to see Lily again. How's she doing?'

'She's excited about this too.'

'So am I,' Jessie said honestly. 'I'll do what I can from here. I'll call you if I think of anyone. Meanwhile, call Carole.' He promised to do so, and to call Jessie again soon. And Jessie made a note to herself to call Carole when she had time.

He called Carole twenty minutes later, and she sounded startled to hear from him. He explained who he was and what he was doing, and how he had gotten there because of Lily and said that Jessica Matthews in Squaw Valley had given him her name. Jessie's name was the key – she opened up after that, and listened to what he had in mind. She said it was fascinating and much needed, but that she had no plan to leave Mass General, and wanted to stay in Boston, without explaining why.

'Would you consult with us then, Dr. Anders?' Bill

asked her, realizing that it was going to be harder than he'd thought to get capable people to move to Denver. 'Perhaps come out and give us some ideas? We're building this from the ground up, and we need all the help we can get.'

'I'd like very much to do that,' she said, and agreed to come to Denver in the next couple of months, when he thought they were ready.

'Could you come before that? Like in the next couple of weeks?' he suggested, and she hesitated, and then agreed, and they set a date. She was going to spend a weekend in Denver, meeting with him and Joe, and brainstorming with them. Bill offered to pay her plane fare, a stay in one of the best hotels in Denver, and a consultation fee, which was a more than respectable amount. She was very impressed by the way he was handling everything. He readily admitted that he didn't know what he was doing, but he was going about it in a very solid, responsible, intelligent way.

Carole called Jessie in Squaw Valley as soon as she hung up, and Jessie smiled when she took the call. She was happy to hear from her – it had been too long since they'd spoken. And she could guess why she was calling. She must have heard from Bill. He wasn't losing any time.

'Okay, now what did you get me into? Who is this guy?'

'He's the father of an SCI patient I had right after

Christmas.' Her face clouded as she thought of what had happened the night she operated on Lily. Tim had died in the accident. 'She has a T10 injury, and her father pretty much accused me of being a quack.' She laughed at the memory.

'And you gave the guy my number?' Carole sounded incensed.

'He was just an anguished parent. He adores his daughter, he's a widower, and from what I can gather, she's his whole life. They live in Denver, and she's at Craig right now. And I guess it inspired him to do a variation of that, on a smaller scale, for younger kids. It's not a bad idea,' Jessie admitted to her friend, 'and he's a smart guy. I think money is no object, so he'll do it right, if he can find good people. He just bought the location, and it sounds terrific. Now he needs good solid advice, and great staff, and who knows? He may come up with something wonderful. I told him to call you. His daughter was on the Olympic ski team, by the way, so the SCI is even more traumatic. He flew around the world after he left here looking for better opinions, but they all told him the same thing I did. You can't blame the guy. If I had the money, I'd probably have done the same thing. And at least he wants to put his money to good use. What did you tell him? Are you interested in the job?'

'No,' Carole said honestly. 'I love it here. And they were very good to me last year – I can't walk out on them now. Which reminds me, I'm sorry I didn't come out for Tim's funeral, Jess. I was still in treatment and sick as a dog from chemo.'

'I figured. How are you now?'

'Cancer free,' Carole said with relief. 'How are you doing?'

'I don't know. We get through the days. The kids are a little rough. It's hard without Tim.' Carole could imagine it would be and felt sorry for her, but at least she had them. Carole never would have children now, and she didn't want to adopt alone, now that she was divorced, so for her the hope of kids was over, which she considered a huge loss. 'I wish you'd come out and see us sometime,' Jessie said wistfully. They had been close friends when they worked together at Stanford.

'I'm going to Denver for the weekend in two weeks to meet your guy. Is he an asshole? He sounds a little rough around the edges if he called you a quack.' Carole sounded worried, and Jessie laughed.

'He didn't say it. He implied it. He has more finesse than that. I operated on his daughter the night Tim died,' she said with a crack in her voice.

'I'm sorry, Jess.'

'Yeah, me too,' Jessie said softly. 'How are you doing since the divorce?'

'I'm fine. I just want to look ahead now. Last year was the worst year of my life. Cancer, divorce, surgery. Maybe consulting on a new project will do me good. I didn't tell your friend I'd been sick. Did you?'

'I said that you'd had health issues, but I didn't say it was cancer. That's up to you.'

'It's none of his business. And I'm fine now. And I'm just consulting, I'm not taking a job, so I don't owe him that.'

'That's fine,' Jessie agreed. 'Let me know what you think after you go out.'

'Thanks for the referral,' Carole said warmly. 'I could use the money. Dylan took most of the furniture, which was a nice touch. Their consulting money will buy me a new couch.' Jessie laughed and was pleased.

'Take care of yourself,' Jessie said gently.

'Yeah, you too,' Carole said, and hung up, and hoped she hadn't made a mistake agreeing to go to Denver. Bill Thomas sounded like an unusual man to her. But hopefully reliable and sound. And if nothing else, she'd have a new couch.

Bill also called Dr. Hammerfeld at Mass General to ask him for recommendations, either for consultants or for people who might want jobs. Dr. Hammerfeld was impressed by what he was doing, and promised to give it some thought, but knew of no one offhand. And Bill didn't tell him that Carole Anders was coming to Denver to advise him, in case she didn't want anyone there to know.

Bill and Lily talked about it every night. She had new ideas for him every day, and so did Teddy when he talked to her. They were both excited about the project.

Thinking about The Lily Pad filled a void for Lily, and distracted her from the fact that none of her friends were coming to see her. Besides Veronica, a few of her classmates finally came once, and were so shocked to see Lily in her wheelchair that they didn't come again. They didn't know what to say or how to handle it so they didn't come at all. She talked about it to Teddy, but not to her father. She was too embarrassed to admit that she had no friends anymore. She felt like a total loser and as though she had ceased to exist for them. And in a way, she had. What had happened to her was just too shocking for them to absorb. Teddy was always sympathetic, and he was her only friend now, at the toughest time of her life.

And it was Phil who turned the tides for her, even more than her father's plans for The Lily Pad.

When she went to physical therapy, he talked to her about the Paralympics again. He had already explained to her that there were five sports in the Winter Paralympics, with several subcategories, and the obvious one for her was Alpine skiing, with the seat attached to the monoski. But this time he asked if she'd like to try it. Her eyes lit up as soon as he said it, and he explained that she could go to Winter Park above Denver and check it out for herself. The idea of skiing again was the most exciting news she'd heard.

'If you like it, and you're serious about it, Lily, you could start training now. The Winter Paralympics are less than a year away.' She was so excited, she could hardly speak.

'When can I do it?'

'How about tomorrow?' he said with a slow smile. He had already reserved a time slot for her, with two instructors who would help her get on and off the chairlift and ski alongside her to make sure she didn't get hurt.

'I'll have my dad bring my ski clothes tonight.'

They went to work on her normal therapy session then, and she called her father as soon as she got out.

'You're not serious, are you?' Bill sounded horrified.

'I am,' she said, sounding defiant, which was unusual for her. But she was desperate to get back on skis and didn't want him to stop her. 'I'm going to try chair skiing tomorrow. It's a little seat on skis. I want to train for the Paralympics, Dad,' she said. She had the same will of iron he did. They were an even match, although they rarely disagreed with each other, but she wasn't afraid to hold her ground.

'I don't want you to get hurt,' he said firmly. 'You've been through enough. Do something else.'

'Lots of people here go skiing, Dad. And I ski better than they do, or I did before. I'm not going to get hurt.'

'And if you do? What if you lose the use of your arms

next time? Like Teddy. Or hurt your head. Lily, no!'

'Yes! Bring me my ski clothes, Dad, or I'll ski in jeans.' And he knew she would. They battled for the next ten minutes, and finally he relented when she insisted that the two ski instructors with her would keep her from getting hurt. 'I want to compete in the Paralympics. I've been training for all these years.' It was the first time she had realized that she could still compete in downhill skiing, even if it would be different than before. Her life didn't have to be as radically changed as she feared. And she was going to fight for it. He finally agreed to bring her clothes. 'Just bring me a plain jacket, Dad. And a pair of black pants.' She didn't want to wear her racing uniform, or her Olympic ski team jacket. 'Do I have a plain helmet in the closet?' She couldn't remember if she did.

'I'll find one. This is crazy, Lily. If anything happens to you, I swear I'm going to kill that physical therapist you call a Marine drill sergeant. This is the last thing I want you to do.' He sounded near tears.

'It's the *only* thing I want to do, Dad.' And he knew she meant it. He looked bitterly unhappy when he brought her clothes over that night in an Olympic bag. But the clothes were without emblems or insignia, and he had found a plain blue helmet at the back of the closet that she used to wear. She tried it on, and it still fit. He didn't tell her that he had been about to give her ski clothes away when they emptied the closet to build the elevator.

He never thought she'd use them again. They talked for a few minutes when he dropped them off, and left. He had things to do that night. Jessie had sent him some résumés to look at, and he wanted to go through them, of neurosurgeons at Stanford and Mass General and one in Los Angeles at UCLA who she thought were possibilities for The Lily Pad, one as a director, and the others as staff.

Lily was heading for her room, with the bag of ski clothes on her lap, when Teddy caught up to her, and asked what she was carrying.

'My ski clothes,' she said, victoriously. 'I'm going to Winter Park tomorrow. Phil set it up.' He had never seen her so excited, and he grinned.

'Are you trying out for the Paralympics?'

'I want to check out how I like chair skiing, and then I'll see. If I can do it, I want to compete in the Paralympics.' He could see how determined she was from the look in her eyes and the tilt of her chin.

'So do I,' he admitted to her, and she turned to smile at him.

'Which event?'

'They have a chair rugby demonstration at the Winter Games, although it's a summer sport. Phil says I can do that. I can use my electric chair for rugby.' Which he couldn't in all sports. 'They won't allow them in basketball, but they do in rugby.'

'It's pretty rough, from what Phil showed me on the

film,' she said with concern, and Teddy laughed. He was a seventeen-year-old boy after all.

'Yeah, but it looks cool, doesn't it?' They both laughed conspiratorially and went to their rooms.

Lily left in one of the vans the next day, wearing her ski clothes, and ready for Winter Park. When they got there, the two instructors Phil had booked for her were waiting. They fitted her onto the small chair on the monoski and strapped her in. They got her on the chairlift, and one of them rode with her. As the chair took off, she felt a strange, familiar feeling and remembered the last morning she had been on a chairlift, in Squaw Valley, minutes before she fell. She was very quiet as she rode up, trying not to think about it and to focus only on skiing again. They got her off the lift easily. She had decided to try the monoski for better control. And as she sat on it, suddenly everything was familiar. She adjusted her goggles, and took the poles in her hands with the small skis at the tips to help balance her. She glided a little to get the feel of it, as one of the instructors talked to her, and then she took off, slowly at first to get acclimated to the monoski and little seat. She was surprised by how easy it was, and how good her balance was in the chair. She hardly needed the poles. After years of training and instinct, she shifted her weight easily for balance, and started to pick up speed. She could see the instructors on either side of her, but she was a natural on the single ski.

It felt just like it always had as she went down the mountain at full speed, with the wind on her face and the snow beneath her skis. She hit a mogul and took it easily. She was fearless as she flew down the mountain and felt as though she had grown wings instead of legs. They got to the bottom too quickly for her. She was laughing and talking and there were tears running down her face.

'I can do it!' she shouted at them. 'I can still ski! I want to do it again!' They took three runs that day, and Lily picked up speed and balance each time as she learned how her weight shifted on the chair. She was a natural, and the instructors could see it. Her years of diligence and training had served her well. She was an obvious choice for the Paralympics, but more than that, she felt as though she had returned to the land of the living. She hated to leave the mountain after the third run, but the instructors had other bookings. She took off the ski and got back in her wheelchair. As she did, she felt like a bird taking off her wings, but at least she knew now that she could still fly. The driver helped her into the van, and Lily sat grinning broadly all the way back to Craig. She had never been as happy in her life. Phil Lewis had given her her life back. She could ski! And no one could take that from her.

Chapter 15

Carole arrived in Denver late on a Friday night, and went straight to the Ritz-Carlton Hotel, where Bill had booked a room for her. She had flown from Boston after work, and she had no idea what to expect from Bill, or what the site for his future rehab center would look like. She had agreed to meet him and Joe at the hotel for breakfast the next day, and then they were going to look at the property he had just bought.

Bill had already been out to see it several times with Steve Jansen, and they both had lots of ideas about how to make it work. They agreed on the use of the two main buildings, and the smaller buildings offered a range of possibilities, either for patients or as offices. The gym was impressive, and Steve had suggested building an Olympic-size pool at the back of the property in an enclosed building, and Bill liked the idea. Steve was immensely pleased with the buildings on closer inspection, and the fine construction that had been done there. They needed very little work, other than handicap accommodations, lifts, ramps, and the kinds of things he was adding to Bill's house for Lily.

Carole was already waiting in the dining room of the hotel when Bill and Joe got there. Her long, straight dark hair was sleek and stylish – and neither of them had any idea it was a wig. She looked pretty and youthful, and Bill noticed that she had a lithe, athletic figure in black pants, a black turtleneck sweater, and high heels. She had tossed her short fur jacket over a chair. And Carole was intrigued as Bill walked across the dining room with a tall, attractive man who looked slightly older than he. Both of them were wearing sport jackets, and she guessed who they were immediately. Bill had a look of command about him that you couldn't miss, but he had a pleasant face, and she noticed he had kind eyes when he introduced himself and then Joe.

Both men ordered a healthy breakfast of bacon and eggs. Carole had coffee, grapefruit, and whole-wheat toast, as Bill brought out the lists of suggestions Lily and Teddy had made for things they wanted to see offered at The Lily Pad, for both younger and older kids. There was a strong emphasis on art and music on Teddy's list, and on sports on Lily's. She had suggested sports teams, competitive games, and a sporting event based on the Paralympics, to be held every year. And Bill also had a list of the recreational activities provided at Craig, some of which would work for younger kids too.

'You should have a peer counseling program,' Carole suggested. 'Maybe even a buddy system, matching up an older child or adolescent with a younger one, so that each child has a "big sister or brother," and also match each teenager with someone in their twenties. It's a tremendous support system. And a college counseling service for kids who have to apply while they're in rehab. And possibly a service to find internships outside the facility so they get used to having jobs right from rehab to make that process easier for them when they get out.' She handed Bill and Joe each a list of counseling-related activities she had come up with, all of which sounded good to both of them. They pooled their suggestions all through breakfast, and Carole gave Bill dozens of new ideas.

'Do you implement things like that at Mass General?' Bill asked with interest.

'We're not set up for it,' she answered. 'I do one-on-one counseling with my patients, although I follow them for a long time after discharge, and even after rehab. I want to know how they're doing, and help them with problems later. I run several groups, which is something you could do with the older kids in your facility. Teenagers have a tough time adjusting to the world, even without spinal cord injuries. With that added to the mix, they have a lot to deal with in school, in dating, with their parents, siblings, peers. Drugs and alcohol are still an issue, as they are for anyone at that age. And I had an experience myself last year where peer counseling made a big difference in my treatment. I had breast cancer,' she said simply, 'and sometimes my peer counselor was more informative and more practical than my physician.' She said it easily, although she hadn't intended to. But she felt comfortable with them, and they both looked impressed. She was an incredibly competent woman, who knew her business, and had given a lot of thought to their project, and had made excellent suggestions. 'I'm healthy now, by the way,' she said to Bill, 'in case you're concerned. My treatment was successful,' she added matter-of-factly.

'I'm glad to hear it,' he said quietly, and meant it. He noticed that Joe hadn't said a great deal through the meeting. He mostly listened to Carole, and looked impressed by everything she said. And the more he heard from her, the more Bill wanted to convince her to come and work at The Lily Pad, and head up all their psychologically related services. She was every bit as good as Jessie had said, and Bill wanted her desperately for The Lily Pad. He mentioned it at the end of breakfast.

'Other than kidnapping you, which I'm not ruling out, what do we have to do to convince you to move to Denver and work for us? We want to run a top-notch, state-of-the-art rehab center for young people, with every possible psychological support service, and art, recreational, and sports programs that will knock your socks off.'

'You already have,' she said to Bill. 'I love what you're doing and what you intend to do, and how you think. What you're planning sounds terrific, but I'm an institutional snob,' she admitted with a grin. 'It's hard to give up working at Mass General. It's a teaching hospital for Harvard and it looks pretty good on my CV,' she said honestly.

'So does starting up a rehab like ours, in full charge of all psychological services. You can hire as many support people as you want.'

'Don't tempt me,' she said, taking another sip of coffee. 'I like everything you've said so far. I'd want to consult for you. I can come out any weekend you need me, or during the week for important meetings, with a little advance notice, so I can reschedule my patients. They allow me to do consulting.' Bill could sense that it was the best he was going to get from her for now, but he had every intention of wooing her away from Boston eventually, if he could. He loved the challenge. And Carole Anders was impressive. It didn't surprise him that she had worked with both Harvard and Stanford.

After breakfast, Bill drove them to the property and walked Carole through every building and then all over the grounds. He had told her to bring rough shoes, as parts of it were muddy from recent rains, and she wore running shoes and looked into every room, closet, shed, and inch of the property with him. He told her what he was going to change and clear and where the Olympic-size pool would be in its own building. They looked at the gym, and figured out which of the smaller buildings would be good for offices. And the two main buildings with all the bedrooms were already beautiful. Carole was in awe of what he'd bought, and his plans for it as a rehab center. Although Craig was efficient and the best in the country, and there were other facilities for children, The Lily Pad was going to be a gem. And she liked his plans to admit some patients on scholarship, according to need. He had all the right ideas, and she fell even more in love with the project as soon as she saw where he intended to put it. It was a beautiful, peaceful, happy place with a great feeling to it, and the buildings, even empty, were cozy and elegant at the same time. It would be a wonderful, positive environment in which to work and live.

'When are you planning to open, by the way?' she asked him as they walked around.

'A year from this summer. I'd like to open our doors in August of next year, if it's feasible, depending on the staff and director we find, and how quickly. That's sixteen months from now. I think we can do it.'

'I do too,' she said, mulling it over, 'since you already have the physical buildings. All you have to do is build in accommodations. You don't have to build from the ground up, which makes a big difference.' It was why he had been willing to pay handsomely for the property in the first place.

'Jessica Matthews has already given me possible names. I've been in touch with them, but there's no one on the list who's the right medical director yet.' He was honest with her.

'It's a shame Jessie won't do it,' Carole said, as they walked back to the car after two hours on the property. They had seen everything.

'I think so too. She said her kids won't leave Squaw Valley, and it's hard to argue with that,' Bill said ruefully.

'I think they're having a tough time without their dad,' she said carefully. 'It's a big blow for all of them. He was a great guy.'

'He died the night she was operating on my daughter,' Bill said, with deep sympathy for her. It had created a strange bond between them. Tragedy had struck them both at the same time. And he still felt guilty about how hard he had been on her, about Lily. He hadn't realized then how capable she was.

'Someone will turn up,' Carole said confidently about the director. 'I'll keep my ears open in Boston.'

'Thank you,' Bill said, and then suggested they stop by at Craig to see Lily, so Carole could meet her. They went to get something to eat on the way and it was almost four o'clock when they got there, and Lily had just come back from an outing. They had gone to a supermarket that morning, and a department store that afternoon. She had two big shopping bags on her lap from Neiman Marcus, as they helped her out of the van and into her chair, and she looked up and saw her father with Joe and Carole, and she smiled, happy to see them. She knew Carole was a friend of Jessie's, and had come to talk to her father about The Lily Pad. He had told Lily all about her.

Lily wheeled her chair into the building, and they went to the visiting center to sit and talk for a while. She still had her shopping bags on her lap, and her father rolled his eyes.

'There's a class I wish they wouldn't teach you here. Shopping. You always did fine without help.' But they had actually taught her how to negotiate stores, get waited on, get through the aisles, find what she wanted, and catch salespeople's attention without being rude or ignored.

'I love to shop too,' Carole confessed. Lily could see it. She was wearing stylish black slacks, and Lily had noticed her short fur jacket and expensive high heels. Carole had style and a good look.

'I wish we had a hair salon here,' Lily suddenly said out of the blue. 'I love your hair, and I haven't had a haircut since Christmas. I love manicures and pedicures, and I haven't had one since I got hurt.' She had noticed Carole's shell pink nail polish too, and perfectly done nails.

'Put that on the list,' Carole said to Joe, who was sitting next to her, and listening to the conversation with interest. He had noticed how impeccably groomed Carole was. 'Hair salon. Or maybe an arrangement with a local hair salon to bring people out to do the girls' hair and mani pedis a couple of times a week. Or field trips to a salon in town.' They were the things that made young girls feel good. 'I was sick last year,' she said to Lily, 'and I couldn't have manicures because of the risk of infection, and I really missed them too.' She smiled conspiratorially at Lily, who really liked her. Carole was warm, open, and direct.

They talked about Craig then and the activities Lily was doing there. Carole was enormously impressed, and even more so when she heard that Lily had started skiing, and was planning to enter the Paralympics.

'I was training for the Olympics when I got hurt,' Lily explained.

'I know. The Paralympics are impressive too. I went once, and it's every bit as stunning as the Olympics, maybe more so. How did you get interested in it?'

'My physical therapist here showed me a DVD. And he arranged for me to go skiing. I'm going to enter in Alpine racing. My dad's not too keen on it,' Lily said, glancing at Bill. 'He's afraid I'll get hurt, but he never worried about that before. And I didn't get hurt skiing.'

'Yes, but things are different now,' he said with a worried look.

'They don't have to be,' Carole said clearly. 'People with spinal cord injuries can do just about what everyone else does, with some adjustment.'

'They teach scuba diving here,' Lily said with a grin, 'and a whole bunch of other stuff. A lot of people play golf. My friend is entering in quad rugby. I wish there were a girls' volleyball team here, but there aren't enough people who want to play right now.' She sounded like any other seventeen-year-old as they sat there, talking about the sports she enjoyed, and her passion for downhill racing. She said it worked well for her with the chair and monoski and was a lot easier than she'd expected.

'When are you going back to school?' Carole asked her.

'In May.' Lily's face clouded over as she said it.

'You don't like school?' Carole asked gently.

'I used to. It's been weird here. My friends don't come to see me. I've lost touch with everyone. I think my injury scares them, or they're nervous about coming to rehab. They're always busy. I thought they'd visit me while I was here, but they don't.' It was a common occurrence, and Carole heard it often from her patients.

'It'll be different when they see you again every day. They can't ignore you then, and they'll get used to seeing you in the chair.'

'Yeah. Maybe,' Lily said, but she was obviously upset about it. She felt forgotten by them all.

They stayed for a long time, and then Lily escorted them around to show them the facility. Carole had heard about Craig for years, but had never been there and was interested in it, and she enjoyed talking to Lily. They stopped at the main cafeteria to get something to drink, and ran into Teddy.

'Where've you been all day?' she asked plaintively.

'Painting,' he said happily, and then she introduced him to Carole, and he greeted everyone. 'Where were you?' he asked Lily.

'Shopping,' she said with a broad smile. 'We went to the supermarket this morning, which was boring. Then we went to Neiman's, Nordstrom's, and Macy's, it was really good.' Teddy laughed and looked happy to see her.

'Are you the friend who's going to compete in quad rugby?' Carole asked him, and he nodded.

'I was thinking about basketball, but I can't use an electric chair. I might do hockey. I haven't decided yet.' Hockey and rugby were both brutal sports, and all three of the visitors were impressed.

He joined them for the rest of the tour, and finally they were back in the lobby, and Carole turned to Lily.

'I really enjoyed meeting you,' Carole said warmly. 'I think The Lily Pad is going to be a very exciting place. I want you and Teddy to think of everything you want there. Your wish list will be our command,' she said, doing a little mock bow, and Lily smiled, admiring her beautifully cut dark hair again.

'Thanks for coming to see me,' Lily said politely, and then kissed her father and Joe goodbye. They left, and she and Teddy headed back to her room. 'I bought you CDs today,' she told him.

'Which bands?' he asked with a delighted look.

'Green Day, Blink-182, Good Charlotte, New Found Glory,' Lily ran down the list with a grin.

'All right!' he said, and leaned over to kiss her on the cheek, and she laughed. She had had a good day, and so had he. He was happy with his paintings. 'I liked your dad's friend, by the way,' Teddy commented as they got to her room.

'Yeah, me too. She's a psychologist from Mass General, who specializes in SCI kids. My dad wants to hire her for The Lily Pad.'

'She seems smart.'

'I love her hair, and her nails,' Lily said dreamily, and Teddy laughed at her as she spread out the CDs she had bought him on the bed so he could see them.

'You're pathetic,' he teased her. 'The woman is a psychologist at one of the most prestigious hospitals in the country, and you like her hair and nail polish.'

'Well, those things count too,' Lily said staunchly, looking at her pale nails that hadn't seen polish in four months. She was too lazy to do them herself, and she hadn't been anywhere to buy nail polish in ages, until today, but she hadn't thought about it. She had bought two sweaters, a jacket, and the CDs for Teddy, and new Nikes to wear in therapy. They were hot pink.

'She's a lovely girl,' Carole said about Lily after they left Craig. She could see easily why Jessie liked her so much. She was bright, kind, polite, nice to talk to. She was obviously devoted to her father, and comfortable with adults. And it was clear that Bill loved her deeply, and wanted to help her in every possible way.

'I worry about her skiing again,' Bill admitted, 'and competing. She's been through enough.'

'It's what she loves,' Carole said gently.

'It's her life,' Bill said.

'Do you ski?' Joe asked her then. He had been admiring her quietly from the backseat.

'I used to,' she said, smiling at him. He was a quiet man, and less forceful than Bill, but she could see that he had great depth to him, and she liked his suggestions about their project.

'You should bring ski clothes the next time you come out. There's skiing very close to the city.'

'I don't have much time while I'm here,' she said regretfully, 'which reminds me, is there a department store where you gentlemen could drop me off? I want to do a quick errand. I can take a cab back to the hotel.' Bill said they were fairly close to Neiman's and offered to take her there.

'Are you up to dinner tonight?' Bill asked her. 'It might be fun to go to one of the local restaurants.'

'That would be nice,' she said, smiling at him, wondering if Joe would come too. She wasn't sure she wanted to have dinner alone with Bill. It might give him the wrong impression. This was a strictly professional trip for her, but she didn't want to decline and be rude.

'What about Table 6?' Joe suggested to Bill, and he seemed to like the idea, which gave her the impression that Joe might come along, which she preferred. Besides, they might have more ideas for their rehab center at dinner. She wanted to use every moment for work.

Bill dropped her off at Neiman's a few minutes later and told her they'd pick her up at the hotel at eight.

'Thank you again for today,' she said as she got out and waved at them both, and then hurried into the store. She knew just what she wanted, and went to the cosmetics department. She picked four nail polish colors, including the one she was wearing, a small manicure kit, quick dry spray for nails, some hair conditioners and gels, and a relaxing face mask. She had them put it all in a box and gift wrap it, and she dropped it off by cab at Craig for Lily a few minutes later and went back to her hotel. She had time to lie down and relax for an hour before she dressed for dinner. And she took her wig off while she lay down. She had seen Lily staring at it that afternoon and wondered if she knew. She would have told her if the men hadn't been there, but she didn't want them to know. She rubbed the peach fuzz on her head, and closed her eyes and took a nap. She still got a little more tired than she used to, but it was getting better, and she was enjoying her life fully these days.

And at seven o'clock she put on a different sweater, a skirt, and high heels, washed her face, put on fresh makeup, brushed her wig, and put it back on. And she was in the lobby when Bill and Joe came to pick her up. Both men were wearing sport jackets, and Joe had worn a tie. He still looked very New York, and Bill was more casual. She liked the way they both dressed. They were handsome men. Her husband had looked like a slightly younger version of Joe. He had the same very eastern style. It suited him, and appealed to her, but Dylan had turned out to be a bad guy. Her life was much better now.

'I want to thank you,' Bill said, as soon as Carole got into the car. 'Lily called me – she didn't know how to reach you, or what hotel you were staying at. Apparently, you dropped off some fantastic stuff to her at Craig. She was all excited about it, nail polish and hair stuff and I don't know what else. She loved it. I gave her your e-mail address so she could thank you. I hope you don't mind.'

And as he said it, a message popped up on Carole's BlackBerry, and she checked it. It was an ecstatic e-mail from Lily, thanking her for everything. Carole smiled.

'I'm glad she liked it. She kind of woke me up to how important those little things are. Sometimes I forget.' She had missed manicures too when she was sick. Now they made her feel human again. And she had already forgotten until Lily mentioned it that afternoon how much she missed getting manicures and having her hair done when she needed it most. They were the little feminine touches that made a big difference.

The restaurant Joe suggested had a quiet cozy atmosphere and great food, and they had a relaxed, easy conversation and somehow wound up on the subject of marriage. Carole and Joe both said they were divorced, and Bill that he was widowed, which Carole knew from Jessie.

'My wife ran off to Nepal to follow her guru,' Joe said with a wry look. 'A midlife crisis, I think. Or maybe I drove her to it,' he said, laughing. He was feeling better about it now that he had moved to Denver, and had a new project with Bill. Life had looked extremely bleak for a while, but he didn't say that at dinner.

'My husband ran like hell when I was diagnosed with cancer. Apparently, statistically that's pretty common. I just didn't enjoy being one of those statistics,' she said. 'But I'm fine. I'm healthy again, and life is good.' She seemed to have a very sane attitude about it, which impressed both men. They were both shocked by the story.

'That's a pretty rotten thing to do,' Bill commented sympathetically. 'You're very reasonable about it. I'm not sure I would be. In fact, I know I wouldn't. I hope you stuck him for a fortune,' Bill said, and she laughed out loud.

'No, I didn't. Maybe I should have. I was too sick to care about the money. And now I'm fine.' She looked happy and at peace, and optimistic, and in fact, she was grateful to be alive. She had a positive outlook that seemed to permeate everything she did. And all three of them were enjoying the evening together.

And as they finished dinner, Lily was painting her nails the same color as Carole's, thanks to her thoughtful gift. She was a happy girl that night, and Teddy pretended to scream in terror when he rolled into her room and saw her in the face mask.

'Is that what you look like without makeup? Shit, Lily, you're scary.'

'Don't make me laugh, I'll crack the mask,' she said through clenched teeth.

'Yeah, whatever, Countess Dracula,' he said, shaking his head, and motored back to his own room.

Chapter 16

Jessie finished work late, as she did every night now. She could never seem to get out of the office early enough to get home, relax for a few minutes, talk to the kids, and cook a decent dinner. Instead, she was always running behind, the grocery stores were closed, the kids were fighting over something when she got in, homework wasn't done, and there was nothing in the house to cook except frozen pizza or hamburgers. Tim had been dead for exactly ninety-one days, and she felt as though her life was out of control.

Adam and Jimmy were fighting over the PlayStation in the living room when she got home, Chris was nowhere to be found but his car was outside so she knew he was in, and Heather was on the phone in her room, paying no attention to her younger brothers trying to kill each other. And the house looked a mess. Jessie went straight into the kitchen and stuck two frozen pizzas in the oven, for the third time that week, feeling like someone was going to report her for child abuse, or neglect at the very least. There was no one to pick up the slack for her now, and the kids didn't do it. They were upset too. Heather's grades had been in the toilet for three months since her father died. She might as well have stayed home from school. Her last report card was all incompletes, Ds, and an F, in PE, for not even showing up.

'Not pizza again!' Adam said with a look of disgust as he walked into the kitchen.

'I'm sorry. I had an emergency at six o'clock, a kid with a concussion. I had to admit him.' She talked to him like he was a fellow physician, instead of a child who needed a mother and a decent meal. 'Tell everyone to come down to dinner,' she said with a look of despair. She felt like she was getting Fs too, in mother, provider, and cook. The only thing she still seemed able to do decently was work. She hadn't killed any of her patients yet.

Chris came to the table, looking worried, and Heather gave Adam a shove when he helped himself first.

'How was your day, Mom?' Jimmy asked her politely, and she smiled. He was the only bright spot in the group, and she knew he was missing his father too. But he was as sweet as Tim had been and as nice to her.

'A little rocky,' she said honestly, and looked around the table. 'How about all of you? Decent day?' They didn't look it, but you never knew. Miracles could

241

happen. 'Did you go to PE?' she asked Heather, who made a face. 'Does that mean yes, I hope?'

'It means I had too much homework and had to come home.' She knew that was an ironclad excuse, or would have been if she hadn't been getting straight Ds. Clearly she wasn't doing her homework either, and Jessie never seemed to have time to check it or help them anymore. By the time she cleaned up the kitchen, did laundry, paid bills, and tidied up, they were all asleep.

'We're going on a field trip to Sacramento next week. To the Hall of Fame Museum,' Adam announced. 'This time don't forget to give me the money.'

'I'll try not to.' The teacher had had to pay for him the last time they went on a field trip, but it was three weeks after Tim died, and Jessie was brain-dead or felt like it. She still did. She never seemed to catch up. And in two more weeks they'd have spring break and would be home alone and have nothing to do, which was worse. She had to remember to hire a sitter for the week, to drive them around and give them lunch. She couldn't expect Chris to do it every day. It wasn't fair to him, and they might kill each other over the PlayStation.

All of them ate quickly, as they always did now, and went back upstairs to their rooms. Jimmy gave her a kiss before he did. The others each rinsed their plate, put it in the dishwasher, and left, except Chris, who lingered to talk to his mother.

'What's up?' Jessie said. She could tell he had something to say to her. She just hoped he hadn't gotten someone pregnant. She could only think of worst-case scenarios these days. What else was there? After Tim dying, anything could happen.

'I got my letters today,' he said with a meaningful look.

'Letters? What letters?' Her mind was a blank.

'My acceptance letters, Mom!' he said, visibly annoyed at her. She was like a zombie these days, which was how she felt by the time she got home. She just couldn't manage working all day, and being there for all four of them, without Tim's help. But she knew she had to, and would get used to it eventually. She still cried herself to sleep every night, and slept in his pajamas. 'My *college* acceptance letters,' he said with emphasis, and she got it.

'I'm sorry. I forgot. So?' She sat down at the kitchen table and looked at him expectantly with a smile. 'Tell me!'

'I got into Princeton, Harvard, and Yale,' he said with a grin.

'Very funny.' He had refused to apply to any eastern schools, and his grades weren't good enough for the Ivy League. He had only applied to schools in the West.

'I got into Arizona,' he said, which he knew was a no from her, because she was convinced it was a party school, and Tim had agreed with her, but Chris had applied anyway. His getting in there was no surprise.

'I didn't get into Berkeley or UCSB.' She was disappointed to hear it. She knew he had only applied to five, although she had wanted him to apply to more, but Tim let him off the hook, softie that he was. 'And I got into Boulder and DU.' He looked pleased as he said it, she knew he wanted to ski, and DU was the University of Denver, which he preferred over Boulder, and so did she.

'You look happy. So what do you think?' She was too tired to get excited and pretend to be overjoyed over two schools she hadn't been wild about in the first place. She wished he had gotten into Berkeley, but his GPA hadn't been high enough, nor his test scores. He had never been a great student. He had improved somewhat during senior year, but it was too late. His junior year had been too weak. 'What are you feeling about those two? I know you liked them both when we saw them.' He seemed to hesitate between the two, which surprised her. He had been leaning toward Boulder before, although neither she nor Tim had loved it, and then he had favored DU. Now he didn't look sure.

'I really like Boulder, but I know Dad liked DU better, so I'm kind of leaning toward DU,' he said, which took her breath away. It was his way of pleasing his father posthumously, which almost ripped her heart out. And she wanted to be supportive of whichever school he chose. They needed something to be hopeful about these days.

'I like it too, but you have to feel good about it,' she said, gently touching his arm, and then his cheek. They exchanged a long look, and she smiled at him, fighting back tears. 'I want you to be happy, baby. Daddy would want that too.' He nodded, and she saw that there were tears in his eyes too. He gave her a hug then, and she choked on a sob.

'I'm going to go to DU. I liked it,' he said quietly.

'Are you sure?'

'Yeah, I am. And two of the guys in my class are going there. We're going to try to room together.'

'It's funny. I have a consulting job there, so I can visit you whenever I go.'

'What kind of consulting job?' He looked surprised. She had never done that before. But she could use the income now, if they paid her. If she went regularly, she was going to charge Bill Thomas a small fee, but not if she just went once or twice.

'Someone's starting a rehab hospital for SCI kids. I'm just giving them advice.' He nodded, not particularly interested, but he seemed pleased with his decision, and he said he might join the ski team, or the swim team. He was a fabulous athlete and excelled at both. It was hard to believe he was leaving for college. It had all happened so soon. She dreaded his going now, and it was less than five months away. 'So are you sure about DU?'

'Yes, I am.' He seemed pleased with the decision,

hugged her again, and went back upstairs. She went to kiss Jimmy goodnight then, but he was already sound asleep when she got there. It happened every night. She stuck her head into Adam's room and told him to brush his teeth and go to bed. And when she checked on Heather, she was back on the phone.

'Is your homework done?' Jessie mouthed at her, and Heather nodded and pointed at the door for her to leave. She considered all her phone conversations top secret and didn't want her mother hanging around to listen in.

Jessie went to her own room, took off her clothes, got in the shower, and let the water run over her while she cried. And then she put on her pajamas and went to bed, thinking about Chris going to the University of Denver. She hoped it was the right decision for him. Even Denver seemed too far away now. All she wished was that she could turn back the clock. They'd all be babies and Tim would still be alive. Instead, Chris was leaving, and Tim was dead. She rolled over and turned off the light. She had gotten through another day.

Chapter 17

Bill called Jessie regularly to report on the progress of his plans, and discuss the suggestions she had made for staff, and she finally succumbed to his entreaties and agreed to go to Denver in May. She had all of the kids stay with friends for the weekend, took Friday off, and flew to Denver on Friday morning. She was worried about leaving the kids, but interested to see what he'd done and what he was doing. Carole was up to her neck in the project by then, and trying to help him find staff too. And Jessie was looking forward to seeing Lily. She was almost finished at Craig, and according to Bill, she had done well there, and was going back to school for the last few weeks of junior year, and would be a senior in the fall, since she had kept up with her work. She was training for the Paralympics, and had skied until the end of the season. She was a remarkable kid. Jessie wished her own worked as hard.

As they had agreed, Jessie took a cab from the airport,

and met him at his house. It was a shambles, with construction still in progress. He had told her he was putting in accommodations for Lily, and he was expecting her home soon, so the heat was on to finish.

When she rang the doorbell, Steve, the architect, had just delivered a model of The Lily Pad to Bill, who was looking at it with delight. Every detail he had described was there. It was The Lily Pad just as he had dreamed it. And he was still smiling about it when he opened the door to Jessie.

'Well, hello,' he said, opening the door wide. 'Welcome to Denver!' The house looked like a bomb had hit it, and they had to climb over lumber to get to the kitchen. She left her bag in the front hall. And as soon as they walked into the kitchen, he introduced her to Steve.

'Dr. Matthews, Steve Jansen. Dr. Matthews has come from Squaw Valley to consult on The Lily Pad.' He pointed to the model, and Jessie stared at it with awe.

'This is amazing,' she said, smiling at both of them. 'It looks like a whole village.'

'It will be, when we're finished. Everything is already there now, it's just not adapted to us yet,' Bill explained. 'The only thing we have to build is the pool, and we're starting that in June. It should be finished by October, before the winter. And we'll be working on everything else this summer too. Would you like something to eat? Coffee? How was your flight?' He looked happy to see her, and she noticed that everything in the kitchen had been lowered for Lily. The kitchen was almost complete, and they were still finishing the elevator. And Bill said he had put in a whole new bathroom for her, and changed her closets.

'She's going to be thrilled,' Jessie said as she sat down at the kitchen table. She had worn jeans and a peacoat and running shoes.

'How's your brood?' he asked her, while pouring her a cup of coffee.

'Hanging in. My son just got in to DU. So now I really have an excuse to come to Denver. I can meet with you and visit him.'

'You can always move here,' he teased her. 'Think how convenient that would be.'

'Yeah, and the others would kill me. How's Carole? Has she been back?'

'She's coming next week. I can't wait to show her the model too. I just got it.' Steve left then, after checking on the elevator again. He promised it would be finished by the end of the week, and Bill said he hoped so. The construction mess would be hard for Lily to navigate. But the work was almost complete. 'I can't believe you're here,' he said to Jessie, with a look of pleasure.

'Neither can I. I figured one of my kids would do something, or get sick, and I'd have to cancel.'

'I'm glad you didn't.' He hadn't seen her since February, but he had talked to her every few days for the last month, with questions, ideas, doctors he'd heard about from other people and wanted to check out with her. She had been very patient with his calls, and so had Carole, who had been an invaluable source of help to them. He knew from Joe that he called her regularly for advice about administrative issues. Bill wanted to put Carole on a retainer, so he didn't abuse her time and good nature, and he would have liked to do the same with Jessie, but so far Jessie had declined.

'Are you ready to see The Lily Pad in the flesh?' he asked after they'd sat at the kitchen table for an hour, talking and catching up on the latest developments in his project. Right now they were just concentrating on remodeling and staffing. The rest, the designing of all the programs, would come later. He hoped to have all construction finished by the end of the year. And he was willing to hire a skeleton staff six months before they opened, but he had to find them first. He was working on that almost full time.

They chatted on the way to the property, and he didn't say it, but he noticed how tired Jessie looked. She had gotten thinner and was almost gaunt, and very pale. He suspected she'd been having a hard time, which Carole had mentioned too. It was to be expected, but Bill knew that being a single parent wasn't easy, and he had had only one child when he lost his wife, not four, and hers were older, active, and needed more attention from her, while she managed a demanding job.

'It was a good time to come,' she commented. 'Things are quiet right now. Ski season's over, so we have no nasty head injuries, except car accidents and things that happen at home. This is the first time I've been away in ages,' she said, and he thought to himself that she looked it. She seemed tired, and he could see what she'd been through. Her eyes were bleak, with dark circles under them, and it was easy to see she wasn't getting a lot of sleep. But she sounded lively and excited whenever they talked about The Lily Pad.

They arrived at the property then, and got out of Bill's car, and she commented on how beautiful it was, which was the first thing everyone said who saw it, and how lovely and peaceful the location was, and how well laid out it was. And as they walked, she saw the buildings and the elegant architecture that fit right into the landscape in total harmony. There was an instant feeling of calm, the moment you entered the space, and it was the perfect marriage of nature and fine architecture.

'This is beautiful, Bill. It's much prettier than I expected, and the buildings are lovely.' He let her into the larger of the houses, and they walked around the spacious common rooms, while he described what he was going to do with them. And she was impressed when she saw the bedrooms.

It took them over an hour to tour the property, and she sighed as she looked at him. 'You're doing something so wonderful here. I hope you know that.' Everything he had described made perfect sense now, and she only had a few suggestions that would help medically. She wanted him to use some of what he'd allotted for offices as space for medical exam rooms, which they would need. She showed him how it would work best, and it all sounded sensible to him and was an easy fix. He pointed out the stakes where they had marked off the pool and the building that would house it. It was perfectly placed and close to the gym, with an enclosed walkway. And the gym was fantastic.

'Wow! It makes you want to stay here forever.' She loved everything she had seen. And there were little gathering areas outside, where the kids could play games or have story time in good weather. There was a large barbecue area too for outside dining. There would be campfires in summer, and the roof over the pool was going to be retractable. 'It's almost like a school or a camp, isn't it? It doesn't feel like a hospital at all.' She was immeasurably impressed.

'That's the idea.' He showed her the therapy rooms then, and all of the changes Carole had requested, which she agreed with. There was absolutely nothing about it she didn't like.

'I wish we had something like this near Squaw. It's tough sometimes sending patients all the way to Denver. It worked for you because you live here, but for a lot of people this is a long way away.'

'If this works, maybe we can open one there one day,' he said, smiling at her. 'But then you can't turn me down as medical director.'

'I wish I could do it here,' she said honestly, looking around, 'but I can't. And Jimmy's not going anywhere for twelve more years. I'll help you find someone, though.' The right person for medical director hadn't shown up yet, but she was sure someone would, and Bill was hoping she was right.

Before he drove her back to the hotel, they stopped in to see Lily at Craig. She was on her way to her tutor and couldn't stay long with them, but she was happy to see Jessie and gave her a big hug.

'I'm so glad you came out here! I missed you,' she said warmly.

'I missed you too.' Jessie smiled at her and could see that she was flourishing. Craig had really helped her, and she looked confident and comfortable with her wheel-chair, and her skiing had done wonders for her. She felt like herself again.

'Did Dad take you to see The Lily Pad?' Lily looked excited as she asked her.

'Yes, he did, it's amazing.'

'I'm jealous. He hasn't let me see it yet. He wanted to fix up some things first. He's going to take me there when I come home.'

'You'll love it!' Jessie said, and meant it. She was enormously impressed by the location and Bill's plans, and everything he had described to her that afternoon. He was a man with a vision, and the courage to see it through.

Lily had to leave them then to meet her tutor, and Bill drove Jessie back to the hotel.

'Are you too exhausted to have dinner tonight?' Bill asked her when he dropped her off.

'No, I'd love it.'

'I want you to meet our administrator. He's an old friend of mine from school. He just moved out here from New York last month. He's been a godsend.'

'I'd love to meet him,' she said as a bellman picked up her bag.

'I'll pick you up at eight.' She waved and followed the bellman into the hotel.

Jessie lay on the bed and turned on the TV when she got to her room. It was the first time she didn't have to do anything for anyone, in years, she realized. All she had to do was lie there and relax until dinner, and five minutes later she was sound asleep.

She woke up with a start at seven, took a shower, and dressed. And at eight o'clock she was downstairs, wearing a short skirt and flat shoes, and a white wool jacket. She looked pretty and relaxed, and her blond hair was in the familiar braid. He had seen her so often in Squaw, and talked to her so frequently since, that he felt like he was meeting an old friend, and she felt that way too as she got into his car with a smile. She had called all the kids before she came downstairs, and everyone was doing fine, so she could enjoy the evening.

'Not too tired?' he asked with a look of concern.

'I fell asleep. I feel great,' she said happily. She needed this respite desperately, from all the responsibilities she was carrying alone now. It was the first break she'd had since Tim died. She was on duty all the time, at work or at home.

'Joe is meeting us at the restaurant. He's been dealing with the planning commission all day. Zoning problems. Thank God he's good at stuff like that – I hate it. We need a million permits. He's a genius at getting the minutiae done, and dealing with all the officials. I just get mad when they put up roadblocks. Joe is a magician, and he makes friends with everyone and gets them to give us what we need. I don't know how he does it. He's a great guy to have on our team.'

'So are you,' she said with a smile as they drove through Denver to the restaurant where he'd booked a reservation. It was lively and full of young people when they got there. He had taken a date there in the last month and had been surprised to run into Penny. She'd given him a big hug, and the woman he'd been with had looked annoyed. It was the only time he'd gone out since Lily was at Craig, and there was no one he cared about at the moment. His mind was on other things. He had just taken the woman out because she was attractive and he had nothing else to do, but he'd been so bored by the end of the evening, he knew he wouldn't take her out again. And as much as he'd enjoyed Penny's company while he dated her, he didn't miss her either. He had too much else to think about, with The Lily Pad, and Lily almost ready to come home. He was much more excited about having dinner with Jessie and Joe and talking about their plans than going on any date.

Bill introduced them to each other, and they went to their table, as Bill asked Joe how it had gone at the planning commission.

'We'll get there,' he said calmly, with a confident smile.

'Better you than I,' Bill said as they sat down. 'I always want to kill someone when I have to deal with officials like that. They're so unreasonable.' Joe laughed, they had been just that all day, but he was a patient man, far more so than Bill. And he had discovered that he and the head of the planning commission had friends in common. It never hurt.

They ordered wine before dinner, and Jessie felt very adult being out with two men, in a nice restaurant, wearing decent clothes and not just jeans, or her hospital coat or scrubs. She hadn't let herself relax in months.

'This is the most civilized evening I've had in ages,' she said with a look of amazement. 'My poor kids have been living on frozen pizza. It's been a mess.' Bill couldn't even imagine what a juggling act Jessie's life was, especially now alone, with major professional responsibilities and four kids. But he could see on her face how much she was enjoying having a night off. He was sorry they didn't live in the same city. It would have been nice to see her more often, and talk about their project as it developed.

Joe and Bill talked about Harvard then, since they had gone to business school there, and she to medical school. It was a common bond they shared. And they all had fond memories of school.

'I don't think I could get in today,' Jessie said modestly. 'It's so much harder to get into decent schools.' But Bill was certain she could have.

'What about your kids?' Bill asked with interest. 'Are any of them likely to go east to school?'

'Not a one,' she said honestly. 'They're California kids, and none of them are great students. Except my little one. He says he wants to be a doctor and go to Harvard, but who knows what he'll want to do by then? Probably be a pizza baker or something. What about Lily? Where do you think she'll apply next year?' He looked worried when she asked him.

'She's always wanted to go east to college, to one of the Ivy League schools, and she's got the grades, but I want her to stay close to home now.'

'What does she want?' Jessie asked gently.

'Probably the same schools she always did, but things have changed.'

'Not academically. There's no reason she can't go east to school. She can get the care she needs there. You don't want her to give up her education because of her injury.' She looked shocked at the idea.

'I want her close to me, and close to home. I'd be worried sick about her there.'

'Then you're going to have to work on that, aren't you,' Jessie said firmly, as their dinner came, and she and Joe struck up a conversation about summers in Cape Cod and Martha's Vineyard.

She brought up the subject of Lily and college again when Bill drove her home. 'You're not serious about making Lily stay in Denver because of her injury, Bill, are you?' She looked worried about it when she asked him, and so did he.

'Yes, I am. This whole thing has been so traumatic, and I want her here where I know she'll get great care, and I can keep an eye on her. I don't want something happening to her back east.' He looked terrified as he said it, and she felt sorry for him, and she knew Lily well enough to know that she wouldn't give in easily. She was too much like him to do that, and she wanted a normal life. That was why she was at Craig.

'You can't keep her in a bubble. She'd be miserable.'

'So she says,' he said sadly. 'It's bad enough that she's

skiing. I have my heart in my mouth every time she goes up to Winter Park.'

'She's not a kid you can tie down or confine, or keep in a rocking chair, knitting,' Jessie said wisely, and he knew it was true. He had seen her chair skiing once, and he was so frightened for her, it nearly killed him. And now she wanted to enter the Paralympics, downhill racing. 'She's your daughter, Bill. She won't give up and sit quietly in her wheelchair.'

'I know. But I think going away to college is too risky for her.' Jessie smiled at him as they got to the hotel.

'I think you're going to have a big fight on your hands if you try to keep her here. As her doctor, I can tell you she'll be okay if she goes away to school. And if that's what she wants, she should do it. She needs to follow her dreams.'

'As her father, I can tell you the stress of it would put me over the edge.' He smiled at Jessie too. 'These kids don't make it easy for us, do they? Yours won't let you leave Squaw Valley for a great job here, and would rather keep you chained up there. And mine wants to drive me into an early grave, downhill racing with a spinal cord injury. I swear, they're trying to kill us.' She laughed at what he said – some of it was true.

'They still have to be who they want to be, within reason. I'm not sure how much voice we get in it, or should. It's our job to let them go when the time comes.'

'Not in a wheelchair,' he said softly. 'I can't do it.'

'You may have to,' she said, smiling at him gently. 'I understand, it would scare me too. But you don't want her living like an invalid, do you?' He shook his head and looked into Jessie's eyes, wishing she were just a woman he had met. But instead she was someone he wanted to hire, and Lily's doctor. She was a wonderful human being, and he felt so comfortable with her. And she was so smart, and so wise about many things. If nothing else, she was a great friend.

'Thank you for a lovely dinner,' she said when he dropped her at the hotel. 'I had a terrific time. I haven't had a night like this in years, just talking and relaxing with friends.'

'I felt that way too. It's a nice break from everything else,' he assured her.

'Yes, it is. What time do you want me at the house tomorrow?' They were going to go through all the CVs he had of therapists and doctors for the center. He trusted her judgment about them more than his own.

'Is ten o'clock too early?'

'It's perfect.'

'I'll get some work done that way, and then we can go over all the résumés I've been collecting.'

'That's why I'm here.' She smiled at him. 'See you at ten.' She got out of the car and waved as he drove away. It had been a perfect evening.

*

Jessie woke at six the next day, as she did every day, and went back to sleep, which was a great luxury. She hadn't been able to do that since Tim died. She got up at nine then, ordered breakfast, and dressed. And shortly before ten she took a cab to Bill's house. And they spent three hours reviewing all the CVs. And at the end of it, she had four people to interview by phone for him. They were all over the country, and only one of them was from Denver, and used to work at Craig.

They had lunch in his kitchen, went back to look at the property again, just to check out some details, and then they went to visit Lily. But she was always so busy, she barely had time to see them. And an hour later they left when she went to driver's ed.

'I suppose I have to let her drive too,' Bill said ruefully as he drove Jessie back to the hotel. It was late afternoon, and had been a very productive day.

'That's up to you,' Jessie said with a quiet smile. 'I'm all for her going to college wherever she wants. Driving is another thing. I'm sensitive on the subject. I wouldn't presume to tell you what to do.'

'I've been thinking of buying her a car. But I haven't decided yet. If I had my way, I'd keep her in her room.' But Jessie knew that wasn't true. It was just hard to tempt the fates again after they'd been so cruel. She felt the same way about her own kids, after the accident cases she saw every day, and particularly now after Tim died. She knew she'd never have the same faith in life again, nor would Bill. He had seen his daughter off to the ski slopes for an ordinary day of skiing, and she had come home a paraplegic. That was tough to live with, and get over the trauma, not just for Lily, but for Bill too. She had the same feelings herself. Tim had taken Jimmy bowling for her and been killed. It was the unreliability of life. Destiny at its worst. 'Can I talk you into having dinner with me again tonight, or is that more than you can stand?' he asked her with a grin as they got to the hotel. She enjoyed his company, and two evenings in a row didn't seem like too much to her. And they had a lot to talk about, about his project.

'I'd love it.'

'Great. Let's make it seven-thirty. I know you have an early flight tomorrow.' She did, and was grateful for the early night.

This time he took her to a great steakhouse. It was lively and rowdy, full of young people and old cowboys. It was an easy place to relax and have an old-fashioned steak dinner. He said he came there often, and Lily had loved it as a kid.

They talked about The Lily Pad again and the four candidates they'd pulled out of the stack of résumés that morning. And then, somehow, Jessie got him talking about his youth in a mining town, the extreme poverty of it, the miners dying, including his own father and brother, and how he had fled to the big city to make his fortune and had done well. She could sense that he'd been a risk taker from the beginning, a little bit like Lily. Her downhill racing, even before her injury, had not been without risk, and she loved it, and was passionate about it. They both marveled at how easily he could have given up his dreams and become a miner and had an entirely different life.

'I'd probably be dead by now, if I had,' he said matter-of-factly.

'What a loss to the world that would have been,' Jessie said sincerely. 'Look at all the good you're doing now.' She wasn't unaware of it, and admired him immensely. In many ways, he was a brave man, even about facing his daughter's injury, once he knew she would never walk again. He had turned it into a blessing for others, or was about to. He lacked polish once in a while, and he could be tough, as when he'd been so angry at her in the beginning, but he never lacked courage. And she understood why he'd been angry. He was a lion defending his cub, which she considered a quality, not a fault.

They talked nonstop all through dinner, and then he took her back to the hotel, thanked her for coming to Denver, and wished her a safe trip home. He got out of the car to say goodbye to her, and she felt him slip something into the pocket of her jacket. She didn't say anything, and then looked at it when she got to her room. It was an envelope with her name on it, and there was a check and a note. It said, 'Jessie, thank you for coming. I couldn't do this without your help. I know you don't want this – use it for your kids. Love, Bill and Lily.' He was a kind-hearted man, and the check was what any surgeon would have charged him for consultation. It wasn't over the top, but it was generous, and she was touched. She sent him an e-mail from her laptop before she went to bed, and thanked him. She said her kids would appreciate it, and in fact, it would help her a lot. It had been a very productive trip. And she had loved hearing what he'd told her about his youth. He was a remarkable man. The coal miner's son who had made a fortune, and used it well. And he was a great father, and a good friend. She was glad she had come.

And on Monday morning, she told Ben all about her time in Denver, what Bill was doing, what the place looked like physically, and the different programs he had in mind.

'It's going to be fantastic,' she told him.

'So are you taking the job as medical director?' Ben asked her with interest. He had wondered if Bill would talk her into it while she was there, but she shook her head.

'I can't. You know that. And what would you do

without me?' she teased him, and he looked unhappy for her.

'I still think you should. You're missing a real opportunity, Jess.'

'Sometimes you have to do that for your kids,' she said philosophically. 'It wouldn't be fair to uproot them, not after losing Tim.'

'It's not fair for you to lose this job,' Ben said stubbornly, wishing he could convince her.

'Stop trying to get rid of me. This is where I belong, not Denver.'

'You deserve another shot at life, and an exciting job. It depresses me every time I stop by your house. All you feel there is Tim's absence. That can't be good for your kids either.'

'Leaving would be worse. Trust me. I know,' Jessie said firmly, and walked into an examining room to see her first patient. And Ben left for the hospital to see the woman with the broken hip he'd operated on that weekend. He felt sorry for Jessie, and all that she'd been through. But one thing was for sure, she was one stubborn woman. He realized now that whatever he did or said, nothing would make her take the job in Denver. She was determined to stay in the house and life she'd shared with Tim.

Chapter 18

Their problems with the planning commission seemed to go on interminably while Joe patiently battled with them, begged, pleaded, massaged, cajoled, reasoned, and charmed. The location of their property was not zoned for a medical facility, and the commission flatly refused to give them the permits they needed. Joe finally took the head of the commission to lunch one day and explained the situation to him, what they were trying to do, and how many kids and young people it would help.

'Think of it this way, the property was zoned as a spa originally. And what we're doing really won't be very different. People staying there for a few weeks or months, taking it easy, swimming, getting massage therapy, relaxing, doing some sports. We're not going to have an acute medical facility. You could almost call it a spa for kids.' Joe would have called it damn near anything to convince him. The head of the planning commission looked at him in disbelief and started to laugh.

'You're a liar, Joe Henry,' he accused him. 'But after all that, your ten thousand phone calls, the kids you want to help, and a very decent lunch, I give up. You can have your zoning, and your permits. You deserve them.' And with that, still laughing, he patted Joe on the shoulder and left.

Joe called Bill on his cell phone immediately and told him the good news.

'You're a genius and I love you,' Bill told him. 'I don't know what you did, but I guess you just wore him down. Thank God,' Bill said, and hung up. It was so typical of Joe to make it happen. He always did. He had an incredible way with people, and never gave up, for the right cause. He just radiated goodness and truth. Bill had been talking to Jessie on the other line when Joe called and she was telling him about the interviews she'd conducted. She hadn't liked two of them, but thought he should hire the other two, an administrative assistant who had worked in a similar facility in another state, and a physical therapist who had fantastic recommendations and credentials, and sounded great on the phone. And both of them were willing to wait until later in the year to come to work, and move to Denver for the job.

'That was Joe on the other line, by the way,' he told her

afterward. 'We got our zoning and permits. He pulled it off. Mr. Magic.' Things were starting to move.

The following day Joe had an appointment with some of the administrators at Craig. He explained to them what they were trying to do. He suggested an exchange of programs, so that some of the patients at Craig could use their facilities, and they could send some of theirs for classes and programs at Craig. It took the sting of competition out of it and made them collaborative, and the people at Craig liked the idea. Bill was thrilled about that too.

And the following weekend Carole came back to consult with them again. Jessie had brought up a whole list of questions and issues that she had sent to Bill by e-mail, and suggested he raise with Carole, mostly about treatment plans, psychotherapists, and the number of therapists Carole felt they should have on staff, in addition to counselors and peer counselors, and how they should run their groups. There were a million details to think of, and Bill was learning more than he had ever thought possible about running a rehab facility. And now that they had their permits, construction was already under way, and Steve Jansen was on the premises every day.

Carole was amazed at the buzz of activity when she came back to Denver. Even though it was Saturday, there were a number of workers there, hammering away. They were working on altering all the bathrooms, which had to be handicap facilities according to code.

'You guys certainly haven't let the grass grow under your feet,' she said to Bill and Joe. There had already been changes since she'd last been there.

And Bill had a whole new stack of résumés for her and Jessie to look at, but still no prospects for medical director, and Bill was worried about that. He wanted a neurosurgeon for the job. It would give them credibility, and he felt it was the appropriate protocol for the position. But so far no one who fit the profile he wanted had turned up.

And Joe was telling Carole what he'd gone through with the planning commission as they walked around the grounds. It was a beautiful spring day.

'You're looking very well,' he said to her, as they sat down for a few minutes in the garden and took a break. There was still a bench there, left over from when it had been a spa.

'Thank you. I'm feeling well.' She smiled at him. 'A lot better than I was last year at this time.' She'd been in the thick of it with her treatment then, and every day had been a challenge and hard to face.

'I don't know how you got through it,' he said with a look of admiration.

'You just do. Like Jessie with what she's going through now. I think they're all miserable without Tim. It will get better, but it takes a long time. It was bad enough getting divorced.'

'It was for me too. And what Karen did was such a crazy thing for her to do. I think she went a little nuts when the kids left. Or maybe she always was. I don't think we'd really talked to each other for years.'

'We did, but Dylan lied to me. He's not a very noble guy. I made a mistake, embarrassing as that is to admit. I thought I was married to someone, and I was actually married to someone else. And the someone else was not a nice person.' She wasn't sorry for herself – it was a statement of fact.

'Have you been out with anyone since the divorce?'

'No.' She smiled at him. 'I was too busy surviving.'

'But you're well now,' he said, drawing the obvious conclusion that she should be dating, but it was more complicated than that for her.

'I'm not dating,' she said simply, 'and I don't want to,' she added, just to make it clear. 'I don't know if I ever will again. A lot happened last year. Internally and externally, physically and mentally. What's left of me doesn't want to date.' She couldn't make it simpler than that. She didn't think he was asking her out, and she considered him a friend. Like Jessie with Bill. They had known each other through painful events, and now they were friends. Carole didn't know Joe as well, and she suspected he had seen hard times too. He had enormous compassion for the suffering of others, which often came from having suffered oneself. But he was starting a new life in Denver, and opening his eyes to life again. Carole's eyes were open, but she wasn't looking for a man. She was content on her own.

'You're too young to make a decision like that,' Joe said quietly.

'No, I'm not, I'm thirty-eight years old. I've been married. It wasn't a success. I can't have kids. I have no reason to date.' It was obviously a carefully thought-out decision. 'Men my age want children, unless they're divorced and already have them, and then they're either a mess, or want more kids. Either way they're not for me.'

'Not all men who are divorced are a mess,' he said reasonably.

'True, but a lot of them are, usually the ones I meet. The choice I've made works for me. I'd have to address some issues and change some things if I wanted to be involved again. I don't.' She didn't explain it, but she felt that in order to have a man in her life again, physically, she would want to have reconstructive surgery because of the double mastectomy, and she didn't want to go through surgery again. She'd had two major surgeries in the past year. And she didn't want anyone seeing her body the way it was now. It was a personal choice, but it was the way she felt about it. But it was too intimate to say to

271

him. 'Trust me, I'm happy this way.' She seemed comfortable with her decision not to date.

'It's a terrible waste,' he said sadly.

'No, it's not.' She smiled at him. 'I'm alive. That's enough. For now anyway. If I ever change my mind and want more than that, I'll deal with it.' She sounded very matter-of-fact about the choices she'd made, and clearly she had made her peace with it. It worked for her. 'What about you? Are you dating, Joe?' She was curious about him too. He was an intelligent, handsome man, and still young enough to share a lot of years with someone. Twenty-five years maybe, or more if he was lucky. It was a long time to spend alone, if he didn't want to. Carole had even more years ahead, if she stayed healthy, but she had no desire to share them with anyone intimately.

'I just moved to Denver and got an apartment. I'm settling in. I don't know a lot of people here yet,' he said simply. 'I like it here, though. It's a nice city. I was tired of New York.'

'I get tired of Boston sometimes, especially in the winter,' she admitted, 'but I love my job. That makes a big difference. I liked California when we lived there. I want to travel more now,' she shared with him. 'I'm thinking about going to Europe this summer. I don't want to put things off anymore. I did that for a long time. Last year I kept thinking of all the things I wanted to do when I got better. I want to do them all now.' She smiled at him and suddenly looked very young.

'I put things off too. That's the trouble with working too hard.'

'Be careful you don't do that again,' she said wisely. 'The Lily Pad will eat us all up, if we let it. But it's going to be fantastic.' She looked excited when she spoke about it, and then she smiled at him and stood up. 'Speaking of which, enough true confessions. We'd better get back to work.' She was making diagrams of treatment rooms for Bill, so he could show the architect what they needed. Joe was busy on the phone as usual, making contacts that they needed in the medical and local community. Bill knew he was the best PR representative they could have. And at the end of the day, Joe drove Carole back to her hotel.

'Would you like to have dinner tonight?' he asked her casually before she got out of his car. She turned and looked at him with a slow smile. Now that he knew her philosophy about dating, she felt comfortable with him. They could be friends. 'I'd like that very much.'

He took her to a good fish restaurant that night, and they had lobster. It had been flown in from Maine and it was delicious. They talked about work, and school, her job at Stanford, the embezzlement that had closed his business, and his partner going to prison. They learned a lot about each other, and then he took her back to the hotel, and she thanked him for dinner. She was leaving in the morning, and he was sorry to see her go. She was easy to talk to, and she had no agenda. She put her cards on the table, and she didn't play games. He found it refreshing. She seemed like a very sane, well-balanced person. Not wanting to be involved made her open and honest about everything. She had nothing to hide. He regretted that she wasn't older and didn't live in Denver. He was twenty years older than she was, and sometimes he felt very old with her. He had seen so much more of life. But so had she, for a young woman, and she was wise beyond her years. It had come at a high price.

At the end of May, Lily finished her course of rehabilitation at Craig Hospital. She discussed it with her counselor, and they agreed she was ready to leave. It was something of a surprise when he said it, and for a minute Lily wanted to say that she didn't want to go. But in many ways she did, and she knew she had learned what she needed to know. It was just scary going back out into the real world. She had felt so protected at Craig. And she knew she wouldn't be when she went back to school.

She told Teddy that night at dinner that she was leaving at the end of the week.

'Already?' He looked shocked.

'I've been here for three months,' she reminded him.

'Some people stay for four,' he said sadly, 'or for years,

like me.' He was devastated at the thought of her going. He had never had a friend like her in the two years since he'd been there. They had bared their souls to each other and been inseparable.

'I'll come and visit,' she promised.

'No, you won't. No one ever does. You'll be too busy.' He looked hurt and angry as he said it.

'I'll never be too busy for you.' She meant it, and he wanted to believe her, but he was overwhelmed with sadness at the thought of her going. 'I'll come to see you after school.' She was nervous about going back, but she wanted to finish the school year with her class and had been working toward it. She was caught up on all her assignments, and was finishing the year with decent grades. She needed them for her college applications in the fall.

They sat in her room and listened to music that night, and every night until she left. She thanked all of her instructors, and she developed a workout program with Phil. And she promised to come back and see him too. He had brought skiing back into her life, and she assured him she'd continue to train for the Paralympics as soon as they had snow. He said he was coming to the games. They were going to be in Aspen, which was easy for all of them in Denver, and even made it possible for Teddy. He had already started training in chair rugby, and Phil was working on it with him as his coach.

The morning Lily was to go home came too soon, and it was agonizing leaving Teddy. She promised to come and see him the next day. They were both crying when she left him. She had given him all her CDs, except the girly ones he didn't want. He hated some of what she listened to, but he loved the rest.

'I'll call you tonight,' she whispered as she hugged him, and then he sped away in his wheelchair as fast as he could. He didn't want to see her get in the car and leave.

As they drove away, she got a text from him: 'I'll love you forever, even if you never come back. T.' She cried when she read it and could tell he thought she wouldn't visit him, but she would. She wasn't going to abandon him, like his parents. She was thinking about him and quiet on the drive home.

'Are you okay?' her father asked her, and she nodded, but she wasn't. She felt like a traitor leaving Teddy and going home.

The car was full of her belongings, and the things she had collected while she was at Craig, posters, blankets, a pillow, her music, her CD player and computer, a teddy bear. Her father had taken some of it home the day before, but there was more. And Steve had been true to his word. All the remodeling had been completed, and the elevator was installed. The kitchen and her bathroom were finished, and the workmen were gone. As her father unlocked the door, she wheeled herself in, and he waited to see if she'd notice all the changes. She wheeled herself up the ramp next to the front steps, and spun around with a look of pleasure and rolled into the kitchen. She hadn't been home in three months. Her father hadn't wanted her to see it, until the remodel was complete. It seemed like forever now that she was there, and she gasped when she saw the kitchen. It was perfect, everything was at her height and accessible for her. She turned to look at her father with a slow smile.

'It's incredible. I can use everything here.' She looked amazed. They had lowered everything in the kitchen to work for her. Stove, sink, cupboards, all of it.

'That was the whole point,' he said, beaming. 'It looks good, doesn't it?'

'It looks fantastic.' The kitchen was even better looking than before and much more high tech.

'I'm so happy you like it. Let's go upstairs.' He wanted her to see the rest. She followed him to the elevator, and he opened it for her, although she could have done it herself, and she rolled herself in. It was big enough for her to turn around in and face any direction. And there was room for two more people in it with her comfortably. They stopped at her floor, and got out, and she wheeled into her bedroom. All her familiar things were there, and she was dying to get on the bed and just lie there and look around, but she peeked into her closets instead, at her father's urging, and everything was accessible to her there too. She could reach all of it easily, and there were poles to help her get things off top shelves and one high rack, but everything else was at her level where she could see it and grab it comfortably, without bending down or stretching up. She stayed in the closet for a few minutes, checking it out, and emerged with a wide smile again. It was going to be easy for her to dress.

She went into her bathroom then, and saw the pink marble wonderland Steve had created for her, and she clapped her hands with delight. It was the most elegant bathroom she'd ever seen, with every possible accommodation suited to her. She could take a shower or a bath, whichever she preferred, and get to the sink and the toilet. There were bars everywhere she needed them. And all of her toiletries were laid out.

'I'm the luckiest girl in the world,' she said softly, and her father shook his head.

'And I'm the happiest father to have you home.' He bent to kiss her, and she announced that she was going to take a bath and change her clothes. And then he wanted to take her to see The Lily Pad. He had waited for months for this, and it was ready for her now. It was still under construction and would be for a long time. But he had had the grounds tidied up for her, as much as possible, and all the debris from the past owner cleared out.

He left her alone then to take a bath, and half an hour later she came down in the elevator, went into the kitchen to make a salad, and was sitting happily at the table in her wheelchair when her father came in. Everything had worked out perfectly. Steve had done a terrific job, and Lily was enjoying all of it. Now their home was completely adapted to her, and she was well aware of what a luxury that was and all that her father had done for her.

They left for the site of The Lily Pad half an hour later, and she was stunned when she got there. It was much more beautiful than she had imagined and looked more complete. He took her through every inch of it and told her all their plans. He showed her the model, and where the pool would be. They went through every building, and the gym. She could already see what a magical place it was going to be.

'I'm so proud of you, Daddy,' she said, and threw her arms around his neck. She hugged him tight, and then she rolled through the main buildings again, and afterward on the way home, she made him stop at Craig. She had a feeling she knew where Teddy would be. In the art department, painting. He was concentrating intensely on a canvas when she rolled in silently behind him.

'I like it,' she said softly, and he turned to look at her in surprise.

'You're here!' His whole face lit up.

'I told you I would come. I brought you something.' It was her favorite CD from home, and she had bought him two of the candy bars he loved that they didn't have at the canteen at Craig.

'You have to come to dinner next week and check out the elevator. My dad had it put in for me. Now you can use it too and come to visit whenever you want.' Teddy just looked at her and smiled. She had come back to see him. She'd only been gone a few hours. 'I'll come back tomorrow,' she promised as she left, and this time he knew that she meant it and she would. He went back to work on his painting with a big smile on his face.

Chapter 19

Lily woke up early on the first day she was to return to school. She was excited and frightened and she had a knot in her stomach about seeing her old friends. It was as though she were too different now, no longer one of them. She had instantly become an outsider once she lost the use of her legs. They felt sorry for her, but they didn't know what to say. And no one had known when she would come back to school – there had been a rumor that she was gone for good. She had felt like a forgotten person, and it hurt her feelings. She had cried over it with Teddy and talked to her counselor about it. She had thought they were her friends. Even Veronica treated her differently now, and she hadn't had a text from her in a month. And now she was going back to class with them as though nothing had happened, but she was doing it in a wheelchair. Her father had offered to have her tutored at home, but she didn't want to do that either. She wanted to be a normal person, in school like everybody else, with a real life. She didn't want to become an invalid at home, and she had learned to manage well in public places. She could handle shopping, libraries, public transportation. She could do all the things she needed to. But going back to school felt like a minefield to her. She was scared. She texted Teddy twice before she left the house. He told her to 'suck it up and be a man,' which made her laugh.

She was already in the kitchen when her father came downstairs for breakfast, staring into the bowl of bran cereal that she had to eat and hated, but she had to manage her diet now for fiber content, and she had been taught how to do that too. She looked up at him bleakly.

'Wow, that's not a happy face,' he said seriously. 'Sleep okay? What's up?' She was wearing a pink T-shirt and jeans, her long dark hair was perfectly combed, and she was wearing pink Converse. She looked the way she would have any other day she had gone to school, except she was in a wheelchair and now everything was different. 'Are you feeling okay?' her father asked, concerned.

'Yeah. I'm fine,' she said but didn't look convincing.

'School?' he asked, and she nodded. 'I figured. You don't have to go, you know,' he reminded her. 'We can get a tutor.'

'I don't want one. And I do have to go.' She had already missed five months of junior year – she couldn't afford to miss another minute if she wanted to go to college in a year. And she had worked hard to stay on top of the work from her school. She knew her father was worried about her going back to school, and wanted to protect her, but that wasn't what they had taught her at Craig. They had given her all the skills she needed to lead a normal life and reenter her world – now she had to use them. 'I just haven't heard from anyone there in a while. It feels weird to face them.' It made his heart ache to see her face and the loneliness in her eyes. 'I wish Teddy were going with me.' He had become her best friend and soul mate in three months. But the time at Craig had been intense, and the friendships formed there were for a lifetime.

She had more in common with Teddy now than with her old friends. And she felt as though all of them had let her down, Veronica most of all, even though she'd known her all her life, and they said they loved each other. Apparently not enough to come and visit or even stay in touch, and talk about what was happening to Lily. Veronica had tried to act like nothing had happened, and had been overwhelmed by the reality of it and couldn't face it, or her friend. And Lily felt uncomfortable about running into Jeremy too. She hadn't heard from him since their breakup the night before she went to Craig. And now Lily had to meet all of them on their turf, after feeling shut out and forgotten by them for months. She was angry and hurt and it all showed in her eyes.

Bill poured himself a cup of coffee and made some toast for both of them. They had a new cappuccino machine in their remodeled kitchen, and Lily had already tried it and loved it. She loved all the changes he had made, and she looked at her father bleakly when it was time to go. She silently went upstairs in the new elevator and got her jacket and books from her bedroom. She came down with them in a denim backpack she had slung over the back of her chair, and she had on the fingerless gloves that she used so she didn't hurt her hands when she wheeled the chair. Everyone at Craig had teased her because she had gotten hers from Chanel.

Lily followed her father down the ramp at the front of the house and out to the car. She opened the car door and maneuvered herself onto the front seat, and he folded up her lightweight wheelchair and put it in the trunk. And she put the radio on, at her favorite station, so she didn't have to think. The drive was no different than it had been a thousand times before, except that it was totally different because of what was in the trunk. And she surprised her father by asking him to stop half a block away from school and let her out there.

'Don't be silly. Let me drop you off in front.' He looked worried and wanted to be sure she got into the building safely.

'I want to go on my own,' she insisted. He didn't like it but did as she requested. He pulled over, and got the chair out of the trunk, and she got into it and glanced up at him with frightened eyes. 'I'll be okay, Daddy, I promise.'

'I know you will. It's going to be easier than you think.' Neither of them believed it, but they pretended to as she rolled away. She told him she'd call when she was ready to be picked up at the end of the day.

A small stream of students were moving past her – she recognized several freshmen and a sophomore. Most of the juniors and seniors drove to school. No one said anything to her as she rolled through the gates and up to the familiar front door. She pulled aside for a minute and rapidly sent a text to Teddy, hoping it would give her the courage to get through the door.

'I'm scared shitless' was all she said.

'Fuck 'em if they can't take a joke,' he texted back just as quickly, and she laughed out loud and looked up to see one of the teachers who was there to watch the students as they came in, to make sure they entered in an orderly fashion, were appropriately dressed, and didn't misbehave unduly. He spotted Lily immediately and came over to greet her. He was the PE teacher, and she knew he must have had door duty for the week since they took turns.

'Welcome back, Lily. We missed you,' he said gently,

and she instantly saw the pity in his eyes. She wondered if he'd have felt sorry for her if he knew she had been skiing for the past two months, three and four times a week, at breakneck speeds.

'Thank you, Mr. Liebowitz,' Lily said politely and rolled past him. She had already spotted several people she knew. There were six hundred kids in her high school, a hundred and sixty in her class, and she was starting to see familiar faces all around her. They were looking over and past her and then they did a double-take as they spotted her in the chair. A few of them waved, and some smiled, but no one came over. It was as though they thought what she had might be contagious, or they just didn't know what to say, 'Hi . . . how've you been . . . sorry you can't walk anymore.' She knew where her first class was, on the ground floor. It was easy access for her, but she'd have to take the elevator after that to get to the others. At least they had one.

The principal came out of her office as Lily rolled past and hurried to catch up with her to say hello. Lily was wheeling her chair as quickly as she could in the swirl of students on their way to class, and she didn't want to bump into anyone and look like a klutz. No one could see it, but she was shaking.

'Hello, Lily. Welcome home!' the principal, Miss Davis, said with a warm smile, and Lily had to stop to talk to her in the middle of the hall. She couldn't avoid it, but hated stopping, and she felt like everyone was looking at her.

'Thank you very much.'

'We're so happy you're back!' She spoke for no one but herself, Lily knew, since she had heard from no one else. She'd had a get well card from all her teachers in the first week after the accident, and heard nothing from them since, other than the homework assignments they sent to Craig. She had been the forgotten person, and felt like it now in spite of Miss Davis's bright smile, which looked phony to Lily.

'Thank you. I've got to go,' Lily said as the bell rang, and whizzed past her toward her class. She had history first period, and had already turned in the required paper, before its due date. She was all caught up. And the history teacher was a young woman who had graduated from Duke the year before and was relatively new to the school. Lily liked her, although she hardly knew her. Her name was Barbara Bailey, and she had a wild mane of red hair and wore clogs summer and winter.

She nodded acknowledgment when Lily rolled in, and then approached her in a matter-of-fact way. 'Would you rather sit in the front or the back or on the aisle?' she asked her as though she'd seen her the day before, and Lily loved it because it made her feel normal and not as though she had just landed from Mars because she was in a wheelchair. She didn't treat Lily like she was sick, which

Lily was grateful for and thought was cool. Miss Davis had spoken to her in a tone that made her feel seriously impaired. Barbara Bailey didn't.

'I'll sit in back,' Lily said quietly, and Barbara Bailey went back to the front of the class to wait for the rest of the students to come in, so she could start. And Lily rolled to a spot in the back row on a center aisle and looked out the window. She could see the last stragglers hurrying into school and saw Veronica laughing between two boys who Lily knew were also on the ski team. Their school was sympathetic to the odd schedules of kids on the Olympic teams, who needed time off to practice and travel to other cities for races and games, and they accommodated them when necessary without penalizing them for it. Veronica hadn't even called to ask what day she was coming back, or if she could be there to help make it easier for her, which would have been nice. And Lily also knew that without her on the team, Veronica was the star now, and probably the favorite to win the gold. It was hard to swallow, but she didn't hold it against her. The really hard part was that she seemed to have no room for Lily in her life. It had been a crushing blow.

They were studying the industrialization of America in history class that day, which Lily found incredibly boring, and her attention kept drifting away as she tried to listen, but she kept staring out the window and wishing it were over. The teacher had just written several things on the blackboard, and when she turned around, she looked straight at Lily with a direct gaze.

'Isn't that right, Lily? Is there anything you'd like to add?' Lily blushed and looked embarrassed in the clutches of the teacher's eyes.

'I – I'm sorry . . . I didn't hear what you said.'

'Try to pay attention, please. I know this period in our history is a little boring, but let's try to get through it, shall we? It's almost the end of the year,' she reminded all of them as her eyes swept the room, while the students sat slumped in their chairs, looking as uninterested as Lily. She had singled Lily out, but Lily smiled as soon as she turned her attention to the others. She loved that Ms. Bailey hadn't given her a pass, or treated her as someone special who didn't need to pay attention. She had treated her like everyone else. Lily wanted to hug her, and a boy in front of her turned and made a grimace of acute boredom, and Lily tried not to laugh at him. And finally the bell rang and they were free. Lily smiled at the teacher as she rolled out of the room, and the teacher returned the smile as she put away her papers.

Three girls Lily knew well came up to her in the hall then, and started chattering about how happy they were that she was back, and she didn't remind them that she hadn't heard from them since January. She knew she couldn't let herself be bitter about it, but she had noticed.

'Nice gloves,' one of them said to her when she saw the

double Cs on them. And she was wearing one of the pink nail polishes Carole had given her. Lily looked as pretty as she always had – she was just sitting in a wheelchair. And she had watched what she ate, so she hadn't gained weight from being sedentary. If anything, she was thinner from the healthy diet, and thanks to Phil Lewis, her upper body looked sleek and toned.

'It's good to have you back, Lil,' one of the other girls said, and looked as though she meant it, and then she lowered her eyes in shame. 'I'm sorry I never called you. I guess I felt awkward about it. I didn't know what to say.'

'Yeah, I know,' Lily said, embarrassed, but touched by her honesty. 'I guess it must have been weird.' She didn't know what else to say to make her comfortable about it now.

'Were you in Squaw this whole time?'

'No, I've been in a rehab here since February, a place called Craig.' There was no reason for them to know about it and the services they provided – she'd never heard about it till she was there either. But it told her immediately that Veronica hadn't bothered to tell anyone where she was, so they might have come to visit. Maybe she just didn't care, or had always been jealous of Lily in some way.

'Ah, finally off drugs!' a tall boy from the basketball team said as he started to speed by, and stopped when he saw her. They had been lab partners in chemistry first semester. He had blown up their project and made her laugh so hard, they got thrown out of class for the rest of the day. His name was Walker Blake. 'You didn't fool anyone here, you know,' he said in a booming voice as Lily grinned at him. She had always liked him and they were friends. 'I always knew you had a drug problem after you blew up our chem project. They told us you were in rehab. I'm not surprised at all. Heroin or crystal meth?'

'I did *not* blow up our chem project! You did, you jerk,' she said, laughing, as the whole mood of the group relaxed.

'I did not. I saw you combine the lethal ingredients to blow the place up! So okay, you can tell us, what were you in rehab for? Smoking crack? The minute I heard you were in rehab, I figured that's what it was about. And it won't do you any good hiding in that shopping cart you're using. You're not fooling me for a minute,' he said, grinning at her, obviously happy to see her, and she was grateful to him for lightening the moment. 'So what have you been doing while we've been working our asses off all year?'

'Actually' – she smiled at him – 'I've been skiing.' His eyes widened as she said it and he thought she was kidding, in the vein of the banter he had started, and she could see he didn't believe her. 'Seriously, downhill at Winter Park, on a monoski with a chair. It's pretty rad.' The others listened with interest. She knew he was an outstanding skier. They had gone on ski trips together with the ski club at school when they were younger, before she was on the Olympic team and had to train with them, and had no time to ski with her friends. 'I'm training for the Paralympics,' she said proudly, and Walker shook his head in disbelief and amazement.

'You're insane,' he said, but he was impressed by her. He always had been, and he was glad to see her looking so well. He had wondered just how badly damaged she was, and if she had a head injury too, and no one had seemed to know. 'I'll go with you sometime if you want. I'd really like to see that,' he said admiringly, as the bell rang again and they all had to get to their next class. 'What do you have next period?'

'Math,' she said, and made a face. It was her least favorite subject.

'I've got chem – not with you, thank God,' he said, and she laughed. 'See you at lunch.' And then he left. He didn't offer to help her, carry her books, push her wheelchair, or get her to the elevator, and she was grateful to him for treating her as he always had, with irreverence.

She left the others and got to the elevator on her own. After a double math class that she hated as much as ever, she had lunch in the cafeteria and everyone flocked around. One of the girls carried her tray for her, although she could have balanced it on her lap, but it was easier not to. Walker stopped by to joke with her, others stopped to say hi, and realized that she hadn't changed as much as they feared, she just couldn't walk, but was managing fine. And finally, halfway through lunch, Veronica showed up and threw her arms around her, and acted like her long-lost friend. Lily was cool to her, but she didn't want a war with her, so she didn't say anything.

And she finished the afternoon without event. She called her father after her last class and waited outside for him. No one paid any attention to her – she was just one of the kids again, even if she was in a wheelchair now. The worst was over, she had survived her first day, and she was happy to go home. She had a lot of homework to do that night. No one had cut her any slack, and she hadn't wanted them to. She was still disappointed in Veronica, but she had been for the past four months. She just wasn't able to make the adjustment to what had happened to Lily. It was too much for her. At Craig, they had said that some people just couldn't handle it, and Veronica was one of them. It was sad for Lily, but she would make other friends, and people like Walker Blake made it easier for her.

She texted Teddy while she waited for her father, and told him it had gone okay. She was tired, and she was about to text him that she had a lot of homework to do, and she would see him tomorrow, and then she remembered that it was the same excuse everyone had given her for months, so she didn't say it. And when her father showed up and she got in the car, she asked him to stop at Craig. She picked up a pizza and a smoothie for Teddy, and she wheeled into Craig and found him at his computer class. He was practically a genius on computers, and he did art projects on them too. He was just finishing when she arrived.

'Well, look at you, after your first day of school.' He smiled at her and thought she looked really cute. 'So, it went okay?'

'Not bad. I'm practically flunking math, and the history teacher caught me daydreaming and made an example of me for not paying attention, and I have about ten hours of homework to do tonight and a math quiz tomorrow, but I wanted to come by and give you a hug at least.' She put the pizza box on his knees, and tucked the smoothie into the back corner of his seat, and he smiled at her.

'No one kicked sand in your eyes in the sandbox?' he asked with interest as they smiled at each other.

'Nope. I thought they would, but they got used to the chair after a while.'

'How was Veronica?' He looked concerned. He knew how much she had meant to Lily and how disappointed she was in her.

'Fake. She gave me a big hug in the lunchroom, and I never saw her again.' She shrugged. 'I missed you today.'

'Me too. This place really sucks without you at night.

I got so bored, I played blow darts with the guy who laughs like a horse and talks about his hot girlfriend and how big her tits are all the time,' Teddy said with resignation. The boy he was talking about had been on the diving team at his school and had an injury similar to Teddy's. They both thought he was obnoxious, but playing darts with him had been something to pass the time without Lily.

'I'll call you when I finish my homework,' she promised, and when she hugged him and left, he knew she would. And then she hurried home. She had a lot to do before the end of the school year, and her junior thesis to finish. It was hell being back in school, and a little piece of Heaven too.

Chapter 20

Lily got decent grades in her last month of school, not as good as she usually did, but she was still in the top third of her class in spite of all the school she'd missed. There was a dance on the last Saturday before the end of school. Walker Blake invited her to it. He had a girlfriend, but he ditched her for the night, and she was a good sport about it, and they danced a fair amount anyway. It was the junior prom, and Lily hadn't planned to go, but Walker talked her into it, and she had a good time. She talked to everyone she knew, and sat with the DJ for a while and helped him pick the music. And Walker spun her around the dance floor in her wheelchair a couple of times and she got so dizzy, she nearly fell out, but he caught her before she did. She caught a glimpse of Veronica with a new boyfriend, but she pretended not to see Lily and never came over to say hello. And in spite of the strangeness of being at her junior prom in a wheelchair, Lily was surprised that she had a good time. It had been nice of Walker to take her, and she told Teddy all about it when she visited him the next day.

'I wish I could go to school,' he said wistfully.

'You're probably learning more here,' Lily said. He read constantly, he loved books about art history, and biographies of famous artists. His dream was still to teach art one day, and he was determined to apply to the University of Denver in the fall, in their fine arts program. Lily was still planning to apply to her favorite colleges in the East, and had avoided discussing it with her father recently.

Almost all her friends had summer jobs. Some of the girls were going to be junior camp counselors. One was teaching swimming, another one was working in her father's office. She and Teddy were the only people Lily knew who had nothing to do that summer. And her father was going to be busy with The Lily Pad. She was planning to spend a lot of time visiting Teddy at Craig, and they had given her permission to use the pool. She was thinking about taking their scuba diving class. And her father surprised her a week after school got out. He said he wanted to make a quick trip to London and invited her to go with him. He was chartering a jet again, so it would be easy for her to go along. She had taken a travel class at Craig, which covered traveling on an airline, so she knew she could have flown commercially too, but her father didn't like to. Chartering jets was an indulgence he allowed himself and could afford.

'How about coming with me?' he suggested mysteriously.

'What are you going to do there?' She still remembered her bad experience at Harrods the last time, but she knew she could handle that now too.

'I'm doing a business deal. If you don't come, I'll be back in a few days. If you want to join me, we could stay longer, although I have a lot to do here.'

'I'll come,' she said, feeling adventurous, and told Teddy about it the next day. She hadn't heard from anyone at school since classes ended, but she knew that this time people were genuinely busy and a lot of them had already gone away. It was going to be a long boring summer for her without a job. The trip to London would be a nice change and something to do. She always enjoyed trips with her dad.

Bill and Lily left for London a week later, and stayed at Claridge's again. Her father had suggested taking an attendant for Lily with them, but she insisted she could manage on her own and preferred it. He took a two-bedroom suite, and they shared a living room, and he took her to Harry's Bar for dinner, which was a club he belonged to. The food was delicious, and it was the first elegant outing Lily had had since the accident. And Bill was impressed at how well she handled it. She wore a short dressy black dress, tights, and pretty flats. It was a warm night, and they both enjoyed the evening at the posh club, and she had managed her wheelchair in tight quarters with grace. And the next day Lily tackled Harrods and several other stores she liked, and came back laden with shopping bags. Her father had given her their car and driver and taken a cab himself. He said he was going to an art auction at Christie's, which didn't interest her, although she knew Teddy would have loved it. She had promised to bring him back postcards from the Tate Gallery and the Victoria and Albert Museum, which he was planning to use in a collage. She had already gotten them for him at a little store near the hotel. She looked victorious when she got back to their suite at the hotel, with all her shopping bags that the bellman brought up for her, and her father was waiting for her.

'Well, I don't need to ask how you did today.' He laughed. 'You must have gotten an A in that shopping class at Craig. Am I broke yet?'

'Not yet,' she said with a smile, but she had definitely done some damage and had fun, and managed all by herself, and was proud of it. It was a big difference from when she'd been there before and left the store in tears as people bumped into her, and salespeople were rude or ignored her, and she couldn't even get their attention. 'How was the auction?'

'Very successful,' he said, beaming at her. 'I got what I

came for. I could have done it by phone from Denver, but I don't buy paintings like this very often.' In fact, he had never bought one as expensive or important, but this painting was special. 'I figured I'd come over and enjoy it.' And it had been a good excuse to do something with Lily, and they were both having fun.

'Did you buy something?' He hadn't told her that he was planning to buy a painting, just that he had business to do in London. He hadn't wanted her to be disappointed if he didn't get it.

'I certainly did.' He smiled as he handed her a photograph of it.

'Oh my God! Daddy, you bought this?' She recognized the artist immediately and the subject. 'A real one?'

'I hope so!' He laughed at the expression on her face and what she said. 'It'd better be at that price. I'll be very upset if I bought a fake.' But there was no risk of that at Christie's, and the provenance was flawless. He had bought one of the water lily paintings by Monet. Not an enormous one, but it was a good size, and a particularly lovely painting. 'I'm going to hang it in the reception area of The Lily Pad. I thought it would look fabulous there.' For a moment Lily didn't know what to say.

'That's incredible.' She threw her arms around him and hugged him. And he pulled her close to him and held her. He knew that if he lived to be a hundred years old, he could never do enough for her, and he was thrilled that she loved the painting, and so did he. He could hardly wait to see it in the entrance of The Lily Pad one day.

She called Teddy immediately and knew he'd be just getting up.

'You're not going to believe this,' she said breathlessly when he answered.

'What? You can walk?' They teased each other about that sometimes, and could, because they were in the same boat.

'No, you moron. Don't be ridiculous. This is serious. My father just bought a painting at Christie's.' She knew that Teddy sometimes followed the results of important auctions online, and would then report them to her, although she was less interested in them than he was. But she was very interested in this auction now.

'What did he buy?' Teddy sounded immediately intrigued.

'A Monet,' she breathed into the phone like a holy word, and she knew that to Teddy it was, and to her now too, because her father owned it, and had bought it because of her.

'As in Claude Monet? You're kidding me, right?' That wasn't possible. His parents had some very important art, but no one he knew owned a Monet. They only existed in museums.

'It's one of the water lily series, and he's going to put it in the entrance of The Lily Pad. You're not going to believe how beautiful it is.'

'Let me look it up online. I'll call you right back.' She giggled when they hung up, and he called her back five minutes later. 'Holy shit! It's incredible!' And he knew it must have cost a fortune because it said 'estimate upon request,' which meant it was a big-ticket item. A *very* big ticket, but he was polite enough not to comment, only on the beauty of the painting, which was remarkable. 'I can't wait to see it.' He sounded breathless with excitement.

'You have to come to the house and see it when we get back.' He hadn't been to their house yet. Lily had been busy with school for the last few weeks. But she was planning to have him over for dinner and to hang out over the summer. They just had to borrow a van to do it, because of his heavy electric chair, which you needed a special lift to move. Because of it, he was a lot less mobile than Lily, who could put her chair in the trunk of any car, and the fancy chair her father had gotten her was light as a feather.

They talked about the painting for a few more minutes before hanging up and then she went to thank her father again for buying it.

'That's something very special for us to have,' he said reverently, and he wanted it to go to Lily one day. It would become an important part of his estate, and could only be a good investment. He was impressed by the purchase himself, and he didn't regret it for a minute. He had no buyer's remorse whatsoever.

They spent the next two days shopping, spending time in Hyde Park, and going to restaurants, and they picked the painting up at Christie's on the last day. He hadn't wanted to leave it at the hotel. It was too important not to have under lock with a guard. And he had already made arrangements with the Denver Art Museum to put it in a vault until they could hang it at The Lily Pad. It was exciting just getting it to the plane and knowing they had it with them on the way home. It had been a wonderful trip for both of them.

She told Teddy all about it when she got home, and as a special treat, Bill arranged to borrow a van with a driver from Craig, and drove Teddy to the museum with Lily once they were home, so he could see the painting. He sat staring at it wordlessly in awe for a long time and then looked at Lily with tears in his eyes.

'It's the most beautiful thing I've ever seen,' he said, overwhelmed, and it touched Bill to see how much he loved it.

Afterward they took him home for dinner, and he was able to go all over the house with Lily, thanks to the accommodations Bill had put in. They hung out in the living room and listened to music, and Lily made dinner for them in the kitchen that was so easy for Teddy to negotiate too. The visit was such a success that Teddy became a frequent visitor during the summer. And he did a painting of his own, inspired by the water lilies, and gave it to Bill to thank him for allowing him to visit them at home. It was a remarkable piece of art for any artist to have produced, let alone one with limited use of his hands. No one would have suspected that from the painting he created.

'We're going to put it at The Lily Pad,' he assured Teddy, 'in the same area as the Monet.' He was very touched by the gift, and impressed by Teddy's talent, which was considerable.

And between Teddy's visits, Walker, who dropped by a couple of times between summer plans, and a few of the girls from her class who visited her, Lily's summer passed quickly. She and her father went to Aspen for a few days at the end of August and when they came home, it was time to go back to school for senior year. It had been an easy, lazy summer, the work at The Lily Pad was progressing well, and thanks to Lily and her father, it was the best summer Teddy had had in two years. He was part of the family now.

Chapter 21

Jessie wanted to take Chris to Denver to settle into his room in the dorm, but she had no one to leave the other children with, and he insisted he'd be fine going on his own. She felt terrible about it, and promised him she'd come out as soon as she could. She'd been telling Bill Thomas she'd come to Denver and consult with him again as soon as her kids were back in school, so she planned to visit Chris then.

Chris looked painfully adult the day he left with two suitcases, his computer, and his skis, and she had shipped his stereo and a bicycle by FedEx. She felt like a bad mother all over again, but she couldn't go with him and manage the other three at the same time. And the friends she would have left them with were on a camping trip in Yosemite. She drove Chris to the airport in Reno and hugged him hard.

'Call me! I want to know how you are.' She was fighting back tears, and so was he.

'I'll be fine,' he said, looking agonizingly like his father. 'Call me tonight.'

'Okay, okay.' She hugged him again, and he disappeared onto the plane for a direct flight to Denver. She went home with a heavy heart. Her first baby had left the nest, and she couldn't imagine life without seeing his face every night. The house was like a tomb when she got home, and the other children looked as mournful as she felt. Heather was lying on the couch, staring blindly at the TV, Adam didn't even beg to use the PlayStation, and Jimmy crawled onto her lap and hugged her the minute she sat down. No one wanted to eat lunch. She tried to talk them into a movie, but no one wanted to go, so she did laundry instead. She was folding clothes when Bill Thomas called her, and she sounded sad when she answered the phone. He could hear it in her voice.

'Is something wrong?' He was instantly concerned, and she was touched.

'Yes . . . no . . . just life, I guess. My oldest just left for college, and we all miss him already. It's so quiet here without him.' And she relied on Chris so much to help her with his siblings, she knew it was going to be hard without him, but at least now he'd have some fun instead of babysitting and chauffeuring for her all the time. She felt guilty for having relied on him so much all year.

'Give him my number and tell him to call me if he needs anything, once he settles in,' Bill said. 'Maybe this would be a good time to get you back here. I really need your advice, Jessie. We've been floundering for the last few weeks. I can't get our medical setup right, and I haven't seen a decent résumé in weeks. How soon can you come?' They'd been talking about early September, and it was here. She brightened at the invitation to consult for him again. It was just the excuse she wanted to visit Chris.

'As soon as you want me. I just have to tell Ben so he covers for me, and make arrangements for the kids. They start school next week. I hired a boy to help me after school now that Chris is gone, but he doesn't start for a couple of weeks. He's an instructor at the ski school. I need him to drive them around.' Heather had just gotten her learner's permit, but she couldn't drive alone without an adult, and Jessie didn't want her driving the other kids.

'Why don't you come the weekend after they start school, or the one after, whatever works for you, and you could make time to see your son while you're here? We could all have dinner together if you like, with Lily. It would be great.'

'I'd like to. Let me get organized, and I'll call you this week after I talk to Ben, and get the kids set up.'

'That's fine.' He sounded relieved, and she had something to look forward to when she hung up.

Chris called her that night after he got his room assignment and met his roommates. He said they were going out to get something to eat, but he wanted to let her know he'd arrived. He seemed so far away and suddenly so independent. She couldn't believe the time had finally come for him to leave for college, and she still looked depressed the next day at work.

'Bad weekend?' Ben asked her when he saw her face.

'Chris left for Denver.'

'I'm sorry.' He could see how upset she was about it.

'Yeah, me too. I hate it when kids grow up,' she said with a rueful smile. 'Which reminds me, Bill Thomas wants me to go to Denver and consult on his rehab again, in the next couple of weeks. Which weekend works for you?' Ben said that either one was fine, and they settled on one in two weeks, and she called Bill that afternoon. He was delighted, and he realized that it coincided with Carole Anders's next visit, and he told Jessie. Jessie was excited to see Carole, it sounded like a fun weekend, especially if she could spend some time with Chris too. She texted him to tell him when she was coming, and called the mothers of the kids' friends, and had it all set up by that night.

The weekend she left for Denver went smoothly. She had a whole bag of things to take to Chris that he'd forgotten, including an extra blanket, and she had slipped in some framed photographs of the other kids. Jimmy made him a picture, which she promised to take him. And she left for Reno straight from work. The various mothers babysitting for her kids had picked them up at school. Ben gave her a pointed look as she left.

'I still think you should take that job,' he said, and she just laughed.

'Yeah, whatever. The consulting is fine. And now I'll get to see Chris.'

'Give him my love,' Ben said, and she took a cab to the Reno airport, and caught the plane to Denver. And she got a cab to the hotel when she got there. Chris said he was busy that night with basketball practice, and she was meeting him the next day for breakfast, before she met with Bill.

It worked out perfectly. She met Chris at his dorm, and met his roommates, who all looked very nice. She brought him the bag of things from home, and they walked around the campus, and then she took him out to breakfast at a restaurant nearby. He looked happy and relaxed and said he was having fun. He couldn't wait till ski season started, but in the meantime he was playing basketball, and was on the swim team. And she dropped him off at school when she left, with a little tug at her heart. She had promised to see him again before she left on Sunday.

And then she took the cab to Bill's, where he was waiting for her with plans, résumés, and adjustments to the model, and he wanted her advice on a dozen subjects. They got right to work at his kitchen table, and were deeply engrossed in architecture plans, when Lily rolled into the kitchen to get some lunch. She was going over to Craig to visit Teddy, and then she was going to a college fair at her school to pick up some applications and brochures. She had promised to get some for Teddy too. And she was happy to see Jessie, who looked equally pleased to see her.

'You look great, Lily,' Jessie told her, as they stopped working for a few minutes. 'How's senior year going?'

'Okay, so far,' Lily said with a broad smile. 'I haven't flunked out yet. I'm going to a college fair today.' Her father didn't comment, and Lily made herself something to eat while they went back to work. And a little while later she left, and then Jessie thought of something and looked up at Bill.

'How is she getting around these days?' She had heard a car door slam and a car drive off. He looked sheepish when she asked the question.

'I got her a car with manual controls. She didn't want me driving her to school. I know, I spoil her, but it really made sense, and she needs some independence.' Jessie smiled at him as soon as he said it. 'She can even get her wheelchair into the car all by herself,' he said proudly.

'You don't need to apologize to me. I think it's a great idea. And she's a very responsible kid.'

'I'm glad you think so.' Lily really had made a remarkable adjustment to her situation, with every possible advantage Bill could give her. And Jessie thought he had done well too. He had come far since January, when he refused to accept the reality of her situation. Now he was building a rehab of his own. It still amazed her.

They went out to look at The Lily Pad together that afternoon, and went over his notes and drawings, and she solved the problems of how to structure the medical wing. They were keeping the medical aspect to a minimum, but they had to be realistic about the kind of care their residents would need, and some would need more than others. They had to have some kind of medical facility. They were just walking out of the building when Joe arrived with Carole. She had flown in from Boston early that morning, and they'd been going over other plans and a list of counselors Carole thought they should hire. And the minute the two women saw each other, they both looked pleased, and gave each other a warm hug.

'How lucky is that?' Carole said immediately. 'That we're here on the same weekend?' She thought her old friend looked tired, and in contrast Jessie thought Carole had never looked better, although she recognized instantly that the stylish dark hair she wore was a wig. She remembered Carole's own hair as a little lighter and softer. But her new hairdo was very chic. She hadn't seen Carole since she'd been sick.

The four of them sat together in the main office after

that and went over the architect's plans and blueprints, Bill pointed out things they were changing on the model, and the swimming pool and the building it was in were almost complete. And then they went down a list of potential employees together. They were getting down to the wire on some of them. Bill wanted their skeleton office staff in place by the end of the year.

'We have no medical director yet,' Carole said with a look of concern. Bill and Joe were worried about it too, but no one they really liked and felt comfortable with had appeared.

'Not unless you can convince Dr. Matthews to do it,' Bill said with an imploring look at Jessie, and she shook her head.

'You guys know I can't. Someone will turn up. We've got feelers out in hospitals all over the country. It's just a matter of time,' she said confidently.

'We're opening in eleven months,' Bill reminded her, and she nodded. And they went on to other things until after five o'clock. The four of them were planning to have dinner, Carole left with Joe, and Bill drove Jessie back to the hotel at six. They both looked tired on the ride back, they had covered a lot of ground all day, and it was hard getting everything done and discussed in the two days she was there.

'You know, I'm serious about your taking the job as medical director, Jessie. Whatever it takes. I'd like to give you a house to go with the job, and a salary that would make it worth your while.'

'I love to be bribed,' she said, teasing him. 'And a house would be great. The one we're in now is falling down around our ears now that Tim's not there to do repairs. But it would mean moving three kids to a new city and new schools. Heather would have to graduate here instead of with her friends. She's a junior this year and she'll be a senior next year. It just wouldn't be fair to them.' And it was a sacrifice she felt she had to make no matter how appealing the job was or how good the salary. 'They don't understand the economics of something like that. Their lives have already been disrupted enough losing their father. I might be able to do it with the two younger boys – they're young enough to adjust, especially Jimmy, who just turned seven, and Adam's twelve. But at Heather's age, she would feel like I'm destroying her life, moving her for her last year of high school.'

'We have some great schools here,' Bill said, but he had lost hope of convincing her. She was too dedicated a mother to do something that would upset her kids, even if it cost her a great job opportunity. Her kids were the priority, just as Lily was for him.

They had gotten to the hotel by then, and he promised to pick Carole and Jessie up at seven-thirty. They were going to meet Joe at the restaurant.

Jessie went upstairs, lay down on the bed, and called her friend. 'Wow, that was a long day. We do so much when we come out here. You must too.'

'We really do,' Carole agreed.

'Do you want to come to my room?' Jessie invited her. 'It's so good to be here together. I wish we could have dinner alone tonight.' It would have been nice to have a girls' evening, and Carole agreed.

'Yeah, I thought of it too, but I didn't want to be rude. They're so nice to me every time I come here.'

'Are you going to move for a job out here?' Jessie asked with interest. It made more sense for her since she was on her own.

'It's a great project and I love what they're doing, but I don't want to leave Mass General. Call me a job snob, but I love the prestige of working for an institution like that.' Jessie smiled at what she said.

'I don't blame you, I'd feel the same way, although I think The Lily Pad is going to be something very special. Bill is pouring a fortune into it, and really doing it right. If we can help him staff it decently, it's going to be fabulous.'

'What about you?' Carole asked her. 'Would you move here?'

'I can't move my kids, not after Tim. Can you imagine how traumatic that would be for them?'

'Kids adjust better than we think, and they have each

other and you. And Chris is in school here now, so you'd all be together, more than you are in Squaw, with Chris away at school.'

'Try explaining that to my daughter. She thinks the center of the universe is Squaw. Tim thought so too.' She laughed, and Carole promised to come down in a minute, and she appeared at Jessie's door five minutes later in jeans, ballet shoes, a Harvard sweatshirt, and a scarf on her head. The long dark locks had disappeared.

'Sorry.' She patted her head when Jessie saw her. 'It's nice to take my wig off for a while. My hair is finally coming in, but it's all wiry and weird.' She took the scarf off, and Jessie could see the bristle all over her head, which was lighter than the wig, just as she'd remembered. 'My hair was never as good as that wig,' she admitted with a grin and sat on the end of Jessie's bed. 'So what's new with you? Anything?'

'Are you kidding? Between work and the kids, I don't even have time to sleep. And half the time I'm on call. It's been pretty crazy for the last nine months, and not a lot of fun.'

'It'll get better,' Carole reassured her, but Jessie didn't look convinced. She couldn't imagine her life getting better again without Tim. It had been a very tough year.

'I don't know how,' she said honestly, 'unless I retire or give up the kids. And it's going to be harder now without Chris – he's been a big help. It'll do him good to get away.

He was constantly taking care of the younger ones. I just hired someone to help. What about you? Is life getting back to normal after Dylan and being sick?'

'Pretty much. I feel really good. I'm back on track, and the consulting here has been great, thanks to you. That's about all I'm doing right now. It's enough.' She seemed satisfied with her life, and for a second Jessie envied her. She still hadn't made peace with losing Tim.

'You're not dating anyone?' Jessie asked cautiously. Carole was a beautiful young woman and five years younger than Jessie.

Carole shook her head with a determined look at her friend. 'I'm done.' She sounded definite about it, and Jessie looked skeptical.

'At thirty-eight? I hope not. Don't be silly. Just give it time.' Carole could have said the same to her, but she didn't. She could see that Jessie was still grieving Tim and their lost life. It was too soon for her.

'I don't need time. It's different for me. I can't have kids. I don't want to get married again. Dylan cured me of that. My body is . . . well, different. I'm not ready to show this to anyone, and I don't want reconstructive surgery. It's too much. I went through enough last year with the double mastectomy and hysterectomy. And I'm happier like this, on my own.'

'I hope you're seeing a shrink,' Jessie said seriously, and knew her well enough to say it. 'You can't give up on your life as a woman at your age.' She had made a tough choice, and Jessie thought it was the wrong one.

'Yes, I can.' She looked satisfied with her decision and seemed to have no doubts or regrets about being alone. 'I can do whatever I want, and I don't have to put up with shit from a guy. It's not as bad as you think,' she said with a mischievous grin. 'I'd been accommodating men for years – my father, the guys I went out with, Dylan. This is a lot easier and a lot more fun than making life wonderful for some crabby guy who cheats on you in the end and dumps you anyway.'

'Not everyone acts like Dylan,' who had had an enormous ego and was a narcissist in Jessie's opinion. Tim had never behaved like that with her. He was a good guy, and surely not the only one in the world to treat a woman well. Carole had just married the wrong one. 'There are some good ones out there.'

'They're all married, and I'm fine like this. It would be different if Dylan and I had stayed married, but I'm not starting out with a new guy with this ravaged body. No way.' Jessie was sorry to hear her say it, and sad for her, she was so definite about it. And then they went on to talk about their respective jobs and reminisce about their work at Stanford Hospital, which had been fun for both of them. And then it was time to dress for dinner.

'I wish we could stay here and order room service,' Jessie said wistfully. It was relaxing and nice just sitting there and talking. She had no women friends anymore after her years with Tim, and no time for them now, chasing her kids all the time, and working as hard as she did.

'It'll do us good to go out,' Carole said as she got off the bed. They consulted briefly about what to wear for dinner, and Carole went back to her room. Jessie was thinking how much she liked Carole, as she got into the shower. She missed having someone to talk to now without Tim.

They met in the lobby half an hour later. Jessie was wearing a short black skirt, gray cashmere sweater, and heels, and Carole was wearing a red leather skirt, black sweater, and sexy boots, and her freshly brushed wig. They were a very good-looking pair. And Bill looked impressed as he picked them up, wearing gray slacks and a black suede jacket he'd bought in Italy, and he had a crisp blue shirt under it with an open collar.

'I feel very lucky being with two very beautiful women,' he said as he walked them to his car. The three of them chatted easily on the way to the restaurant, and Joe was waiting when they arrived. They talked about The Lily Pad all night, although Jessie noticed that Joe looked at Carole differently from the way Bill looked at either of them. She could easily see that Joe had a soft spot for Carole, and she mentioned it to her as they walked back into the hotel afterward.

'Don't be ridiculous,' Carole brushed off the suggestion. 'We just work well together.'

'Yeah, you may think so.' Jessie laughed at her. 'I think
he has something else in mind too. Do you like him?'
Jessie was curious, and Carole just laughed.

'I think he's fine. I'm not dating, remember? And he's
too old. But it doesn't matter. I'm not in the market for
a guy.'

'I don't think he's looking for a woman either after his
experience with his wife. I think he just likes you.
Sometimes that's how things happen,' Jessie said wisely.

'Trust me, nothing's happening. When are you
leaving?' Carole asked her.

'After I see Chris tomorrow.'

'Let's try and come out at the same time again,' Carole
suggested. 'It was fun.'

'Yes, it was,' Jessie agreed, and hugged her as she left
the elevator. 'Call me sometime. I miss you, Carole.'

'Yeah, me too,' she said, and waved as the elevator
closed. It had been a very pleasant evening, and every
time she came to Denver, Carole got more excited about
The Lily Pad, and now Jessie felt the same. It was an
exciting project, and the man who was organizing it was
a wonderful person. And his passion for what he was
doing was contagious. They were all on fire with his plans
and following his dream.

*

Jessie saw her son the next morning for breakfast, as promised, and hugged him tight before she left him.

'I'll come back soon, I promise,' she said as he put her in a cab.

'I'll be fine,' he said with a wistful expression. He knew he would be, but he was worried about her. She was so tired and stressed all the time, and so overwhelmed now without his father. He had given the others a stern talking to before he left, not to be difficult and to try and help their mother whenever they could. No one had paid attention to him except Jimmy, who had solemnly promised to do whatever he could to help her, and was trying hard to do so.

Jessie slept on the flight to Reno, and took a cab home. She got her car out of the garage then and picked up all three kids. They stopped at a Burger King for dinner, and they told her about their weekends. Heather had a new boy she liked, and all of them said they had had fun at their friends' houses. She told them all about Chris's room and his roommates and what they'd done, and what the campus looked like, and then she told them about The Lily Pad. They weren't too interested in the project, which seemed remote to them, but they were happy she was home, and so was she. She had enjoyed catching up with Carole over the weekend and hoped to see her again soon. She was glad they had the connection now with Denver, and the excuse to occasionally meet

for the weekend, if they could coordinate their schedules
again.

Jessie did all their laundry when she got home. She
checked that their homework was in order. She read
Jimmy a story and tucked him into bed. She reminded
Adam and Heather not to stay up too late, and then she
lay on her bed for just a minute before she undressed –
and woke up in the morning, still fully dressed with the
lights on. She had needed the sleep. She often fell asleep
that way now.

She showered, dressed, made breakfast, and got
everyone off to school, and then she left a sheet of
instructions for Barry, the young ski instructor who was
coming in that afternoon to babysit the kids. He'd been
recommended by the mother of one of Heather's friends
who had hired him the year before to watch her two boys.
She and her husband had gotten divorced, and her ex had
moved to San Francisco, and she said Barry had been a
godsend for her. Jessie hoped he would be for her too.
Especially without Chris now, she needed help, and she
couldn't afford a full-time housekeeper without Tim's
salary to complement hers. Barry at the house after school
until she came home from work was all she needed. He
was twenty-two and had a car, which was even better,
since she needed hers for work. He had promised to take
Jimmy to the dentist for a checkup that afternoon.

She left the house and got to work before Ben, in

time to see her first patient. She had two surgeries scheduled after that, and it was four o'clock before she got back to the office, and six before she finished. And then she dashed home to see the kids. She didn't know what to expect, but when she walked in, she found utter chaos.

Adam and Jimmy had had a pillow fight in the living room, and there were feathers everywhere, and Jimmy's lip was bleeding and he was crying. Heather had baked cupcakes to take to school, and had left a huge mess in the kitchen, and burned half of them. She had put the stereo on and it was blaring. There was a half-eaten pizza in a box on the table, and Barry was avidly playing with the PlayStation and letting them do whatever they wanted. He had a bottle of Evian next to him, and took a long drink as he went to the next level of the game and didn't even see Jessie come in. She stood in front of the TV glaring at him, and he grinned at her, as the boys went silent and scampered upstairs.

'Just what exactly is going on? Is this what you call "watching my children"? What were you watching, them trying to kill each other and destroy my house, or Heather burning it down?'

'Sorry,' he said, taking another sip of the Evian, and then he stood up, and Jessie thought he looked unsteady, and suddenly she wondered if what was in the Evian bottle was really water. She picked it up off the table before he could stop her, unscrewed the cap and smelled it, and looked at him with horror.

'What is that?' It had a familiar smell. She knew it was alcohol but she couldn't identify it.

'Tequila,' he answered simply. He was a drunk, but not a liar.

'Are you crazy? You drove my kids today, and you were *drinking*? Are you insane? Do you want to kill them? Get out of my house! I should report you to the ski school. Do you realize I operate on people all the time who get hit on the road by drunks like you?' And then she held out her hand. 'Give me your car keys.'

'Huh?'

'You heard me. Give me your car keys.' She was so livid that he was afraid to argue with her. He fished them out of his pocket and handed them to her.

'I only started drinking when we got back here.'

'That's nice, I'm sure that seems fine to you, but it doesn't to me. You were responsible for my children, one of whom is seven. He's a little kid, and he was bleeding when I walked in. I don't care if you walk home – you're not driving if you've been drinking. Come back and get your car tomorrow. I'll leave the keys under the doormat. Now you can go.' He looked frightened of her as he slunk out. He had never seen anyone so angry, and he'd been afraid she might hit him, but she wouldn't have. She started cleaning up the living room after he left, and burst into tears. And one by one the children came downstairs.

'I'm sorry, Mom.' Adam apologized first, and Jimmy was right behind him. It scared them to see their mother crying – they were big gulping sobs. She'd had enough, and she knew she couldn't manage without Tim, or Chris, and her son couldn't give up college to help her.

'Me too,' Jimmy said softly, and Heather came down the stairs and helped Jessie pick up the feathers and the burned cupcakes in the kitchen.

'I was going to clean up before you got home, but I forgot,' she said, embarrassed. They had pushed their mother too far, and they could see it. They didn't know what to do to make it better now as she continued to cry. She couldn't stop as she tidied everything up and they helped her.

'Do you realize that kid was drunk?' she said in outrage, looking at all of them. 'And he's not a kid, he's a man. He should know better. He was drinking tequila while he was supposed to be taking care of you.' She grabbed the Evian bottle, emptied it into the kitchen sink, and threw the empty bottle in the trash.

'We'll cook dinner, Mom,' Jimmy said, and she realized that he could cook frozen pizza as well as she did. She felt like she kept letting them down again and again because she couldn't cope. She knew she had to get a grip, but she didn't know how, and then she quietly left the kitchen and said she'd be back in a few minutes. She walked upstairs to her room and locked the door. She knew now that she had no choice. No matter how upset they would be about it, this was worse.

She sat down on her bed and called Bill Thomas in Denver on her cell phone, and she didn't even realize she was still crying. He answered on the second ring, and he was startled to hear her voice. He could tell that she was crying.

'Are you all right?'

'No,' she said, and sobbed again. 'But I will be. I can't do this anymore. It's too much. Not by myself.' She was still sobbing, and he felt sorry for her. 'I'll take the job as medical director. I'll take the house if you still want to give it to me. I need the money – I can get a decent housekeeper that way. And maybe I can still practice, or join an office of neurosurgery and operate part time. I'll figure that out later. Just know that I'll take the job. I need to let Heather finish the school year here, but we could move in June. Will that work for you?' It all came out without stopping for breath, and he was stunned by everything she was saying. He hadn't expected that at all.

'Are you sure? I don't want to take advantage of you at a low point. Why don't you think about it tonight, or for a couple days?' She sounded desperate, and he was sorry for her. She was having a tough time.

'No, I always knew I wanted the job. I just couldn't do it to my kids. But this is worse. I can't manage here without Tim or Chris. I just hired some kid to watch my children, and I came home and found him drunk on tequila, and a total mess here.' Bill wished he could give her a hug as he listened – she sounded as though she could use one.

'Why don't you take it easy tonight, and we'll talk tomorrow? If you don't want to leave Squaw, there has to be another way to work it out.'

'I really want the job.'

'And I really want you as our medical director, but I don't want to exploit your situation and have you regret it later.'

'It doesn't get much lower than this. Or maybe it does. But I'm ready. I think moving to Denver will do us all good. Ben's right, it's too depressing in this house.'

'All right, let's talk in the morning,' he said kindly. 'And Jessie, take it easy tonight. The kids are going to be okay, and so are you, whatever you do.'

'Thank you,' she said sadly. 'I'm sorry I'm such a mess.'

'We've all been there,' he said gently. 'I'll talk to you tomorrow.' They hung up, and she lay on her bed for a minute, wondering if she was crazy or had done the right thing. She took a breath, blew her nose, and then went downstairs and cooked dinner. And the kids were so worried about her they were angels that night.

When Jessie woke up the next morning, she thought about her call to Bill Thomas the night before. She knew she had sounded crazy, but it felt like the right thing. Her life was over here – it had only worked with Tim, and now it didn't. And she knew that at first, the kids would be upset about moving to Denver, but it was a fresh start for all of them, a new house, new schools, a new job for her, and they would be close to Chris.

She called Bill back even before she showered and confirmed what she had said the night before.

'I was worried about you last night,' he said gently.

'It was a bad night.' There had been nine months of them since Tim died, and she knew that moving to Denver wouldn't change that, but it was an exciting job, which would be good for her. 'It's still the right thing. Maybe I had to get to this point to be willing to make a change.'

'I'll try to make it as easy for you as I can, and June will be fine. And I have the perfect house in mind for you.' He had seen it recently, and had been thinking of buying it for any director they hired, as an incentive to take the job. Free rent, in a beautiful home in one of the best neighborhoods in town, not far from his own house, and it was in an excellent school district.

'Thank you. I'll try to make you glad you hired me. I want to do a really great job.' She sounded earnest, and he was touched.

'You already are.' He was enormously relieved. She had just solved his biggest problem, finding a director for The Lily Pad. 'What are you going to tell your kids?'

'Nothing for about six months. They don't need to worry about it now. I need to check out the schools. Elementary and middle school for Jimmy and Adam, and high school for Heather.'

'Don't worry. We have some wonderful schools,' he said calmly. 'Heather would be going to Lily's high school. We'll work it out, and I'll help. Just get things organized at your end. This is a big leap ahead for us. When do you think you can come here again?' They had a lot of work to do together now.

'In a few weeks,' she said, thinking about it. 'Just don't say anything to my kids if you call.'

'I won't,' he promised her. 'And Jessie, I'm thrilled.'

'So am I,' she said honestly, and she suddenly felt lighter. She knew she was doing the right thing.

She went downstairs and put Barry's car keys under the mat. Then she cooked breakfast for the kids, and after they left for school she called Carole and told her the news.

'You made a great decision,' Carole congratulated her. 'I'm proud of you. I know it must have been hard to do.'

'Not really. I just lost my mind. After that it was easy,' she laughed. 'What about you? When are we going to convince you?'

'Now, now, you've been the director for five minutes, and you're already coercing me.' She laughed, and so did Jessie.

'I wish I could . . . I hope I can . . . We need you in Denver.'

'They need me here too. I'm just glad you took the job, Jess.'

'So am I.' She had a feeling of peace that she hadn't had for months, and her kids would adjust to it. It didn't seem so insurmountable now. Sometimes kids had to move, and they survived. She knew that hers would too.

She told Ben about it when she went to work, but swore him to secrecy since she wasn't going to tell her kids for a while. And he was thrilled too. He gave her a big hug and beamed at her.

'I'm so happy for you! You don't belong here, Jess. You never did. You need to move on.' She discussed the issue of practicing in Denver. She'd have to get a Colorado medical license, and find an office that would let her do surgery part time. She didn't want to give that up. Ben assured her it wasn't impossible to find, especially with credentials like hers.

She felt better all day when she thought about what she'd done. She still felt a little guilty toward her children, but she was convinced now that it was the right thing for all of them.

Bill called her again that afternoon to make sure that she hadn't changed her mind, and she laughed.

'No, I'm sorry I was such a nutball last night. I

shouldn't have called you then.' She was embarrassed, but he was a friend now too.

'You were fine, and you're not a nutball. You're human, and you have a lot on your shoulders. I'm just glad you took the job.'

'So am I.' She was smiling this time. And she had decided to rent their house. That way if it didn't work out in Denver, they could always come back, but she didn't think they would. But keeping the house was a safety net for them and a smart thing to do. It was going to be a big change.

'There's an expression I've always loved, "What blesses one blesses all." I believe that. Your taking the job is a blessing for me and The Lily Pad, and hopefully it will be a blessing for you and your kids too.' The Lily Pad had already blessed a lot of people – Joe, Carole, and all the people Bill had hired so far. And it would bless all the kids who stayed there for rehab. It had only begun to bless all those involved. 'I'll call you in a few days,' he said, and hung up, and everything felt lighter to her now. She even stopped at the grocery store on the way home and made them a decent dinner. She realized as she set the table that she hadn't done that since Tim died. Now that she had accepted the new job, things were finally starting to look up.

Chapter 22

Lily worked hard at school into the winter months. She stopped and saw Teddy every day after school faithfully, knowing how much it meant to him. It had become a ritual, and he was working diligently with Phil Lewis to train for chair rugby, and playing practice games. They were rough, but Teddy loved it, and Phil was tireless at coaching him. Teddy was determined to be in the rugby demonstration at the Winter Paralympics that were being held in Aspen at the same time and in the same location as the Olympics. Lily had gone to see almost all of Teddy's games and they looked brutal to her, but Teddy had a great time doing it and was incredibly deft at moving his chair with the joystick and catching the ball with the sticks in his gloved hands. They applied a sticky substance to the ball so it was easier to hold on to.

And things were going well at school for her. She made new friends, and at the first snows, she started skiing again. She had contacted her old coach and explained what she was doing. He was stunned to hear from her and was still mourning her tragic accident when she asked if he would train with her again. He had gone into retirement after she fell.

'You're skiing again? That's not possible.' Despite what her father had told him, when he had seen her after the accident, he had realized she would never walk again.

'Yes, it is possible,' she laughed. 'Come and watch.' He came to Winter Park where she skied. She wanted to enter the Alpine skiing event, which was downhill racing, on the monoski fitted with the chair, and her old coach was in awe of what she could do, and the speeds she achieved. She was as strong as she used to be, and as fast on her new ski, dangerously so in fact. It terrified him, but he was thrilled to see what she was doing. He was Austrian, and had been a ski instructor in his youth, and a famous Olympic coach later on. He had worked with her for five years and prepared her for the Junior Olympics.

'I want you to help me win again,' she said to Oscar after the first time he'd seen her on the chair ski, and she showed him films of the Winter Paralympics. She still had a hunger for the gold. 'Will you do it?'

'Does your father know about this?' He looked worried. He knew how devoted Bill was to Lily and how protective of her.

'Yes, and no. He came to watch once in the beginning, but he doesn't know how serious I am about it. And I've gotten better and faster since he saw me. Last spring I was in rehab when I did it. But now I really want to train. Every day, if you think we need to.'

'Yes,' he said with a stern tone that was familiar to her. Sometimes it used to annoy her, but now she was thrilled. It meant he was taking her seriously. 'And we will go to Aspen and ski the mountain there. But I want to learn more about how your new chair ski works, and just how fast we can go. I will speak to some people at the Paralympics and maybe some of the skiers. I will do research.' And she knew he would be merciless with her once he did, which was just what she wanted. She wanted him to push her as hard as ever, so she would win.

Oscar did the research he had promised, and they started training in late October, every day after school, and she'd go to visit Teddy briefly after that, and then go home to do her homework. She told the head of the PE department at school what she was doing, and he let her out early whenever he could so she could train. After school she met Oscar at Winter Park, and they skied until the lift closed, and all day on weekends. She was tireless, and doing exercises at home to strengthen her arms and upper body, she was in better shape than she'd ever been. And her father was skeptical about what she was doing, but didn't object, since Oscar was skiing with her, and he knew he couldn't stop her. He had no idea how hard she was pushing herself, or how fast she skied. Bill had heard about the Paralympics, but assumed it would be a very tame event. It was obvious he'd never seen it, and for now Lily preferred it that way. He paid Oscar's coaching fee, and left Lily to have her fun. He was busy every day and on weekends at The Lily Pad.

By November, Lily was training as intensely as she had for the Olympics, and keeping up with her schoolwork. She was also busy filling out college applications, and she ran for class president. Walker Blake won and appointed her vice president, which looked good on her college apps, along with her previous skiing history, and her training for the Paralympics now, which wasn't why she did it. She did it for the love of it. And the day she'd made a breakthrough when Oscar helped her increase her speed, she wanted to tell Teddy all about it on her way home.

She went to look for him in the gym and couldn't find him anywhere. She found him in the infirmary instead. He had caught a bad cold after a rugby game, when he had sweated a lot and got in a draft. He was wheezing and they had to press on his chest to clear his lungs. And Lily knew how dangerous a cold was for him. He had a fever when she saw him, and she sat with him for an hour until he went to sleep.

She was worried about him, and when she came back

to see him the next day, they had moved him to the hospital facility at Craig, and he looked worse. They were afraid of pneumonia, and as she sat with him, she was terrified he was dying. A nurse told her that they had called his parents, which she knew was a bad sign, and she wondered if they would show up. And he was worse the next day. Lily sat stroking his face and his shoulders so she knew he could feel her touch.

'Hey, you, we're in training, remember? You've got to get better soon,' she said softly, and he nodded again and drifted off to sleep. And they kept waking him to clear his lungs, since he couldn't do it himself. Phil Lewis came to see him several times a day too, and Lily could sense that Teddy was slipping away. And his parents still hadn't come. She called her father and arranged to spend the night with Teddy, and even skipped her sessions with Oscar for a few days. She was afraid that if she left Teddy, he would die. He was nearly there. And on the second night when she slept in her chair next to him, she woke in the middle of the night, and he looked frighteningly still.

'Oh my God,' she said, sure that he had died. 'Teddy? . . . Teddy!' She shook him gently and started to cry, and he opened one eye.

'What? Stop shaking me, you jock. You're loosening my teeth,' he said with a grin in a hoarse voice. The fever had broken in the night. He was still very sick and was in the hospital for two more weeks, but by Thanksgiving he was back in training again with Phil.

'You scared the hell out of me, you know,' she told him after he recovered.

'Yeah, me too,' he admitted, and neither of them commented on the fact that his parents had never come. They had called him a few times, but he had been too sick to talk, and that was it. It was a sad statement about his parents and for him.

He shared Thanksgiving with Bill and Lily, and Joe came too. He had decided not to visit his kids that year, and stay in Denver. He had too much work to do, and didn't want to leave. It was Lily's first Thanksgiving in a wheelchair, but she felt as though she had much to be grateful for. And she spent the weekend in Aspen with Oscar afterward, learning the mountain there on her new ski, and he was pleased. She had done well.

And in Squaw Valley it was Jessie and her children's first Thanksgiving without Tim. Chris came home for the holiday, and she had just seen him two weeks before in Denver. She was there about once a month now, and they were forging ahead with new hires and new plans. Carole had been to Denver twice more, and she spent time with Lily and Teddy and made lists of all the things they would want in a rehab. She questioned them mercilessly about every kind of entertainment, recreational activity, device, sport, counseling feature, high-tech gadget. Teddy said he would love to run a peer counseling group, and Lily's emphasis was on sports, and an annual event, like the Paralympics but on a smaller scale, with more sports categories, and medals for the winners. It was a long list, and gave Carole a lot of information to work with, and she discussed it all with Joe afterward. He was impressed and a great sounding board for her plans.

Carole and Jessie had overlapped several times. They were all busy with their respective areas. Jessie was focusing on hiring the staff with Bill, and they were putting together a remarkable team. And Carole and Joe were designing programs, and once they refined them, they discussed them with Jessie and Bill.

'What about Phil Lewis, Dad?' Lily suggested one night at dinner, after she'd seen him at one of Teddy's rugby games. 'He'd be great as head of your physical therapy department.'

'Do you think he'd be interested?' Bill looked intrigued. He knew that Lily and Teddy loved him and he had done wonders with them.

'I don't know, ask him. He's the best.' She had come to see his merits, just as Teddy had, and Bill liked the idea of approaching him. He invited him to lunch several days later, and was pleased at how interested Phil was. He came out to The Lily Pad to see it for himself and fell in love with it, and he accepted the job. Lily and Teddy were thrilled.

'As long as my parents let me transfer to The Lily Pad,' Teddy said with a worried look.

'They have to,' Lily said with a fierce glance.

After Thanksgiving she got serious about her college applications. She applied to Princeton, Harvard, Brown, and NYU, and her first choice was Princeton. Her father wanted her to apply to the University of Denver, and she wouldn't. She still wanted to go away to school. But she helped Teddy fill out his application to DU, it was the only school he was applying to, and he prayed he would get in. He wrote a brilliant essay about what his artwork meant to him, and he submitted two of his paintings as part of his application, and Lily thought they were his best. He added that he was training for a demonstration at the Paralympics in chair rugby, and he asked Phil to write one of his recommendations. It was an impressive application, and he had good grades, and good test scores, as did Lily. But she didn't know if her grades were strong enough for Princeton. She put her skiing history on her application, listed her previous medals, and added a photograph of herself on her chair ski.

She showed her applications to Carole the next time she saw her, and she was impressed, but not surprised.

'If any school turns you down, they're crazy,' she said. Lily started mailing them before Christmas, although the deadline wasn't till January but she wanted to get a head start. She had to explain that she had been injured and in a rehab hospital for five months of junior year, but her grades had been good in spite of it, although they were better now, in senior year, even though she was spending hours training with Oscar every day, and he was satisfied with her progress. It all took so much time. Her schedule left her little free time to spend with friends, and it bothered her sometimes that she was never asked out by any boys, but she was so busy training, doing homework, and finishing her applications that she scarcely had a moment to think about it. And she still visited Teddy every day.

Lily managed to do her Christmas shopping on the last weekend before school closed. She bought a beautiful coat for her father, because he never liked to shop for clothes himself, and a warm sweatshirt for Teddy to wear after his games, and a stack of music, and she bought a sweater for Carole, and a warm scarf for Joe, and she bought a pair of fur earmuffs and sent them to Jessie for when she came back to Denver, but said she could wear them in Squaw too. Bill hadn't told her that Jessie was moving out in June to be the director of the center, since her own kids didn't know yet, but he had bought the house he had promised her, and on Jessie's last trip out before Christmas, he drove her there one evening on their way back from The Lily Pad.

'I need to make a stop. I hope you don't mind,' he said casually, as they drove to his place to have dinner with Lily.

'That's fine,' Jessie said, going over some of the notes they'd made that day. They had just hired two more physical therapists, one of them specializing in young children.

'Do you want to come in?' Bill asked her as he pulled into the driveway. It was a neat three-story house, with a well-tended garden and two big trees in front. It was white, with a heavy brass knocker on the door, and a big backyard that was fenced in. It looked like an ad for the perfect family house. Jessie glanced up as he asked her, and shook her head with a smile. The house was lit up – she didn't know that he had asked the broker to do it that night. The sale had gone through a few weeks before.

'No, I'm fine, I'll wait here. We did so much today, I want to make sure I got my notes right and didn't screw it up.' She felt like she was doing homework every night, but she loved it. It was exciting knowing she would be part of it as the director.

'Actually, I wanted to introduce you to a friend,' he said, and waited for her to put her notes away. 'It'll just take a minute.' She put the notes in her bag and suspected nothing as she followed him to the front door, and was mildly surprised when he knocked with the big brass knocker, opened the door, and walked in. The broker had left it open, per Bill's instructions. And she was even more surprised when she saw that the house was empty and there was no furniture, but all the lights were on. It looked freshly painted, and there were beautiful dark hardwood floors, a big front hall, a wide staircase, and a big living room with a fireplace. Even empty, the house had a friendly feeling to it, and she turned to Bill with a puzzled expression. Why was he meeting a friend in an empty house? Bill stood there smiling at her, as her eyes widened.

'Welcome home, Dr. Matthews,' he said with a warm smile and handed her the keys. 'As the director of The Lily Pad, I am happy to present you your new home. I hope you'll be very happy here, Jessie.' Her eyes filled with tears, and she threw her arms around him and hugged him. She had never seen such a beautiful house, and the thought of living there with her children undid her. She kept hugging him and thanking him, and he showed her around. There was a handsome master suite, and four additional bedrooms. There was a family room upstairs and another one in the basement, a living room, a dining room, den, and a big country kitchen. Each bedroom had its own bathroom, and there was a powder room downstairs, and a two-car garage. It was a dream house, and Jessie felt like she'd won the lottery, not just a job.

'I'm overwhelmed. I don't know what to say,' she said, breathless, as they returned to the front hall. 'I've never even dreamed of a house like this.' The neighborhood was a perfect family, residential area, a few blocks from where he lived. 'Bill . . .' She stood there crying again, and he put an arm around her shoulders, as they walked outside. She had never been so moved in her life, or felt as lucky.

'I hope you'll be happy here, and at The Lily Pad, for a long time.'

'I don't deserve this,' she said humbly. No one had ever done anything like it for her before. She could live there rent free as long as she was the medical director of The Lily Pad.

'Yes, you do,' he said with a broad smile. She could hardly wait to bring her children there – it was so much nicer than the house they had now. They were going to love it, even Heather, once she got over the shock of moving. Jessie was still speechless as they drove back to his house, where Lily was waiting for them. She had made a very nice dinner and was turning into a very decent cook. Lily noticed that Jessie said very little, but she looked happy, and finally got more talkative at dessert. She asked them about their Christmas plans. She could hardly wait till Chris came home for Christmas break from DU.

'We're going to be here,' Bill said comfortably, 'just the two of us.'

'And Teddy,' Lily added.

'And Teddy,' Bill corrected himself, 'and then Lily and I are going to Aspen for a few days with her coach. I want to see this chair skiing she's been doing, getting ready for the Paralympics.' He still expected it to be a relatively calm event, and had a shock in store.

The holidays were quiet in both Denver and Squaw. Jessie's Christmas with her kids, their first without their father, was predictably hard. And they were relieved when it was over.

On the day after Christmas Bill drove Lily to Aspen with Oscar, and they rode up the chairlift together that afternoon. Lily was undaunted by it now. And at the top of the mountain, as her father watched, she took off like lightning, using her poles with the little skis on them for balance, as she had learned to do. Her balance was still perfect, and her speed astounding as she flew down the mountain. Bill watched her with tears in his eyes. He had no idea of what she could do until he saw it for himself.

'Holy God,' he whispered as he watched her, and followed at his own speed. Lily was as fast as she had ever been, and as skilled, and maybe more so. A year after her injury, she was as fast as the wind, and Bill had never been as grateful in his life. She was an amazing girl, and he realized that Jessie's prediction for her was coming true – she was going to lead an amazing life. She already was.

Chapter 23

By the time Bill, Oscar, and Lily left for Aspen the week before the Olympics in March, everyone they knew was so excited they could hardly stand it.

Bill had reserved a house for them right in town, with an apartment below for Oscar. Jessie was flying in from Squaw and meeting Chris there. Carole was coming from Boston, and Joe wouldn't miss it for the world, and was going to stay at a hotel. Walker Blake had organized a dozen people from school to attend Lily's Alpine race in the Paralympics. Teddy was coming with Phil, and participating in the chair rugby demonstration to promote the summer games. He wasn't competing this time, but he planned to in the summer, and the rugby demonstration was a featured event and a big deal. They were filming it for ESPN.

Lily was as excited as she had been when she entered the Junior Olympics, and when she was accepted on the adult Olympic team. And she was more nervous this time. She wanted to do well and make everyone proud of her. The pressure was enormous as she trained with Oscar every day.

'Forget the medal,' Oscar said to her on their first day in Aspen. 'Just do what you've been doing. Have fun. *Enjoy* it!' he said, trying to loosen her up for the event. He could tell how tense she was and didn't want it to affect her skiing. And on their second night there, at a restaurant where Lily was having dinner with her father, she ran into Veronica. She seemed very full of herself, after winning a bronze medal in the Olympics the week before. She gushed when she saw Lily, and Lily was visibly annoyed after she walked away. She was wearing the jacket that Lily had been wearing a year before, and Lily was wearing the red and blue uniform jacket of the Paralympics, and proud of it. It had been designed by Ralph Lauren for the games.

It was a tense time for everyone competing, and Aspen was crammed with people who had come from around the world to see the games. There were film crews everywhere, and Lily had had requests for interviews, and all she wanted to do was train and practice before her big race. She had been working hard for this for five months, at the state athletic training program at Winter Park, and six years before that.

Carole and Joe came up from Denver together and

were staying at the same hotel, near the house Bill had rented, and they had dinner with Bill and Lily, and the following day Jessie arrived with her oldest son, and stayed at the same hotel too. Jessie introduced Chris to Lily, and they hit it off right away and talked about school, music, skiing, and he said he was on the ski team at DU, and was impressed by her Olympic history and the schools Lily had applied to. She was obviously a smart girl, but not stuck up like a lot of the girls he knew and had met at school.

'Do you want to ski tomorrow?' Lily asked him casually, and he was interested to see how she did it, and agreed to go with her, before she started working with Oscar at noon. Her coach was all in favor of taking a morning off, and thought it might do her good so she could relax.

The next morning Chris came to pick her up at the house, and went to the locker with her where she kept her ski and poles. He watched with interest as she put the monoski on, fitted it with the chair, and rolled her wheelchair into the locker, and she took off with ease once he had his boots and skis on. He was a good skier, but had to work to keep up with her, and they went up the ski lift together, chatting easily, while he asked her about the Paralympics. His mother had been telling him about it, and Lily told him about Teddy playing rugby.

'Do you miss Squaw Valley?' Lily asked him amiably

on the chairlift. He was good-looking, and she liked talking to him, and he didn't seem to care that she was in a wheelchair. He thought she was beautiful, and he was intrigued to ski with her and see how she managed on the monoski with the small seat.

'I miss Squaw sometimes,' he said easily. 'But I'm having fun in Denver.' He had been on the skiing team in Squaw too, but he said he hadn't been good enough for the Olympics, unlike her.

He gave her a hand off the chairlift when they got to the top, and she moved into position with ease, as he got ready next to her. They took off, slowly at first, and then at full speed. He was a perfect match for her, and they skied easily side by side. She raced with him for a while, and then they eased off and relaxed. She was an exquisite skier, and he was impressed as he watched her handle the monoski and her poles and race down the mountain with him. She skied faster than he did but gave him a break here and there, and they both looked exhilarated when they got to the base, and went up the lift again.

'Wow! You are some skier!' he complimented her, and she smiled and adjusted her helmet, and he shared a candy bar with her, and then they took off again. They got three good runs in before she had to leave him and meet Oscar, and Chris looked as though he had seen nirvana when he met up with his mother and Bill.

'How was it?' Jessie asked him. 'Did you have fun?'

347

'She is an incredible skier!' he said to both of them, and her father agreed.

Lily stopped at one-thirty, met them for lunch, and then went up with Oscar again, and she invited Chris to join them, and Oscar was pleased. Chris was just what she needed to distract her from her intensity and anxiety about the race. And by the time Phil and Teddy came to Aspen the next day, she was in a great mood. The three young people had a good time together, and then they joined forces with Walker and his group late that afternoon, and suddenly the house Bill had rented was filled with Lily's friends, and then some of the Paralympic competitors Lily had met came too, and the place was a zoo of music, food, voices, and laughing, talking kids everywhere.

'I feel like I'm running a school!' Bill commented to Jessie, with a grin. He could hardly get to his own room.

'Get used to it,' Jessie said to him. 'You will be soon.' He laughed at what she said.

They all went to the opening ceremony that night, and it was deeply moving, as all the competitors entered, and at the end the Paralympic flame was lit. The games had officially begun.

They managed to have a quiet dinner with Carole and Joe afterward. It was the night before Lily's event. The young people were happy on their own, and Lily had to get to bed early. And after dinner, Joe, Carole, Bill, and

Jessie took a walk around Aspen. The two men walked together, and Carole and Jessie looked in the shop windows at jewelry and furs and all the high-priced temptations of Aspen.

'I've got something to tell you,' Carole said with a mischievous look as they stopped in front of one of the shop windows. Jessie wondered if she had changed her mind about dating Joe. He looked enchanted every time he saw her, and Carole seemed to be comfortable with him, although she seemed determined so far to treat him as a colleague and friend. 'I'm considering leaving Boston. I've gotten so involved in The Lily Pad, I want to move to Denver, and take the job out here. Maybe I'm nuts to leave Mass General, but it just feels right to me now. What do you think?' Jessie's face exploded into a smile.

'Hallelujah! Are you kidding? I'd love it! Have you told Bill?'

'No, I told Joe I was thinking about it today. I'm debating about giving notice when I go back. I want to give them a month. If I do, I could move here in April. And I like Denver. It's a nice city, and with you moving here, and Bill and Joe, I have friends here. It's a start. Maybe I need a new beginning.' She looked pensive as she said it. It was a big decision for her. Huge.

'Don't we all,' Jessie said with a serious expression. 'That's the best news I've heard all year. I hope you do it.'

'I'm pretty sure I will. I've been mulling it over seriously since Thanksgiving.'

'Does Joe have anything to do with the decision?' Jessie asked cautiously, but Carole shook her head.

'At least not yet,' she said honestly. 'He's very sweet to me, and he's been calling me in Boston. But he hasn't been pressuring me about the job or anything else. I just like it here. And so much bad stuff happened to me in Boston. I'd rather be here, helping to get The Lily Pad off the ground.'

'So would I,' Jessie said. 'I can't wait till June. I'm going to tell the kids when I go home. I figure that gives them enough time to get used to the idea.' The months since she'd made the decision in September had already flown, and she was coming to Denver a lot. Bill was paying her for the consulting, and he was starting her on the payroll as medical director in June. But her finances were already greatly improved from the consulting, and so were Carole's. It had already changed both their lives. 'Well, welcome to the team,' she said, giving Carole a hug. It sounded like it was a sure thing she was moving to Denver, and it would make it more fun for Jessie too. And the two women had become closer than ever since working on The Lily Pad together.

'What are you two ladies talking about?' Joe asked, as he and Bill joined them. Joe gave Carole a warm look, and she smiled.

'Work,' they both said at the same time.

'Don't you two ever think about anything else?' he scolded them, and they laughed. They were hard workers and smart women, and both brilliant in their fields, and he admired them a great deal.

They went back to Bill's rented house after that, and the young people cleared out. Many of them were competing in events the next day, or training before their races. Teddy was staying in a hotel with Phil, and they all had lodgings close by. Chris was just leaving when Bill got home from dinner. He seemed reluctant to leave Lily, as Bill went to his room. They seemed to have a lot to say.

'Good luck tomorrow,' Chris said to Lily with a warm look in his eyes, and then he leaned down and kissed her cheek. She was still smiling when he left.

'I'd say you have an admirer,' her father commented later, when he saw her in the kitchen. Lily was excited about her race the next day, and Bill poured them each a glass of milk before bed.

'I like him. He's nice,' she said shyly. He was the first boy who had shown a romantic interest in her since she got hurt. Jessie had been right apparently – there were boys out there who would like her and maybe even want to date her, even though she was in a wheelchair. It was exciting to think about.

She lay in bed that night, thinking about the race the next day and hoping she did well. It was hard to sleep, and she was up at dawn. Her Alpine race was going to be the second event of the day, after Nordic, which was cross-country. Teddy's chair rugby demonstration was scheduled for the second day. It would give spectators an opportunity to see a sample of the events at the summer games.

'Ready?' her father asked her, as they left the house together, and she nodded. She looked scared, and he tried to give her confidence as they went to meet Oscar. They had to get to where the ski team was meeting, and she had to join the other members of her team. There were competitors from all over the country and around the world, and when they talked about her officially, they always said that she had been scheduled for this year's Olympics and favored to win, and had won bronze in the Junior Olympics four years before. Both were a big deal, but so was this, and it was serious competition. The entrants were just as intense about it as competitors in the Olympics and trained just as hard.

They all took the chairlift up the mountain, and as she waited with her team, Lily wondered if she was ready. She didn't want to make a fool of herself or her team. Their coach spoke to them all before they started, and she got in the lineup with her number on her back. She was number nineteen. And she knew that her father and Jessie, Chris, Carole and Joe, and Teddy and Phil were all waiting for her at the finish line at the end of the run. Walker was there with a huge crowd, and had promised to cheer and hoot loudly when she came down. She was so nervous she could hardly think, and Oscar was hovering as close as they would let him.

She watched the first racers take off, and was impressed with their style and their speed. Several of them had competed before, and the previous gold winner was in this race too. Her injury was slightly less acute than Lily's, and she could walk with braces when she wasn't on skis, but it made no difference once they were skiing. And then suddenly it was her turn, and with a silent prayer she took off and just concentrated on the mountain and what she was doing. The time flew, and before she knew it, she was at the base. She was exhilarated and out of breath, and she saw Teddy and the others beaming at her. She went over to Teddy as soon as she could, to wait for her results, and her father came to praise her for how well she'd done. His eyes were shining with pride. And Chris gave her a thumbs-up.

'How did I do?' she asked Teddy breathlessly as she took off her goggles.

'You looked like a bat out of hell to me.' He beamed at her.

They announced her speed minutes later, and her timing had been good, not as good as the previous champion, but very close. Her coach had come down the mountain, and he was thrilled with her numbers and her speed.

'We're going to win the silver,' he said in his heavy accent, with tears in his eyes. 'You watch.' But nothing was sure until all the others did their runs. And at the end of the event, they would announce the winners. It was an interminable wait as she listened to each one's score. But Lily was still up there, as they announced each one, and then they gave the final results. Lily had come in second. She had won the silver medal, and suddenly she was sitting in her chair ski as they put the ribbon with the medal around her neck, and the anthem was playing, and she was crying, and when she looked over, so were her father and Oscar, and they were hugging, and then everyone she knew came over to kiss her and congratulate her when the medal ceremony was over. It was even better than winning the bronze in the Junior Olympics. This was one of the greatest moments of her life. Walker grabbed her and picked her up right off the ground with her ski dangling while she laughed. She leaned over to kiss Teddy when he sat her down, and Chris put an arm around her and looked into her eyes with a wide smile.

'I was really proud of you!' he said with a voice full of emotion, and there were tears running down Jessie's cheeks. A year before in the hospital at Squaw, she had never expected to see this, nor had Bill or Lily.

They stayed for the rest of the races and then went back to Bill and Lily's house to celebrate. She had to join her teammates for dinner that night, but she stayed at the house while her father poured champagne for everyone, and Chris stood very near her. It had been the most incredible day of her life. The gold medal winner had congratulated her. She was nine years older than Lily and had been doing this for eight years. She told Lily she was sure she would win gold one day too.

It was a long, exciting night full of congratulations and celebration. The next day they all went to watch Teddy play chair rugby, and Lily had her heart in her mouth watching him, as she always did. It was so aggressive and so violent, she was constantly afraid he'd get hurt. But he scored a goal and his team won, and everyone was impressed by what they did, and Teddy had a great time. They all did. And ESPN interviewed Teddy after the game.

It was a magical moment and Lily couldn't wait to compete again in four years. It made her even more deter-mined to start a sports program at The Lily Pad, where they would have competitions with medals once a year. It gave everyone something to strive for, and four years was too long to wait. They all stayed for the full ten days of the games in Aspen and went to many of the events. And Lily had a ball with her team. The closing ceremony was deeply moving. Lily was wearing her silver medal, and she knew it was something she would never forget. And after it was over, she thanked Phil for everything he'd done.

The day after the closing ceremony, they all went

home. Chris told her he'd call her in Denver. He wanted to go skiing with her again, and suggested they go out to dinner.

'That would be fun,' Lily said, smiling at him, as he left for Denver with his mother. And Jessie stopped to talk to Carole for a minute before they left.

'Have you decided?' Jessie whispered.

'I'm in. I'll give notice when I go back.' Jessie smiled broadly, hugged her, and gave her a thumbs-up, and then she rushed off to drive Chris back to DU. She had been watching him with Lily, and she could see a romance blossoming between them, and she was extremely pleased. She couldn't think of anything better, for either of them. And she was thrilled that Carole was moving to Denver. Now she would have a good friend there when she moved herself. And best of all, Lily had won the medal she had worked so hard for.

Lily was wearing her medal around her neck, as she slept in her father's car all the way back to Denver. He looked over at her and smiled. He had never been happier in his life.

Chapter 24

On a Saturday morning in March, after she was back from Aspen, Jessie screwed up her courage, sat down to breakfast with her children, and told them her decision. She had been dreading it all week, but she knew she was doing the right thing.

'We're *what?*' Adam looked at her in amazement.

'We're moving to Denver,' Jessie said calmly, trying not to feel guilty at the look on his face. 'I took the job as medical director of the new rehab facility there. It's a very good job. We will live in a beautiful house that goes with it, and I hope we'll all be happy there.' She waited for the storm to hit, and predictably, it did.

'Don't you care what we think or how we feel? I have friends here! We all do!' Adam shouted at her. He had just turned twelve. He played soccer and Little League and was on a ski team.

'Of course I care how you feel. But you can do all the

things you do here, in Denver. You can ski, do Little League, all of it. And there is a very good school for you and Jimmy.' Jimmy was sitting at the table, looking shell-shocked, and worst of all, Heather was sitting in total silence with tears rolling down her cheeks.

'How can you make me move for senior year? How can you be so mean?' Heather asked with a horrified expression. Jessie felt like a monster. It was the reaction she had expected and was dreading. And she didn't totally disagree with her, and still felt guilty about it.

'I know, baby, it's hard. But it's a great job, and we'll be able to do a lot more things than we can now. It's hard for me without Daddy to help.' She said it as gently as she could, and Adam looked outraged.

'Then get a better job here. Dad would never have made us do this.'

'Probably not,' she said honestly. 'But I think it's a good decision, and we'll be able to see more of Chris, since he's in Denver too.'

'I want to stay in California to go to college,' Heather said miserably.

'You can come back here for college. And I'm not going to sell our house. I'm going to rent it. So we can always move back here if we want to.'

'If *you* let us,' Adam said, giving her an evil look. He was just adolescent enough to hate her. And Heather was in the depths of despair. She jumped up from the table then, ran to her room, and slammed the door. Adam did the same a minute later, and Jimmy sat at the table, looking confused, and he reached out and patted his mother's hand.

'They'll get over it, Mom,' he said kindly, and she put her arms around him.

'Why aren't you mad too?' He was the angel in her life.

'Because everybody can't be mad at you. That wouldn't be fair.' He was always the sweet spot in the group.

'Thank you for being so nice about it. I think you're really going to like the school and the new house, and we'll come back here to visit,' she reassured him. He nodded and then went up to his room too. It killed her to see how sad he looked going up the stairs.

Heather as good as declared war on her that day, and from then on. For the next month Jessie got the cold shoulder from Heather, was insulted by Adam, and Jimmy just looked despondent. She felt like the worst mother in the world. And she called Carole to whine about it. Carole had already found an apartment she loved in Denver, and her attitude was great. She was packing up in Boston, and excited about the move. And she insisted that she and Joe were just friends when Jessie asked again. But for now Jessie was more concerned about her kids than Carole's move.

'My kids are going to kill me, literally or figuratively.

Heather hates me, Adam is pissed, and Jimmy looks depressed.'

'They'll be fine when you get to Denver,' Carole said confidently. 'I saw Chris the other night, by the way.'

'You did? Where? Was he playing hooky?'

'No, he was having dinner. At Bill's. With Lily. I think he likes her.'

'I think he does too.' Jessie smiled. When she told him about the move, he was shocked, but less upset than the others, as long as she wasn't selling the house.

'They went to the movies afterward. And Bill says he's been over several times. He took Lily on a date.'

'Well, that's one piece of good news. I approve. She's the nicest kid in the world. She's got every reason to be a spoiled brat, and she isn't. She's a great girl.' Jessie hadn't seen her since she won her medal, and she was due to go back to Denver very soon, once her kids settled down. 'What am I going to do with this bunch, other than shoot myself or change my mind?' She was discouraged by how distressed they were about the move.

'You'd be wrong to change your mind. Just hang in. They'll get over it. Give them time,' Carole encouraged her.

'Wonderful, you try living with them. Heather says she won't go. She stays at her best friend's house almost every night and says she wants to move in with them and go to school here next year. I can't let her do that.' Jessie sounded stressed at the idea.

'She won't do it,' Carole reassured her. 'She just has to express herself. Better that than hidden aggression. She wants to punish you.'

'Well, she is. Actually, I'd like hidden aggression a lot better – hers is a little too overt.' Jessie sighed, and Carole assured her that Heather would relent eventually, but the war continued week after week. If anything, Heather got angrier and more hostile with her mother. Even though Jessie had expected it, it was painful to live with.

When Jessie went to Denver two weeks later, Carole proudly showed her her new apartment. She loved it. And all Jessie could talk or think about were her battles with Heather.

When she went to see Bill, she discovered that all was not smooth sailing between him and Lily either. It was the spring of the young people's discontent. Bill had said that he was having a problem with her. Jessie hoped it wasn't Chris, and that he didn't object to his seeing Lily. But she was eighteen, and a very sensible girl. And her son was a good boy and wouldn't do anything to hurt her. Before her father got home, Lily came downstairs and asked for Jessie's help.

'I can't reason with my dad,' she said as she pulled up to the kitchen table with a look of despair, while Jessie wondered if Heather said the same thing to her best friend's mother. Jessie had talked to Lily and Lily was sympathetic about Heather's fury about the move. She said Heather would get over it, but Jessie was beginning to wonder if that was true. 'I'm still waiting to hear from all the colleges I applied to, and Dad says he won't let me go away,' Lily explained to Jessie with intense frustration.

'Why not?' He had said as much to Jessie, but she wanted to hear what he was saying to Lily.

'I don't know. He's ridiculous. Something about he doesn't want me to get hurt. It makes no sense. Why would I get hurt going to school?' They both knew how protective he was, and he wasn't ready to let his little girl go away, particularly in a wheelchair.

'Did he always say that?' Jessie asked carefully.

'He never really liked the idea before, but he would have let me. He had no excuse not to. Now he won't, because of my SCI. It's such bullshit.' Jessie could tell how worried and angry Lily was. They had been arguing about it for months. 'I've got good grades and scores. What's the point if he won't let me go to a decent school?'

'And you don't want to stay home?' Jessie wanted to be sure.

'No, I want to go away to school. Jessie, will you talk to him, and try to get him to be reasonable?' She looked at her with pleading eyes.

'I'll try, but he's a pretty stubborn man, especially about you. My kids aren't too happy with me these days either,' she volunteered, and Lily looked sorry for her. She liked Jessie a lot, and thought her kids were lucky to have her. Chris said nothing but good things about her. He loved his mom a lot. 'Except for Chris, they're all furious with me about the move. Well, Jimmy isn't, but he's looked heartbroken since I told them,' which almost seemed worse to her.

'Heather hates me at the moment. She thinks I'm ruining her life.'

'Yeah,' Lily nodded sympathetically, 'moving away for senior year would be tough. But Denver is pretty cool. She'll like it here. It's too bad we won't be in school at the same time.' She looked unhappy again, then, 'I hope I'll be away, in college back east. Will you talk to my dad?'

'I'll try.'

And she did that afternoon. Bill was adamant about it. He felt that Lily had been through enough. She was too vulnerable on a campus in a wheelchair with drunk boys all over the place, and he wanted her at home. He wanted her to go to DU.

'She didn't even apply there,' Jessie said sensibly. 'She's going to lose the year entirely if she doesn't go to one of the schools she applied to,' all of which were in the east.

'Then she can go to City College or take a year off. I am not letting her go east.' He looked determined when he said it, and Jessie remembered that look of the fierce protector from Squaw a year before.

'Bill,' Jessie said quietly, 'you've done everything possible to integrate her back into the world. You sent her back to her school – you didn't have her tutored at home. You sent her to Craig to learn all those skills so she could go out in the world and go away to school. And you let her compete in the Paralympics, and let's face it, downhill racing is a dangerous sport, for anyone. And you won't let her go away to college? What are you afraid of, really?'

'That she'll never come back,' he said with sad eyes. 'I lost her mother. I don't want to lose her. What if she moves to Boston or New York?' Jessie smiled at what he said.

'Look at what you've given her, and done for her. Look at this house, the life she has here, the rehab center you're starting that she's excited about. The skiing she does here. Do you really think she won't come back? Trust me, she will. She just wants to try her wings a little, and get a good education. You can't blame her for that. And besides, she loves you. She'll come home.'

'I never went back after I went to college,' he said somberly.

'This isn't a coal mine. And she adores you. She'll come back like a homing pigeon after college, and every chance she gets.'

'I wish she'd just stay here,' he said unhappily.

'You're better off letting her go, then she'll want to

come back. This way she may really rebel,' Jessie warned him. She was afraid of it with Heather too.

'I don't know. How are you doing with yours?'

'They hate me,' she said matter-of-factly. 'Well, no, Jimmy doesn't, but the other two think I'm public enemy number one. It's not a lot of fun.'

'Lily is pissed at me too,' he said with a sigh. 'Besides, I'd miss her so damned much. She's my whole life,' he admitted mournfully, but Jessie already knew that about him.

'No, she isn't. You have The Lily Pad now to keep you busy, and friends, and work, and you're not going to lose her. She loves you too much to stay away for long. You're her hero,' Jessie reassured him.

'Not at the moment,' he said with a wry smile.

'Why don't you see where she gets accepted, and decide how you feel about it then? But try to keep an open mind.' He nodded, and she knew she had done the best she could for Lily, but Bill wasn't an easy man to convince, and he was terrified to lose his daughter.

Jessie had dinner with Carole that evening, at her new apartment. It was a nice girls' evening, which they hadn't had in a long time. Jessie brought up the subject of Joe again, and Carole was still firm in her decision about not dating, but she sounded as though she had softened a little.

'You don't know what it's like to be so different. I feel

disfigured,' she said quietly, referring to the mastectomy. 'I don't feel like a woman anymore.' Jessie knew that was the crux of it for her.

'If he loves you, he won't care.'

'I don't want to go through a bunch of painful surgeries for a guy.'

'You don't have to. There have to be ways around it – sexy nightgowns, wear a bra with your prosthetics. You don't have to pose for the centerfold of *Playboy*. Look at Lily, it's about finding new ways to do old things and not letting an injury ruin your life. Lily has set one hell of an example for all of us. There has to be an easier solution than reconstructive surgery if you like the guy, and I'm beginning to think you do.'

'Maybe I do,' she conceded cautiously, 'but I also don't want to get hurt again. I got pretty badly burned by Dylan.'

'That's a chance we all have to take. Even if you find a great one, he could die.' They both thought of Tim as she said it, and Jessie's eyes were sad.

'What about you?' Carole asked her. Tim had been gone for fourteen months and the last thing Jessie wanted was another man. All she wanted was peace with her daughter. That was hard enough to achieve at the moment and her main concern.

'It's too soon,' Jessie said simply. 'Tim is a tough act to follow. He was the best.'

'You can't win. Either they're shits and you're afraid the next one will be too, or they're fabulous and no one else will ever measure up,' Carole said ruefully, and Jessie laughed.

'That pretty much sums it up.'

'What about Bill? He's a good man, and I never see him with any woman.'

'He doesn't want one. He's got Lily. And we're friends. I like it like that, and now he's my boss. That's too complicated for me.' Carole agreed. And Jessie clearly had no interest in Bill or anyone else. She was still sleeping in Tim's pajamas and hadn't packed up his clothes. She was starting to face the fact that it would be a good time to do it when she moved. She wasn't going to send his wardrobe to Denver. It was time to let go, at least of his clothes.

Jessie didn't see Lily again before she left, but she texted her that she had talked to her dad but couldn't guarantee the results.

Three weeks later she got an ecstatic call from Lily. She had gotten into Brown, Princeton, and NYU. She had the choice of three great schools, all on the East Coast. 'My dad is having a fit,' she reported to Jessie.

'Where do you want to go?' Jessie asked her.

'Princeton. Hands down.'

'What if you take a trip there with him and look around? Maybe he'll feel better.' It was the only thing Jessie could think of to suggest.

'He went there with me on my college tour before I got hurt. He thought it was fine then. Now he doesn't. And they even have handicapped services on campus. I checked. What now?'

'I don't know. Try to talk to him and tell him how much it means to you.'

Lily talked to Carole about it too, and she said to give him time. But she had two weeks to accept or decline, and Bill hadn't budged an inch. And she didn't want to accept a place at college without his permission. He had to pay for it, after all. And what if he wouldn't?

And then Teddy got the news that he had gotten into DU. He called his parents about it, and they were shocked that he had applied to college. And they were so relieved that he wasn't asking to come home, or them to come out, that they said he could go. He had been accepted in the fine arts program, which was what he had wanted. And he said he was going to try for a master's after that. He had big dreams. Craig had fostered that in him. And so had Phil and Lily.

Lily took him out to dinner that night to celebrate, and told him her woes about her father.

'Now you're going to college,' she said mournfully, 'and it looks like I won't.'

'He'll give in,' Teddy predicted. 'If not, you can come to DU with me.'

'That's what he wants. He wants me to be a baby forever.' She looked unhappy as she said it, and she took Teddy back to Craig after dinner. 'Did you ask your parents about moving to The Lily Pad?' she asked when she dropped him off.

'That's my next call. I figured one thing at a time. They consider me this vegetable they left out here, who can't function on his own. They were totally shocked when I said I wanted to go to college. They think of me as Stephen Hawking, without the brain.' It hurt her to hear him say it, but it seemed to be true. They had no idea who he was, or what he was capable of, nor what his dreams were, and didn't seem to care. She thought they were cowardly, selfish people. Teddy deserved so much more.

'They'd really freak out if they knew you play rugby,' she said, laughing. 'Vegetables don't play rugby. You kick ass out there,' she added, and he laughed too.

'Yeah, I do, don't I,' he said proudly. Lily got out of the van then, and the attendant took Teddy into the building, and Lily went to get her car and drive home.

Her father was waiting up for her when she got there, and he walked into her bedroom as she got into bed. He had just watched a DVD of her winning the silver medal in Aspen, and he had been proud of her all over again.

'You'd better get to work on that sports program you told me you'd set up for us at The Lily Pad,' he said gruffly.

'Why now? I was going to start this summer after I graduate.'

'You may not have time.'

'Why not?' She looked confused.

'Because you won't be here after the summer, if you're going to Princeton.'

She looked at him carefully, as their eyes met. 'Am I?'

'I guess you are,' he said with a sad smile. 'I watched you tonight in that Alpine race that won you the silver medal. You've got wings, Lily. It's time for you to fly.'

She threw her arms around his neck then and hugged him, with her eyes closed, as he fought a lump in his throat. 'Thank you, Daddy . . . thank you . . . I promise I'll make you proud of me.'

'You don't have to,' he said with tears in his eyes. 'You already did.'

Chapter 25

'And don't forget Jimmy's backpack!' Jessie shouted to
Heather up the stairs, and then looked around the living
room in Squaw for a last time. All of the furniture was
already gone. It had left for Denver two weeks before and
was arriving in two days. The only thing left were their
beds and a few cartons from the kitchen. She had
stripped the beds that morning, she had used ancient
sheets that she had just thrown away, and the beds were
being picked up and donated to Goodwill. Ben had
promised to come by when they picked them up. And she
had bought new beds for them in Denver that were
already there, in their rooms. Their bags were packed and
waiting in the front hall. She had sold her car to Kazuko.
She had just bought a new one in Denver, thanks to Bill,
and the generous salary he was paying her as medical
director.

The shuttle to take them to Reno was due any minute,

as the kids trooped down the stairs carrying their bags for the plane. Heather had Jimmy's backpack, and he was carrying the stuffed dog he slept with. They acted like they were leaving the *Titanic* with all their treasures. And Heather hadn't spoken to her mother in two weeks. So far nothing about the move had been easy, except the house waiting for them there and her job. But she could understand how they were feeling. Even to her, leaving this house felt like losing Tim all over again. It had been so interwoven with him, and he had loved their place so much. The people who had rented it were moving in on the first of July, and it was strange and sad to think of strangers living in their home. She hoped they'd be happy there. She and her children had been, until Tim's death.

The only thing that cheered her as she looked at their faces was knowing how much they would love the new house. She had tried to tell them about it, but they didn't want to hear. They would just have to see it now to understand. It was much nicer than the one in Squaw. And everything was beautiful and clean and fresh. A whole new world.

They were silent on the ride to the airport, and when they got there, Heather bought magazines, and she was texting frantically all the way to the plane. Right up to the day before they left, she had threatened not to come. And Jessie had been seriously afraid she would refuse to, but she didn't. In the end, she packed her suitcases, although she had cried for the last week, with each goodbye.

Adam was listening to his iPod, and Jimmy was holding his mother's hand. And they were all going to watch movies on the plane. All Jessie wanted to do was sleep – it had been an exhausting few weeks, and emotionally draining.

Jessie had sold her practice to Ben and already filed for her Colorado medical license. After she got it, she would talk to some neurosurgeons in Denver about joining their practice part time. But for now she wanted to concentrate on The Lily Pad. She had a huge amount of work to do before their 'soft' opening in August. They were going to open the largest house first, and wait six months to open the other, as they continued to hire staff and add programs. They were planning to roll out their full range of services over the next six to nine months. Bill was in his office there now every day, and she would be too. And Joe and Carole had had offices there since March. Phil Lewis was starting as the head of their physical therapy department on the first of July. And the full medical staff had been hired. It was all coming together now at full speed. What Jessie needed to do now was settle her kids. And she had hired a housekeeper to be there full time to drive them around, and cook dinner for all of them. On the salary Bill was paying her, she could afford to do that.

And all she had to pay at the house were utilities. And Ben had paid her fairly for her half of the practice. Her finances were finally in good shape, for the first time in a year and a half.

The flight to Denver was uneventful, other than the dark looks Heather gave her. Bill had sent a van and driver for them when they arrived. While pretending not to, the kids looked around with interest as they drove into town. Chris had promised to come to dinner that night. He had just started a summer job in a law office. Bill had helped him get the job. He was mostly filing and pouring coffee, but it was good experience for him, and he was thinking about law school. His first year at DU had gone well.

'When are we going to get there, Mom?' Jimmy asked, clutching his stuffed dog, and looking at Jessie.

'Soon.' They were all tired from the trip. And then Jessie saw the house, and the van pulled into the driveway. All three children seemed surprised.

'Whose house is that?' Adam asked with suspicion. 'Bill's?' It looked fancy to him.

'No, ours,' Jessie said as she got out, and helped Jimmy down from the van.

They walked up to the front door, and Heather brought up the rear. Jessie unlocked it, and they all stopped in the front hall, and noticed the large living room with the fireplace. And then they peeked into the dining room and the kitchen. It was all as pretty as Jessie remembered, and they were impressed.

'Wow, this is nice,' Jimmy said, and Adam looked like he agreed. Heather didn't say a word and pretended not to notice.

'Your bedrooms are upstairs. You can pick the ones you want. There are three on my floor, and one on the top floor.' She thought the one on top would be best for Chris, it was big and airy and had more privacy, but if Heather insisted on it, she would give it to her, to make peace. Chris was planning to move in when their furniture came, since he had to move out of his dorm room that week. Their timing had been perfect, and carefully orchestrated by Bill and Jessie, to fit their needs. Their kids had just finished school, and Lily was graduating in a week, so Jessie would be able to be there.

She wandered around her bedroom floor then, glancing into the other bedrooms, and saw Heather lying on one of the new beds with a look of ecstasy. She had gotten them all king-size beds, which they hadn't had before. The boys had had bunk beds in their old rooms, and Heather had had twins, which had been fine when they were small. The minute Heather glimpsed her mother through the open doorway, she got up with a scowl and disappeared into her bathroom. But the instant of happiness Jessie had seen seemed hopeful.

Jessie was amazed at how quickly they each selected a

room. Heather took the largest one, next to hers. Adam found one he liked better, and Jimmy liked a smaller, cozier room because, he said, it reminded him of his old room. And Chris got the top floor, which she had thought would work best for him. None of the younger ones wanted to walk up an extra floor. They checked out both family rooms then, and ran up and down the stairs, exploring every floor. Jessie sat down on her own bed, and looked out the window at the peaceful view, feeling lucky again to have such a beautiful house. She was lying there, thinking about it, as Heather walked into her room with a serious expression.

'I hate that you made us move here, but the house is nice, Mom,' she conceded. Jessie looked at her and smiled. For Heather, it was a big admission. 'I still want to go back to Squaw,' she said sadly.

'I'm glad you like it. You can go back to visit.' Heather shrugged then and disappeared back to her own room without further comment. Adam showed up a few minutes later with a puzzled look on his face.

'Why did he give us such a fancy house?' he asked his mother, as though there were something suspicious about it.

'It goes with the job. Anyone who took the job as medical director would get it. He wanted someone good to move here. It's called an incentive,' she said, and he nodded.

'Heather is taking pictures of her bathroom,' he added, which sounded like good news to Jessie. It was white marble, with a large oval tub and a huge shower. Jessie's bathroom was even bigger.

They were still looking around and settling in when a car pulled up behind hers in the driveway, and Jessie saw Bill and Lily get out. She heard the doorbell ring and went to let them in, and she saw that Lily was holding a huge basket of food and snacks for them on her lap, and Bill was carrying two bags of groceries and some wine.

They all came downstairs to meet the visitors, although Jessie was embarrassed by Heather's sullen expression.

She introduced her children to Bill and Lily, and they all went into the kitchen, and Bill put the basket on the island in the middle, and the groceries on the counter. The boys were chatting with Lily, and she offered Heather a tour of the school the next day, which, much to Jessie's delight, Heather accepted, even if grudgingly, but Lily didn't seem to mind. She could see that Heather was upset.

Jessie looked past them at Bill then, who was watching the interaction and gave her a discreet thumbs-up, and she grinned and nodded. It was going well, and they loved the house, even Heather, although she hated to admit it.

And ten minutes later, Chris showed up, and looked

happy to see Lily, which was an unexpected treat for him.

'Come on, Chris, I'll show you your room,' Jimmy said, pulling on his brother's arm. 'It's on the top floor.' That made it difficult for Lily, unless Chris carried her. In the end, Chris did exactly that, swept Lily up in his arms, and carried her upstairs, as Jimmy followed.

'Welcome home,' Bill said to Jessie after they left, and she smiled at him.

'Thank you for the gorgeous house. I think my kids have almost forgiven me. The boys anyway. And Heather is getting there. She loves her room.'

'Wait till your furniture comes – it will really look like home to them then.'

'Yes, it will,' she said, leaning against the kitchen counter. 'How are things at The Lily Pad?'

'Booming along. It's a beehive over there now. We're almost ready. All we need are patients.'

'They'll come,' she said peacefully. 'I'm not worried.' And she knew that eventually they'd have patients from all over the country, just as at Craig.

Bill and Lily stayed for about an hour, and then they went home, and Jessie heard Chris tell her he'd stop by later. Bill suggested they all have dinner together the following night. He offered to do a barbecue, and Adam and Jimmy looked delighted. Chris said he would help, and Heather didn't object. They hadn't had a barbecue at home since their father died.

'Lily's cool,' Adam announced as he helped himself to some of the food from the basket, while Jimmy took Chris upstairs to check out his room at last. He'd been begging to show it to him since Chris arrived. The boys were definitely settling in and were already wondering if any of the neighbors had kids their age. Bill had said he didn't know but was sure there were some. The neighborhood was all families.

They ate the groceries for dinner that Bill and Lily had brought them, and after that they all went to their rooms, lay down on their big beds, and watched movies on their computers. Heather called all her friends and secretly told them how beautiful the house was. She had already invited two of them to come and visit in July and August, and they had promised to come. Things were looking up. And she was curious to see the school with Lily.

Jessie called Carole and told her things were going well with the kids. Heather was still angry, but it was obvious she liked the house and she had conceded that much to her mother. And Jessie knew her visit to the school would be a major factor.

The next day Lily picked Heather up and took her around her school, and showed her where everything was. She introduced her to some juniors who would be seniors with her in the fall, and to several cute boys. Heather was duly impressed and reported to her friends later how hot the boys were at her new school. And for the first time, she actually looked happy when she got home. Two of the girls had asked for her cell number, and if she was on Facebook, which Heather said she was.

And that night they went to the Thomases' for dinner. Bill barbecued chicken and steaks for everyone, and they sat down at a big picnic table outside, while Lily moved around them with ease, and made salad in the kitchen. Jimmy followed her and looked at their kitchen with fascination when he saw that everything was at the right height for Lily.

'Wow, you can reach everything!' He had never seen a kitchen like that before.

'Yes, I can. My daddy did that for me.' Lily smiled at him. He was as cute as Chris had told her.

'That's rad!' he said, and she laughed as Chris came to help her carry things outside.

'Is he bugging you?' Chris asked with concern about Jimmy, and she shook her head with a grin.

'No, we're friends. He likes our kitchen.'

They had fun at dinner, and the following day their furniture arrived from Squaw Valley, and Jessie spent the day organizing everything. It looked like home to all of them by that night. Her furniture fit perfectly, and the kids had everything they needed in their rooms. When Carole came by, they were almost settled, and she helped Jessie unpack the kitchen. It had gone remarkably smoothly.

'Looks like you're all set,' Carole said when they finished, and Jessie thanked her for the help.

When she left, Jessie realized that it was true. They had everything they needed. *Except Tim,* she thought to herself, and then she turned off the lights and went upstairs. And for the first time in seventeen months, she didn't put on his pajamas. She had brought them with her, but she folded them carefully and put them away in a drawer. It was enough now just knowing they were there. She didn't have to wear them anymore.

Chapter 26

The new housekeeper, Mary Sherman, arrived the day after the movers, and Jessie introduced her to the children and spent the morning with them until they got acquainted. Mary was in her forties, and had worked for two families Bill knew. She made a nice lunch, and offered to drive them to the park and take them to a movie, and as soon as they left, Jessie went to work. Real life had begun.

And Bill was right. The Lily Pad was a hive of activity, with everyone buzzing around, opening files, working on computers, putting away medical supplies and sports equipment. There were a thousand things being done by an army of people, and Jessie walked into her new office with a smile and a sigh of relief. She felt as at home here as she did in the new house. Everything felt fresh and new, people were excited, and they had two months until they opened. But it was all in good order.

Jessie got busy sending e-mails to neurosurgeons she knew around the country, telling them what they were doing, inviting them to visit, and asking them to send patients. Their roster of medical and rehab personnel was impressive. And the website they had put up was informative and inviting. Joe had done a great job with it. It turned out that he not only had a knack for overseeing construction and dealing with people, but he was a whiz with computers. The Lily Pad was giving him a chance to use his many talents. And Jessie was proud of everything they had done in the past year. The Lily Pad was already a spectacular place.

'How's it going?' Bill asked her when he wandered into her office at the end of the afternoon. He'd been working on some financial matters with Joe, and he was happy to see Jessie in the office next to him, and be able to talk to her and ask her advice anytime, not just on the phone or when she came to Denver for a weekend.

'I think everything's on track.' She smiled at him. She was totally at home and in her right place. 'I can't wait till we open. It will really be exciting when we have patients.'

'What if no one comes?' he said with a look of panic.

'That's not going to happen,' she reassured him. 'We have some great staff here, people with top experience. When physicians see our personnel roster and read their credentials, they'll know.'

'And you're here,' he said with relief. Every now and

then he still wondered if it would all work, but Jessie seemed so sure, and others had told him the same thing. This was a new world for him.

'They'd even come without me. I'm just window dressing.'

'Well, the window is looking mighty good, thanks to you,' he said gratefully as he sank into a chair. 'Everything go okay with the kids today?'

'Perfectly. They like Mary. They love the house. The boys are happy, and Heather will get there. Lily was terrific to take her to school. I think that really helped. She seems less anxious and angry. Life is good.' He looked pleased. 'I could never have done this, without you and the house.'

'And I couldn't have done it without you,' he said sincerely. The people she had recommended and helped him choose were first rate. 'Are you planning to take any time off this summer?' he asked her, and she shook her head.

'We're opening in August, remember? Maybe a long weekend with the kids, but that's about it. I was thinking of giving a Fourth of July barbecue, though. To celebrate our new home and the people we know here. I'll let you know if we get it together.'

'And Lily would like you all to come to her graduation next week. I'm very proud of her,' he said with a smile.

'So am I,' Jessie said softly. 'We'd love to come.'

It was a perfect event on a sunny day, and Bill gave a

luncheon in his garden afterward. Lily looked radiant in her cap and gown. It was a real victory for her. Bill and Jessie both cried when she got her diploma.

And when Jessie asked her kids about giving a Fourth of July party, they liked the idea. They wanted to meet people, so she had Heather create invitations on her computer, and handed them out over the next few weeks. It was basically going to be an old-fashioned picnic in their new backyard. And by the time the day came, fifty people showed up. Chris and Adam were making hamburgers and hot dogs, Heather and Jessie had made a vast array of salads, corn on the cob, french fries, and biscuits, and Jimmy helped set out the pies and desserts, and handed out ice cream bars from a big cooler, while people helped themselves to wine, beer, iced tea, and lemonade. It was exactly what she had promised, a traditional Fourth of July picnic. And when Chris finished cooking, he sat down with Lily to relax. She was drinking lemonade, and he poured himself a glass of iced tea.

'The hamburgers were great,' she complimented him as he took off his apron and grinned at her.

'My mom and dad used to love giving parties in Tahoe. It's kind of fun doing it again.' His father used to man the barbecue, and now it was up to him as the man of the family.

'My dad and I are going up to a lake tomorrow, to go fishing. Do you want to come?' Lily asked him shyly.

'Sure, I'd love it.' He looked pleased to be asked, and gently took her hand in his. 'I'm glad we moved here,' he said awkwardly. 'Now I can see you all the time.' Except she was going away to school. He could sense what she was thinking, and he had thought about it too. 'I'm going to miss you when you leave.'

'I'll come back a lot,' she promised. 'And at least you'll be here for holidays now. Maybe you could come to visit me in Princeton sometime,' she said cautiously.

'I'd like that,' he said quietly and put an arm around her, as she moved her chair closer to him. She didn't feel awkward in it anymore, or around people. She was completely at ease, and he was with her. It didn't bother him that she couldn't walk. He honestly didn't care, and she was a better skier than he was, even on her sitting ski. He was very proud of what she could do, and what she'd accomplished. And she was contributing time and effort to The Lily Pad. While they were talking about it, Teddy came over in his power chair. He had been chatting with all the guests and was the life of the party. He had sat down to eat with Carole and Joe, to discuss the art program he was designing that would be exciting for all ages. He had been at The Lily Pad every day, making lists of art supplies they'd need. They had hired two full-time art teachers, and they had two big rooms to work in. He was planning to work there after school and on weekends, to help out, as an internship for credit.

'What are you two up to?' Teddy asked them.

'We're just hanging out,' Lily answered easily. Teddy and Chris got on well, which was nice for her. She loved being with them, and Chris was perfectly at ease with Teddy. Jimmy came over a little while later, and snuggled up to his older brother. He had ice cream all over his chin, and Lily wiped his face and gave him a hug before he scampered off again to find his mother. The three of them sat together, while the party wound down, and eventually just the two families were left. It had been a perfect day.

'Do you guys want to come over and use the pool?' Bill asked as an afterthought. It was still hot at six o'clock. The Matthews kids looked thrilled at the suggestion, and they moved the rest of the group to Bill's house. Teddy had left by then, with his attendant from Craig. And once everyone was in the pool at Bill's playing water polo, Lily got into the pool, and chatted with Jessie. Her father was playing with the boys, and Heather joined in. She had looked happy all day. They were all having fun, and they foraged in the fridge later for dinner, and had a casual meal in the kitchen. It was a wonderful Fourth of July for all of them, and Lily hated to see them leave after dinner. Bill could see that she and Chris were growing increasingly attached to each other.

'I invited him to go fishing with us tomorrow, Dad, if that's okay with you,' she said easily.

'He's a nice kid, I like him. I get the feeling you do too,' he teased her gently, and she nodded with a grin. 'How's that going to work when you go away to school?' he asked her, hoping it might bring her home more often if they continued dating.

'I don't know. We'll see. We both have a lot to do. I guess I'll see him when I come home.' Bill nodded and still wished she weren't going away, but he had gotten used to the idea. Jessie had convinced him that letting Lily go away was the right thing to do, even if it was hard for him. It was healthy for her to want to.

The three of them had a good time together the next day at the lake. They caught several fish, and Bill cleaned them when they got home and cooked them for dinner. They were delicious, and afterward Chris took Lily to a movie. He stopped the car and kissed her a few blocks after they left her house.

'I've been wanting to do that all day,' he said hungrily, and she smiled at him.

'Me too.' They had wanted to be discreet around her father. They had been falling in love with each other for the past four months, and it was turning from a slow fire into a blaze. They were young and had everything to look forward to. And it felt like more than a summer romance to both of them. Jessie had noticed it too. And she and Bill talked about it on Monday at work.

'It looks like the noble houses of Thomas and

Matthews have a romance going,' Bill said as they ate lunch in Jessie's office, which was becoming a habit he enjoyed. He always had new things to report to her, and she kept him closely informed of what she was doing.

'I know,' she said, about Chris and Lily.

'Do you approve?' Bill asked her.

'Very much so,' she said, smiling at him. 'You?'

'He's a great boy, and he's wonderful to Lily. I just don't want either of them to get hurt or disappointed,' he said, looking concerned.

'If only that were possible,' she said with a bittersweet look. 'We can't protect them, or even ourselves. Life happens. We make the best of it, like you, or me, or Lily. That's all you can do.'

'Are you doing okay now, without Tim?' He usually didn't like to mention Tim and upset her, but she seemed to be better lately, and she didn't look as tired as she had when she was living in Squaw Valley. She seemed happier and relieved that her kids were adjusting, even Heather, who was looking forward to the visits of her friends from Squaw. She was still sad about moving to Denver, but she had had some good times since she'd been there and seemed less angry at her mother.

'It's easier here,' Jessie said quietly. 'I would never have had the courage to get out of that house. But it was the best thing for us. Ben told me that a long time ago. But I couldn't have done it at first, or even for a long time, till

I was ready. It's a whole new life here. I still have the memories, but I don't have to look at the bed he slept in every day. It's a relief.' She looked freer now, and less troubled. He had noticed it for the past few weeks. Carole walked into Jessie's office then, with some more counseling résumés to show her, and Joe was close behind her. They seemed to work together all the time now. They were always working on some project or other with each other. Bill and Jessie had both noticed it, but never commented on it, and this time he couldn't resist mentioning it to Jessie when they left.

'Do we have an office romance too?' he asked with an amused look, and Jessie glanced at him quizzically.

'She says not. It's a complicated issue. But it does seem that way, doesn't it?' There was something different about them, closer and more intimate, without words.

'It does to me too, but he hasn't said a word to me. But Joe is very private.' Bill knew him well.

'So is she. But she doesn't want to date anyone, after her divorce and everything else she went through.'

'Well, I think something's going on. Maybe it's my imagination,' Bill said, and went back to his office. They had other things to think about before they opened, but he would have been happy for his friend if he had found a woman who cared about him. And Carole was a good woman.

'Do you think they know?' Carole asked Joe when they

went back to his office to work on the opening party they were planning. She gave him a guilty look, and he laughed at her.

'Maybe. And what if they do?' It had started a few weeks before, in June, finally, right before Jessie moved to Denver, and they hadn't told anyone. Carole still couldn't believe she had gotten past all her own obstacles and objections, but little by little, over many months, Joe had swayed her, and she was glad he had. She had never felt as comfortable with anyone, and everything she had been so concerned about before seemed unimportant now. He accepted her just as she was, and she had fallen in love with him, after swearing she never would again. And even the difference in their ages didn't matter. They felt made for each other. 'We'll have to admit it sooner or later, you know,' he said gently, smiling at her across his desk. They found a thousand excuses to work together every day. They made a good team, at home and in the office. They were going back and forth to each other's apartments, and Carole insisted they come to work separately, so no one would figure it out in the office.

'I feel funny telling Bill and Jessie. She's still so lonely without Tim. I don't want to upset her by putting our happiness in her face.' Carole looked concerned.

'I think she'd be happy for us. We paid our dues, Carole,' he reminded her. 'Especially you.' He leaned over and kissed her. 'We deserve this.'

'Yes, we do,' she agreed, and they went back to work on the guest list for The Lily Pad's opening. But somehow, she just didn't have the heart to tell Jessie. So for now she and Joe were keeping their romance a secret, and in some ways it made it more exciting. She smiled to herself as she thought about it. It was fun being in love, at any age.

Chapter 27

The opening party Carole had planned for The Lily Pad was more elegant than anyone had expected. Local physicians were invited, and the upper echelons at Craig. She convinced Dr. Hammerfeld to come from Boston, and business associates of Bill's showed up. Ben Steinberg and Kazuko came from Squaw Valley. They had invited physical therapists and nurses. The head of Lily's school, Coach Oscar, and Steve Jansen, the architect, invited several friends. Teddy was there. Lily's friends included Walker and his girlfriend and Jessie's children. In the end, there were three hundred people milling around the grounds and admiring what they'd done, and enormously impressed by what they hoped to do. They were opening their doors in two weeks, and they had no patients yet, but they had an army of well-wishers and supporters. They all agreed the next day that the party was a big success, and Bill thanked Carole profusely.

'It was a joint effort,' she said modestly. 'Everyone worked on it. And Joe helped me organize it,' she said, looking at him with a warm smile. 'And we want to plan a fund-raising gala for next year.' It gave Bill the courage to finally ask Joe later that day when they were alone. It was none of his business, but Joe was one of his oldest friends, and he hoped he was happy. He seemed to be, and he lit up like a Christmas tree around Carole. It was impossible not to notice, and she looked radiant.

'Is something going on with you two?' Bill asked as they crossed the grounds to their respective offices.

Joe hesitated for a moment and then nodded. 'I'm in love with her. I have been since the day I met her. I didn't think she'd ever want me. It just shows you how life can turn around.' He looked at his friend seriously then. 'I never told you, but I had a loaded gun in my hand the night you called to tell me about Lily. I was going to kill myself that night. And then you told me about her accident, and I realized how self-indulgent and self-pitying I was being, and that you were dealing with something much more important. I put the gun away after we talked, and I got rid of it after that. I just thought my life was over and I was better off dead. And then I came out here to visit you, and you put together The Lily Pad, after my vague suggestion. I got involved in it, and it changed everything. And then Carole showed up and changed my life. I've never been happier than I am with her.'

Bill looked shaken by what Joe had told him. 'Why didn't you tell me things were that bad? Why didn't you call me?'

'It's just when we need it most that we don't reach out for help. And I look at what Carole went through, and I realize how insignificant my problems were, even if I thought they were monumental and worth ending my life over. They weren't. And thank God I didn't. Look at all the good things that have happened since you called me and I came out here. It's a whole new life.' It struck both of them that it took so little to either destroy a life or rebuild it. There was only a hair's difference between the two. And Bill was grateful that Joe had made the right choice. He shuddered to think what might have happened that night if he had called him five minutes later, or not called at all. Joe would have ended his life. And instead he had started over and was happy. 'I never expected something like this to come along at my age. And Carole says she didn't either, and she's twenty years younger. You just can't give up. Things can change at any moment, just like they did for me.' And then he looked at Bill pointedly. 'You should make an effort to get out there too one of these days. You can't stay alone forever. You're still young, and Lily will be off to her own life soon.'

'I know,' Bill said, and looked unhappy at the thought of it. 'I don't know what I'll do without her.'

'You'll keep busy here, but that's not enough. Work isn't everything. I learned that the hard way.'

'It's enough for me, as long as I have Lily,' Bill said seriously, and Joe knew he meant it. All he could wish for him in addition was the kind of happiness he had found with Carole. She was the perfect woman for him at this point in his life. She might not have been earlier, or he for her, for a variety of reasons, but she was perfect for him now. She was everything he wanted, just as he was for her. It was just the right match.

They went back to their offices then, and Bill was haunted by Joe's admission about the gun, and what he had almost done that night. And what a terrible waste it would have been. Bill didn't tell Jessie or anyone about it, but he was deeply moved by the story.

Their first patient came to them through a local neuro-surgeon, two days after their official opening in mid-August. Jessie got the call, about a little boy who had been in a car accident with his parents four weeks earlier. They had both been killed, and he had a T9 spinal cord injury, slightly worse than Lily's at T10. He was eight years old and was in the care of his grandmother. They got another call from a local surgeon two days later about a twelve-year-old girl who had fallen off a horse. Within a week they had five patients. And by the end of the month they had ten.

Bill looked at Jessie with amazement when he walked into her office. 'It really was a case of "If you build it, they will come," ' he said, smiling at her. 'They're coming.' And they got three more patients on Labor Day weekend. One of them was a fourteen-year-old boy who had had a diving accident in a pool. And then a surgeon in Los Angeles sent them two patients, both of whom arrived by private plane. By the first week of September, they had sixteen patients between the ages of eight and nineteen. It was exactly what they had hoped for. The staff handled each case with precision, skill, and dedication, while Jessie supervised. Bill was thrilled by what was happening. The Lily Pad worked!

It was a busy week for him and Jessie, at home and the office. Heather started school and loved it, which was a huge relief to Jessie. Chris went back to DU, and Jessie settled him in the dorm herself this time, and Bill was flying to Princeton with Lily that weekend. The house was a shambles of packing and preparation, and shopping she had done, and his assistant and their daily housekeeper could hardly keep up with her. Lily was in full swing racing around town getting organized. She went to say goodbye to Jessie and Carole the day before she left, spent the afternoon with Teddy, and she had dinner with Chris that night. He took her out, and on the way back, they talked about what would happen now.

'I don't want to tie you down, Lily,' he said sadly.

'You're going to college to spread your wings. I don't want to hold you back.' She was devastated as he said it, and looked up at him with her big lavender eyes.

'Are you dumping me?' He was horrified by what she said.

'Of course not! I wanted to give you your freedom if you want it. I just thought . . .'

'I love you, Chris.' They hadn't said that to each other yet, until that night. 'I can still have a good time in college. But I'm not going to meet someone like you. I know we're both young, but I don't want to lose you. And maybe one day, when we're older . . .' She let her words drift off, and he took her in his arms and kissed her. It was all he had needed to hear, and hoped for. He couldn't imagine her wanting to wait for him, especially at Princeton.

'When you're really ancient,' he teased her, 'like twenty-five maybe, we'll talk about this again. Meanwhile, Lily Thomas, you're my girl, you got that? I'll see you when you get back. I'll call you tomorrow when you get there. And tell those hot Princeton guys, you belong to me. And you've got nothing to worry about here. Okay? Are we square on this?' His eyes were dancing with happiness and love for her.

'Completely,' she said, with stars in her eyes too, and he kissed her again. She could hardly make herself get out of his car when he got her chair out.

'I love you, Lily,' he said when he kissed her for the last time.

'I love you too, Chris.' She rolled into her house then, waved at him, and gently closed the door behind her. It was late, and she hoped her father would be asleep.

He wasn't. He was lying in bed thinking how empty his life would be without her. And he was awake long after she drifted off to sleep, thinking of Chris.

They flew into the Mercer County airport the next day, in a Canadian Global Express, and a van and driver met them and drove them to Princeton. Lily was in high spirits all the way, and Bill was quiet, listening to her and enjoying her company. She didn't say anything about Chris, and he didn't ask her. He knew. He had been young once too.

Lily went to the orientation desk and got her room and dorm assignment, and Bill was grateful to discover that because of her wheelchair, her room was on the main floor of Whitman College, and the driver helped them get all her bags and boxes inside. Bill worked on setting up her computer while she put away her clothes. The room was small, and she had been assigned a roommate, Chiara from Connecticut, and he was startled to see that she was also in a wheelchair when she came in, with a disability similar to Lily's. They eyed each other suspiciously for a minute, and then they both laughed and started talking. She had been in a car accident at sixteen, and was impressed by Lily's story and the fact that she'd been in the Paralympics. She had heard about them but never seen them. And her parents chatted pleasantly with Bill while he set up the computer, and Chiara's father brought in a small fridge.

By eight o'clock the girls were all set for dinner. Lily said goodbye to her father, and her roommate Chiara hugged her parents. The girls were clearly ready for their parents to make a discreet exit and leave them to the excitement of their new life. The two girls were chatting happily as they left, negotiating the paths easily in their wheelchairs, and talking about what eating clubs they hoped to join one day. Lily had read all about them and already knew she wanted Cottage. Chiara said she wanted Ivy. They were the clubs that were a more distinguished version of fraternities and sororities on campus. But they couldn't join until the spring of their sophomore year, and could use the clubs only as juniors and seniors.

Bill looked at Chiara's parents ruefully as he stood up, after hooking up the stereo and computer. 'I guess that's our cue to leave before they get back. We're no longer needed.' He had a lump in his throat as he said it.

'Looks like it,' Chiara's father said with a grin and put an arm around his wife. 'It's our first time at college. We've got three more at home.'

'She's my only one,' Bill said bleakly, and with all the

dignity he could muster, he left without bursting into tears. He found the driver and headed back to the airport, and two hours later they were in the air, heading back to Denver, and he had a stiff drink. He had never felt so lonely in his life.

They landed at two in the morning local time, and Bill was home by two-thirty. He walked into the house, and the silence was deafening as he gave in to the tears that had been choking him all night. And then he saw that Lily had sent him a text message: 'Thank you. I love you, Daddy.' That only made it worse.

Chapter 28

'How was it?' Jessie asked him with a look of concern the next day. She could see the answer on his face. He looked like someone had died.

'It was okay. She was happy as a lark when I left,' he said grimly.

'It was bad when Chris went away last year too. You get used to their being gone after a while.'

'You've got three others. My house is like a tomb.'

'You'll just have to try and keep busy,' Jessie said gently. She could see how upset he was.

She, Carole, and Joe tried to entertain him in the ensuing weeks, and invited him to dinner. He had a good time with them, but it was always the same when he went home. No Lily. And she was so busy, she hardly called him, and he didn't want to nag her. He was the childhood cocoon she had shed.

Carole and Joe had come out of the closet by then, and

Jessie was happy for them about their romance. She didn't envy them, and didn't want one of her own. She was happy with her kids. And Carole and Joe always asked about Lily. Bill said she was doing well and having fun – he could hardly wait for her to come home for Thanksgiving. And Jessie knew that Chris felt the same way – she could tell by the way he asked about Lily. He admitted to getting calls and texts from her, but he missed her.

And Jessie was aware how much Teddy missed her too. He had convinced his parents to let him transfer to The Lily Pad, and after they researched it, they agreed. Jessie had spoken to them at length, and they were intelligent and thorough. He had moved into The Lily Pad right before Halloween and had arrived in a bumblebee costume he had painted himself and delighted the younger children.

There were two boys his age in residence and one girl, and one boy slightly older. Teddy was enjoying hanging out with them when he wasn't at school, working in the art room, or playing rugby. He was busy at DU. And The Lily Pad was booming. They had twenty patients at the moment, and were expecting more in the coming weeks. They were almost ready to open the second residence hall, as soon as they hired more staff. Teddy was helping with the art program with the younger children on weekends, and they all loved him.

Everything was going smoothly on all fronts. And Jessie had invited everyone to dinner for Thanksgiving, Joe and Carole, Teddy, Phil Lewis who had nowhere to go, Bill and Lily, and all four of her children. She was planning a festive meal and going to cook it herself, even though she was on call. And Carole promised to fill in for her as chef and hostess if she had to go to work.

When Lily came home on Wednesday night, she was treated like a returning movie star. Her father had sent a plane for her, which she had admitted to no one at school – she pretended she was taking a flight from Newark.

Chris came to see her at the house late that night, and her father couldn't get enough of her the next day before they went to Jessie's house for turkey dinner. And all of Jessie's children were happy to see her, as were the adults. Everyone had missed her. She announced at dinner that she had decided on her major. She was going to take psych, and wanted to go for a Ph.D. afterward and become a psychologist like Carole, to work with SCI kids, hopefully at The Lily Pad. Her father was proud of her when he heard it, and hoped she'd find somewhere closer to home to get her Ph.D. But that was still a long way off.

They were talking about it as she held hands with Chris under the table, when Jessie's BlackBerry rang, and they called her in. They had a new intake they needed her to see and assess.

'Well, that's the end of me,' Jessie said with a big smile, looking at Carole. 'You can take over from here.' They had had turkey, but not yet dessert, and everyone had enjoyed the meal so far. Jessie had set a beautiful table and prepared a delicious meal with Heather's help. She and her mother were back on good terms now. She still missed Squaw, but loved her new school and had a boyfriend who was making Denver fun for her, and she was making lots of new friends and keeping in touch with her old ones.

The desserts were already lined up on the kitchen table. It was easy for Carole to serve them once Jessie left. Heather and Lily helped her, as did Chris. And while they cleared the table for dessert, Heather told Lily how much she loved her school. Lily was happy to hear it. And then she turned to Chris and asked him if he wanted to go skiing the next day, and he was thrilled. There was already snow in Winter Park, and Lily had been aching to ski.

There were a million things she wanted to do while she was home, most of them with Chris, and a few with her father. He realized as he listened to her how grown up she had gotten. Things had already subtly shifted. She wasn't his little girl anymore. She was her own woman, and Chris's to some degree, but mostly her own. Chris could see it too, but he was growing up too. They seemed more like a couple now than they had before she left, and Bill wondered if it was 'official.'

They all left before Jessie got back, and Bill had invited everyone to Christmas dinner at their house. And the whole group looked pleased with the invitation. He and Lily went home then and chatted about what a nice Thanksgiving it had been. And she yawned as soon as she got in. The house felt different to him, just knowing she was there. With Lily at home, it was a much warmer place to be. Without her, he felt lost, but he didn't say it to her. He was trying to grow up too.

She went skiing with Chris the next day, and they went out to dinner after she visited with Teddy. And on Saturday Bill took Lily and Chris to dinner with Jessie. Her other children had other plans, and sleepovers, and Heather was out with her boyfriend. So the four of them went out for a quiet dinner, and then Chris and Lily sat in the den at her house, talking. And on Sunday morning, she left. It was all over much too quickly, as Bill said to Jessie on Monday.

'How does it end so quickly? One minute they're babies, and the next they're grown up. I feel like I missed the whole movie.'

'You didn't,' Jessie reassured him. 'You're still in it. You just don't know it. It's not over yet.' And then they talked about The Lily Pad and her intakes over the weekend. Bill was aware of each child that was there. They discussed every aspect of the center with each other. Jessie had her Colorado license by then, but she had done nothing about entering another practice. She hadn't had time yet. The Lily Pad kept her too busy.

The next weeks flew by, and three weeks after Thanksgiving, Lily was home for Christmas vacation, and this time Bill knew she'd be home for two weeks, so he was more relaxed about being with her.

And on Christmas Eve, they all sat together at Bill and Lily's table. She and Chris had put a tree up, under Teddy's artistic direction, and they all shared a Christmas feast. Bill thought, as he sat there, that it had been the fastest year of his life. So much had happened. Lily had won the silver medal, The Lily Pad had opened, Jessie had moved to Denver, Carole and Joe had fallen in love, Chris and Lily were a couple, Lily was at Princeton. It had been an amazing year.

Chapter 29

If the year before had gone quickly, the months between December and June virtually flew by. They opened the second residential house, and had thirty-two patients at The Lily Pad. Jessie gave up the idea of joining a local practice, she had no time, although she wasn't sure she wanted to give up surgery. By June, Chris had finished two years of college, Teddy and Lily their first year, and Heather was about to graduate and attend UC Santa Barbara in the fall. And Carole was planning a gala to benefit The Lily Pad, in October, with Joe's help. She had given up her apartment and moved in with Joe. All of their lives seemed to be moving at dizzying speed, and Bill was slowly getting used to Lily being away, and the idea that she was growing up, painful as it was.

She had helped them organize their annual sports competition, from Princeton. They had five coaches under the direction of Phil Lewis, and the event was planned for November, on the Thanksgiving weekend, so people from out of town could easily attend. There would be medals given in every category.

The Monet water lilies looked spectacular hanging at the entrance to The Lily Pad, and Teddy's painting hung near it. And Bill had had a black granite wall installed, also near the entrance, with the names of their biggest donors, to honor their contributions. He had called it 'The Winners' Circle,' and Steve Jansen had just finished it. In time, they planned to put their sports medal winners on the wall too. Bill went to look at the wall with Jessie, and they listed donors from platinum to bronze. Jessie stood looking at it with awe, and Bill was pleased.

'Your name should be up there,' she said to Bill as she smiled at him.

'No, it shouldn't. I'm not really a donor, in that sense,' he said modestly. 'All these people have given us money to do something very special here. I'm the founder. That's not the same.'

'You made us all winners,' she said gently. 'Without you, none of this would have happened.'

'And without you, it couldn't exist.'

'Yes, it could. You'd have found some other neurosurgeon, overpaid him or her, offered them a fabulous house, lured them to Denver, and given them the opportunity of a lifetime to do something wonderful for SCI kids and help them lead amazing lives when they leave.' It was what had happened to Lily at Craig, and now it was happening here too. And Lily was off to a great life. But so was everyone there, loving what they did. 'You gave us the greatest gift of all, purpose, passion, joy.' She was still smiling when they walked back to her office, and she turned and saw that he was looking at her strangely as she glanced up at him.

'Jessie . . .' His voice was very gentle as he walked toward her and stood close to her. 'Don't you think we've waited long enough?'

'For what?' She looked confused.

'For passion and joy, what you just talked about. We've helped everybody start their lives over, better than before. Maybe it's our turn now. We've been doing this together for a year, longer if you count all the times you came to Denver before you moved here. I've been waiting for you for all this time.' Tim had been gone for two and a half years. 'I don't want to wait anymore.' He touched her face gently then and kissed her. Her eyes opened wider, and she kissed him back as he pulled her closer into his arms and held her. He had wanted to do this for so long and had known it wasn't the time then, but now he knew just as surely that it was. 'I love you, Jessie.'

'I love you too,' she said softly, leaning against him. She didn't have to fight anymore. She wasn't alone. They were together. They were winners, just like the others. The Lily Pad had blessed them all.

Pegasus

Danielle Steel

In the German countryside, on the cusp of the Second World War, everything is about to change for two lifelong friends . . .

As widowers, the two men are raising their children alone – Nicolas's two lively boys and Alex's adored teenage daughter – but lead contented, peaceful lives. Until a long-buried secret about Nicolas's ancestry threatens his family's safety.

To survive, they must flee to America. The only treasures Nicolas and his sons can take are eight pure-bred horses, two of them dazzling Lipizzaners – gifts from Alex. These magnificent creatures are their ticket to a new life, securing Nicolas a job with the famous Ringling Brothers Circus. There, he and the white stallion, Pegasus, become the centrepiece of the show, and a graceful young high-wire walker soon steals his heart.

But as the years of war take their toll, Nicolas struggles to adapt to their new life, while Alex and his daughter face escalating danger in Europe. When tragedy strikes on both sides of the ocean, what will become of each family when their happiness rests in the hands of fate?

A Perfect Life

Danielle Steel

An icon in the world of television news, Blaise McCarthy seems to have it all: beauty, intelligence and courage. But privately, there is a story she has protected for years . . .

Blaise's daughter Salima, blinded by juvenile diabetes, now lives in a year-round boarding school with full-time assistance. When the school closes suddenly, Salima returns home to Blaise's New York apartment with her new carer, Simon. Simon rapidly shakes up their world, determined to help Salima find the independence she never thought possible. As all three face challenges that change the way they see one another, the bond between mother and daughter deepens as never before.

Then Blaise's personal and professional worlds collide: a young rival at work attempts to take over and the well-guarded secrets of her home life are exposed. Suddenly her life is no longer perfect, but real. Can mother and daughter together learn how to face a world they can't control?

Power Play

Danielle Steel

Fiona Carson has proven herself as CEO of a multibillion-dollar high-tech company, but she still has to meet the challenges of her world every day. Devoted single mother, world-class strategist, and tough negotiator, Fiona weighs every move she makes and reserves any personal time for her children. Isolation and constant pressure are givens for her as a woman in a man's world.

Meanwhile, Marshall Weston basks in the fruits of his achievements. At his side is his wife Liz – the perfect, supportive corporate spouse – who has gladly sacrificed her own law career to raise their three children. Smooth, shrewd, and irreproachable, Marshall is a model chief executive, and the power he wields only enhances his charisma. And to maintain his position, he harbors secrets that could destroy his life at any moment.

Both must face their own demons, and fight off those who are jealous of their success. Their lives as CEOs of major companies come at a high price. But just how high a price are they willing to pay? Who are they willing to sacrifice to stay on top? Those they love, or themselves?

First Sight

Danielle Steel

New York. London. Milan. Paris.

Fashion week in all four cities. Endless interviews, parties and unflagging work.

At the centre of it all is Timmie O'Neill, whose renowned line, 'Timmie O', is the embodiment of casual chic, in fashion and for the home. She has created an international empire that consumes her life.

In a world where humility and compassion are rare, Timmie's humour, kindness, integrity, and creativity are inspirational. Yet as blessed as she feels by her success, she harbours the private wounds of a devastating childhood and past tragedy.

Always willing to take risks in business, she never risks her heart – until an intriguing Frenchman comes into her life during Paris Fashion Week. There is every reason why they must remain apart. But neither can deny the electricity that sparks whenever they meet.

Are they brave enough to face what comes next? And will they do it together – or apart?

Until the End of Time

Danielle Steel

Bill, a dedicated lawyer working in New York, leaves everything he trained for to follow his dream and become a minister in rural Wyoming. Jenny, his fashion stylist wife, leaves the milieu and life she loves to join him. The certainty they share is that their destinies are linked forever.

Fast forward thirty-eight years. Robert is a hard-working independent book publisher in Manhattan, looking for one big hit novel. Lillibet is a young Amish woman, caring for her widowed father and three young brothers on their family farm. In secret at night, by candlelight, she has written the novel that burns within her. When it falls into Robert's hands, he falls in love first with the book, and then with the woman he has never met.

These two remarkable relationships come together in unexpected and surprising ways, as lovers are lost, and find each other again. In this extraordinary novel, bestselling author Danielle Steel delivers a story about courage, change, risk and hope . . . and love that never dies.

The Sins of the Mother

Danielle Steel

After building an empire that has made her a legend in business, Olivia spends months each year planning a lavish holiday for her family, now adults. More than anything, she hopes to express her love and her regret at all the important times she missed during her children's early years.

This summer she has arranged a dream trip on a luxurious yacht in the Mediterranean. But old resentments die hard, and Olivia is still running the business full time.

As each of these individuals confronts the past and the challenges of the present and future, they also learn to accept the enduring, unconditional love of their family – and a mother who is both strong enough to take more than her fair share of the blame, and loving enough to accept them as they really are. The question is: can they do the same for her?